BETH BOLDEN

Chapter One

Week One

Dylan Leonard traveled light.

In the three years he'd spent in the NFL, he'd learned that everything could change in a moment, and it was always better to be able to stuff everything that mattered to you into a single duffel bag.

It sat at his feet as he watched Kelly Garcia, the travel coordinator for the Miami Piranhas, have a mini meltdown right in front of him.

"I don't understand," she said into the phone, her voice sounding increasingly frantic, "what do you mean, *not habitable*?"

He watched as she nodded, scribbling down notes onto a notepad in front of her, her mouth a grim line.

"Well, when will it be?" she asked, annoyance leaking into her brisk voice. He could hear it even if he hadn't known her very long—approximately five minutes. Maybe four. If it was even possible to know someone you'd only observed talking to someone else.

He'd been shown into her office by Coach Dawson, who'd promised that she'd get his temporary living arrangements squared away. Except, from the way she'd distractedly waved him in, already on the phone, it didn't seem like anything was going to get squared away anytime soon.

Finally, she let out a heavy, resigned sigh, and hung up. From the way she didn't quite meet his eyes, Dylan knew it wasn't good news.

Just another day in the NFL. Traded to a brand-new team, because after only three years of solid kicking, you've been replaced by some rookie phenom. Already washed up at twenty-six. Welcome to the National fucking Football League.

"Dylan, I'm really so sorry about this, but the condo we keep for temporary housing, it's . . ." Kelly hesitated. "Well, it's uninhabitable. I guess there was a water main break, and it needs to be . . . I don't know what needs to be done, but it can't be used. I can put you up in a hotel, we have a really nice hotel we use for the team to stay at before games . . ."

Dylan didn't want to tell her that the thought of going to another impersonal hotel, after years of them, after he'd finally started creating a home in Las Vegas, only to have it ripped away in an instant when his agent had called him to say he'd been traded, made him want to grab his duffel and fade into the Miami night and not come back.

But it did.

You should not be this bitter, not after only three years.

But he was.

He also wasn't willing to give up the dream yet.

You're good. You're fucking solid. So solid the Piranhas were willing to give up a player for you, Dylan reminded himself.

So instead of giving the middle finger to Kelly—who didn't deserve it—and the rest of the Piranhas organization—who didn't either, especially considering how much Dylan had liked the few words he'd exchanged with the head coach, Asa Dawson—he nodded.

"The hotel would be fine," he said. It wasn't, but he'd dealt with so much already, this just felt like another small compromise in a long list of them.

They were heading into the first regular game of the season. He wouldn't be spending much time away from the Piranhas facility, but he'd still make it a priority to find a place to live, ASAP.

Living in a hotel wasn't really living. It was just existing. And Dylan had had enough of that.

"Kelly?"

Dylan looked up and saw a big guy, with short dark hair, and tattoos peeking out of the tight white shirt he was wearing. He was built like a tank, all big thick biceps and broad shoulders, with a surprisingly gentle smile.

"Oh, hi, Logan," Kelly said, sounding even more flustered. "I know I said I'd get you those tickets . . ."

"It's no rush," Logan said, and his voice was kind, and his eyes even kinder as he stepped into the office. "You seem a little . . . flustered, and it can wait."

Dylan had been around a lot of football players. He'd been in the NFL for three years, then there'd been five years of college before that, at Michigan State, and high school even before that.

He was used to guys who walked into a room and dominated it with their sheer size.

But they didn't usually have kind eyes or a smile that immediately set everyone at ease.

Those were not typically skills those big guys possessed.

"It's fine, I'm fine," Kelly said, "it's just that this . . . well, this is Dylan, he's our new kicker, and I was going to get him set up in the temporary condo, but there was a water main break and it's unlivable, and now I've got to call the hotel . . ."

"The hotel?" The guy glanced at Dylan. "You can't send him to the hotel." He paused, then extended a hand. Dylan shook it, impressed by both his firm grip and the even wider smile that bloomed across his features. "I'm Logan Banks. Center. Great to meet you, Dylan. Welcome to Miami."

"Trust me, I don't *want* to send him to the hotel," Kelly said.

"Then don't," Logan said. "He can come stay with me. I've got plenty of room."

Kelly looked at least as surprised as Dylan felt.

"I'm a good roommate, no stinky socks left out in the living room, and I never drink the last of the milk. And," Logan added with a wicked smirk, "I don't bite. At least unless someone asks nicely."

"Uh," Dylan stammered. Unsure. He didn't *know* this guy. But he seemed nice enough, and the idea of going to the hotel was so crappy, what could it hurt? Besides, no matter where he went—either to the hotel or to Logan's house—he wasn't going to be staying long. As soon as he could unload his Vegas condo, he'd be finding a new one in Miami.

"Trust me," Logan said, leaning a hip against the edge of Kelly's desk, "you do not want to go to that hotel."

"What's wrong with the hotel?" Kelly asked, confused.

Logan shot her a look that told Dylan that he completely, totally, understood his issue with the hotel. "It's any hotel, Kel," he said kindly. "They all suck. At the hotel, we're just a number, and let's face it, we're a number the rest of the time too. It just sucks."

"Ah," Kelly said.

Logan turned back to Dylan. He still hadn't made up his mind, but to his own surprise, he was leaning towards getting up and actually going with this guy.

Anyone who possessed such a genuine smile couldn't be all bad.

Even if he *did* leave smelly socks in the living room.

"What do you say?" Logan asked. "I live only a few minutes away from the practice facility, I have like five guest rooms I'm not using, you could practically have your own wing. And," he added, grinning extra bright, "we could carpool!"

"You don't know anything about me," Dylan said slowly. "What if *I* leave dirty socks out in the living room?"

"Are you gonna?" Logan asked archly, raising an eyebrow.

Dylan laughed. He wanted to like this guy; in fact, he had a feeling it had already happened, without even intending to.

"See, I didn't think so," Logan said, reaching out and clapping him on the shoulder. "I usually have a good feel for these kinds of things, and I think we're gonna get on great."

"Okay. Sure. Yeah . . . I'd really appreciate it, if you wouldn't mind putting me up for a few nights."

"Just a few?" Logan questioned, and Dylan felt himself flush with embarrassment. He'd planned to be out of Logan's hair as soon as possible, but he'd never wanted him to realize that was his intention.

"As long as it takes," Dylan corrected.

Logan grinned. "Exactly. You're welcome for as long as you need, dude. Unless it doesn't work out, and then I'm sure I'll be the first to tell you that you need to get your ass moving."

Dylan was surprised. Actually, that was an understatement. He was *shocked*.

Kelly, clearly listening to their conversation, rolled her eyes. "Yes, he means that," she inserted. "He's painfully honest."

"Yep," Logan acknowledged. Not even looking the tiniest bit ashamed of this fact. "But don't worry, you won't be homeless. We take care of our own here."

"You just got here, Logan, only a month or so back, you *don't* know how it is," Kelly reminded him with another eye roll.

"We're establishing the culture here early, feel me?" Logan said with satisfaction. "If it doesn't work out with me, at my place, I'm sure it'll work out with someone else."

Kelly might not have understood, but Dylan did.

All he'd learned, in the last minute, was that he liked the guy even more than he had before. He'd be honest, no hard feelings, if he wanted Dylan to go, but he'd never kick him out and leave him on the street. Even though that wasn't really possible. Worst-case scenario, he'd end up at Kelly's impersonal hotel. But he didn't think that was going to be the case.

Dylan rarely had these good feelings about people. He'd learned in his last three years in the NFL that most of the guys were out for themselves, first and foremost. And he couldn't even blame them for that. After all, if you didn't put you first, nobody else would.

You had to be the advocate of your own career, because if you weren't, you'd end up fucked.

"That sounds good to me," Dylan admitted. "Really good. I hate the hotels . . ." He glanced over at Kelly. "Sorry."

She threw up her hands. "This is news to me, but I get it. It's impersonal."

"Exactly," Logan said. He turned to Dylan. "That all your stuff?"

"Yeah," Dylan said. "I travel light."

Logan nodded, clearly understanding why. Though if Dylan remembered correctly, and had put the right name to the right face and the right history, he'd been with only two teams in his four-year NFL career—the Vikings, and then the Piranhas, though like Kelly had said, he was new to Miami.

Just like Dylan.

But unlike Dylan, he hadn't dealt with the uncertainty of not being drafted, of having to crisscross the country, trying out for teams, and then finally, hoping that he'd landed in a spot that could be home, only to wake up early this morning to the knowledge that he'd been traded three thousand miles away.

"You gonna get those tickets for me, Kelly?" Logan asked, as Dylan stood, slinging his duffel onto his shoulder. He glanced over at Dylan. "They're for some friends of friends, but I said I would . . ."

"Oh, yeah. Yeah. I will. Tomorrow." She glanced over at Dylan. "If it doesn't work out for any reason . . ." She hesitated. "You just tell me, okay? The apartment will be livable at some point, I'm sure, and if it isn't, I *can* always find you a hotel room. Or maybe something else. It's just . . . it's late, and . . ."

"Really, it's okay," Dylan said, putting her out of her misery. She clearly felt bad that the only option she'd had for him had been the dreaded hotel.

"You're too nice," she said, standing and extending her hand. "Welcome to Miami, Dylan."

He shook it. "Thanks," he said. Then turned to Logan. "You ready to go?"

"Yeah, actually, I am. Early day today, actually, it was supposed to be our day off but . . ." Logan shot him another one of those lopsided grins. A sweet one, the total opposite of his big, bulky build. "I came in anyway."

Dylan eyed his exposed arms as they walked out of Kelly's office. "I'm not surprised," he said wryly. "You look like you never miss a day."

Logan flexed, shooting Dylan a goofy exaggerated body-builder look. "Oh, you know it, baby."

Dylan laughed. "Well, I work hard too. Have to be the hardest worker, or . . . well, you know. And even then . . ." He trailed off. Still feeling the smart of being replaced in Vegas. He'd known things were not good the moment the Raiders had drafted that young kid out of Grambling State. They were convinced he could consistently kick sixty-yard field goals, and he *could*, or at least he'd been able to in practice.

But Dylan knew, the way that kid didn't yet, that it was a totally different animal to kick in a game.

To do it consistently.

To come out and do it whenever your team needed you to.

To be essentially forgotten, until you were suddenly thrust into the spotlight, the most important player on the team.

"Yeah, it doesn't always matter," Logan said, and he put his hand, casually, on Dylan's shoulder. Supporting him, understanding him.

Football players were a surprisingly touchy-feely bunch, but Logan seemed to be even more than most. Dylan didn't mind it at all.

Then, suddenly, Logan stopped short, and the expression on his face changed from easy amusement to something else.

"Hey," he said, his voice abruptly gone serious. "I do have to tell you something . . . I guess you should know before you stay with me."

"What is it? You do, in fact, leave your stinky socks in the living room? You routinely drink the last of the milk?" Dylan had to make it a joke, because all of a sudden there was something heavy and uncomfortable in Logan's gaze, and he didn't like it.

He liked the easygoing guy, the one with such a ready, comforting smile, that he'd met before.

"It's not the socks, or the milk. I'm . . . well, you should know I'm gay."

Dylan paused for a second, not quite following. "And?"

The single word seemed to fluster Logan even more. "And you might not want to stay with me, if you knew. So, I thought you should know. I'm not out . . . though I think I might want to be someday. It's why I came here, to Miami."

"One of my best friends is Jamie Wright," Dylan said, naming the kicker he'd become friends with during a tryout with the Los Angeles Riptide. Jamie had been out since college, and was famously dating another ex-kicker, Neal Fisher. "I don't give a shit who you like to sleep with, unless you do it loudly, and in the very next room the night before a game."

"Oh. Okay. I just wanted to make sure . . ." Logan's smile was back, but it was a little shaky.

Dylan couldn't help but remember what Jamie had told him once about coming out. "Sometimes," Jamie had said, late one night, between beers four and five, "it feels like coming out doesn't just happen once. It happens dozens of times. Hundreds of times. Sometimes to everyone you ever meet. And I'm *out*. Have been for fucking years."

Jamie hadn't explained what it might be like for someone who wasn't, who had to constantly judge people's decency, their acceptance. Who had to determine if they could be trusted with their secrets, who had to make these judgments with every single person they got close to.

With every person they invited into their home.

Because who'd want to hide in their own goddamn house?

"It's fine. You're fine," Dylan said firmly. This time he returned the touch, right away, reaching out and squeezing him on the shoulder, because he didn't want Logan thinking that even though he'd said it was okay, he didn't want to touch him anymore.

Logan cleared his throat. "Wright's your friend, huh? And he's with Neal Fisher. I liked Neal a lot, the one time I met him. Haven't had a chance to meet Jamie yet, though."

"He's so great, like freaking rock solid," Dylan said. "*And* they're kind of annoyingly adorable together."

"One of those couples, huh? We've got one of those. Tristan and Wade, two rookies, who can't keep their hands off each other." Logan chuckled, wryly. "Just make sure Kelly doesn't put you next to them when we're on the road. She did that to me once and *never again*." Logan shuddered.

"Noted," Dylan said, amused.

He'd heard Miami was way less conservative than other NFL teams—and the gossip must be true, if there was actually an out and open couple on the team.

"You got a car?" Logan said, resuming their walk down the hallway towards—Dylan presumed, anyway—the exit.

He was sure in a few weeks all these hallways would be familiar, but for now, they felt more like a maze.

"Yeah, it's getting shipped here from Vegas," Dylan said with a nod. "So I guess til it gets here, I can either take an Uber or . . ."

"Or," Logan teased, "you can tolerate me driving you around."

"Or that," Dylan agreed with a sheepish smile. "I don't want to be a bother . . ."

"Dude, you're here to save the day," Logan said, taking an abrupt left down another hallway. "We don't have a kicker right now. Not since Jonah tore his Achilles. Zach, the punter, has been practicing, in case we needed to make a kick in the last game, but it's been a mess."

Logan pushed open a door, and suddenly Dylan found himself in the Piranhas' locker room. "Sorry," he said offhandedly. "I just gotta grab my bag."

"No worries," Dylan said, turning around, taking in the bright blue and yellow walls, and at the end of the room, a young woman was clearly turning one of those lockers into his, setting out a vinyl decal with his name written on it.

"Hey, Lyanna," Logan said, calling down to her. "Come meet our new kicker."

She grinned, flipped her braids behind her shoulder, and walked over. Her grip, as they shook hands, was firm. "I was just setting up your locker," she told him. "Sorry, it's all the way down at the end . . ."

"What? All the way down at the end? No way. You gotta move him up here," Logan said, as he pulled a small bag out of his own locker. "I'm gonna need him close."

Lyanna raised an eyebrow. "Oh, and why is that?"

"He's my roomie," Logan pronounced proudly. "And we roomies gotta stick together."

"I'll see what I can do," Lyanna said, sounding amused. Dylan almost told her to forget it, that he was fine down at the end, but there was something about Logan's championing that felt *good*. Felt right. Soothed his bitterness like a balm.

"That would be really great," Dylan said. "It would mean . . . well, it'd mean a lot to me."

Lyanna smiled. "I get it. Never easy to be traded. But don't worry, you're gonna fit right in."

"You're the best," Logan said, giving her a high five. Then he turned to Dylan. "You ready to see Casa Banks now?"

Dylan nodded, discovering that he *was* actually curious to see Logan's house.

Logan led them outside, into the player parking lot, and unlocked a matte black Land Rover, opening the back hatch so they could throw their bags in.

Logan wasn't the first NFL player that Dylan had ever hitched a ride with, and even though they all, universally, drove expensive cars, some of them were neater than others.

But Logan's was pristine. Like he'd just vacuumed it out.

And that boded well, Dylan decided, for whether he *did* actually leave his smelly socks in the living room or drank the last of the milk.

He also hadn't exaggerated how close he lived to the practice facility and the attached stadium. It was a quick five-minute drive on the freeway, and then they were exiting, leaving the high-rise buildings of downtown Miami behind, driving into a more suburban neighborhood, with waving palm trees lining either side of the street.

"This is your first year here and you've already settled in?" Dylan asked as Logan pulled into a long driveway. No gate, but the house was set back quite a bit from the main road, behind a long curved circular drive.

It was big, but not enormous, with stucco walls and a red tile roof. Logan hit a button, and a garage door around the side began to open.

Logan nodded. "I thought about renting, but I hate not being settled. And I intend to stay here for awhile, if the Piranhas'll have me."

From everything Dylan had heard about the lineman, the Piranhas would be lucky if they could keep him.

He turned off the car and got out, and Dylan followed, but before he could protest, Logan had grabbed both of their bags from the trunk.

"Come on," he said with an easy smile. "I'll show you around." He pointed to the empty space in the garage, next to the Range Rover. "You can park here, when your car shows up, I'll make sure to get you a fob that opens the garage. Oh, and a code to get into the front door."

Dylan nodded, taking in the house as Logan moved through the mudroom, to the kitchen, to the living room—where there was nary a dirty *or* smelly sock to be found. It was all clean and neat, and not as painfully impersonal as Dylan had expected, considering that Logan had just moved here himself, a few months back. There were plenty of framed pictures, scattering across the built-in bookshelves on one end of the living room. Logan with two guys who must be his brothers, because they looked nearly like clones. And in some of them, an older girl, with long reddish-brown hair.

"My brothers, they both play too," Logan said, coming up behind Dylan as he glanced at the pictures. "Levi plays right tackle for the Seahawks, and Landry, tight end for the Bills."

"That's impressive," Dylan said. He'd been an only child and had always envied those big families, with lots of kids.

"Lyla, my sister, she finds all the attention annoying," Logan said. "She thinks it gives us all big heads." He shrugged. "I guess it kinda does?"

He'd heard of both Levi and Landry Banks, so maybe some of those egos were justified. But then Logan, who was just as good, if not better, didn't seem to have any ego whatsoever.

"What about you?' Logan asked as he led him up the stairs. "Any brothers or sisters?"

"Nope, just me and my mom, for basically ever," Dylan admitted. "My dad left, well, I'm not sure he was really ever around, honestly. But we got along okay, anyway."

"Better than just okay, I'd guess," Logan said thoughtfully. "I can see it, in your face." He pointed down the hall. "Master suite's down that way. And this is yours. There's a big bedroom, and a bathroom, and feel free to use this spot as like a place to hang out or whatever, if you don't want to come downstairs." Logan gestured to the couch and TV that was set up in the landing area right outside the bedroom.

Dylan nodded. He appreciated Logan making sure he knew he had his own space—that he wasn't *required* to hang out with Logan.

But he already had a feeling that he'd want to spend any time off that he had with Logan.

He was such a nice guy, friendly and open, and Dylan hadn't been sure what to expect at all when he'd been traded, but he sure hadn't expected to meet someone like Logan.

"Towels and stuff should be in the closet in the bathroom," Logan said. "When I first moved in, my mom came and made sure I was all stocked." He turned to Dylan, who'd thrown his bag on the bed. It *was* a big bedroom, with another flat-screen TV on the wall opposite the bed, and a large walk-in closet.

It was so much nicer than staying in the hotel, and Dylan felt himself swamped with gratitude—and something else, too. A question that had cropped up from the very first offer that Logan had made and that had only grown louder since he'd come home with him.

"Hey, you want a beer?" Logan asked. "It was a *day*, and I don't usually drink much during the season, but well, seems like today might be the right time to break that rule."

"Sure," Dylan said, and followed him back downstairs to the kitchen.

The fridge was pretty empty from the glimpse Dylan had as Logan pulled out two beers, flipping their tops off with an expert flick of his wrist.

"Cheers," Logan said, tipping their bottles together.

Dylan took a long drink. Liked that they were just hanging out here in the kitchen. It made the question easier to ask.

'Cause he was gonna *have* to ask it.

"So I've been in the NFL for three years," Dylan said, "and I gotta ask. *Why?*"

"Why?" Logan raised an eyebrow. "Why, what?"

"You really didn't have to do all of this." Dylan waved his hands around. "I know how it is. I've been around. Players aren't this friendly. This nice. Not regularly. Everyone's . . . well, everyone's out for themselves, you know?"

"I know." Logan's gaze was serious as he leaned over the counter. His dark eyes were magnetizing. "And I think that kinda sucks. Don't you?"

Dylan exhaled in a long whoosh. He *did* think it sucked. His first view of the NFL had been that horrible tryout with the Riptide, when they'd been way too anxious about their kicker situation. While it *had* improved from there, he wouldn't say that he'd found any team particularly welcoming either, even the Raiders, whom he'd played for much of those three years.

He and the punter in Vegas had stuck together. Special teams guys usually did. Nobody else seemed to even realize they were there—except when he had to go make a high-pressure kick in a game, and while he'd only missed a handful of times, he'd felt the cold shoulder from the rest of the team.

None of them had really given a shit about him.

They'd definitely not have offered him a place to fucking *live*.

"Yeah, of course it sucks," Dylan said slowly. "But why me?"

"You needed it," Logan said. "I walked into Kelly's office, and you were just sitting there, looking a little shell-shocked—which nobody could blame you for, by the way, being traded, *wow*, it would really suck—and I could help, so I did."

"Just like that?" Dylan questioned.

"I told you, I'm decent at reading people, and you seem like a good guy. I think we could be friends."

"So just . . . serendipity?"

Logan grinned. "Exactly." He tipped his bottle against Dylan's again. "I couldn't have said it better myself. Sometimes you're just in the right place, at the right time, and the right opportunity presents itself."

"Is that why you came to Miami?" Dylan wondered.

"I guess so? I wanted out of Minnesota. Couldn't be myself there. Couldn't even dream of it. The team never would've accepted it. But I knew Miami would be different."

Dylan nodded. Jamie had told him more than once how lucky he felt he'd ended up on the Riptide, which was welcoming to all sexualities. Of course, they'd kinda had to be, considering that their quarterback and their now quarterback coach had come out at the Super Bowl by kissing over the Lombardi trophy.

"You could've gone to Los Angeles, too," Dylan suggested. "And there are some other teams that I know are more accepting."

"The Riptide?" Logan laughed. "And replace Bran Phillips? Hell no, he's a fucking legend. I watch his tape, all the time. No, Miami was the right fit for me. And hopefully . . ." He hesitated. "It'll be a good fit for you, too."

Dylan drained the rest of his beer. Glanced around. He had friends, of course. He counted Jamie as a good friend. Maybe even a best friend. Truthfully, he'd been kind of a loner his whole life, and becoming a kicker hadn't really changed that situation.

But now he had someone who genuinely wanted to be his friend.

Who even knew what the word serendipity meant.

For the first time since he'd gotten the call early this morning, Dylan thought things might actually be looking up since he'd gotten traded.

"I think so too," Dylan agreed with Logan. He waved his bottle. "Let's have one more, to celebrate me getting a new team—and a new friend."

Logan grinned and didn't hesitate before grabbing another pair of beers.

Logan Banks was not a morning person.

He woke up, stumbled down the stairs, and had his head in the fridge, debating pulling the milk right from its shelf and downing the rest of it without bothering to find a glass when a voice startled him.

"Am I gonna find out you drank the last of the milk?"

It took Logan a long moment—he wasn't proud of it but he *wasn't* a morning person, okay?—to realize who was in his house. In his kitchen.

It was Dylan, the new kicker.

They'd stayed up later than he usually did, sharing a few beers—which absolutely explained that low-level-tired headache throbbing in his temples—and shooting the shit about all the mutual people they knew who'd played ball in college and the NFL.

The moment he'd flown into Miami, he'd liked a lot of the guys here. Sebastian Howard was great, an absolute fucking legend, and Rob Jeremiah, the left tackle who'd been here a few years, he was solid, too. And he and Pax, the quarterback, had clicked right from the beginning.

But he'd never connected with someone as quickly as he had with Dylan.

He certainly hadn't expected it when he'd walked into Kelly's office and seen him sitting there.

It wasn't sexual or romantic at all—something he'd kept reminding himself last night, when they'd been in the dim kitchen, Dylan's dark hair that desperately needed a trim falling into his eyes, his light green gaze bright and intent—if only because Dylan was clearly straight. Accepting *yes*, queer *no*.

Of course, if Logan had suspected that he was, he'd never have invited him to stay with him. That led to disasters. No, he knew he could be comfortable with Dylan. Knew he could tell him the truth about things, and get the truth right back.

That, Logan told himself firmly, was more important than a fleeting hookup.

Friendship was forever.

"I promise I will *split* the last of the milk with you," Logan said, pulling the remainder out of the fridge.

He turned to set it on the counter and for a second, just a single second, something jolted through him.

He called it a something because something was amorphous. Something wasn't defined. Something didn't mean that it had *actually* happened.

Dylan stood there, hair wet and still falling into his eyes, wearing only a pair of black boxer briefs. He was slim but muscular, a trail of dark hair disappearing under the waistband. But it wasn't all that that made Logan feel something. It was his legs, long and slim and carved out of fucking marble, just a light dusting of hair accenting them.

Fucking legs. He didn't even give a shit about legs. And yet . . .

He is not your type and you are not attracted to him, Logan ordered himself to believe.

Besides, it was just a second.

He *liked* Dylan. *As a friend*.

And *friendship is forever*, he added. He had a feeling he was gonna need to get that phrase tattooed onto his eyelids so he wouldn't forget it anytime soon.

"Glasses?" Dylan asked, glancing around the kitchen.

Logan pointed to a cabinet and wrenched the top off the milk with perhaps more force than was entirely necessary.

When he poured the milk into the glasses Dylan had grabbed, some slopped over the side, and Logan nearly grimaced, but before he could, or grab a paper towel to wipe up the spill, Dylan just laughed.

Carefree. Happy. *Real*.

And Logan realized that he hadn't last night. Not like that anyway. He'd had shadows of bitterness in his eyes. He'd been uneasy and insecure, in a way that anyone would be after they'd just had their whole support system ripped away.

Logan hadn't given it back to him—nobody could possibly rebuild that fast—but he'd shown him that one existed. He'd shown him his own.

"Not a morning person?" Dylan asked as he grabbed a paper towel and wiped up the spill.

"No, not really," Logan admitted sheepishly.

"That's okay," Dylan said. "'Cause I am. I can make breakfast?"

"You *cook*?" Logan was unable to help the worshipful edge to his voice.

Right here was the perfect man. He was handsome, he was funny, he laughed and the whole world turned. And he could fucking cook, too.

Not the perfect man.

The perfect *friend*.

"I do," Dylan said wryly. "Helps with the not-starving part."

"Right, right. I admit . . . smoothie in the morning, usually. And then I pick something up at the cafeteria at the practice facility. I could burn water, looking at it."

"What do you like to eat in the morning?" Dylan asked, and then neatly bumped him out of the way with a hip, peering into Logan's mostly empty fridge. "Well, nothing it seems," he added with a chuckle.

"We'll go to the grocery store tonight, on our way home," Logan promised, even though the thing he hated most on earth was the grocery store. All those slow people, pushing their carts even slower, knowing what they wanted and how to cook it—or even worse, *not* knowing what they wanted and taking ten thousand years to make a fucking choice at the meat counter.

But maybe with Dylan next to him, it wouldn't be so bad.

"Well, you've got eggs, at least," Dylan said, pulling a carton of them out of the fridge.

"Occasionally, I will stoop to boiling an egg," Logan admitted.

Dylan rolled his eyes. "How else do you like them?" He hip-checked Logan out of the way again, not resting on any ceremony whatsoever, pulling open every cupboard he could reach, clearly searching for pans. Which, Logan knew his mother had bought for him. No idea where they were, but he knew they *did* exist.

Yesterday, Logan had not expected a gorgeous, slim, dark-haired man with eyes the color of a light spring morning to be half-naked in his kitchen.

It was that fact that kept tripping him up. That was all.

"Uh, scrambled is fine," he said. "Or over easy. Or fried. I like eggs. However they come."

"Sounds good," Dylan said with a nod. He pulled a frying pan out.

"Oh, that's where they are," Logan said, and Dylan laughed.

Light and easy again, like Logan had made this difficult transition easier.

Like he'd made it bearable.

"You make the smoothies," Dylan said. Paused and then turned towards him again. Eyes so bright, Logan's fingers sliding uselessly against the condensation on the sides of his glass. "If you can handle that?" he added archly.

"I make a mean fucking smoothie," Logan said.

Dylan nodded, and turned towards the stove.

As he pulled out the blender and the makings for his famous smoothie recipe, Logan couldn't help but think that it didn't feel like the first time they'd ever shared a kitchen this way, making breakfast. It felt like the tenth time or the hundredth time or the thousandth.

And he hoped that it wouldn't be the last either.

Chapter Two

Week Two

"Shit, no, you gotta . . ." Dylan collapsed into laughter as Logan tried, really poorly, to turn around on the screen with the controller. "You are really fucking bad at this. Didn't you guys play video games when you were growing up?"

"Well, sorta," Logan said, scratching his head. After they'd gotten home from a long day at the practice facility, he'd anticipated crashing on the couch and watching a movie, but then Dylan had shown up, waving this new game he'd just gotten, and Logan, who didn't normally consider himself a sucker, was *always* a sucker for that smile on Dylan's face.

He'd initially settled down, wearing his "couch uniform" of just a pair of bright blue athletic shorts, but as he'd tried to figure out how to maneuver his on-screen character in the first-person shooter, he'd ended up mostly on the floor, tongue sticking out of his mouth in concentration.

And it hadn't helped. Not a fucking bit.

He was still spinning around helplessly on the screen, and had died four times in a row, without taking a single shot.

Normally he'd hate this, but Dylan made everything better.

In the past week, he'd even mostly gotten the tiny, miniscule way he'd been attracted to Dylan out of his system. He'd focused on the friendship, and how comfortable and free it made him feel.

"What does *sorta* mean?"

"*Sorta* means that we had an old system, like a Super Nintendo, and we almost never played it, 'cause it sucked. Crashed all the time," Logan admitted.

He didn't like talking about this normally, but in the last few weeks, he'd discovered that he could talk to Dylan about nearly anything. Even things that he'd never talk about with anyone else, he found himself saying without a second thought to Dylan.

"You didn't even have an Xbox?" Dylan didn't hide his surprise, but to Logan's own, it didn't sting like he'd expected it might.

"Man, we were dirt poor in Texas with four kids and my dad laid off a lot of the time," Logan admitted, tossing his controller down, finally admitting defeat. "My mom always told us to get outside. And maybe that was good, 'cause all that playing outside did one thing: made us strong. Made us fast."

"Got you to the NFL," Dylan finished for him. "So, what you're saying is we gotta start way more basic than this."

Logan shot him a look. "Ya think?"

Dylan laughed.

But not *at* Logan. He knew better than that.

He'd known, impossibly, the moment he'd walked into Kelly's office, that Dylan was going to be a good guy.

And he was.

A good guy.

A great friend.

A fantastic teammate.

"We need to start with something easier for sure," Dylan said, and got up, maneuvering around the half a dozen pillows that had fallen from the couch to the floor, right along with Logan's body, and went over to the stack of game boxes sitting by the gaming system he'd added to Logan's TV when he'd discovered that he didn't own one.

"What's easier?" he asked, actually curious.

"Um," Dylan said, sorting through the options. "I think I've got it!" he cried out triumphantly, holding the game aloft like it was the Vince Lombardi trophy.

"What is it?"

Dylan returned to the couch, flopping down, and scooting over until he was hanging practically over Logan's shoulder. He dangled the game in front of Logan's face.

"Lego Star Wars?" Logan made a face. "You really are a nerd, aren't you, Leonard?"

Dylan didn't take offense, though, just cackled.

"Dude," he said, "I'm a *kicker*. I think the nerd credentials are well established."

Logan couldn't really help it. He'd gotten a lot better about not checking Dylan out—because friends did not check out friends, that was practically emblazoned on page one of the friendship manual—but from the beginning, Dylan had copied Logan's couch uniform, so all *he* was wearing was a pair of black shorts that clung to his ass and his thighs, and well, Logan was only fucking human, okay?

Dylan didn't need to spend the time in the gym that Logan did, but he still put in decent hours.

And it showed.

Nerds didn't have calves like that. Or triceps. Or pecs.

"Don't look much like a nerd to me." Logan let his gaze drift down obviously, exaggerating the waggle of his eyebrows and Dylan laughed again.

"Maybe not, but don't let it fool you. I'm a nerd, through and through," Dylan said, flopping down onto the couch. "So, are you in? Lego Star Wars or bust?"

"Am I gonna have to know the story?" Logan questioned.

Dylan's jaw dropped. "You've never seen *Star Wars*?"

"Guilty as charged."

"Well, first, we're gonna remedy that *ASAP*," Dylan said with relish. "I can't believe I get to pop your cherry."

Logan froze, his hand still on the controller. "Uh," he said. "Hate to break it to you but that's been done . . ."

But I could pop yours, that voice that didn't want to co-operate, inserted slyly. And now Logan was fucking thinking about it. A dark head, between his legs, tongue flicking out uncertainly. A hand pressed to the middle of his chest, as Dylan squirmed on his dick.

Stop. Do not cross Go.

"Your *Star Wars* cherry, silly," Dylan said, laughing, punching him lightly in the arm.

"Is that a thing?" If it was, then Logan wanted it to be Dylan who did it. Logan wanted him to do all kinds of things.

It was a problem, even though he kept trying to pretend it wasn't.

"Sure, it can be," Dylan said, one of those quicksilver grins lighting up his whole face.

"So why this game?" Logan asked, trying to pluck the game from Dylan's fingers, but he was too quick, and pulled it away. "'Cause it's easy?"

"Well, it's simpler, sure, but it also requires less hand-eye coordination," Dylan said, and Logan shot him a glare. But Dylan only laughed. "We're being honest here, dude. Set you on a football field, and you'd destroy most everyone, but with a video game controller in your hands?"

"Fine, fine, fine," Logan said with a resigned sigh. He grabbed for the game again, and Dylan wasn't quite fast enough this time, and when Logan got ahold of it, he didn't let go.

Yanked both it *and* Dylan over the side of the couch, and Logan froze as the other guy landed basically in his lap.

He 100% did not mean to freeze. It wasn't in his nature to freeze.

After all, they had a touchy-feely friendship. Logan had never shied away from touching Dylan and vice versa. It worked for them.

But now he was *in his lap.*

And he wasn't moving.

Logan could count every shade of green in Dylan's eyes as they stared at each other. His hand hovered right over Dylan's back. He wanted to push him in, pull him close, but no matter how touchy-feely they *were,* they weren't in the habit of embracing. Not like this.

Not with Dylan straddling him, not only wearing a pair of athletic shorts each.

Then Dylan reached out, pressing a palm against Logan's chest. Right where his rose tattoo sat, right over his heart. Not pushing him away. Not using him to get up. Just resting it there.

Like he couldn't help it, he just wanted to touch.

You're wrong. He doesn't want to. Not like that. Not like you want him to.

Logan opened his mouth to make a joke, but his brain was empty, and nothing came out.

Dylan leaned forward a fraction. Licked his lips.

There was something soft and hazy and affectionate in his gaze. Something curious.

And then he spoke. "Guess," he said, voice low, "that your reflexes really do suck, Banks."

Logan gave a shaky laugh. Here was the joke that he was supposed to have made, but even after making it, Dylan didn't seem very inclined to move.

"Guess they do," he said.

He didn't even sound like himself. He sounded all breathless and anticipatory.

He'd hooked up with plenty of guys. Even guys he'd really wanted, at the time.

But none of them had ever felt like this, even before the first kiss. All shaky and hesitant and aching.

"It's okay," Dylan said softly. "I like you anyway."

"Even without *Star Wars*?"

"Listen." Dylan's voice was earnest, and his gaze . . . Logan could barely meet it, but he couldn't quite look away either. "I'm gonna remedy that. But even if I never do . . ." He licked his lips again, and Logan's stomach clenched. "Yeah, you're good in my book, Banks. Real good."

He couldn't possibly be thinking about kissing, too.

Dylan was *straight*.

Except he didn't look real straight right now, sitting in Logan's lap, continually glancing down at his lips.

The thing was, Logan couldn't sit here forever, like this, and keep it PG. His dick, unfortunately interested in Dylan from the first moment, even though he had told it to *chill*, was going to join the party sooner rather than later.

"Uh, thanks?" Already it felt like he didn't have any fucking blood in his brain.

Dylan tilted his head, questioning.

Fuck it, Logan thought, and gave up the argument, settling his hand wide and warm against Dylan's lower back.

Any straight guy would've noped right out of that.

But Dylan didn't move.

Maybe he didn't give a shit. Maybe he and Jamie, his other gay friend, cuddled like this all the time. A fierce sense of possession roared through Logan at that thought. He didn't like that *at all*, even if it was unfair. Even if Dylan could cuddle with whoever he liked.

"Is this . . ." Dylan trailed off.

And goddamn it, he swayed even closer.

Another minute, and there was no way Logan was going to be able to keep his erection from prodding at Dylan's ass.

A loud ring echoed through the silence and Dylan jumped, scrambling up. "Uh," he mumbled, and Logan understood. He was just as frazzled.

His phone rang again, vibrating insistently against the glass top of the coffee table in front of them.

"That's uh, a family ring," Logan said.

"Oh, yeah, your brother, right?" Dylan said, and Logan could tell he was trying not to make it awkward. The phone kept blaring and Logan still hadn't moved.

Wasn't sure he could without tripping over his own goddamned feet or his mouth, for that matter. How was he gonna talk to Levi like this?

"Yeah," Logan said, finally pushing himself upright and glancing over at the phone screen.

"I'll let you get that . . . better get a decent night's rest," Dylan mumbled, and before Logan could stop him, tell him that he could talk to Levi any old time, he was gone, disappearing out of the room.

The phone stopped ringing. Finally.

But Logan reached for it anyway, redialing Levi's number.

"Hey, you busy with something?" Levi asked as soon as he picked up.

Logan looked over at the doorway, the one Dylan had just disappeared through. "Uh, nothing important," he said. "Dylan and I were just playing some video games."

Levi snickered. "He gonna help you get any better?"

Last summer, he'd discovered to his horror that Levi, while *also* never having video games growing up, had become really good at them. He'd whipped his butt several times.

That memory was partially why when Dylan had shown up with the system that he hadn't protested very long or very hard.

He clearly needed the practice, because while he could absolutely smash Levi into submission in every other way that counted, apparently he couldn't do it with a controller in his hands.

Anything that gave Levi the upper hand was unacceptable.

"Don't worry, next time we play," Logan said, "I'm gonna kick your ass."

It was way easier to think about the friendly rivalry he had with his brothers than to think about what had just happened between him and Dylan.

"You keep hopin' that's gonna happen," Levi teased.

"Hope's for wusses," Logan retorted. "What's up, baby bro? You doin' okay in Seattle?"

"Yeah," Levi said, but there was a slight hesitation—so slight that maybe nobody else would've heard it, but Logan did, because he'd been watching out for Levi for most of his life.

"Cut the shit," Logan said. "What's up?"

"I just . . ." He heard Levi sigh, heavily. "What do you do when someone on your line won't pull their weight?"

"Is that what's going on?" Logan kicked himself. He hadn't watched Levi's game tape from last week because he'd been too busy hanging out with Dylan. When was the last time he hadn't made time to watch his baby bro's tape? Logan couldn't remember.

"Sorta. He just . . . he's kinda an ass, upfront, so I expected him to be a dick in the locker room, you know? But then during practice, he's not blocking, during last week's game he gave up two holding calls, and didn't really give a shit."

"Listen, I know that it might seem like he doesn't," Logan said, "but trust me, every one of us gives a shit. Even if we never show it."

"He doesn't." Logan had rarely heard Levi's voice this hard. They had their brotherly rivalry—but at the core, it was friendly. "So, you talk to your coach about this?"

"He brushed me off. Thinks Nathan's just dealing with some shit, but that he won't let it get on the field. He *let* it get on the field, Logan. I saw him. Half the downs I was fucking double-blocking and he's just given up, yards downfield."

Logan knew his brother never gave up on a play. It was something they had in common.

"You gotta elevate it. Don't confront him. It's not your job to coach him."

"Really? Ya think?" Logan could hear Levi's eye roll even through the phone. Just like his sarcasm, it was impossible to miss.

"I thought you called to ask my advice," Logan said.

"Shit, I just hate this," Levi said. "It's never been like this before. We were always . . . well, a fucking unit, you know? Blood, sweat, and tears. All of that. You ever have a guy on the line who wouldn't cooperate? Wouldn't play his heart out?"

Logan thought about it. "No," he said, finally. "No, but I think you just gotta let it play out. Keep up. Put your own heart into it, and he's gonna show his true stripes, sooner rather than later."

"I hate that you're right," Levi said.

Logan couldn't remember the last time Levi had sounded so young. So defeated.

When he'd been in Minnesota, he'd been closer to Seattle, which had felt like a bonus, because he could be there for Levi, if he'd ever needed him. But while Minnesota *was* closer to Seattle, it wasn't like it was really all that close.

Both he and Landry were too far away now.

Levi needs to learn to make it on his own. This is his life, and he's an adult now.

He was, even if Logan didn't want to think of him that way.

"You're just gonna have to deal with it," Logan said.

Levi was silent for a long moment.

"You've been busy," he said.

"In case you missed it, we lost two games in a row, and things kinda suck here," Logan said.

"You still think you made the right decision, going to Miami?"

Logan didn't have to think twice about it. He could still feel the heat echo of Dylan's body, pressed against his own. And it wasn't just that, but the way he'd laughed. The way one night, after the second loss, they'd just sat here together, staring at the TV, at old Jeopardy reruns. They'd made each other feel better without saying a single fucking word.

It was Sebastian Howard, coming back into his own.

It was Pax, fighting through not only his own insecurity, but Davis' as well.

It was Beau and Coach Dawson and everyone who was working their asses off to make sure they succeeded against everyone's fucked-up expectations.

"Yeah," he said, without hesitating. "Yeah, absolutely. It was the right call for me."

"Because you want to come out."

"Not just that, but yeah. I think I could, here. The support system's here, and it's great, honestly."

"Good, I'm really fucking glad for you," Levi said warmly. For once, for a brief moment, their brotherly rivalry was silent. "And besides, you've got Dylan now, right?"

Logan really didn't want to talk about Dylan. Especially not tonight. Not when what had just happened between them was so fresh.

So fresh you're gonna go upstairs, after you hang up with Levi, and you're gonna take a shower, and you're gonna come your brains out, just thinking about Dylan sittin' pretty on your lap.

"Dylan, yeah," Logan said. "He's great."

"And you're okay with sharing your place with him?" Levi sounded skeptical.

"We're barely ever here," Logan said with a chuckle. "Don't you spend like ninety-five percent of your time at the practice facility or travelin' to a game?"

"Yeah, yeah," Levi said with a chuckle. "Guess I do. But that's workin' out okay?"

"It's awesome. No complaints. Nice to have someone to hang around with, ya know?" Logan didn't say it, but the way Levi hummed under his breath made it clear he understood.

Logan remembered how hard it had been to lose the daily companionship—near constant for his childhood and beyond—of his two brothers. They'd shared everything, and then Landry had left, and then Logan, and then Levi.

Lyla was the oldest, two minutes older than Landry, and she'd never wanted to be involved in her brothers' shenanigans, but the three of them? They'd been inseparable, until they weren't.

"Yeah, I get that," Levi said.

"Just hang in there, okay?" Logan said. "I think Landry plays y'all in a few weeks, right? He'll take you out for a beer and you can talk it out."

"Landry doesn't get it. It's not the same."

Logan got that too. "Yeah, I know. He's one of those diva tight ends. Thinks he owns the goddamned place."

"Yep, damn straight he does." He could hear Levi smile. "But . . . it'll be good to see him."

"Thought so," Logan said, trying not to sound too smug. "And our bye week isn't that far away."

"November eleven, that's months away," Levi said incredulously, which the fact that he *knew* which week the Piranhas had off said it all. Logan hadn't even been sure which week in November it was.

"Still, maybe I'll fly over and catch a game. Bring Mom and Dad and Lyla."

"That'd be nice," Levi said. "Think about it. You've got a lot on your plate. Tryin' to win some games. Dealin' with that new roommate of yours." His voice went sly at the end. Which either meant that he suspected the truth, or he just wanted to give Logan shit.

Either way, Logan wasn't happy about it.

"Listen, we're just friends."

"Sure you are," Levi teased.

"Just 'cause I'm gay doesn't mean I want to get up on every guy I see," Logan argued. And it was true, he didn't. He was particular, like anybody else in the world was particular. But he also happened to be inexplicably, annoyingly attracted to Dylan, just like Levi kept hinting he was.

"Oh I know," Levi said knowingly. "But there's something in the way you talk about him . . ."

Ugh. Logan really hoped his brother was full of crap. Because if anyone found out—if *Dylan* found out—he'd be embarrassed. There was no way around it. They were *just friends.*

"Just . . . let it go, okay?" Logan said. He began pacing around the room. This conversation was making him think about what had just happened; and that was bad. It was just . . . it had just been an accident. And then Dylan had been . . . surprisingly comfortable. That was it. It didn't mean anything else.

"Sure thing," Levi said. Clearly pleased with himself.

"I gotta go," Logan said. "It's late."

"Thanks for the advice."

"Say hi to Landry for me and give him plenty of shit, okay?"

Logan could hear Levi's grin through the thousands of miles that separated them. "Like I'd do anything else."

Levi hung up and Logan was left standing in the living room by himself.

Part of him *knew* he needed to go talk to Dylan. Reassure him that he wouldn't make things uncomfortable, that it didn't have to change their friendship.

He was the one who fell into your lap and then stayed there, Logan reminded himself.

Clearly Dylan didn't think it was a big deal. So maybe he shouldn't make a big deal out of it either.

Week Four

Dylan had told himself a million times in the last two weeks that it was no big deal.

Sure, straight guys sat in other guys' laps all the time.

Sure, they had momentary, semi-insane urges to kiss their friends. Their *male* friends.

Right after it had happened, Dylan had escaped upstairs and immediately called the one person who could make it all make sense: his best friend Jamie.

But when questioned about why Dylan would be feeling all these things, Jamie hadn't done much other than chuckle. "I'm just gonna say," he'd added, *so* unhelpfully, "that sexuality is fluid. We don't know enough about it to understand exactly how or why it works. But it sounds like you're attracted to Logan."

Dylan had absorbed this, and spent the last two weeks wondering if it was actually true.

Was he attracted to Logan?

He liked him, so damn much, as a friend and a teammate, and even as a roommate.

And there was that too, wasn't there? He'd planned on finding his own place and moving out in a few days. It'd been a few weeks now, and he didn't want to leave. Logan didn't seem to want him to either, and they'd settled into a routine.

Every time Dylan even suggested that he look for a new house, Logan always said the same thing: *why?*

Why indeed.

But now there was this other wrinkle in their relationship.

Logan hadn't said a word about it the next morning, and so Dylan hadn't either. But it hung there, unspoken, between them.

On every ride to and from the stadium and the practice facility.

Every time they hung out in the living room.

When they played Lego Star Wars.

Even when Dylan had set Logan down with an enormous bowl full of popcorn and they'd watched *A New Hope* together.

Dylan glanced over now at where Logan lay on the weight bench, biceps bunching with each rep, and couldn't help but think, *maybe I am. Maybe I'm attracted to him, a guy, for the first time.*

Logan was gorgeous. Objectively, completely gorgeous. Thick and muscular, and something about his tattoos made Dylan's heart beat a little faster. Which was crazy . . . they were just tattoos! But he lay awake at night, and thought about each and every one of them. What they all meant. What Logan's skin might taste like, if he touched any of them with his tongue.

He'd meant what he'd said to the guys when Sebastian had taken them to their favorite sushi place the other week: *I'm not against it. I guess it would have to be the right situation. The right guy.*

The joke was on him, because when he'd said that, he was already thinking, *I think I've met the right guy, and I'm in the right situation.* But he didn't know how to tell Logan that.

Didn't know how to even begin that particular conversation.

Instead, he'd asked Logan last week what his type was. Wondering, even though he shouldn't, if *he* could be Logan's type.

But Logan had dodged the question instead of answering it. Leaving Dylan just as in the dark as he'd been before.

He'd been waiting til the prime opportunity presented itself to try to shed some light on the situation. Not when they were alone in Logan's house—no, that was definitely a mistake. He might do something crazy, like throw himself at the guy. Even if it turned out that he *wasn't* Logan's type.

No, he'd wanted a situation where they were technically in public, but protected from doing anything he might regret.

This, the weight room early on a Wednesday morning—so early nobody else had come in yet—was perfect.

Logan finished his set, and pulled off his old t-shirt, wiping his face with it. Dylan, doing tricep curls, messed up his rhythm.

"You know, you never answered my question," Dylan said casually. Like it was no big deal. Like he hadn't lain awake half a dozen nights since it happened, thinking about it.

"What question?" Logan always had a smile for him. Always a kind eye. Looked out for him.

Even if they were never anything more, Dylan would be glad they'd met for that and that alone. He'd been a welcoming force and a friendly face at a time when he'd needed it. Every time he was uneasy—it still happened, Dylan found it hard, after the way his career had begun and then the trade, to really settle completely—Logan was there to say a few supportive words.

"You never told me what your type is," Dylan said.

Logan paused as he stretched. It was just a brief second, but Dylan saw it because Dylan was attuned to everything he did.

Every movement he made.

Every smile that crossed his face.

If this was what being attracted to a friend felt like, he both loved and hated it.

Some moments, it felt like Dylan couldn't even *breathe*.

"You worrying about me finding a date?" Logan teased.

Trying, Dylan was positive, to keep things light. Easy. Uncomplicated.

Well, they'd passed from simple to complicated weeks ago.

The first time Dylan had stood in the shower and let himself think about Logan when he jacked off. What he'd smell like. What he'd feel like. How different he'd be, but somehow, still everything that Dylan craved.

Yeah, they were long past simple, easy, or straightforward.

"Yeah," Dylan said, "maybe you're a monk?"

"No, just don't typically hook up during the season." Logan rarely sounded standoffish. In fact, Dylan realized, this was the first time. Logan didn't want to talk about this.

Maybe he doesn't want to talk about this with you.

"Is that all you do, then? Hook up?" Dylan asked.

"Yeah, usually." Logan shot him a look. "Why you so interested? You want to go out? Bring a date home? Fine by me." Except, Dylan thought, *was it?* Sure, Logan had said it but he hadn't sounded like he *meant* it.

He'd gotten a lot better at telling when what Logan said and what he meant didn't line up. It didn't happen often, but he was at least seventy-five percent sure that they weren't today.

"No, actually, I don't," Dylan said. "I just heard Sebastian say something to you the other day, and I realized you hadn't had anyone over. You couldn't have even gone out, 'cause we . . . well, we've been spending so much time together I don't know how I could've missed it."

"You didn't miss it. I haven't gone out, and it's fine." Logan's voice was still steady, but there was a look in his eyes that Dylan hadn't seen before. He really didn't want to talk about this, and if Dylan was *any* kind of friend, he'd let him have this and let it go.

But he didn't *want* to let it go, because this wasn't just about Logan, this was about him, too.

"So you really aren't going to tell me your type?" Dylan asked.

Logan gave a short bark of laughter. "Why do you even care?"

"I don't know. We're friends? Friends talk about this shit."

Logan stood up and walked over to the mat, grabbing a medicine ball. Apparently wanting to give Dylan even more hell, because whenever he did abs . . . well, that day a few weeks ago had truly been the prompt for that first shower jerkoff session.

"You're not a bad friend if you don't want to hear about me with guys," Logan said. Giving him an out. Because that was exactly who Logan was.

I don't want to hear about you and other guys because I'm . . . well, I think I might be jealous.

Sebastian's comments that he'd overheard had made it clear that Logan definitely had a hookup kind of reputation. No relationships. Only sex, only occasionally.

Maybe they'd only been friends for a little bit now, but Dylan already suspected that deep down, Logan wasn't a hookup kind of guy. He was a relationship guy. His friendship with Dylan proved that.

Logan was a good guy. The *best* kind of guy. He deserved to get what he really wanted, deep down.

"You think that bothers me?" Dylan challenged. "Jamie tells me about him and Neal all the time. It *doesn't*."

For a long minute, Logan did his ab exercises with the medicine ball, and didn't answer.

Maybe, Dylan thought worriedly, he'd pushed him too far.

Honestly, it was too much to hope that maybe Dylan's attraction—even as inexplicable as it was—was returned.

Logan finished up his set, and set the ball aside. Turned towards where Dylan sat on the weight bench. "This about the other night?" he asked.

"What other night?" Except that Dylan knew exactly what night he was referring to.

No way was he referring to *Star Wars* night. Or the last ten other nights they'd spent together on the couch. No, he was definitely referring to the night when Dylan had ended up in his lap and had *liked* it.

Logan rolled his eyes. "You know what I'm talking about, Dylan. Don't play dumb, because I know how fucking smart you are."

"Oh, so we're gonna talk about it now?"

"You want to?" Logan asked, raising an eyebrow. "'Cause it sure seems like you do."

He hadn't, actually. He'd just wanted to . . . Dylan actually didn't know what he'd wanted from any of this. To understood where he stood? To believe that he wasn't alone?

That when Logan went to bed, alone, he couldn't sleep either, because he was too busy thinking about Dylan?

But he wasn't ready to say any of that. It was too much, too soon. Dylan wasn't proud of it, but he definitely felt freaked out.

Like the world had just turned upside down too quickly for his equilibrium.

"That's what I thought," Logan said when Dylan didn't say anything. "Now, let's get back to our workout."

He shouldn't have been annoyed.

No, 'cause you're the one who chickened out. You brought it up and then you totally panicked.

But he was, anyway.

They finished their workout in silence, and went their separate ways, Logan to the offensive line meeting and Dylan to the special teams meeting.

Dylan didn't say he was avoiding Logan necessarily, but if he skipped lunch in the cafeteria, grabbing an energy bar out of his locker instead, and then went onto the practice field to get some extra kicks in before everyone else showed up, then so be it.

But by the time they met up, post-practice, Dylan wasn't mad anymore. He just felt guilty. He'd brought it up and then balked. That wasn't Logan's fault. He couldn't even blame him for being annoyed about it.

"Listen," Dylan said as they walked to the car, "I'm sorry. I didn't mean to push about that . . . it wasn't ever my intention."

Logan turned to him, a genuine smile on his face. Dylan felt that same flip-flop of his stomach, that he didn't want to feel but that *kept freaking happening*. "I'm sorry too. Sorry I snapped. Friends?"

Friends was *great*. Friends was what Dylan kept telling himself he really wanted, before he kept getting caught up in everything else.

Before he'd landed on Logan's lap and *liked it*.

"Yeah," he said, stopping and pulling Logan into a quick hug. Feeling the heat and the solidness of him for an instant before he let go. "Friends."

CHAPTER THREE

Week Six

Whenever the phone rang so early in the morning, it was a bad sign.

It was an even worse sign when Logan groggily reached over to the bedside table for it and he realized it was Simon Lang, his agent, who was calling.

"Simon," Logan answered, his heart already pounding, his stomach lurching sickeningly, "what's wrong?"

Because it had to be something wrong.

Simon wouldn't ever call at five a.m. if there wasn't something wrong.

"You remember Ricky, right?"

The bottom dropped out of his stomach entirely.

"Yeah, of course I remember Ricky."

Ricky had been a guy, young and ambitious, trying to make it as an influencer, who he'd hooked up with in Minnesota occasionally. He hadn't ever bothered to have Ricky sign an NDA, because it had just been a few times, and at that point, Ricky had been adamant that he wasn't going to come out anytime soon. He'd not necessarily felt *safe*, but *safer*.

"I just got a heads-up," Simon said with a deep, weary sigh, "that he's publishing some kind of expose about you and him."

A thousand moments flashed through Logan's head in that one single, endless moment. All the times he'd hoped that he might be able to come out on his own terms, make his own choices, dictate the path of his own life.

Only to have all of that ripped away.

"We can't stop it?" Logan asked, even though he knew that if Simon could, he'd have already done it.

"No," Simon said heavily. "It's mostly about his career. Everything he's doing on TikTok. Though he gets in a few good wallops on you."

"What does he say?"

Logan didn't even know what Ricky *could* say. They'd never been serious. A handful of hookups, with never any promises between them. And when Logan had decided to sign with the Piranhas, leaving Minneapolis for Miami, he'd sent Ricky a quick text, letting him know that things were done between them. Not that they'd ever really begun. Ricky had always wanted to spend more time together than Logan had.

Honestly, he hadn't even *thought* about Ricky since moving to Miami.

Which really . . . Logan realized . . . said it all.

"That you abandoned him in Minneapolis. That you promised to help and support him in his career and you abandoned him there, too. That he's made something of himself in spite of you not because of you. I think that was the quote."

"What," Logan declared flatly. "What the fuck. No. I never promised him a goddamned thing. We hooked up a couple of times, that was it. Nothing else. I never even . . . we weren't even *together*."

"That's definitely not what he's claiming," Simon said with resignation. "He's talking a full star-crossed love story. Absolutely heartbroken, etcetera, etcetera. Fits in with this new song he's gonna put up on TikTok."

"Oh, that's such fucking bullshit," Logan said. "Not only does the guy have to out me, he's gonna lie about it, too?"

"Seems he is," Simon said. Paused. "I am so sorry, Logan, I knew you wanted to do this on your own terms. When you were ready. It sucks that it happened this way."

It did suck.

It sucked even more than Logan could deal with right now. Later, when he didn't feel so numb, he would probably realize the extent to which it sucked. But right now, he couldn't think of any of that.

"What can we do about it? Issue a statement?"

"We're going to, absolutely," Simon said. "Crisis meeting first thing, at seven, at the Piranhas offices. Helen, the head of PR, is going to take point on this. I trust her, and you should too. I won't make it for this meeting, but I'm flying in a few hours after."

"What does Helen want to do?"

"Helen," Simon said carefully, and that was what worried Logan more than anything—the careful edge in his agent's voice, "is going to do what's best for you and for the Piranhas."

"You mean, she's going to do what's best for the Piranhas," Logan said.

Simon sighed. "Normally, I'd worry about this more, but currently the Piranhas have three players out of the closet, along with the coach's son. I think in this situation, your goals and her goals are going to align pretty closely, plus, I know she was around, working for the Piranhas, when O'Connor came out of the closet," Simon added, referring to the Piranhas quarterback who had come out many years earlier as bisexual, becoming the first out player in the NFL. He'd retired two years ago, but his presence was still felt, throughout the whole league. "She's got experience with this. I trust her to take care of it."

"If you trust her . . ."

"Logan," Simon said patiently, "I do. And you should too. Besides, I'm gonna be there, in a few hours. You got a friend you can lean on til I get there? I know Levi and Landry . . ."

"They won't be able to come. Might be able to get Lyla on a plane," Logan said, though he didn't really want to ask her. She had a life. A job. She couldn't go flying off to protect her little brother all the time. "I've got a friend though." And realized that he meant it. Dylan would be there for him. It wouldn't be just him either. Sebastian would go to bat for him, and Beau. Wade and Tristan, too. Definitely Pax. Logan had a feeling that Pax would understand where he was coming from, all too well.

Logan knew that even Coach would understand. Just last week he'd pulled him aside and given him a little pep talk after his confrontation with Micah Rose, the new rookie corner.

"We preach acceptance and damn good football here," Coach had said, patting him on the shoulder. "I appreciate you standin' up for Beau in there. For makin' sure everyone knows that's not how we do things here."

Logan realized now that that *wasn't* how they did things here.

Barely anybody would blink an eye, when they found out that Logan Banks was gay. Even the fans wouldn't give a shit. In fact, they might even like him better now.

It would not have been this easy, if Ricky had done this while he was still in Minnesota.

There was, Logan decided, at least *that* silver lining.

"So you're gonna be okay til I get there?" Simon asked, clearly concerned.

"Oh, I'm gonna be just fine," Logan said, and knew that he meant every word he was saying. It was all gonna be just fine.

He'd meant to do this anyway. Did it suck that Ricky had taken away his chance to do it the way he wanted? Yeah, of course it did. But the point was, it had happened.

He was *free*.

He tried to focus on the intoxicating rush of it—and not the frustration that Ricky had screwed him over—as he walked down the hall to Dylan's room and knocked on the door.

After a few more knocks, it opened to reveal a sleepy Dylan. "What's going on?" he asked. "We don't have to get up for hours yet."

They didn't. Logan supposed he could have waited til right when he needed to leave for the meeting with Helen. But he also didn't want to go downstairs and eat breakfast alone, either. He wanted . . . well, he wanted Dylan.

Yeah, you do, a sly voice reminded him, but he pushed it away.

Dylan was his friend. Especially this morning.

"I just got a call," Logan said. Trying not to focus on the way Dylan brushed his still too-long hair out of his sleepy eyes. "Some guy I hooked up with in Minnesota, he wrote an article about us. About me."

Logan could see that it took a moment—a *long* moment—for Dylan to understand what he was saying.

"An asshole you hooked up with just *outed* you?" Dylan said incredulously. "What a dick. Man, I am so sorry." Before Logan could register what was happening, he had an armful of sleepy Dylan.

For a moment, he just stood there and *felt*.

Felt Dylan, and his warm, sleepy softness. Felt his love. His support. His loyalty. It wrapped around him, and more than anything else, it comforted him.

But slowly, the comfort started to morph into something else.

They'd hugged before, of course, but nothing like this.

Not an extended hug. Not an . . . well, an embrace. Because that was what it felt like.

Like Dylan didn't want to let him go.

His head came up to his shoulder and yeah, Logan realized, that was his chin resting on his shoulder. His arms wrapped around his shoulders. His body pressed so utterly close to Logan's own. He could feel every inch of it. Skin against skin.

The moment *that* thought went through his brain, it was game over.

He let go and Dylan stumbled backwards a half a step. Like he hadn't expected it to end. Like he hadn't wanted it to.

He didn't say anything, and neither did Logan. They just stood there, staring at each other.

Dylan wasn't in his lap this time—but it felt the same, like the moment stretched out between them, all the possibilities laid out between one breath and the next.

It would be so easy to just lean in and kiss him.

Logan wanted to. God knew he wanted to. But he'd told Simon that Dylan was there for him, and he *was*. What kind of friend would he be if he took advantage of Dylan's support like that? If he pushed, when all he should be doing was gratefully accepting?

Finally, Dylan broke the silence between them. "What are you gonna do?" he asked.

"I have a meeting in an hour, with Helen, who does the PR for the Piranhas," he said. "My agent's flying in, but I don't think he'll be in time for the meeting. As for what we're doing, I guess we'll probably put out a statement."

"You okay with that? You could just ignore it." Dylan leaned back against the edge of the doorframe.

"I could. I could definitely pull a Sebastian and say I don't want to talk about it, but . . ." Logan hesitated. "I *want* to talk about it. I would have done this, anyway, but on my own timeline, maybe next offseason, if I'd gotten the choice."

Dylan nodded. "Okay, then you should. Maybe this wasn't your idea right now, but own it. Make it yours. Don't let that asshole guy make any more decisions for you."

"You know what? I won't." Logan found himself smiling. "You're great, you know that?"

Dylan smirked. "So everyone keeps saying. You want breakfast?" He paused for a second, and then just shook his head. "Nope, you're gettin' breakfast, that's what's happening. Happy Coming Out Day breakfast for you, Logan Banks. And then, you know what? I'm going to the meeting with you."

"What?" Logan was surprised.

"Yeah, you shouldn't be alone in there. Sure, Helen probably has your back. But you said Simon won't be there?"

"Not yet, no. He's got to fly in from New York."

"Then I'm coming. I'll be your advocate."

Logan wanted to roll his eyes, but honestly, deep down, he was touched.

"You'd do that?" he asked as they made their way down the stairs, towards the kitchen.

"Of course I would. I'm hoping I just have to sit there in menacing silence, my very presence being enough to keep everyone in line," Dylan teased as he pulled the fridge door open. "But I have every intention of intervening if necessary."

Logan laughed. He couldn't help himself. The idea of Dylan being menacing? A threat? It was funny, but it was heartwarming too, because it would be in his service.

"If you really want to, I'm sure it's fine that you come with me," Logan said.

"What do *you* want?" Dylan asked, opening a carton of eggs. "'Cause as far as I'm concerned, that's the most important thing right now."

"Would you really . . ." Logan cleared his throat. He hadn't realized how much he *hadn't* wanted to go to the meeting with Helen by himself, until Dylan had offered. "Would you really do that?"

Dylan set a pan on the stove and began to crack eggs into a bowl, whisking them. "Course," he said. Then turned to Logan with a brilliant smile on his face. "I think a Happy Coming Out Day breakfast *also* includes sausage, don't you think?"

Logan spluttered. "You are *filthy*," he said, but reached into the fridge, pulling out the packet. "I forget 'cause you look all innocent and sweet, and then that shit comes out of your mouth."

"It's part of my charm," Dylan said with a grin. "Now, put on the coffee. It's fucking early and I am gonna need all the caffeine in the world if I'm gonna be your protector."

"Sure thing, boss," Logan said.

Six weeks ago, he'd never have imagined that suggesting Dylan stay with him for a few days would turn into this. But now he couldn't imagine living in this house without him.

"You should text your brothers, too," Dylan suggested as they sat down to eat a few minutes later. "They might get questions, if the article is coming out today."

"But they're gonna get all . . ." Logan trailed off, complaining.

"Protective?" Dylan teased. "Yeah, that's kinda part of the Banks charm, I've discovered."

"After we figure out what we're doing, I'll tell them then," Logan said, fully aware he was putting it off. Levi was still dealing with that uncooperative guard on his team, and Landry would absolutely, one hundred and ten percent go AWOL from the Bills, all to protect Logan.

Dylan raised an eyebrow, but didn't argue.

He didn't have any brothers or sisters of his own, but he'd gotten a front-row seat to the chaos that was the Banks family.

Even Landry was asking about Dylan now. Wondering, in that quiet, stern way of his, what was going on between them. "Y'all don't sound like just friends," Landry had said, just the other day, "you sure that you don't . . ."

"I don't," Logan had said firmly. But he was wondering if, in fact, he *did*. But most of the time he managed not to think about it, because that would suck.

Even worse than Ricky outing him.

Yeah, falling in love with his straight best friend would be the *worst*.

Logan seemed relaxed all the way up til the moment they walked into the conference room, and Helen stood to welcome them, a tense expression on her face.

Then, Dylan kinda thought he would've turned and run back to the car if he wasn't right there, behind him, a friendly hand on his back, guiding him into the room.

"Hey," Logan said wryly, "sorry to get you out of bed so early." She *did* look like she'd been up all night, with dark circles under her eyes, but this was also part of her job, Dylan assumed. Crisis management. "Dylan wanted to be here for me, so I said it was okay."

"Of course. Totally fine. I get it," Helen said, nodding sympathetically. "Simon said he'd be on his way later today? But I'd like to try to get much of our response nailed down now, so there's no questions on what we're doing or saying. Since it's Tuesday, there'll be media hanging around today and tomorrow, and they'll have all seen the story." She gestured to a large screen at the end of the conference room, and Dylan realized then why Logan had tensed.

There it was, blown up in nearly life size, an article that proclaimed, *TikToker Ricky Barnes and his Personal Heartbreak.*

Logan had never even mentioned Ricky, though on the way to the practice facility, Dylan hadn't been able to help himself. He'd asked about Ricky, trying to be conscious of Logan's feelings, curious to know how they'd been involved. But Logan had claimed they'd hooked up a few times, and that was it.

Now, though, Dylan got a real good look at the guy Logan had liked.

He was cute and petite, with elfin features and a shock of bleached-blond hair, styled perfectly. Wearing a bright pink shirt unbuttoned nearly to the waist.

Dylan glanced down at his own plain blue t-shirt, and knew from the quick glance he'd gotten in the mirror that his dark hair was at least a few months past needing cut. It was the wrong time to think about it—he was supposed to be here for Logan, as a friend, and whatever support he needed—but at least he had an answer to the question that had haunted him.

He knew what kind of guy Logan liked now.

He's nothing like you.

It was better this way, Dylan decided. Their friendship was important to him, and he didn't want to fuck it up. They'd come close, two times before—that night when he'd accidentally landed in Logan's lap and *liked it*, and then when he'd tried to ask what Logan's type was, and he'd gotten flustered and upset—but now he was glad that they hadn't crossed the line.

"Let's start," Helen said, "with what our first response should be to this story. Have you read it?"

Logan shook his head.

"I forwarded the text of it to your email, but we can just go over the essentials, if you'd prefer," Helen said briskly, all business, which Dylan found he appreciated. Overwrought drama, even if it was deserved, wasn't going to get anything done. And Helen was right; it was Tuesday. Media would be crawling all over the facility today and tomorrow, and especially now that they knew about this story.

Everyone was going to need to have a story and a pat answer.

"Essentials are fine." Logan made a face. "I already know enough to know that most of the stuff about me is a total lie. We never dated. We hooked up maybe half a dozen times. I never promised him anything, I definitely never promised to help him with his career. We barely ever discussed it. Talk . . ." Logan flushed. "We didn't talk much when we were together."

Dylan told himself that he was burning with injustice for his friend. And he *was*. But he was also burning with . . . with something else. With the idea of crawling into Logan's bed and not talking at all.

"I see," Helen said, her voice neutral. "That is something we can correct of course. He doesn't look good outing you like this, but they're framing it like you broke his heart and this is the only way he could get your attention. Especially considering . . ." To Dylan's shock, she glanced right at him. "Especially considering what he claims in the article."

"What else does he claim?" Logan's voice was hard. Unrelenting.

"He says he's seen you in pictures and videos with another man," Helen said diplomatically. "He's claiming that you ditched him in Minnesota and then moved on with someone else. Someone in Miami."

Logan laughed humorlessly. "Who on earth would I possibly have time to be involved with?"

Helen shot Dylan another one of those unexpectedly apologetic glances, and Dylan had a feeling he knew where this was going. "Well, the man you're living with, for starters," she said.

"What," Logan spat out. "Ricky thinks I'm dating *Dylan*?"

"You're living with him. There's a number of shots with your arm around him. Touchy-feely kind of stuff," she said and held up her hand when Logan's face turned murderous. "It's not a problem, and I'm not saying you did anything wrong, I'm only saying, that's his assumption. So we can correct it, of course, and make it clear that not only did you never date Ricky, you aren't dating Dylan either."

"Yeah, we will. Immediately," Logan growled. "That's gonna be the first line. *Logan Banks is single*." He turned to Dylan. "God, man, I am so sorry. You're not even . . . you don't need to be fake outed, along with everything else."

"He's not the only one who picked up on it, Logan," Helen said gently. "It's . . . well, when I called around to my other media contacts in the Miami area, there's another story brewing, this one's just about you and Dylan. I think the reporter said it was titled, *Miami's Hot New Couple You Never Saw Coming*."

"Yeah, they never saw it coming because it's bullshit. We're *friends*." Logan, who'd finally settled in his chair, shot it back and stood, beginning to pace around the room. He looked madder than Dylan had ever seen him before.

"Listen, it's fine, if we need to deal with the other stuff first . . ." Dylan didn't even get the words out before Logan shut them down.

"No," he said, pounding a fist on the table. "*No*."

"We can certainly start off there," Helen said, clicking a pen and pulling a notebook closer to her, beginning to make notes. "Talking about how you wanted to come out on your own terms, and that you're disappointed with Ricky for taking away your agency here. Then, clarifying all the things that the article gets wrong, starting with your relationship with Ricky, and then continuing on to . . ." She paused, hesitating. "Though . . ."

"Though *what*?" Logan demanded.

"Though, I'll be honest . . . the article is a bad look. It's easy to issue a denial, of course, but it doesn't take away the taste," Helen said with an apologetic look. "It's too bad, honestly, that you're not really together, because that would be *such* a good story. Easy to put a positive spin on something that isn't so positive now."

"You're not serious," Logan said incredulously. "He outed me."

"He did, and that *was* shitty, but I'm serious about the other thing, because whoever wrote this did a masterful job of making him look like a heartbroken saint and you like the devil. But we won't go there," Helen said frankly, "because you've made it clear that's not a possibility, and we know that Dylan isn't . . . well, that you're only friends, so it doesn't matter."

Dylan had promised himself that he wouldn't interrupt the meeting unless it was important.

But this felt important, so he raised his voice. "If we were together, do you really think that would help Logan?" he asked, directing the question towards Helen.

"You can't possibly . . ." Logan spluttered, but Dylan ignored him.

Ignored the voice inside his own head that was screaming that this was the dumbest idea he'd ever had.

If it was so dumb, why did it feel so right?

"I don't even think you'd have to be together, you just wouldn't deny the accusation that Ricky makes," Helen said bluntly. "But I know it's not an option, since you're not interested in dating men, Dylan."

"I wouldn't mind actually," Dylan said before Logan could explode.

He didn't think Logan had a temper, he'd never seen it, not in any of the time that they'd spent together, but he could practically feel it bubbling up now.

"You . . . you don't mind?" Helen sounded shocked. Dylan had a feeling she wasn't shocked very often.

Dylan shrugged. "Why does it matter? Isn't queerness a scale? Just because I haven't dated a guy before doesn't mean I wouldn't date Logan. If it helps his image for everyone to think we're dating, then I don't have a problem not issuing a denial. We'll know the truth, and we'll make sure that the team knows the truth."

"Dylan," Logan said through clenched teeth. "This is a terrible . . ."

"Idea?" Dylan grinned. "Maybe. But it could help you, and I want to help you."

Logan's expression softened. "I know you do, and God knows I appreciate it, but I don't need you to pretend to be something you're not, just to make me look good. That's not on you, man. You've been there for me enough . . . I wouldn't want to do that to you."

"How do you know it's something I'm not?" Dylan hadn't wanted to be so blunt about it. He'd wanted . . . well, there were so many things he wanted, most of them things he couldn't explain, couldn't put words to. But he knew, without a doubt in his mind, that he wasn't completely straight.

He wouldn't be fantasizing at night about putting his hands all over his best friend if he was.

"This is . . ." Logan's jaw tightened. He looked away. "Can you give us a minute?" he asked Helen.

She still looked stunned, like the last thing she'd expected was for a football player who was straight to *voluntarily* agree to appear to be not so straight.

Dylan supposed her shock wasn't misplaced. Despite the advances the NFL had made since Colin O'Connor had come out—since *she* had helped O'Connor come out—there was still a decent amount of toxic masculinity in the sport. It was unavoidable, even though nobody liked talking about it.

"Uh, sure, of course," she said, picking up her pad and pen, her skirt swishing past them as she walked out the door, closing it behind them.

Dylan knew he should be able to look Logan in the eye. After all, he was the one who was offering to . . . well, be his fake boyfriend.

Because that was what it was, wasn't it?

Helen could talk nicely about how they just wouldn't be correcting the assumption, and he could say they'd tell everyone they knew the truth, but for general purposes, he'd have a boyfriend.

Logan would be his boyfriend.

Dylan took a deep breath and glanced up, meeting Logan's eyes.

If he couldn't do that, how could he do anything else?

"Explain," Logan said in a terse voice. He still hadn't sat back down, and every muscle in his glorious body was tense, like he wanted nothing more than to flee the room, just like Helen had. "And," he added, "don't you dare tell me this isn't a big deal."

"I know it is," Dylan said. "I'd never disrespect you *or* anyone else I know by saying it isn't. I just . . ." He shrugged. "You heard Helen. I can *help* you. This asshole's done a number on your reputation."

It killed him that out of everyone on the planet, the fucking nicest guy, the guy who'd give the shirt off his back, who would invite a stranger into his home because he needed a place to stay, would get badmouthed like this.

Logan didn't deserve it.

"None of that matters," Logan said.

"It fucking matters to *me*," Dylan retorted.

"I don't think you get it, what you're agreeing to, what everyone will think," Logan said, enunciating each word, like suddenly he was confused and Dylan was an idiot and didn't get what he was agreeing to. But he did.

"I know exactly what everyone will think. I told you . . . it wouldn't necessarily be a lie."

"Just a few weeks ago you proclaimed you weren't queer."

"And you've never done that when you were confused?" Dylan pushed back. "When you were overwhelmed by the newness of it? I've had . . . well, I've had some thoughts. I don't know what they are. But I know that I can't sit here and tell you that I'm going to be lying to the world about who I am."

"No, just who you're dating," Logan muttered.

"Make up your mind which bothers you more." Dylan knew why Logan was being stubborn about this; he wouldn't be the man he was if he didn't push back.

"Fuck, it *all* bothers me," Logan said, beginning to pace again.

It was almost normal now, to let his gaze drift down, to see the way his muscles bunched and flexed as he strode around the room.

That, Dylan knew, was *not* something straight guys noticed about their friends.

They wouldn't want to do more than just look. They wouldn't want to touch, like he did.

"What bothers me the most," Logan continued, like he didn't even realize that Dylan was checking him out—and Dylan hoped he'd never know—"is that this is something you think you *have* to do. Some kind of payback for me letting you stay at the house."

Of course Logan would think that.

Dylan didn't even think—didn't *overthink*. He stood and intercepted Logan right as he crossed behind him. Put his hands on his shoulders. Ignored the muscles twitching under his touch. Looked right into Logan's dark eyes. He was beautiful, inside and out. Dylan couldn't help feeling a pulse of understanding for Ricky. He'd had this man, even if for a few nights, and he'd lost him.

But that didn't explain or excuse the shit he'd given him after. Or the shit that Dylan was going to clean up.

"It's not about that," Dylan said in a low voice, staring right into Logan's face. "I promise you that it isn't. It's about the fact that we're friends. That when I needed you to be a friend, you were. And now that you need me, I want to be there for you."

"But"—Logan sounded absolutely wretched—"it was *easy* for me to be there for you. All I had to do was give you an extra bedroom. Fuck, it was more than easy, it was more for me than for you, because I got *you*, man. For what? You taking a room that wouldn't have gotten used anyway?"

"You can't compare," Dylan said, shaking his head. Not loosening his grip on Logan's shoulders. Maybe he wasn't as strong as the center, but he wasn't weak either. And he wouldn't be weak now, not when this counted. "You really cannot fucking compare."

Logan's gaze softened. "What you gonna do about it, Leonard?"

"What am I gonna do? I'm going to be your fake boyfriend, that's what I'm gonna do."

"You really want to do that?" Logan said with a sigh. Glanced away for the first time.

"I do," Dylan said, resisting the urge to move his hands, and turn Logan's face back. He wanted Logan to see just how much he gave a shit. But maybe it was better this way. It was going to be difficult enough to maintain their friendship when they were pretending to be more without putting their hands all over each other, too.

Except you do anyway, that's part of how you got into this mess.

"I don't want this to ruin a good thing," Dylan added. "We're friends, right? Friends, always?"

Logan smiled for the first time since they'd walked into the conference room and he'd been confronted by *TikToker Ricky Barnes and his Personal Heartbreak.* "Yeah, man, you aren't gettin' rid of me now. You down for matching friendship bracelets?"

Dylan felt relief bubble up inside of him. This was gonna work. He knew it. And nothing, absolutely fucking nothing, had to change.

"I'm down," he said, "for anything."

Chapter Four

"Let me get this straight," Tristan said and then broke off into laughter. "Well, I guess it's not that straight at all," he added when he finally managed to stop giggling.

"It's not," Logan said, trying to be serious, but he couldn't help the few chuckles that escaped him either. "But it's not . . . it's not really like that, you know? He's just doing me a solid. We're not actually together. Just friends, still."

"Sure," Tristan said, his grin knowing. "You're just besties, you just live together, you hang out together all the time, you touch *all the freaking time*, and now you're pretending to be boyfriends. One hundred percent platonic!"

Logan ground his teeth together. Tried not to agree with Tristan because it didn't feel platonic to him either. But he was going to have to tough it out.

Gonna be difficult to pretend to be something you secretly, desperately want, a desire you've buried so deep because you knew it couldn't ever happen, is happening.

"I think it's great that Dylan's doing this for Logan," Wade inserted quietly, his support evident. Same as Tristan's was, just entirely different. "But I *am* sorry you didn't get to do this on your own terms."

"Me too, but I think it's gonna be okay. Actually, it feels good to just be free," Logan said.

"I bet it does," Paxton said, joining their group on the side of the field. Practice was just starting, and he'd been taking advantage of the players gathering to tell them what was going on.

So far he'd gotten several different reactions—none of which were about his sexuality.

Nobody seemed to give a shit about that—but everyone had an opinion about his relationship with Dylan.

"I thought you were already dating him?" was the most common response.

"Water's just fine," he said, nudging Pax, reminding him that while the closet was fine, being *not* in the closet was also fine. He knew the guy wasn't straight, but Pax never talked about it. Kept his sexuality—like all his other issues—locked down real tight.

"Yeah, yeah." Pax rolled his eyes, but his tone was friendly.

"We gonna practice or not?" Coach Randy called out as he walked over to the group. "I hear we've got a winning record, and I'd like to keep it that way."

"Yep," Pax said, flipping open his wrist guard with the plays written on it. "You ready to get some work in, guys?"

There was a round of nods.

Tristan spoke up. "I don't know, I'd be down to hear more about Logan and Dylan."

Kenyon elbowed him in the side. "Nicholson, you are a real pain in everyone's ass, you know?"

"I know." Tristan beamed, like he was proud of this particular fact, and Logan thought he probably was.

"And don't ever change, okay?" Kenyon finished, wrapping an arm around the rookie receiver.

The offense had already learned that Tristan was great, especially in tense moments, for diffusing tension in the huddle. Pax, while a fantastic leader, always focused, always looking ahead, never letting bad shit get to him, was not particularly good at that. Logan knew Pax, and knew that was something that bothered him. He always wanted to be good at everything. But Logan wanted to tell him that as long as they had someone who *could* diffuse the inevitable tension, it didn't matter that it wasn't him.

But he hadn't said anything because Pax could be . . . well, he could be overly wrapped up in shit sometimes. Wouldn't listen to anyone.

Well, he *would* listen to Davis, but then Davis wasn't going to suggest to Pax that he should give himself a break. Probably because Davis had never let himself off easy once in his whole damn life.

"What we runnin' today, Coach?" Logan asked. Really not wanting to talk about him and Dylan anymore. Not even wanting to *think* about it. Because as soon as they got home, after practice, the reality of it was going to be inescapable.

"I want to see some more running plays," Coach Randy said. "We need to get Kenyon more involved in the passing game. Out patterns, some pitches, even a few sweeps. I want more screens. The 49ers' defense is brutal and they're gonna be on Pax right away on Sunday, so we need to get the ball out fast."

"Sure thing," Logan said. He'd already been thinking that the blocking was going to be brutal, and with Coach Randy's comments, he realized it was going to be even more brutal still. He made a mental note to text the other line guys and talk about meeting early or staying late to work on some of their formations, to make sure that they'd be able to withstand the onslaught that the 49ers' defense intended to bring.

It was their job—but *mainly* Logan's job—to make sure that nobody touched Pax.

So he could do what was needed to generate yards and then points.

"Okay," Coach said, clapping, "let's start."

The offense jogged onto the field, and Pax called out a play, tucking himself behind Logan as he crouched down, fingers light on the ball, but still gripping it.

His most important job was to get the ball into Pax's hands at exactly the right time, in exactly the right way.

Coming into Miami had meant working with a new quarter-back—but Logan had liked what he'd seen from Paxton Kelly before he'd ever considered changing teams. In the end, it hadn't been as tough of a transition as he'd feared. He and Pax worked well together, their mutual perfectionism meaning that the first few weeks were brutal with all the extra practices, getting the snap of the ball perfect, but once they'd gotten the rhythm down . . . nothing could alter it.

They'd performed this motion so many times it felt like breathing now, and Logan let himself fall back into the pattern they'd perfected, snapping the ball into Pax's hands, and then immediately rising to his feet to block the first onslaught of defenders coming their way.

There weren't any today because they were still just walking through the plays, trying to get the details worked out, but as he put his hands up to where the invisible defender should have been, he felt relief that he could still lose himself in football like this.

Dylan wasn't what Logan would call a distraction, but he'd been occupying his thoughts a lot lately, and now it was impossible for him not to simply move in, rent-free into his head. *Naked and rent-free,* his brain unhelpfully supplied.

He heard the play unfolding behind him, Coach Randy shouting as Kenyon looped around the back, taking the handoff from Pax and heading down the sideline. It was easy, without any defenders, but it was good to get the details worked out first.

"Good, good, let's try it again," Coach Randy called out, clapping in approval. "Next one on the list, Pax."

Logan didn't mind helping the position guys work their shit out, but he also knew it would be a lot more fun—AKA a lot more challenging—in a bit when the second-string defense guys showed up and they could actually run some of these plays against more than just air.

They went through variations of ten more plays, Logan losing himself a little bit more and more into the rhythm of practice. When Coach Randy was happy with the plays, he called for a break, while they waited for the defense to finish their own drills, and as Logan sucked down Gatorade, he couldn't help himself.

He glanced over at where the special teams guys were gathered.

Watched as Dylan nailed a ball right between the uprights from a good fifty yards back.

He wasn't the biggest guy on the team—but it was impossible to forget how much power he contained when he kicked. It wasn't just power he unleashed, but it was that he released it so deliberately, all of it directed exactly where he wanted.

Kick successful, Dylan high-fived the punter, who'd held for him, and then he turned, and he met Logan's gaze.

They were a good sixty yards away. But Logan still felt the impact of those green eyes.

I've had . . . well, I've had some thoughts.

He'd been too distracted by trying to convince Dylan that he didn't have to do this at all, but now Dylan's words came back to him in full force.

Like he was hearing them for the first time.

He'd had thoughts. Thoughts about guys.

No—you cannot assume the thoughts were about you.

But he wanted them to be. He just couldn't ever ask, not now, not when Dylan was doing this incredible thing for him. Saving him from the mess that Ricky had created.

"I heard about what happened."

Logan looked up and Beau was standing there, his earpiece pushed up on his head, tablet tucked under his arm.

"You okay?" Beau asked, taking a few steps closer, until their shoulders were nearly touching as they gazed out at the field.

"Yeah," Logan said. It felt like all he'd done all morning was talk about it. How he felt about being outed. How he and Dylan were dating. How they *weren't* dating.

He'd just wanted to lose himself in the game he loved for a little bit, but he also wasn't surprised that Beau would come over and check in with him. That was the kind of guy Beau was.

Maybe Beau had come out of the closet on his own, at seventeen, but when he'd done it, everyone and their dog had expected that his daddy would kick him out of the house.

Guess they didn't know Asa Dawson all that well.

"I know you wanted to do it on your own terms," Beau said. "So I'm sorry about that."

"I did," Logan acknowledged. Then sighed. "But the end result is the same. I'm free. Finally."

Beau raised an eyebrow. "Are you though? Coach told me some crazy story about you and Dylan pretending to date? Dylan isn't even . . ."

"I don't think anyone knows what Dylan is except for Dylan," Logan said, cutting his friend off. "And he's helpin' me out, out of the goodness of his heart. When he definitely doesn't have to."

"Course he doesn't," Beau agreed. "But he cares about you. You guys are close. Anyone can see that. And I read that article . . ."

Beau didn't have to say anything—it was written all over his face.

Logan still hadn't read it yet. He couldn't bring himself to do it. He'd heard enough excerpts tossed around that he didn't need to subject himself to the whole damn thing.

"Funny," Logan said, finishing his Gatorade, "he told me that we didn't need to sign NDAs because he didn't want to come out anytime soon, either. For his *career*."

"People suck, Logan. I'm sorry. Really, I am."

"I'm not even mad that he outed me. I'm just . . . I wish he hadn't dragged Dylan into this."

Beau nodded. "Except," he said thoughtfully, "I have a feeling that Dylan would have dragged himself in, anyway. That's the kind of guy he is. The kind of friends you two are."

Logan hated that Beau was right. Also hated that after he said it, he turned and walked off, so that he couldn't even argue.

Even if he'd had a leg to stand on.

Because both of them knew he didn't.

"Come on," Coach Randy called out, waving them over, several defensive players trailing behind him. "Let's run some plays."

"You ready to go?" Rob, the left tackle, asked him as they jogged out to the center of the field. Pax was running behind, his head tucked up right next to Davis, as they watched something on his tablet.

"Yep," Logan said.

"Not distracted?" Rob asked.

He liked Rob a lot. He was a solid left tackle. Rarely let a defender get past him, and helped Logan anchor the line. He'd been another advantage that Miami had held, when he'd been deciding where he wanted to play.

Logan shot his friend a grin. "What do you think?"

"I think you probably got a lot on your mind," Rob said, as they watched Pax finally grab his helmet and head their direction. "But I know you. You never let it get to you."

Logan nodded. "I want to win this game. Kick those West Coast jerks' butts."

"Then let's get it done," Rob said.

Pax tossed Logan the ball, and the familiar feel of it under his fingertips grounded him.

Focused him.

He tilted his head up and saw Evans, one of the backup linebackers, through his face mask.

Coach Randy blew the whistle, and Pax counted off the play, Logan's hand tensing and then relaxing with each count, and then he snapped it, muscles straining as he lifted himself, pushing out his hands against Evans, as he struggled to get around him.

But Logan didn't let him. In fact, he pushed *him* back.

Blocking well was hard enough, but blocking great was a fucking art form. It didn't just take brute strength, it took finesse. And it was different with every player; sometimes it was different with every play.

Logan didn't just have to keep his body in great shape, but his mind too.

If he didn't concentrate, and pay attention to the way the defensive line shifted before each play, then he wouldn't be prepared. And if he wasn't prepared, then the middle of the line would crumble, and it would only be a second, maybe two, before Pax was on the ground.

Logan worked as hard as he did to make sure that never happened.

"Next," Coach Randy called out.

They lined up again, and Logan caught his breath, catching the ball as Kenyon tossed it in his direction.

They repeated it again, and then again, and then ten more times.

Until Logan's head had emptied completely except for two thoughts: *ball* and *block*.

"That's good, that's real good," Coach Randy called out, clapping his hands. "I like the look of these."

"You'd better," Logan breathed out unsteadily as he jogged back to the sideline, slower than he was proud of.

He grabbed some water, and sucked it down, trying to even out his breathing. He could hear Tristan and Wade laughing with Kenyon a few yards away. Pax and Davis breaking down the plays they'd run. What had worked, what hadn't.

"Hey, lookin' good out there."

Logan glanced over and saw Dylan approaching. He was pulling off his practice jersey, and the tank he wore under it rode up, exposing his pale toned stomach.

Logan choked on the water trickling down his throat.

He'd been able to handle Dylan and his various stages of undress before. They were football players, after all. They got naked in front of each other on a regular basis.

But now? Now that, according to Ricky and the rest of the fucking news media, he was supposed to look at Dylan and think *yeah, that's hot and that's mine*?

He couldn't help himself.

Shit.

"Thanks," Logan said, when he finally finished clearing his throat.

"You okay?" Dylan asked, giving him a solid whack on the back. It was exactly what they'd have done a week ago, even two days ago, but now it was turning Logan inside out.

"Oh, just fine," Logan said. "Everything's fine."

Dylan was quiet for a moment, and they just stood there, Logan feeling stupid with his water bottle in his hand and probably a dumbstruck expression on his face. Dylan looked peaceful, relaxed though. Like this wasn't bothering him. Like he didn't mind it at all.

And wasn't that the fucked-up kicker in all this?

"You tell some people?" he asked, turning towards Logan.

"And some people told me," Logan said gruffly.

"Anyone give you shit?" Dylan wanted to know. He tugged at his jersey again, and Logan resisted the urge to reach out and hold it down.

He didn't need any more glimpses of skin.

He felt like one of those asshole gentlemen in the fucking nineteenth century, both scandalized and sensationalized by a single glimpse of an ankle.

"If you mean, did anyone say any homophobic crap, no, of course not. You think Coach would tolerate that?"

Dylan shook his head. They'd all been present in the locker room during halftime at the last game, when Logan had confronted the rookie corner, Micah Rose, over something he'd said to Beau.

Logan hadn't just done it because he was pissed that 1) Rose kept making everything about himself and 2) nobody needed to hear that shit. He'd also done it because if you nipped a problem in the bud, before it could become any more serious or wide-spread, then it stopped before it could even begin.

Nobody else would challenge him or Beau or Sebastian or Tristan or Wade, or any of the other queer guys in the locker room again.

Logan had made sure of that.

"Though," Logan added, with a smirk, "Rose did come up to me today to tell me he was real sorry."

Dylan grinned. "He was real sorry, huh?"

"I think he might be afraid of me," Logan said. He was fucking counting on it. "Also, I don't think he's got a real problem, anyway, I think he's just . . ." He waved his hands around. "You know. Strugglin'. Like a lot of us do at the beginning."

"Did you?" Dylan asked after nodding his agreement.

"Struggle? Naw, Landry wouldn't have let me," Logan said. "I was lonely though, at the beginning. The other guys on the line helped, but I was used to, well, used to having everyone around, you know? College felt different."

"Closer," Dylan agreed. "It felt closer. More tight-knit. In the NFL . . . it's everyone out for themselves."

"Yep."

"Though," Dylan said thoughtfully, "it's less like that here than on other teams. Anyway, I know Beau's keepin' an eye on him. Micah. And Sebastian too."

Logan was surprised. And not much surprised him. "Really?"

"I think Sebastian came to the same conclusion you did, that he's not really a homophobic asshole. That he could use mentoring more than ass-kicking."

Logan hummed under his breath. He liked to think nobody was that close-minded, but he knew they did exist.

"You ready to go home after practice, or do you have more meetings?" Dylan asked.

Right. They'd driven in this morning together, as they did most mornings.

Tuesday through Thursday usually meant tougher practices, honing the team's plan for Sunday's game.

Fridays were lighter, with the walkthrough on Saturday.

He knew Helen had prepared their statement to release tomorrow afternoon, late in the day, and ordered him to avoid the media, today, if he could help it.

He should go home after practice.

None of the other linemen would question him leaving earlier than usual, considering he was generally the last guy out.

"I think I might just take off," Logan said slowly. There was no really good reason for him to stay. "You good with that?"

"Oh yeah," Dylan said. "Maybe we can grab some dinner on the way home."

Before, when they'd been friends—and *only* friends—it wouldn't have been a big deal. They'd grabbed dinner together dozens of times over the last six weeks.

But now he thought about what that meant. Who might see them. What they might have to *do* to keep up the charade.

Nothing, a fucking uncooperative voice in his head suggested slyly, *everyone already thought you were together. Just keep lookin' at him the way you can't stop lookin' at him, and you're covered.*

"Really," Dylan said, shooting Logan a look of frustration at his silence. "Is this how it's gonna be now, you overthinking all of this? Just because we didn't correct someone's stupid-ass assumption?"

"No." Logan hesitated. "I don't know."

"I didn't offer to do this because I wanted things to get weird," Dylan said, lowering his voice, coming a step closer. His arm was pressed against Logan's side now, and he could smell him. Grass, and dirt, and his sweat.

"I know," Logan said apologetically. "God, I know, I'm sorry."

"You don't get to apologize for this or for anything else today," Dylan said firmly, and then he wrapped an arm around Logan's shoulders, tugging him closer. "Okay?"

Maybe Dylan was right and nothing had to change, not when they didn't want it to.

Not even if everything felt like it had when Dylan had admitted in that soft, uncertain voice. *I've had . . . well, I've had some thoughts.*

"Okay," Logan said. Then added in a more confident voice, "I guess I gotta treat my man right, take him to dinner."

Dylan grinned. "Damn straight you do."

Even though Logan was putting up a confident front, Dylan could sense as they walked into the steakhouse that he wasn't feeling nearly as confident as he kept pretending he was—but if that was what he needed to get through this, then Dylan wasn't going to begrudge him.

Still, he wanted Logan to know he was there for him.

Logan had picked this place, one of the more popular steak restaurants in Miami, and Dylan had been surprised.

"You want to go somewhere else?" he'd asked as he'd pulled into the parking lot, but Dylan hadn't wanted to—even if he'd been surprised.

"Maybe they can find us a dark corner," Logan added, a teasing edge to his voice.

And then all Dylan could think of was that. *Oh God, a dark corner. Think of everything you could do in a dark corner, unbothered, unseen . . .*

But none of that was happening. Logan had made that clear enough.

Though after spotting them, and greeting them, the hostess did in fact take them to their darkest, most isolated alcove.

"See? I got some pull here already," Logan joked, even though he didn't sound all that convinced.

From the way the hostess eyed them, Dylan was pretty sure she'd read the article, and she wouldn't mind seeing what they got up to in this shadowed corner.

Dylan knew he should say something clever and funny. Make Logan laugh. He'd had no trouble doing that before this morning but now his brain was empty, and an awkward silence descended between them. He picked up his menu, reading it carefully even though he already knew what he was going to order.

The truth was, Dylan didn't know *what* to say. It might have been instinct to suggest that they not correct Ricky's assumptions, but he *hadn't* really thought it through.

Or at least, he hadn't anticipated that it would make everything so damn awkward between him and Logan.

Maybe he never should have admitted that he'd been having thoughts about guys.

"You can always change your mind," Logan said abruptly in the silence.

Dylan lowered his menu. "What? Why would I?"

Clearly Logan had felt the awkwardness too.

"Listen, you don't have to do this. I don't want to fuck this up," Logan said, leaning forward. His gaze had always been magnetic, but now Dylan couldn't quite look away, and as much as he was trying to deny why that was, he knew. And that, he theorized, must be why things had gotten awkward between them.

Logan must have guessed that the thoughts he'd mentioned were about him.

Great job, Leonard. Way to fuck up the best friendship you ever had.

Then, he'd compounded the problem by volunteering to be his boyfriend.

"It's funny," Dylan said, "because that was just what I was thinking."

It wasn't particularly, or clever, but Logan laughed anyway.

"Are we both sitting here angsting about how awkward this is going to be, which is only making it awkward?" Logan asked.

"I . . . I think so," Dylan said, unable to help the answering laugh that bubbled out of him.

"God, we're stupid," Logan said. He was grinning, and suddenly, Dylan realized that the awkwardness was gone.

"Can't disagree."

"You wanna split some of those fries?" Logan asked. This place had the best fries—perfectly crisp on the outside, soft and tender on the inside, and piled high with roasted garlic aioli and snow drifts of freshly grated parmesan cheese.

They were not normally on the season diet, but they'd splurged with them once before, and Dylan couldn't deny he'd been thinking about tasting them again.

"Fuck yes," Dylan said. "You *are* my favorite person."

"But gym early tomorrow," Logan said, like he didn't already look like he was carved from marble. Not even a full plate of those fries would change that.

Dylan had never liked going to the gym. He did it because he had to. But he found he kinda enjoyed going with Logan.

And not just because the view was always top-notch.

The waiter appeared then, and they ordered. Big steaks for each of them, then the fries and Dylan added a salad.

"I'm assuming you talked to Landry and Levi."

"And Lyla," Logan added, rolling his eyes. "They're all ready to kick some ass."

"You're their favorite brother, of course they are."

Logan looked surprised. "I'm not their favorite brother. That's Levi. He's the baby."

Levi *was* the baby, and Landry and Lyla worried about him, of course, but Dylan had seen and heard enough to know he wasn't wrong in his assessment of the situation.

"Maybe, yeah, but they all gravitate towards you." *Like we all do*, Dylan thought.

One thing Dylan had learned about Logan in the last month and a half was that he was absolute shit at taking compliments. "Anyway, they're all staying put. I had to really talk Landry down. But he's in a contract year. He doesn't need me fucking with that."

Dylan had a feeling that Landry would sacrifice more than just an advantageous contract if his brother needed him, but he also had a feeling that Logan wouldn't believe him.

"Lyla's not even coming?"

"She's busy. Besides," Logan said, tossing him a quick grin, "I've got you, don't I?"

Dylan was floored—and honestly, fucking *honored*.

"Am I an honorary Banks now?" he asked teasingly, raising an eyebrow.

"You taking care of me? Lyla would award you the title herself."

"I think," Dylan said, "that it's so freaking awesome how you guys look out for each other. Makes me wish even more that I'd had brothers and sisters."

"Hey," Logan said, tilting his head, "you do now. Honorary Banks, right?"

"I'm honored, honestly," Dylan said.

"And hey, think about all those fucking terrible pranks that Landry and Lyla pulled on me and Levi that you get to skip," Logan teased.

It was funny; he'd never met any of Logan's brothers or his sister—but he felt like he knew them, just from all the stories that Logan had told him about them.

From the stories, he *was* glad he'd missed out on their sibling pranks—and their sibling rivalries.

They'd all mellowed with age, but Dylan had heard enough to know that at points it had been intense.

The waiter appeared then with their food, and for a few minutes, they were quiet, demolishing their steaks.

Dylan swiped a fry through the garlic aioli and hummed in happiness as he deposited it in his mouth. "These are so good, they should be a crime," he said.

Logan nodded, and then with a sly glint in his eye, took his fork with its chunk of steak, and swiped it through some of the residual aioli on the plate.

"Hey!" Dylan cried out. "Thief!"

He blocked Logan's fork with his own, and for a second, they fenced with the silverware, Dylan trying to tangle up the tines with his own so that he couldn't get away with the theft.

It was petty, maybe, but it was fun, and even if they weren't in Logan's living room, it wasn't like they were in the middle of the restaurant either.

"Uh," a voice said uneasily behind them.

Dylan glanced up to see a few girls standing there. Teenagers, from the look of them, looking like a bouquet in their colorful flowered dresses.

"You're Logan Banks," the one in front said.

Logan looked like he'd just been caught out. He dropped his fork with the offending piece of steak to his plate. "Yeah," he said.

Dylan realized what the apprehension on his friend's face was. This was the first time he'd met fans in public, *after* Ricky Barnes had taken all those shots at Logan's character.

"And you're his boyfriend," another one said, tilting her head towards Dylan.

Dylan froze.

"Can we have a picture?"

"With you? Of course." Logan recovered faster than Dylan did. But then the trio shook their heads in unison, like they all knew what they wanted.

"Together, the two of you," the leader said. "We think you're so damn cute."

"Um," Logan hesitated.

Dylan could see the train wreck coming. Could see the hesitation wrecking the positive spin they were trying to put on the story, dragging Logan's reputation back down to where Ricky had sunk it.

"Sure, of course," Dylan said cheerfully. "Where do you want us?"

They all broke out in big smiles. "Oh, just there is fine," the leader said, whipping out her phone. Dylan leaned in, and before he could overthink or God forbid, *change his mind*, pressed a quick kiss to Logan's cheek.

He hadn't shaved this morning—it had been *so* early when he'd been woken up with the bad news—but to Dylan's surprise, the scruff on Logan's face wasn't rough at all, but soft, and his lips, out of their own volition, just *lingered*.

"Aw, they're so adorable," one of the girls murmured.

When he'd moved in, he'd felt Logan's muscles tense, but now he relaxed, and to Dylan's shock, he wrapped an arm around Dylan's shoulders, tugging him in a bit closer, fingers digging into his shirt.

Dylan was more flustered than he wanted to admit, and when he finally pulled away, all the words he knew he should be saying stuck in his throat.

Instead, it was Logan who'd seemingly found his. "That what you wanted, girls?"

They all nodded, their eyes totally lighting up. "Good luck this week," the leader said.

"Thanks," Dylan said, finally finding his voice.

Then, just as suddenly as they'd been invaded, they were alone again.

But when the girls had left, they definitely took part of Dylan's peace of mind with them. Because he'd known what Logan felt like before this, but it hadn't ever been that intense. He'd wanted, more than he'd ever thought possible, to press his fingertips to Logan's cheek and turn him just enough so that it wasn't just his scruff that Dylan was kissing, but his lips.

"Ah, well, that went . . ." Dylan watched as Logan searched for the right words. As he reached for his water glass and gulped half of it down.

"Well?" Dylan finished for him.

"I guess I didn't expect them to be so interested in . . . well, in *us*," Logan said weakly. "You think that's gonna be common?"

Dylan had no idea. There were equal amounts of eagerness and dread warring inside of him at the thought that it *might* become common. That he might be able to do it again. That maybe next time, Logan would be the one to kiss *him*.

"I guess you'd know that better than me," Dylan said slowly. Still not sure whether he should be excited or apprehensive.

Logan chuckled. "I've got no fucking clue either," he admitted. "But I can't think it's a bad thing. I was sure they were coming over to lecture me or something."

"I bet," Dylan said, understanding.

Then he knew, without a doubt, that it didn't matter if every occurrence wrenched his internal tension higher and tighter—he was gonna be glad each and every time people ended up being supportive of his friend.

"But it . . . well, you're right, it turned out okay, right?" Logan shrugged. "It didn't . . . it didn't bother you, right?"

Oh, he was plenty bothered.

Hot and bothered.

But Dylan knew that wasn't what Logan was asking.

"Of course not," Dylan said. "Not in the least."

"Okay, good." And Logan looked so goddamned relieved, that Dylan knew he'd made the right call.

CHAPTER FIVE

LOGAN WAS NOT PARTICULARLY surprised when the next morning, Beau found them in the locker room, right after they'd finished their workout, and said that his dad, Coach Dawson, wanted to see them in his office before practice started.

Dylan, on the other hand, looked comically terrified, shock filling his pale eyes, his lips clamped around the straw stuck into his protein smoothie.

"You think . . ." Dylan hissed as they rounded the corner in the hallway outside Coach's office. "You think we're in trouble for that pic?"

Logan had very deliberately not thought about the picture they'd taken at the restaurant.

Or the way Dylan's lips had felt against his cheek.

Of course, that meant that was all he'd thought about as he lay in bed last night and tried to sleep.

"Naw," Logan said, pausing outside Coach's office. "He probably just wants to check in, 'cause you know, the statement's coming out this afternoon."

"Oh, yeah," Dylan murmured, like he'd forgotten that it hadn't already happened.

Like he didn't have a few hours where he could still bow out.

But Logan knew he wouldn't. Last night had proven that pretty definitively.

"You ready?" he asked Dylan in a quiet voice, nudging him with his shoulder.

"To face Coach?" Dylan nodded. "Now's as good a time as any."

When Logan knocked on the partially open door, Coach immediately called out, "Come on in, boys."

Coach was sitting on the corner of his desk, a knowing gleam in his eye.

Logan had to wonder how long he'd been listening to them talking outside his office. It was a good reminder that Coach knew everything.

Even things they didn't want him to know.

"Take a seat," Coach added, gesturing to the chairs set in front of his desk. "I just wanted to chat real quick. Helen's told me what happened, Logan, and I'm sorry. I know you wanted to do this on your own terms."

Logan nodded. He had. But other than Dylan getting dragged into it, he wasn't . . . well, he couldn't really be angry about it, because there wasn't any point. Even though he hadn't picked the timing or the scenario, he couldn't deny that the outcome was exactly what he'd wanted.

"It's actually not so bad. I've gotten used to the idea of everyone knowin' now," Logan said. "And I wanted to do it anyway."

"Still doesn't give anyone permission to reveal it without your say-so," Coach said firmly. "Helen tells me you're releasing a statement today." He picked up a piece of paper from his desk. "You've read the final version?"

Logan nodded. Words weren't ever his strong suit, but Helen had done a really great job of crafting all of what he'd felt into one concise statement.

There'd been a firm rebuttal of his relationship with Ricky, and all the accusations Ricky had leveled at him—but mostly she'd focused on what was important to Logan, and expectations of the future.

Specifically, she'd penned a line: *As much as I understand the intense interest in my personal life that this article has generated, I still ask that my privacy be respected and my personal life remain personal.*

He hadn't confirmed or denied anything. But everyone, of course, would assume that any allegation that he didn't specifically refute—AKA that he was dating Dylan—was plain and simple fact.

"And you, Dylan . . ." Coach sighed. "Helen tells me that you actually *offered* to help Logan out here. But I want you to know, it's not necessary. If you change your mind . . ."

Clearly, Coach had not seen the picture from last night.

He'd seen it, first thing this morning, when he'd opened his email and there it was, a forward from Helen, who said it was spreading through social media.

He hadn't been able to help the way his gaze had lingered on the photo, even as small as it was on his phone screen. The surprise on his own face. The undeniable joy in his eyes. The way Dylan's own had fluttered closed.

The possessive arm he'd slung around Dylan's shoulders.

"I'm not going to change my mind," Dylan said firmly. "I don't have a problem doing this."

"You're sure, then," Coach said. "And you, Logan? Nobody says you have to do this. I know y'all were close friends before that.

No need to . . ." He hesitated, and Logan swore he saw something he'd never imagined he'd see in his coach's eyes: understanding. Then as soon as Logan had identified the emotion, it was gone. "No need to compromise your friendship, just to refute this jerk's claim."

"It's not compromised, Coach," Dylan said very earnestly. "It's even stronger than ever."

Coach sighed. "And now I get to give my real fun speech, I'm sure you two know the one. It's a little *less* relevant considering y'all aren't actually dating, but the point remains: what happens between you doesn't impact what happens on the field. Okay?"

Logan was friends with Wade Lewis and Tristan Nicholson—both rookies who also happened to be in a relationship, a *real* relationship, so he'd heard their version of Coach's speech secondhand. His friend and safety Sebastian Howard had gotten it too, of course, when he'd admitted to Coach that he was dating his son, Beau.

Coach didn't really seem to mind interpersonal relationships on the team. He only cared about one thing: making sure their messiness didn't ever spill onto the field. Didn't ever impact the game or what Coach was trying to accomplish here.

Logan couldn't blame him.

Asa Dawson had come from a wildly successful collegiate program. His reputation was ironclad; everything he'd touched before the Piranhas had turned to gold. But college was completely, utterly different from the NFL, and Logan knew a lot of people assumed he'd fail in Miami.

But what they didn't know was nobody was as singularly determined to succeed as Coach.

"It won't," Dylan swore earnestly.

"Besides," Logan added, "we aren't even on the field at the same time."

"Doesn't mean," Coach retorted sternly, "that the drama won't impact your individual playing time. I just ask that you make sure it doesn't." He paused, his face softening. "Really, I'm not too worried about y'all. Logan, you're a rock. And Dylan, you came to us for a reason, because we had faith in you and that hasn't changed. But for equality's sake, I had to give y'all the same speech I gave Tristan and Wade and Sebastian and Beau."

"You weren't worried about them either," Dylan guessed. "Not really."

That was the thing about Dylan. He was so smart, unexpectedly. Nobody expected someone who kicked a ball for a living to have so many insightful observations. But Dylan always did.

Coach eyed him, and then his smile grew, slowly.

"I'll neither confirm nor deny," Coach said, but the sly twinkle in his eyes gave him away. "Now, you two have got a practice to get to. And I," he added, that twinkle growing even more pronounced, "have a pregame speech to write."

It was only two days before the big game against the 49ers, and though practice had been tough this week, Logan thought it hadn't been too ridiculous.

The hardest part of the week had been the mental adjustment to "everybody knows"—but it hadn't been only the new realization that hiding his sexuality was in the past, but the new boyfriend he'd apparently acquired.

It wasn't so much the new role Dylan had assumed that had Logan floundering, but the fact that deep down, he couldn't deny that he *liked* it.

Of course, nothing had really, truly changed. They still car-pooled together in the mornings, they still grabbed dinner to-gether most evenings, Logan continued to suck at playing Dylan's video games, and Logan still had to resist drinking the rest of the milk.

There were two adjustments: *one*, whenever they were out, Logan found himself thinking about what they *looked* like, and he'd realized that even though they weren't acting any differently than they had been before, people accepted them as a couple, and *two*, he couldn't stop those words of Dylan's from repeating on a near-constant loop in his head. *I've had . . . well, I've had some thoughts.*

He had to forcibly stop himself, at least half a dozen times, from asking Dylan what the thoughts were *specifically*, and also if the thoughts were about him.

That, he reminded himself, *is the opposite of keeping Dylan a friend. It's pushing yourself on him, when he's just trying to figure his shit out, and he's doing what he can to help you.*

"So," Pax asked, leaning against the locker next to Logan's, waiting as he finished getting ready, "you bringin' Dylan to the dinner?"

"Why would I bring Dylan to the offensive line dinner?" Logan asked incredulously. "He's not on the offensive line."

"But he's with you now," Pax said, so reasonably that Logan almost believed it himself. Yeah, it made sense: Dylan belonged with him now.

"We're not really together, you know that," Logan said, dropping his voice lower. Not that everyone didn't already know the truth.

Pax shrugged. "There's a reason everyone thought you were."

"Yeah, except that Dylan's not queer," Logan retorted. That was the moment Dylan's hushed confession came back to him, again. Because truly, it never really left. He'd had thoughts. Thoughts that weren't straight. That meant he wasn't straight.

"I don't think anyone knows what Dylan is, except for Dylan, and besides, I know you like him," Pax said, still so reasonably that Logan found his annoyance growing.

"Oh, you know I do?" he retorted, gritting his teeth together as he got dressed. Dylan was, thank *God*, still in the showers. He didn't need to hear Pax's totally reasonable conclusions.

"None of us are blind," Pax said. "Bring him to dinner, okay? Sebastian brings Beau to the defense dinners."

Logan nearly argued that Sebastian did that because Beau really *was* his boyfriend, but he could already tell that this was going to be a circular kind of argument, and on top of that, there was Dylan, towel wrapped around his waist, emerging from the showers.

"Fine," he grumbled. "I'll bring him."

"Awesome," Pax said, sounding pleased. "We're leaving in a few."

Logan nearly asked him if he was bringing Davis, but that was a low blow. Everyone knew that they couldn't date, no matter how many longing looks their quarterback shot his coach—and it was just mean to remind him of that particular fact.

"What was that about?" Dylan asked casually as they finished getting dressed.

"Well, remember how I was going to the offensive line dinner, before we went to the hotel?" Logan asked.

Dylan nodded.

"So are you, apparently."

Dylan frowned. "But I'm not . . ."

Logan waved a hand. "Just . . . go with it, okay?"

"Is this one of those 'we're supposed to be dating' things?" he asked.

Logan had a feeling it was actually one of those *we wish you were actually dating* things, probably courtesy of Tristan, passed along by Pax, neither one who could leave well enough alone.

"Yeah," Logan said shortly.

"Sounds good to me," Dylan said. Not sounding even the tiniest bit upset or worried that they'd have to play up the couple angle more in front of a bunch of people who were supposed to know the truth, but didn't care.

Maybe it'll be fine, Logan's brain whispered to him, unhelpfully, *maybe he'll even enjoy it.*

It was generally a tradition for the starting quarterback to take the offensive line to dinner each week, as a thank-you for protecting his ass.

Logan had heard rumors that last year's dinners hadn't been very well attended, but now, with Pax's improved leadership, everyone went.

Occasionally, they'd even have other players join, like Kenyon, or Tristan and Wade. Beau and Sebastian had even joined them a few weeks back, even though Sebastian didn't play on the offensive side of the ball, and Beau was technically a *coach*.

"This is great," Dylan said as they walked into the downtown pub-style restaurant with its mahogany paneled walls, and dim lighting.

"We're in the back," Pax said, gesturing towards what looked to be a private room separate from the rest of the restaurant.

"Are these always at such cool places?" Dylan asked in a low voice as they filed into the private room. The table was long, and Logan told himself that he wasn't doing anything but what was expected of him as he pressed his hand to Dylan's lower back, guiding him towards the head of the table.

"Pax does a really good job," Logan said. "Always finds some place neat to bring us."

"I had a feeling," Dylan said, grinning. "He's such an over-achiever."

"Welcome to the offensive line," Logan teased. "We aim to succeed."

The host, a young man in his mid-twenties, was guiding them around the table, and he glanced up at them, his smile wide. "You guys are too cute," he said. "I never bought what Ricky said about you two."

Logan felt himself tense, but Dylan was so much better at these kinds of interactions than he was, and he shot the host back an equally friendly smile. "Thanks," he said. "I mean . . ." Dylan shot Logan a sideways glance, full of secret amusement, "you can't help who you fall for, right?"

"So true," the host said seriously. "I'm Matt. If you need any-thing at all, let me know, okay? Extra water, a private corner to make out in, a napkin for an autograph . . . even a selfie taker, I am *real* good at those."

"You think he *meant* that?" Logan hissed as they sat down and Matt left.

"Which part?" Dylan asked, apparently unconcerned. His hand settled on Logan's shoulder, a friendly reassuring touch. But was it all that friendly? Logan was suddenly worried that it *looked* like he desperately wanted a dark corner he could make out with Dylan in.

Maybe what he'd thought was just friendly touching was actually more.

"The making-out part!" Logan exclaimed.

Dylan's green eyes twinkled. "I think he could probably arrange it, if you were wanting to," he said seriously. His hand squeezed. "Hey, it's all good. We're fine."

"You're definitely fine," Logan said, before he could stuff the words back into his mouth.

Dylan grinned, clearly pleased. "That makes two of us, then."

"You two gonna stop flirting anytime soon?" Pax asked, from the head of the table, his eyebrow raised as he pinned them with a single look.

"Flirting?" Logan felt caught. Was that what they were do-ing? Why did it feel so goddamn natural if they weren't just being friendly?

"I think it's adorable," Rob said, from the other side of the table.

Rob knew the truth, but was apparently down with the group that were currently giving them hell.

In fact, the entire offensive line knew the truth.

"Oh, they're cute as hell," Brock teased. "You two gonna start a TikTok account like Tristan and Wade?"

"No, no, definitely not," Logan said, finding his voice.

"I don't know, we could." Dylan sounded speculative, and not against the idea at all. "Maybe we could win over some of Ricky's fanbase."

Pax laughed, followed by the rest of the table.

The waitress arrived then, and began distributing the menus, and Dylan took advantage of the quiet to murmur behind his own menu, "I get so angry when I think of the shit that asshole is saying about you."

"He doesn't matter." Logan tamped down the anger he felt whenever he thought about that two-timing sonofabitch.

"I'll drink to that," Dylan said, clicking his water glass against Logan's. "Come on, this is at least a little bit fun, isn't it?"

"What is?"

Dylan's smile was conspiratorial. "Being *adorable*."

Then his hand landed squarely across Logan's shoulders, and tugged him even closer.

Logan didn't know if he agreed, but the one thing he did find it was hot.

And he didn't know what to do about that at all.

Maybe Dylan shouldn't be enjoying faking being Logan Banks' boyfriend so goddamn much, but he was. It was undeniable.

"You two enjoy your meal?" Matt asked as they headed towards the exit. He had one hip leaning against the host stand, and a twinkle in his eye. "What about those dark corners? You find one of those?"

"You wish," Dylan said, the words tripping so easily off his tongue. Way too easily. He shouldn't be thinking about kissing Logan. Except how could he not?

It didn't matter that Logan was a guy. It only mattered that he was Logan.

"I kinda do," Matt said. "Can we take a selfie? I'd love to post about you two on my Instagram."

"Course," Logan said, speaking up, his voice gruff, just the tiniest bit rough around the edges like *he'd* been thinking about the kissing too, and not just the kissing they'd do in a second, Dylan's lips pressed to his cheek.

They posed quickly, and even though it was the second time they'd done this, and he should be used to it by now, it still rocked him from the inside out as his mouth met Logan's skin.

You want your mouth all over every part of his skin, Dylan's uncooperative mind supplied. *All fucking over.*

If he'd thought he was straight, that ship had definitely sailed.

He didn't know he could've been so wrong about himself, but it was undeniable by this point.

"Oh, this is so great," Matt cried out as he looked at the picture. "I love you two. You're doing so much good for football. Proving you don't have to be . . . well, whatever, to play great."

"That's the idea," Dylan said gently, seeing the flash of hurt in Logan's eyes.

He might not be talking about it, but he *was* upset that he hadn't been able to come out on his own terms, in a way that would've been meaningful to him.

He hadn't talked about it much, but it was unmistakable.

Dylan didn't want to push him into talking about it, but he needed to, even if it wasn't with him.

"Well, we gays are real appreciative," Matt said.

"I'm glad," Logan said in a heartfelt tone.

When they got outside, Logan turned to Dylan. "That wasn't too terrible, was it?"

"No, it was great," Dylan said, meaning it. *Especially the part where I got to kiss you, even if it was just your cheek, again.*

"They didn't make you feel uncomfortable, did they?"

Dylan laughed. "No, no, not even remotely. I didn't do anything I didn't want to do." *That I wouldn't love to do without an audience, alone in some dark corner. Maybe Matt could still hook us up.*

"I don't know what the rules are," Logan confessed.

"What rules?" Pax appeared next to them.

Logan groaned. "Not you again."

"Me again," Pax said with an unrepentant grin. "You two looked like you were enjoying yourselves."

"It was a great dinner," Dylan said. "Thanks for inviting me, Pax."

"Of course," Pax said, waving his hand. Like it was no big deal. Dylan had a feeling he'd done it to see Logan squirm. But Logan, once he'd relaxed, had clearly enjoyed it too.

Which frankly asked more questions than it answered.

"Where's Davis?" Logan asked, an evil gleam in his eyes.

"Oh, at the hotel already. We're doing our own walkthrough tonight, just me and him."

Logan raised an eyebrow. "Sounds cozy."

Pax rolled his eyes. "Just because you two are having the most obvious honeymoon period of all time doesn't mean the rest of us are hooking up, too."

"Right," Logan said, and didn't sound even the tiniest bit convinced.

Chapter Six

Coach didn't give a pregame speech every week.

But, by the skin of their teeth, the Piranhas now had a winning record, and there was nothing like winning a few games to make you want to win a lot more.

So Logan, sitting on the bench in front of his locker, wasn't surprised at all when Coach dragged the rickety chair to the center of the room, clearing his throat loudly to grab the team's attention.

"Sixth game, y'all. I know at the beginning of the season it felt like we'd never get here. But after today, we're a third of the way through the season now. And . . ." Coach hesitated, then a bright smile broke over his face. "Honest to God, I couldn't be prouder. Y'all fought hard, for every single win, and even more impressively, you fought through even those losses. But you know what? Our work isn't done. We've got a winning record—but I think we could do more. And I think I'm not alone."

A cheer went through the locker room.

"I want more than just a winning record. I want to make the playoffs," Coach continued. "I want to win the division. I want to prove to every single person who didn't believe in us that we aren't so easily dismissed. And I think . . . I think you want that too. So let's make it happen."

The roar that erupted was deafening and the team ran onto the field, under an archway of waving blue streamers that simulated the ocean—or so he'd been told.

At the other end was the fighting Piranha mascot, decked out in its yellow and turquoise, whipping the crowd into a frenzy.

"I always tell myself that thing couldn't look any weirder, and then I see it again," Dylan said catching Logan's shoulder and pointing with his gloved hand to the Piranha as they jogged over to the bench.

"Caribe?" That was the fish's nickname. Apparently it was another name for a piranha. Logan didn't know whether that made it better or not.

"There are way weirder mascots," Dylan said. "The Stanford Tree? Jamie told me all about that one. And that Steelers guy, with the hammer? But hands down, weirdest mascot award has to go to Caribe. I think it's his face?" They both looked over at the mascot, mugging for the crowd with its oversized fins, and Logan laughed.

"Okay, maybe not *just* the face," Dylan conceded with a grin. "I gotta get warmed up." He tipped his head towards Logan, and Logan had to fight the urge to wrap a hand around his neck, tug him even closer. Even as close as he was now, Dylan never quite felt close enough. "Good luck today."

"You too," Logan said, "though you'll hardly need it. 'Cause you're awesome. What did Coach say? He has faith in you?"

Dylan's eyes softened and he pushed his hair back. Logan was going to get him a headband or something, if he kept refusing to cut it. *If* Logan kept "forgetting" to remind him.

Sue him, he liked it long.

Okay, what he *really* wanted was to push his fingers through all that hair and pull Dylan down, til their gazes met. Til their lips couldn't do anything but touch, finally.

And that, *exactly that*, was what Coach had told him couldn't happen. He couldn't let himself get distracted by either his own feelings or the slight but tantalizing possibility Dylan might feel the same way.

"Yeah," he said. "Let me guess, you do too."

"The most," Logan said confidently, 'cause he did.

There was nobody on the field he'd trust as much as he trusted Dylan.

Even the rest of his linemen.

Even Pax.

But he *knew*, without a single doubt, if Dylan jogged onto the field to kick a winning field goal, he'd do it.

"Go kick some defensive butt," Dylan said, patting *him* on the butt before he took off.

It was something Logan should've been used to.

Players touched each other everywhere. It was why he hadn't felt it was strange or weird that he and Dylan were so touchy-feely with each other.

But then, he supposed, most players didn't *keep* touching each other, once they were off the field and out of the locker room. Those players also weren't embarking on a fake relationship either.

"Hey," Pax said, walking over, his helmet dangling from his fingertips. "You ready to go, Banks?"

"Me?" he asked. "I was freaking born ready."

Over the next half an hour, Logan warmed up with the linemen, taking a few practice snaps with Pax. He wouldn't say he had a super strict pregame routine—not like Dylan did. Dylan was a perfectionist, and liked to hit a graduated routine of further and further field goals, topping off at about sixty-five yards. Instead, Logan concentrated on keeping himself chill and calm, but focused.

He made his rounds through the various groups on the field, checking in with everyone. First up, he tossed a ball around for the receivers, sending Tristan sprinting down the field to catch one. His spiral wasn't nearly as tight as Pax's, but when Tristan caught it anyway, shooting him a happy-go-lucky grin, he couldn't help but smile right back as he moved on, high-fiving Kenyon and the rest of the running backs, then turning towards where, on the other end of the field, the defense was warming up.

Sebastian was stretching near Rose and Evans and a few of the other defensive backs.

"Hey, Banks," he called out, "you ready to kick some California ass?"

Logan jogged past, nodding his agreement. "Absofucking-lutely," he called back.

He skirted around where Dylan and the special teams group was set up, because he knew how focused Dylan liked to be before a game.

He was the opposite of Logan, who liked to touch every aspect of the team, even with just a smile or a quick quip.

But even though they were totally different, they were both methods that worked.

By the time Dylan kicked off, sending the ball through the end zone posts, Logan's jittery nerves had calmed, and he felt ready to go out and do his job.

As the offense took the field for the first drive, Logan's world narrowed to two distinct and equally important tasks:

Protect the ball.

Protect Pax.

From the first play, the 49ers' defensive line did what Coach Randy had predicted—they pushed, and *hard*, rushing in with such determination and force that even Logan, who prided himself on never giving an inch, couldn't help but be pushed back.

Pax got rid of the ball almost immediately, tossing it on a screen to Kenyon. He got three . . . no *four*, yards, Logan registered, as they lined up again.

It became clear from that first, difficult drive, as they made their way down the field at a snail's pace, gaining two, three yards on a good play, and nothing on a bad one, barely making first downs each time, that this was a game that would be played in the trenches, one inch at a time.

By the time they reached the 49ers' forty-yard line, Logan's arms and legs were already screaming. He'd always prided himself on making sure not only he, but the rest of the line was the fittest on the field, but as he glanced down, he saw it wasn't just him. They were all struggling in their effort to hold back the onslaught.

It was third and seven, as Pax pulled them together into the huddle.

"Guys," he said, consulting the list of plays on his wrist guard, "we're gonna try to get the first down, but let's get whatever we can. Set Dylan up for a field goal."

No doubt about it, Logan thought as they lined up again, his fingertips tightening over the ball, Dylan and his reliable leg were going to end up being their savior this game.

The play Pax had called was a quick buttonhook out, with the idea that Tristan would lead the defenders away from Wade, who'd catch it and just get enough yards for a first down.

It was a well-designed play, and it worked great—but this time, the moment Pax dropped back, Logan could see the left tackle struggling to block the linebacker, blitzing hard, aiming to sack Pax and put him *and* the ball on the ground.

Logan saw Pax glance over, take in the situation, and he threw the ball, a little earlier than the play had designed. Wade caught it, but he was at least a yard short.

"Damnit," Logan muttered under his breath. As they jogged off, they passed the kicking unit.

Dylan already had his helmet on, his gaze focused as he gazed over at the goal posts and the ribbons attached at the top.

Logan didn't know much about kicking, but he knew that wind definitely played a factor, so it made sense that he'd be attuned to it.

It's on you now, Logan thought as he took his spot on the bench, grabbing the water bottle someone tossed him. *You gotta do it for both of us.*

Dylan took a last breath, and let it filter slowly out of his lungs. It was the same thing he did before every single kick, without fail.

Repetitive motion, making sure that each and every movement he made was exactly the same, a routine he could always count on, was the foundation of his kicking game.

He dug his cleat into the turf, and then watched as the long snapper popped the ball back, and at the exact right second, his foot connected with the ball, sending it soaring through the uprights, and scoring the Piranhas three points.

He never breathed again, not until the ball was off and away—and most of the time, he was lucky enough to say, he breathed easy, because he usually made the kicks he attempted.

But every kicker missed sometimes. It was inevitable. Occasionally there might be a bad snap, or terrible wind, or just a nasty angle that put a weird spin on the ball. Sometimes a kicker just plain fucked it up.

Shit happened, and Dylan knew his kicks weren't always a guarantee, but he'd gotten lucky so far in his career—*and* he'd worked hard. Though there was always some luck involved. His reputation as a solid kicker under pressure was what Coach had said attracted the Piranhas to him.

They hadn't cared if he was a kicking phenom who claimed he could make sixty-five-yard kicks on a dime, even in inclement weather.

They liked that he could be consistent.

So you better stay consistent, Dylan thought as he ran off the field. *That's your meal ticket here. Making the kicks when they need you to make the kicks.*

Up til now, he'd done that.

But the possibility always sat there, hovering in the back of his mind, that he wouldn't. He never listened to it. Was even afraid to give it a voice. But that didn't mean that the voice didn't exist.

Didn't mean that he couldn't feel it back there, waving its hands, desperately wanting attention, every time he stepped onto the field.

Each time, the decision was simple though.

I don't care what you think, and I'm not listening to you.

But it took a conscious decision. Each and every time.

He kicked off, pinning the opposing team at their ten-yard line. Coach must have been real pleased, because when Dylan returned, job done for now, to the sideline, he actually glanced up from his clipboard and patted Dylan on the head. "Great kicking," he said. "Rock fucking steady."

Dylan nodded, pleased that Coach was pleased.

The longer Coach stayed pleased, the longer he stayed employed.

He also nodded at Logan, who was sitting over on the other end of the sideline, going over some plays with Pax on one side, and Tristan and Wade on the other. He barely glanced up, but for a second, their gazes connected and he felt pride surge through him, reflected from Logan's own eyes.

As he made his way to his own part of the sideline, where his kicking net was set up, Dylan couldn't help but gloat a little at how that felt.

Logan Banks gave a shit about him. Logan Banks was fucking *proud* of him. He'd known, of course, that Logan felt that way, because it was impossible to be his friend and not know it, but today felt new, like a whole new experience.

Maybe that wouldn't mean what it did to anyone else, but it meant something to him, because to him, Logan wasn't just a really great offensive lineman, part of a growing familial football dynasty, he was a great guy. The best kind of guy. Loyal and kind and dedicated.

The kind you'd want to have your back.

And, that really unhelpful voice added, *the kind of guy you'd want to find in a dark corner and see if that naughty gleam in his eyes is all a tease or if it might be for real.*

Dylan shook his head, trying to clear it.

He didn't need to be thinking about Logan like that. But ever since the dinner they'd shared, a few nights ago, and the picture—the picture that Helen had gone out of her way to send them, cautioning that it was spreading through social media like wildfire—he'd found it difficult to think about anything else.

The first casual thoughts he'd entertained of him and a guy, they were growing from mere curiosity into a kind of need that he didn't think he'd ever experienced with a woman before.

He didn't just want to know how Logan felt under his hands, he *needed* to know. And that kind of undeniable need, it had both the power to open his eyes, and a destructive mirror that could destroy his friendship with Logan.

And this, Dylan told himself firmly, *is why you don't think about personal shit during games.*

Trying to refocus his mojo, Dylan forced himself to do the series of stretches he always performed after each kick. Making sure he was limber. Making sure he was ready, next time he was called on.

And if he kept his gaze off the bench where Logan sat?

Well, there was nothing wrong with a little self-preservation.

Especially when, to his surprise, his number got called a second time that quarter. And then again, at the beginning of the next quarter. And a *fourth* time, right at the end of the first half.

Four field goals in one half. They'd all been reasonable distances, but it was still an accomplishment and a first for him personally.

But as Dylan sat in the locker room at halftime, he had a feeling that nobody else was as pleased as him, because the offense was struggling.

Thus, the four field goals, and not four touchdowns.

If you asked him, he'd prefer to be kicking extra points, too, but he'd also do whatever the team required.

Coach raised his voice above the noise of the locker room.

"Y'all," he said, "I know you're disappointed. No touchdowns. But I want to remind you . . ." His voice grew stronger. More emphatic. Dylan couldn't help but admire Coach's ability to orate on the spot. It was truly impressive. "It doesn't matter whether we win by a point or by twenty. We *win*, no matter how it's accomplished. If we send Leonard out there to make four more field goals, and we win twenty-four to seven, it's still a W, and we'll still take it. Right, Leonard? You gonna go out there and win the game for us?"

Dylan raised his head. "Sir, I'm happy to do whatever we need to get the job done. But it's not just me. Pax and the guys . . . they're under serious duress, and they're still movin' the ball enough to give *me* an opportunity."

Coach nodded with approval. "That's damn straight. There's a battle goin' on, and we're winnin', but just enough. We gotta keep on fighting the good fight, and we'll come home with the victory we deserve."

A determined yell went through the locker room, and carried them out onto the field for the second half.

Usually, games were long bouts of semi-boredom, punctuated by short bursts of intense activity and nerve-wracking moments where the game literally rode on his shoulders.

But this game was a total fucking exception.

After the sixth field goal, Dylan specifically stopped keeping track of how many he'd kicked. Because if he counted, he'd start thinking of Rob Bironas' record for successful field goals in a game, and then he'd be all up in his ass about it.

And with the game on the line, and the responsibility for the win resting heavier and heavier on his shoulders, Dylan couldn't let that happen.

Instead, he curled into himself, into his little bubble in front of his net, and jogged out onto the field each and every time he was called, hyper-focused on the task at hand. He wouldn't let himself look anywhere near the bench, because then he'd see Logan, and he'd *see* the importance of the kick in his eyes, and it would add so much additional pressure that he wasn't sure he could avoid it swallowing him whole.

Coach Roger, the consultant-slash-assistant that Coach had hired to consult with special teams, approached him as the clock wound down. Dylan could see the offense struggling still to make it down the field. He knew Paxton wanted to get his touchdown. Wanted to not saddle Dylan with more responsibility for kicking yet another field goal. But it seemed, as his last pass fell uncaught to the ground, it wasn't going to happen that way. A glance at the scoreboard told Dylan the Piranhas were currently winning by four, but with the fourth quarter nearly over, he was going to make one last kick.

Coach Roger stuck his thumb towards the field. "You ready to go, Leonard?"

He nodded. Nailed one last warmup kick into his net.

He refused to think if this was number eight—which would tie Bironas' record—or if it was nine, which would exceed it.

Instead, he focused on putting one foot in front of the other, and then on the ball as the special teams formation set up. Not on the way every teammate patted him on the helmet as he left his bubble. Not on the roar of the crowd as he jogged onto the field.

He lined up. Checked the ribbons fluttering on top of the goal posts. Very little wind. It had been a clear sunny day in Miami, and dusk had fallen, the lights shining on all sides of the stadium.

The official blew the whistle, and Dylan took his single breath, letting it out slowly, and with it, every ounce of hesitation and doubt.

Pushing off, his foot hit the ball straight on, and he watched, a little in shock and more in awe, as the ball sailed right between the uprights.

The whole stadium shook, and for a second Dylan thought, *I must have broken the record.* For a split second, *less* even, he felt a pulse of something like disappointment for breaking Bironas' record, especially after his story had ended in such tragedy. But then he saw a flashing graphic out of the corner of his eye, and he realized he hadn't broken it at all. He'd *tied* it.

That, Dylan realized, was somehow even better.

He'd always really looked up to Rob Bironas, and now they'd share something together, even if Rob was no longer around.

He turned, and to his surprise, he was absolutely fucking mobbed by players. And it shouldn't have surprised him at all, but the first player to reach him?

It was Logan, who was yelling and fist-pumping in the air as he wrapped one arm around him.

Chapter Seven

"So you *really* didn't know that was to tie the record?" Logan asked skeptically as he pulled into the garage. "You didn't even keep track?"

Dylan shrugged. "If I kept track . . . if I thought about it . . . I might *think* about it."

"And you might overthink it?"

"Yeah, exactly."

After gathering their bags from the back of Logan's SUV, they went into the house. He'd drunk what felt like a ton of Gatorade and water after the game, but the one thing that always seemed to quench his thirst was in his own refrigerator.

Logan dropped his duffel on one of the barstools and was just detouring to the fridge when his phone rang.

It was Levi.

They hadn't talked in a week, when Levi had called to report that he hated that guard on his team a *little* less. It had probably also helped that the offensive coordinator had intervened.

Levi had been full of smug pleasure that it had finally happened, and they'd joked for half an hour before he'd had to go to practice.

"Hey, baby bro," Logan said, tucking the phone between his ear and his shoulder, pulling open the fridge and finding the chocolate milk.

One of the beautiful things about living with Dylan was that he made sure there was always a full jug of it after a game.

Bless Dylan and his total lack of dislike for the grocery store—and his ability to think ahead.

"Hey, you got a special delivery yesterday," Levi said. "I was surprised you didn't call me about it, and then I realized you were probably already at the hotel, for the walkthrough before the game."

Even during home games, the teams usually asked that they stay in the team hotel—making sure that nobody did anything especially crazy. It also cultivated routine and made away games seem a little less different.

There was nothing that Logan liked better than sleeping in his own bed, but he'd also gotten used to the idea that at least the night before a game, he was in a different one.

"Yeah." Logan pulled out the chocolate milk. Dylan had already grabbed two glasses from the cupboard and he shot him an impudent look. "What kind of special delivery?"

He could practically hear Levi's glee through the phone. "Something special. For you and Dylan. He there? Put him on speaker."

Despite his protestations to the contrary, Levi—and Landry and Lyla—were all convinced that he and Dylan were some kind of star-crossed Romeo and Juliet love story.

Frankly it wasn't just them.

It was awkward and more than a little embarrassing.

"Okay—but you'd better congratulate him before any of your bullshit," Logan said, setting the phone on the counter and pressing the speaker button. "Dylan tied the record for most kicks in a game."

"Did you really?" Levi was a Banks—and thus competitive and utterly obsessed with records of any kind.

"Yeah. Tied Rob Bironas." Dylan sounded pleased but tired.

"That is fucking badass." Levi paused. "Who is Rob Bironas?"

Logan rolled his eyes. "You're ridiculous," he said. "He's a kicker, *obviously.*"

"Obviously," Levi retorted. "Anyway, go get your special delivery. I want to hear you when you open it."

"Is it going to explode?" Logan asked skeptically as he picked up the phone and walked from the kitchen to the front door. "Make a huge mess? Make me want to fly to Seattle and dismember you?"

Levi cackled. "No explosions, unless you count . . . well . . ." His voice went sly, and Logan, who knew his brother better than he liked, didn't feel like his suspicions had been alleviated at all.

"Unless we count what?" Dylan asked as Logan opened the front door.

The brown box sitting on the front door mat his mom had picked out seemed innocuous enough.

"Explosions of the *luuuuurve* variety," Levi teased.

Oh God, he was absolutely going to fly to Seattle and murder Levi. Slowly. Painfully. And enjoy every second of it.

His face flushed as he set the box down on the kitchen counter, not wanting to touch it. "You didn't send me sex toys again, did you?"

"Why would I repeat a prank, especially when it was so good? Nope. Not sex toys."

Logan told himself that Dylan didn't look the tiniest bit intrigued by the sex toys.

Don't ask. Please don't ask.

"Oh great," Logan muttered. "Something equally embarrassing, I'm sure." He tore into the brown paper tape with a thumbnail.

"Just now that y'all are dating, I wanted to make sure you had some . . . guidance," Levi teased. "I know you're fucking clueless at this, Logan. You could use all the help you can get."

"We're not dating," Logan reminded him. "We just aren't correcting Ricky's article. That's all."

He couldn't look at Dylan. Not now. Not when the hunger for it to be true, for it to be just what Levi said it was, was probably written all over his face.

"Oh, that's all," Levi said airily. "Well, open it and tell me what you think."

Logan ripped the box open, only to reveal a smaller, more colorfully printed cardboard box. "A . . . *date* box?"

"You don't date, bro, you don't have a fucking clue what you're doing. I signed you up for this, so poor Dylan there doesn't have too terrible a time of it."

Logan felt Dylan peering around his shoulder, and even though the package wasn't sex toys, he still kinda wanted to murder Levi.

"What do you mean, you *signed me up for this*?"

"It's a subscription service. Every two weeks, you're gonna get a new one," Levi said, cackling. "Keep it fresh. Keep it hot, you know. That's important for a new relationship."

"What even . . . is it?" Dylan said, poking at the cardboard box. It said something on the front about how everything you needed for a sweet, fulfilling night in was included.

And yet, supposedly it wasn't sex toys.

Levi was right, you are *bad at this,* Logan realized, *when you think about a good night in and all you think about is sex toys.*

But the last thing he should do was make Levi think any of this was acceptable—even if he was right.

"It's a date in a box. Everything you need to keep that relationship going, one lovely, romantic evening at a time," Levi said. "Or at least that was what I was promised."

"God forbid it's not everything you were promised," Logan said dryly. "Hey, if you want to waste your money, I'm not going to judge."

"I don't consider it a waste," Levi said self-righteously. "I'm helping out my brother out of the goodness of my own heart."

"Uh-huh," Logan said sarcastically, to cover for his complete and total humiliation. No wonder Levi had wanted Dylan to be here for this. "Well, I'm sure these will gather dust in my closet real well."

"That's not the way to treat your new boyfriend, Logan," Levi reprimanded.

"He's not . . ." Logan started to argue again, but gave up halfway through the sentence when he realized that Dylan was laughing next to him.

"You have to admit," Dylan said, when he finally finished cackling, "that this is pretty fucking funny."

"No," Logan said.

"See, I knew I liked you, Dylan," Levi said. He sounded *very* pleased. Maybe even eclipsing the amusement from the sex toy debacle.

"I have to go," Logan said firmly. "Fuck off, Levi." He hung up.

He was just going to go die in a hole now, thank you very much.

"Hey, I thought it was funny," Dylan said. He looked like he meant that, his expression betraying not even a hint of embarrassment. Probably because for him it *was* just a joke. He didn't secretly hope that it was real, even though it couldn't possibly be.

Not like you, you great big idiot.

"Sure," Logan said. He grabbed the box. He wouldn't throw it away, because he couldn't bring himself to do that—growing up poor meant getting rid of perfectly good things was impossible—but he would shove it in his closet. Back in the darkest corner. Where he'd never have to see it.

"Hey, I've got to call my mom, tell her about the record," Dylan said. But he was still smirking. "But first . . . what sex toys?"

Logan made an outraged sound and Dylan dissolved into laughter again. "Hey, dude, I just love your brother."

"He's a pain," Logan said, telling himself that he was absolutely not jealous of Levi. That would be pathetic.

"But he's *your* pain," Dylan said.

"Well, you were part of this prank, so you're definitely a surrogate Banks now," Logan said. "How's that feel?"

Dylan grinned. "Pretty damn good, actually."

Logan told himself as Dylan went upstairs that the pleasure on Dylan's face didn't have anything to do with the fact that he'd just called them fucking *brothers*—only that he hadn't had any of them growing up and now he did. Even if they were just borrowed from Logan.

Logan knew he should be sleeping.

It had been a long day—and a fucking *long* game. Not every game was played in the trenches, but this one had been.

Every single down had been a struggle.

After the game, Pax had suggested they all go out to celebrate their kicker's incredible achievement, and there'd been some talk—mainly from Tristan and Wade—about buying Dylan eight shots to match his eight field goals. But Dylan had cried off, saying he was tired.

Logan couldn't deny *he* was tired too. It had been a fucking wild week, culminating in one of the toughest games he'd ever played in.

After Dylan had left to talk to his mom, Logan had puttered around the house, even though he knew he should just go to sleep. Flipping through all the hundreds of channels on the TV, not finding anything that caught his interest, and when Dylan's door had remained shut—*and that's his prerogative, and there's nothing wrong with that, he's allowed to celebrate with his mom,* Logan had reminded himself—he'd finally taken his tired, aching body to bed.

But sleep evaded him.

Instead he stared at the ceiling, shadowed in the dim light from the streetlamp on the corner that always peeked through his blinds, no matter how tightly he shut them, and tried not to think how he'd felt, watching Dylan kick that final field goal.

It hadn't been to win the game—but it hadn't mattered. Not to Logan.

He'd felt his heart in his throat, and then he'd felt it fall to his stomach, and then lower, when Dylan's foot had connected with the ball.

There was no doubt he'd wanted it for Dylan. More than he wanted to look at too closely. But somehow, he'd wanted it for *him* too.

Which didn't make any fucking sense.

But he still couldn't dismiss the thought.

Logan rolled over and tried to ignore not only the grumble in his mind, but the grumble in his stomach. He'd shoveled in tons of pasta post-game, trying to compensate for the energy and calories he'd lost, but he found he was still hungry.

And thirsty too.

He groaned, turning back over.

Ignoring the pervasive thoughts was hard enough. Ignoring his physical needs was impossible.

Finally, he swung his legs over the edge of the bed, and not even bothering to grab a t-shirt to cover his chest, walked down the hall and down the stairs towards the kitchen.

Dylan had taken over grocery shopping after he'd discovered that Logan was allergic to the store, and so now their fridge was usually stocked, and the fruit bowl on the counter was always full.

He'd have a few bananas and a big glass of chocolate milk, and maybe two out of his three hungers assuaged, he could fall asleep.

But when he rounded the corner to the kitchen, he realized he wasn't alone.

Dylan was leaning over the counter, flicking through something on his tablet, the glow lighting up his face.

He glanced up. "Oh, you couldn't sleep either?" he asked.

Logan shook his head. "Too tired and yet too keyed up, all at the same time," he said, grabbing a banana from the bunch hanging on the hook above the fruit basket.

"Yeah, seriously," Dylan agreed.

He peeled his banana and ate half of it, the two of them just standing together in companionable silence.

It was surprising—yet not at all, Logan realized—that just being in Dylan's presence seemed to relax him. Finishing the banana, he skirted around him, and pulled open the fridge, grabbed the chocolate milk.

He shook it experimentally, checking how much was left, and out of the corner of his eye, he saw Dylan's lips curl into a smirk.

"Just drink it all, you know you want to," Dylan teased.

"I was really thinking, why bother with a glass," Logan said, twisting the lid off and taking a big gulp, "'cause I was always gonna finish it."

"For someone who claimed he wouldn't ever drink the last of the milk when we first met, you do it at an alarming rate," Dylan pointed out dryly. But he was smiling.

"Apparently, you make me thirsty," Logan said.

Dylan made him a lot more than thirsty. And that was the real problem, wasn't it?

They'd gotten tangled up, in more knots than just friendship. It had started with that night when Dylan had ended up in his lap, and now it was here, with them in a dark, shadowed kitchen, Logan trying not to think how absolutely gorgeous the slender, muscular line of Dylan's bare back was, as he leaned over the counter.

How much he wanted to trace that perfect slope. With his fingers. With his mouth. With his *teeth*.

Then Dylan looked up at him, and there was a knowing in his eyes. Like he'd caught Logan looking and he knew exactly what that look meant.

"Have you read this?" he asked, frowning and pointing to his tablet.

"Read what?"

Logan leaned over, and felt a jolt. Dylan was reading Ricky's article.

"You should . . ." Dylan started to say.

But Logan didn't let him finish. "No," he said firmly. "*No.*"

"My mom told me about it, said she read it," Dylan said. "She was surprised, considering everything, that I hadn't read it. I couldn't sleep, so I thought . . . why not?"

Logan deliberately took a slow drink of milk. Trying not to let the sudden anxiousness take him over.

Or if that was impossible, to at least keep it off his face so that Dylan wouldn't know.

He didn't need to read what Ricky had said about him. Didn't need to agonize over the lies that he'd told, all for attention.

"I can't . . ." Dylan took a deep breath. "I can't get over how angry this whole thing makes me. He paints you as this like . . . asshole player, who doesn't give a fuck about anyone or anything, and that's not you, man. I know you and Helen put out a statement, but this is . . . to be perfectly honest, I wanna go kick his ass."

It was impossible *not* to smile, a little bit, at that.

Dylan was so fierce. So loyal. So *mine*, Logan's mind added before he could stop it.

"And that," Logan said, "is why I haven't read it. 'Cause it'll piss me off, and I don't want to be pissed off about it. I want . . . *ugh*," he said, smacking the counter, "I want to be *glad* it's happened, not pissed off. And even if I am, it doesn't fucking change a thing."

"I get it." Dylan's expression was sympathetic, but not in a way that galled. It just made Logan feel warm inside. Protected. "You want to focus on the good part of it."

"And not on the part where he outed me and then forced you into a position that you shouldn't have ever been in?" Logan asked wryly. "The part where he won't shut his fucking trap about us on TikTok?"

It was a hypothetical question. Logan knew it. He'd even guess Dylan knew it. But he answered it anyway.

"Yes, to the first," Dylan said slowly, "but truly, I don't mind the second. And he didn't force me anywhere. He forced you, maybe, but not me. I chose to be here. With you."

Dylan couldn't know what those words were doing to him, in the dim light of the kitchen. Logan's fingers clenched around the edge of the granite countertop because he didn't want to forget himself. Forget that they were *friends*, first.

Friends, first and last and everything in between.

"What about the third?" Logan asked, clearing his throat.

"The third?"

"Where he won't shut up," Logan said, so annoyed that he wouldn't.

"How do you even know what he's saying?" Dylan asked. But Logan knew he must have looked. Levi had, claiming that so far all his posts had just been rehashes of the article, and a few snippets of a song that sounded very dramatic and brokenhearted—that was supposedly about Logan.

He certainly was excellent about playing up the devastated angle, but Logan didn't really buy it. How could he? They'd never had some great romance. A few hookups, a few satisfying orgasms, that was it. They'd barely even *spoken*.

"Levi keeps sending me texts, telling me he's gonna go kick his ass," Logan said with a resigned sigh. "I keep telling him not to stoop to his level, because he'd probably turn it into some kind of live broadcast."

"He would," Dylan agreed.

"I don't like it," Logan said. "That asshole, talking about you . . ."

"Hey, it's fine, I don't mind, besides, he gave us an opportunity to reach out to guys like Matt, you know? And speaking of that . . ." Dylan swiped across the screen on his tablet. "I'm assuming that

Helen sent you the pictures we've taken. The one the first night, and the one on Friday, at the offensive line dinner? She mentioned they're spreading through social media."

Logan hadn't wanted to talk about it. Hadn't even wanted to bring it up. Because if they started talking about it, they'd have to *keep* talking about it, and he was afraid if he got started, he wouldn't want to stop.

He wouldn't want to confine it to just *talking*, either.

But Dylan had been the one to broach the subject, so he nodded. "Yeah," he said. "I saw."

Dylan looked up, and his gaze was purposeful, his light green eyes intent with *something*. That something pinned him down, kept him stationary when he knew he'd be better off moving away, putting some distance between them.

But he didn't move, because he didn't think he could.

"It's gotten me thinking . . ." Dylan said.

Logan almost retorted: *thinking, that's bad*. And maybe a week ago, he might have. When things had been light and easy and free between them. But now it felt like he was navigating around sudden curries and eddies that he couldn't understand, couldn't explain.

"Thinking about what?" Logan asked, his voice low and gruffer than he'd intended.

"That it won't be the last time we have to do that," Dylan said quietly.

A thought that had also crossed Logan's mind. More times than he wanted to count.

Logan nodded. Not sure he trusted his voice to come out as steady as it needed to.

"I realized that it wouldn't be the last time and it probably wouldn't be *only* on the cheek next time, and I thought . . ." Dylan cleared his throat. "That the first time we do it, shouldn't be like that. Uh, shouldn't be in . . . in front of other people."

Logan's mind went blank. Completely fucking blank.

Was he saying . . . he didn't want the first time to be a performance? He wanted it to be . . . real?

No, Logan told himself firmly, *that's not what he means. He means, we don't want to look like fucking idiots. The last thing either of us wants is for him to look shocked, the first time he kisses a guy.*

"You *have* been thinking about this," Logan said, before he could clamp the words down, keep them in.

Dylan's gaze was guarded. Like he didn't want to give too much away. But Logan wanted to take it all, to *steal* it. "Yes."

"And you think we should kiss, now?"

Dylan cleared his throat. "I'm not saying *now* now, but yes, we should, before . . . before we get put on the spot, and we give ourselves away."

What Dylan couldn't possibly realize was that the moment their lips met, it was inevitable Logan was going to give himself away.

It didn't matter if they did it here, in this dark kitchen, with nobody the wiser, or if they did it in full view of the entire Piranhas team, with a full complement of media reporting on it.

"You're sure you're ready for this?" Logan felt like he wasn't just asking Dylan this; he was asking himself.

And he was afraid of what the answer might be.

"You're sure you're ready for this?"

Dylan gazed at his friend. His . . . well, he couldn't deny the term anymore . . . his *crush*. Because Logan didn't just make him feel warm and friendly; he made him feel hot and wanting.

"I think so," Dylan said, rising up from where he'd been leaning over the countertop. Taking a step closer to Logan. He shouldn't say, *I've been kinda dying for this.*

Logan licked his lips, and gazed down at him. He wasn't short, not by any means, but Logan was a big guy. But even then, it was easy to forget that, because he was so kind and, in many ways, gentle. He'd never once made him nervous.

Except right now.

Dylan told himself he shouldn't be nervous.

He'd kicked eight freaking field goals today.

Eight.

After that, kissing a guy shouldn't be a big deal.

Except it wasn't just any guy he was kissing.

It was Logan.

Who hadn't looked particularly shocked or dismayed at Dylan's suggestion. Instead, he'd looked intrigued, eyes lighting up.

He didn't know if it was possible that Logan wanted him—but it seemed they were both going to find out right now.

Logan still hadn't moved, so Dylan took another step closer, angling his head, fitting his body against Logan's, until each place they were touching felt like a mini explosion of sensation: his shoulder against Logan's collarbone, their forearms brushing, one thigh nudging another.

He'd wondered, before this moment, if it would feel weird, to be doing this with a guy. But it didn't. No part of it felt even the slightest bit strange. He felt like he was coming home.

All he'd have to do was tilt forward, just a fraction, and their mouths would be touching, too.

He'd kissed plenty of women before and he'd never felt the anticipation rumbling inside like an earthquake, until he wasn't sure he could contain it anymore.

He kept expecting Logan to just take that final inch and be the one to kiss him, but he didn't.

He was waiting, heart thundering away in his chest, because Dylan could feel it, thumping away, for him to make the final move, to close that last little bit of distance between them.

He wouldn't ever push, Dylan realized, because that wasn't who Logan was.

You need to trust yourself and trust him.

Dylan realized that he did. He trusted the way he'd been feeling about this, about Logan, about *men*. And there was nobody on earth he trusted more than Logan.

He leaned in, and pressed his lips against Logan's.

For a second, neither of them moved. Neither of them, Dylan was pretty fucking sure, even *breathed*.

It was everything he'd expected and imagined and fantasized about, and it was more, too.

Logan was warm and solid and soft, so much softer than Dylan could've dreamed. He reached up, and with wandering fingertips, stroked the scruff of his cheek, tilted his head, and pressed their mouths together more insistently.

Dylan didn't know what woke Logan up, but maybe it was the pressure, because suddenly, he was kissing him back, lips moving confidently but gently. Carefully. Like he didn't want to scare Dylan off.

But Dylan was so far past being scared off.

He angled his head and deepened the kiss, groaning a little as his tongue brushed Logan's. It was still so slow, like molasses, but it also somehow managed to be the hottest kiss he'd ever had. And then Logan's hands, those big, warm, competent hands slid down his back, curling around his waist, tugging him even closer, and Dylan couldn't hold back the groan that escaped out of him.

Somehow, he'd known it would feel like this. A kiss shouldn't feel so safe and so exhilarating, all at the same time, but this one did.

Logan's grip tightened, each fingertip digging into his skin, into the smooth cotton of the boxers covering his hips, and suddenly the slow hot kiss wasn't quite as slow anymore. He was taking it over, hunger rising between them, and Dylan gasped, rubbing his thigh and his hardening cock, almost on instinct, against Logan's.

He could barely think anymore. Just *it feels so good, he feels so good*, running through his uncooperative brain in a sluggish, feverish loop.

It had begun slow, but it ended fast.

One moment, they were kissing, and the next, they weren't. Logan tore his mouth off Dylan's, and then his hands were gone, and he was on the other side of the island, lips red and wet, pupils blown, an erection that matched Dylan's tenting his boxer briefs, and shock written all over his face.

Clearly, he hadn't expected it to be like that.

Dylan hadn't been surprised though. He'd known it would be. How could Logan have thought it wouldn't?

It's why he'd wanted to do it now, when they were alone, and not as some kind of weird pseudo-performance. 'Cause he'd known his own desire, and had hoped, from the way he sometimes caught Logan looking, that he wasn't alone.

That hope had turned into a full-blown reality.

But from the expression on Logan's face, Dylan wasn't sure it was a reality he'd wanted to face.

"Well," he said, somewhat stupidly. Sue him, most of his blood wasn't currently residing in his brain. "Well, we did that. Uh . . . good practice."

Now can we practice some more? A lot more? Preferably on some kind of soft, horizontal surface?

Logan was still staring at him. Still hadn't said a goddamned word.

Maybe it had been a mistake—*but*, Dylan reminded himself, *you had to do it. You were gonna end up doing it one way or the other, and if you'd kissed for the first time in front of other people, that would have been so much fucking worse.*

Disastrous, for sure, because if anyone looked at Logan right now, they'd know the truth.

Except, maybe not.

Because as hard as Dylan stared at his friend, even he couldn't figure out what the truth was. Was he upset? Stunned? Turned on? Desperately wanting to do it again? A confusing mix of all four?

"I guess it won't be too terrible to do that again, at least," Dylan said. Why hadn't Logan *said* something?

He was the one who'd just kissed a guy for the first time, and he wasn't freaking out. Not even remotely.

Logan's tongue darted out, licked his bottom lip. Dylan felt the impact of it hit him, square in the solar plexus, like he'd just been tackled. His tongue had been on *that* tongue. His lips on those lips.

How was he ever going to think of anything else when they were together?

Maybe that's why people said that curiosity killed the cat.

Except, Dylan thought wryly, this time it hadn't killed the cat. It had turned the cat *on*.

"No." When Logan finally spoke up, it was in a low, rough voice. He sounded hot and bothered, and yep, when Dylan took a chance and glanced over at his crotch, he was definitely still turned on.

Well, that made two of them. But what excuse could he possibly come up with to green-light kissing a second time?

Just because you liked it. Because you loved it.

But under Logan's intense gaze, Dylan didn't have quite enough courage to admit that, even though he wanted to.

Still . . . what would it hurt? Logan wouldn't hurt him. He'd never dream of it. If he didn't want to, he'd say no gently. Kindly. Carefully.

Dylan opened his mouth to suggest it, against all his better judgment, but that was the moment that Logan finally decided to say more than one fucking word.

"Gettin' late," he said, "I'm off to bed."

Dylan bit his tongue so he wouldn't squawk *alone?* back at his friend.

Because yes, that was clearly where he was going, *alone.*

Tamping down his disappointment, he smiled at Logan and said, as carefree as he could possibly manage, "Have a good night, man."

Watched as Logan tossed the empty milk carton into the recycling bin, and then made his way out of the kitchen.

Dylan couldn't deny it anymore; he was both ecstatic and also disappointed. But was that really Logan's fault? Could he really blame Logan? Just because he was gay didn't mean he was into every guy. It didn't mean that Logan had to be into him.

It was just a real problem that Dylan had discovered that he was *also* into guys—one guy in particular.

The one guy who wasn't really into him.

Chapter Eight

Before the kiss, Dylan hadn't been able to sleep.

He'd been sure that all the excess sexual frustration that he shouldn't be feeling—but *was*—would make it even tougher to fall asleep.

But the truth was, he'd come back upstairs, settled back into his bed, and to his surprise, fell right into a succession of dreams that left him feeling . . . unsettled.

That, Dylan told himself, as he rolled over the next morning, *is a lot better term than horny.*

'Cause he was.

So fucking horny.

And not the kind of horny that a quick fist around his cock in the shower would fix.

No, he wanted to touch, and be touched in return. By one person specifically.

To distract himself, Dylan grabbed his phone. There were a handful of texts on the screen, all sent to the Piranhas group chat.

The first was from Tristan: **hey, we need to go out tonight, celebrate Leonard's record properly. I'm still down: eight shots for eight field goals.**

The next came from Wade. **Do you want him to be unconscious for practice on Tuesday?**

And the third, Dylan's heart stuttering, even as he tried to keep his breathing even, was from Logan. **Why don't y'all come over this afternoon? We'll grill burgers, and you can harass the record holder in person.**

Everyone—from Tristan to Wade to Pax—seemed to love that idea. Pax said he'd bring the beer. Wade said he'd bring his mama's famous potato salad. Tristan said he'd bring himself, apparently a gift to the whole gathering.

The last message had been sent less than a minute ago.

Dylan pulled himself out of bed, groaning a bit at his tired, sore muscles. Sure, he hadn't been through the wringer yesterday, like some of the guys, like Logan specifically, and the other guys on the o-line, but kicking eight field goals, plus all the kickoffs, had taken their toll.

He stretched a bit, and then debated for only a minute, before throwing a t-shirt on. Normally, he and Logan walked around the house in just boxers or briefs, not worrying about appearances, but after last night, Dylan thought a layer of cotton protection between him and Logan might be a good idea.

Logan was downstairs, eating cereal at the kitchen table, hunched over the bowl. He too, Dylan realized, was wearing a t-shirt and shorts. Maybe he'd done that because he was going out after breakfast, or maybe . . . maybe he'd decided just like Dylan that too much exposed skin might lead to something.

"Hey," Dylan said, detouring towards the fridge. "I saw the texts. A barbeque sounds like a good idea. I was going to the store anyway, get us stocked for this week. So I'll pick up some stuff." He pulled out a handful of boiled eggs, tapping their shells against the side of the sink.

Logan glanced up at him. "It's your party, you shouldn't be buying the groceries."

"You *hate* the grocery store." Dylan shrugged. "Like I said, I was going anyway. Not a big deal to pick up some hot dogs and burger patties and buns."

"If you're sure." Logan didn't sound sure at all. "I could go with you . . ."

Dylan knew he hated the store. He'd discovered this around week two, when he'd watched Logan visibly wilt at the suggestion that they go together. It was an odd dislike, but somehow made Logan more endearing. And Dylan kind of loved that he knew these sorts of things, the secrets that Logan kept from everyone else.

"Nope, I got it," Dylan said. Finished peeling his eggs. Poured himself coffee, and came to sit down at the table. His normal seat was kitty-corner to Logan's. Their knees often bumped together when they sat like that.

And okay, maybe Dylan had been lying to himself that up until the last week their friendship had been strictly platonic, because that wasn't platonic at all. But if he sat opposite Logan instead . . . well, what would that even mean? That he was afraid of touching him?

It was bad enough that he'd put a shirt on this morning. That Logan had put on a shirt *and* real shorts.

Daring Logan to say anything, Dylan slid into his regular seat. And then deliberately let his knee bump Logan's.

"Need me to grab anything else?" Dylan asked.

Logan didn't flinch, not exactly, but he looked like he wanted to run away.

Also like he wanted to lean in a little closer.

Fascinating.

"Pax said he was getting beer, and I think the other guys are bringing stuff too."

"Yeah," Dylan said with a nod. "But anything else for the week?"

Monday was the day they usually had off, especially after a win. Sometimes Dylan would go in anyway, if Logan was, but it seemed that he'd decided against it today.

"Oh, the usual stuff, I think," Logan said. "Eggs?" He hesitated. And seriously flushed bright red. "Sausage?"

Dylan chuckled. "I got you, man."

Oh, Logan was really cute like this.

No wonder Ricky had been distraught when he'd gotten dumped.

"I'll clean up the backyard a bit. Get the chairs out. Make sure the grill's ready to go," Logan said.

"No workout today?"

"I may just do some stretching," Logan admitted. "I feel like I went through a war."

For Logan to admit that—Logan, who was in crazy good shape—said everything about what the game had been like. They could probably all use a break after yesterday.

"I bet," Dylan said, drinking his coffee. "But you're not injured?"

Logan shook his head. "Just sore. You? No side effects from being awesome and tying the record?"

"Eight field goals? Man, I kick more than that in an afternoon of practice," Dylan admitted.

Fifteen minutes later, he was pushing a cart through the produce section, when his phone rang.

For a split second, Dylan's heart stuttered. Was Logan calling him?

No—he glanced at the screen—it wasn't Logan.

It was Jamie.

He'd texted him last night, congratulating him on matching Bironas' record, but now he was calling.

Conveniently, because he'd just been thinking that maybe the person he needed to talk to was Jamie.

"Hey," he said, answering the call and tucking the phone between his ear and his shoulder. He reached out and grabbed two big bunches of bananas and set them in the cart.

"I know," Jamie said, his voice amused, "that I told you that you were amazing last night, and that I always knew you could thrive someplace, but I wanted to say it again. Much louder."

"That *is* what a phone is for," Dylan said, amused.

"I was a little nervous for you, heading to Miami," Jamie admitted, "but I was clearly wrong. Miami's where you're meant to be."

Dylan hummed under his breath, tossing a bag of baby carrots into the cart.

"But don't get me started," Jamie continued, after barely taking a breath, "about this crazy fake boyfriend idea."

He'd called Jamie when the news had come out. Had kept the conversation to a bare minimum, because Jamie was like a sweet mother hen. He'd worry about you, and cluck like the world was ending tomorrow, but in the end, he'd do it because he cared about you. But because the conversation had been so short, Dylan hadn't given Jamie any real opportunity to start clucking.

He was gearing up to do some serious clucking now.

"We kissed last night," Dylan said, tossing a bomb into the conversation before Jamie could go too far down the clucking path.

"You . . . you *kissed?* Like kissed kissed?"

"You know what kissing is. You put your mouth on another person's mouth . . ."

"I know what kissing is," Jamie interrupted. "I didn't realize you were doing it with Logan."

"We weren't. But . . ." Dylan hesitated. "I thought maybe we should test it out, you know?"

Jamie was silent for a moment. "Test it out?"

"I told you I was having thoughts . . ." He'd said that same phrase with Logan too. But he knew it was more than just a stray thought or two. It was enough thoughts, put together, that it wasn't just a random occurrence. He had these feelings, and he didn't quite know what to do with them.

Well, that was a lie. He knew what he wanted to do. But the fact they were around at all confused the hell out of him.

"You did," Jamie said. Dylan could hear the change in his voice—from clucking to supportive. That was why they were friends; really, why they'd become friends in the first place. They'd both arrived at the Riptide kicker tryouts and they were supposed to be adversaries, competing for the same spot, but it had never felt that way, and Dylan chalked all of that up to Jamie's kind, giving heart.

"Do you want to talk about what that means?" Jamie asked, hesitantly, when Dylan didn't say anything.

"I'm not having like . . . I don't know . . . a big gay freakout," Dylan said.

"I didn't think you were." Jamie's voice was wry.

"I must be . . . well, I guess I must be bisexual," Dylan said, as he pushed the cart aimlessly around the produce section. "That makes sense."

"It's not like you have to have all of the answers now, or even some of them," Jamie reminded him gently. "And your labels don't even have to stick. They can change, as you learn more about who you are."

"But that's the whole problem," Dylan said, suddenly aware of a rising panic inside him. "I didn't know this about myself. I'm twenty-seven years old. I've been around half-naked or totally naked guys for half my freaking life. And just, now, *suddenly*, I'm bi?"

"I don't think it's all that sudden, to be honest," Jamie said.

"It *feels* sudden," Dylan retorted.

"Listen, sometimes . . . sexuality isn't black and white . . . it's shades of gray. It's a sliding scale. Just 'cause you're bi doesn't mean you're equally attracted to men and women. Doesn't mean you're even sexually *and* romantically attracted to them in the same way." He sounded very sure, and what he was saying also made sound logical sense. There was a reason they called it a *scale*, after all. "I'm just saying it's not that you didn't know yourself. Logan's just . . . an extraordinary circumstance, and that's okay."

"It's okay that I want to desperately get into Logan's pants?"

"Oh?" He could *hear* Jamie raise his eyebrow, even across the phone line. "That's how it is, huh?"

"I told you I kissed him."

"You said you were testing. Like practice, I thought."

"That's true. That's how . . . well, that's how I suggested it, initially."

"But?" Jamie already knew what he was going to say. They both knew what he was going to say. Dylan knew he had to just *say* it.

"But the truth is . . . I wanted to kiss him. I like him, you know?"

"As a friend?" Jamie asked archly. "Or more?"

There was part of Dylan who wanted to stuff that knowledge back into the deep, dark corner it had come from, but there was a bigger part of him that was ready—even eager—to face it. To explore it.

Let's be honest, you're just really fucking horny.

"Not just as a friend. There have been the thoughts. And uh . . . dreams, too. And now the kissing . . ."

"You have a crush on Logan Banks." Jamie said it matter-of-factly, with zero clucking.

"Yeah," Dylan said. "Yeah, I do."

"You kissed him, and you want to kiss him again."

"But *how*," Dylan retorted. "I . . . I suggested we do it because well, I didn't want to do it for the first time in front of other people, or as part of well . . . you know what. But now . . ."

"Now you can't find a convenient excuse other than *I'd like to do it again*?" Jamie asked archly.

"He liked it. I swear he did. He was . . ." Dylan cleared his throat. "We were both . . ."

Jamie chuckled. "You both liked it. Got it. So what's the big deal?"

"He's a friend, Jamie. You know that. A really good friend. We're living together."

"But you could move out tomorrow, if you needed to. You've got plenty of money. You sold your old place in Vegas. It was obvious once you decided to stay put for the time being that you didn't want to leave. And it wasn't hard to figure out why."

"Because we're friends?" Dylan pointed out, all too aware of how weak an argument *that* was.

"Sure, that's totally why." Jamie's sarcasm told the whole story there. How completely, utterly unbelievable Dylan's suggestion was. "See, I'm just not sure what the problem is. You like him. He clearly likes you, because despite the rumors, we gays don't just go around kissing everyone who suggests it, or liking it either. Yes, you're friends, but you know what that is? That's icing on the cake. That's an extra cherry in your Shirley Temple. That you were friends first."

"You don't think it's a mistake?" Dylan, currently standing in the butcher section, trying to debate on how many brats to get, couldn't quite believe that Jamie wasn't clucking up a storm right now.

"You're a smart, cautious guy," Jamie said. "You don't tend to shoot from the hip. And you've thought about it plenty. If you want this, then you really want this. And that says it all, I think. Just tell him how you feel."

"Even if he might think it's a mistake?" Dylan decided to go for broke. He tossed four packs of brats into the cart. Followed by two dozen hamburger patties.

There it was. The worst fear, and he'd said it out loud.

It was hard, in the harsh light of morning, to not think that Logan had run away last night. Away from any possibility of more.

And then he'd shown up this morning in *real shorts*.

Not just his briefs.

"You're never going to know if he does, unless you ask," Jamie said firmly. "And if he just wants to be friends . . . I'm not saying that doesn't suck, because it absolutely would, but at least then you'd know."

"Yeah, I would." Dylan still wasn't sure he was willing to take that risk, no matter how good the kiss last night had been.

"And maybe he's afraid, too," Jamie offered. "I don't have to tell you how terrible it is to start liking a friend, especially a *straight* friend."

"But I'm not . . ."

"Right, we both know that," Jamie said. "And you said you'd mentioned it to him, when he asked. But having thoughts about kissing guys, and admitting you're not straight—those are two different things."

"So you think he might not think I'm ready?"

"I don't know what he thinks. All I'm saying is that yeah, he could be afraid. Just like you're afraid."

Dylan considered this as he headed towards the deli counter. He'd get some pre-made coleslaw, and then pick up a couple dozen chocolate chip cookies from the bakery. *Oh*, and he should get some ice cream too. Everyone loved ice cream. And watermelons. You couldn't have a barbeque without watermelon.

"I'll think about it," Dylan said.

"Just don't think too long," Jamie cautioned.

"I won't," Dylan promised.

As Dylan picked up the rest of the stuff for the barbecue, throwing in some chicken breasts and steaks for him and Logan for the week, Jamie chatted a bit about how the Riptide's season was going—good, of course, as always—and how he should make sure to find the segment his boyfriend, Neal, a former kicker, had done on Dylan's record-setting Sunday.

"You'll love it," Jamie said, and Dylan could hear the love in his voice.

"Maybe not as much as you," Dylan teased.

"Fair. That's fair," Jamie conceded.

"Too bad we're not playing each other this year," Dylan said. "Could be fun."

"Would've been," Jamie agreed. His voice went a little sly. "Maybe in the playoffs, huh?"

"Ugh, don't even talk about playoffs yet, you're gonna jinx us," Dylan complained. "We're just happy to have a fucking winning record, at this point."

"Keep going the way you are, and you're gonna have to think about it," Jamie teased.

"That's a problem for tomorrow," Dylan said. "Listen, I gotta go check out."

"Check out? Where are you? The store? Really?" Jamie laughed. "You're such a mom, it's adorable. No wonder Logan likes you."

"Better than a hen," Dylan said.

"What?"

"Gotta go, bye," Dylan said, before Jamie could figure out what he'd said. Or what it meant.

That was also a problem for tomorrow.

The problem for today?

Figuring out what the hell he was going to do with all these feelings swirling around inside of him.

Logan wasn't proud of himself.

He'd wanted to celebrate his friend's achievement, sure, but he hadn't invited half the team over to his house because of that.

He'd done it, embarrassingly, because he didn't know how to be alone, just the two of them, with Dylan anymore.

Not because he didn't want to be. But because what was stopping him from just leaning over and kissing him? From pinning him to the counter between the fridge and the stove and laying one on him that he wouldn't forget?

Dylan clearly hadn't hated it when they'd kissed last night.

There'd been a moment, before he'd escaped upstairs, that he'd thought, insanely, that Dylan might even want to do it again.

So of course, he'd done the one thing he could think of—he'd run away.

Not your finest moment, bucko, Logan thought.

And now, he'd invited two dozen people to the house, because he didn't know how to get through an afternoon and an evening without addressing the elephant in the room: *we kissed and you liked it, and I freaking loved it.*

Because he had. Way, way too much.

His whole life he'd been afraid of falling for the wrong guy, so in the end, he'd kept them all at an arm's length, every hookup. Ricky hadn't been all that different, in retrospect. He'd done to him what he did to all the guys he had sex with. Kept them at a distance, never let them get too close.

But Dylan had been inside, wormed all the way in, before Logan had even realized that he could feel that way about him. And once he'd realized it, it was too late to push him away. This time it had been too late; he'd absolutely fallen for the wrong guy.

The straight friend. The thing he'd been trying to avoid from the moment he'd realized, in third grade, that he liked boys, not girls.

The truth was, this avoidance tactic was only going to last for a couple of hours. Then the guys would go home, and he and Dylan would be alone again.

They'd be alone again tomorrow morning. And tomorrow night, when they got home from practice.

And for so many nights and mornings after that.

Even if Dylan moved out, which Logan absolutely did not want him to do, they'd still see each other all the time.

You are gonna have to figure out a way to deal with this.

This same fucking admonition had been repeating itself in his head all morning, and through the afternoon.

Logan let the lid on the grill close as Dylan poked his head out the back door. "Hot and ready?" he asked.

Oh yeah, hotter than you know. Why don't you come over here and find out?

Then Dylan flushed, instantly, when he realized what he'd said.

"Uh," he said. "I mean . . . is the *grill* hot and ready?"

"Yeah," Logan called back. Clearing the roughness out of his voice. God, they were going to have to talk about this. They couldn't keep creeping around each other, afraid to say anything, because of how it might come out.

If he and Dylan were going to stay friends—and he wanted that, more than ever—they were gonna have to figure this shit out.

Logan refused to accept anything else.

Even if it meant he had to tamp down every stray desire, every stray feeling, until the only person who felt them was him.

Dylan emerged from the house again, carrying a huge tray full of brats and burgers. "Here you go," he said. "Tristan and Wade are here, and I think I just saw Pax's car pull up."

"Tell him to bring the cooler of beer I know he brought out here," Logan said. See, he could do this. He could host a party, with his best friend—even a best friend he'd kissed in a dark kitchen the night before—and it didn't have to be weird.

"We're good at this, you know," Dylan said, handing him the tray. He'd changed into a pair of khaki shorts, fitted to his fucking incredible legs, and a green tank top that made his gorgeous eyes even more arresting.

He shoved a hand through his dark hair—still too long, and still exactly the length that Logan wanted to tangle his fingers in—and grinned. "And I like doing it, actually. This was a great idea."

"You," Logan said, brandishing his grill spatula, "are not supposed to be *working*. This is supposed to be for you."

Dylan just rolled his eyes. "And I can't enjoy it because I bought some brats and some pre-made burger patties? Sliced some tomatoes and chopped up lettuce?"

"Just . . . try to relax and enjoy yourself, okay?" Logan felt guilty. It had been his idea to do this, and he'd done it without even considering that he had no real idea how to host a barbecue, and he'd ended up shoving most of the burden onto Dylan's shoulders. They were *capable* shoulders, but that didn't make him feel any less guilty for doing it.

"Sure thing, boss," Dylan teased as he grabbed the empty platter.

The back door opened again, and out spilled Tristan, Wade, Pax, and Sebastian, with Beau close behind.

Pax and Sebastian were each carrying one end of an enormous cooler.

"See, I didn't even have to tell Pax to bring the drinks out," Dylan said impudently, with a curl of his lips that Logan was just dying to kiss off.

He'd have wanted to do it before, he could admit that, at least, but now he knew what those lips would taste like. How Dylan would moan when his tongue slipped between them.

Fantasy was one thing; reality was entirely another.

Reality meant living with the dirty knowledge of it, day in and day out.

Reality meant wanting to do it again, as soon as possible.

"I gotta make sure everything's ready to go, and then I swear, I'll have at least a quarter of the beers that Tristan is going to try to pour down my throat," Dylan teased.

"You make sure of that," Logan said. "I'll manage things out here."

"See?" Dylan said, and to Logan's shock, he leaned in and kissed him on the cheek. Like he'd done twice before, once for those teenage girls, and the other night, at the pub for the offensive line dinner. But there were no fans here, only their friends. Who were all looking on in interest as Logan nearly dropped his spatula, and Dylan sauntered off.

"Got beer here," Pax said, flipping the lid open, and shooting a good-natured glare in Logan's direction, "and some pop and tea for those of us that don't like to drink during the season."

Sebastian, the cooler deposited, wandered over. "You two look real friendly," he said.

"Haven't we always?" Logan retorted.

"True, true," Sebastian said. "I'm just thinking . . . well, you don't want to hear what I'm thinking, do you? You look like you've been doing too much thinking, yourself."

"Do I? Shit." Logan didn't want anyone to know. Because if anyone else managed to figure it out, there was no way he was going to be able to keep the truth from Dylan.

Sebastian raised an eyebrow. "There somethin' you need to tell me, Banks?"

"No," Logan said firmly.

"I told Tristan to let me ask, 'cause you'd be more likely to tell me, man to man, than man to part Tasmanian devil," Sebastian joked.

Logan eyed where Tristan had opened a beer and was chatting excitedly to Wade and Beau. But his gaze kept drifting over to where Sebastian and Dylan stood by the grill.

It was true; Tristan was never going to let this go.

Why had Dylan done it? Why had he given all their friends—and Logan's heart, for good measure—the wrong idea? Logan felt annoyance and frustration surge inside him.

"Can you watch these for a minute?" Logan asked, but before Sebastian could answer, he'd slapped the spatula into his hands, and was marching into the house.

The only one in the kitchen was Dylan.

He turned, just as Logan walked in. "Oh, are those done already?" he asked.

Like nothing was wrong.

Like him kissing Logan on the cheek in front of their friends was no big deal, like it was the kind of thing they did all the time. Like the line between what was fake and what was real wasn't blurring with every second they spent together.

"No," he said. Took a few steps closer, until he was nearly crowding into Dylan's space. *So you can keep your voice down,* he told himself, even though he acknowledged that the real reason was that he'd been fighting all day to stay out of Dylan's personal space, and he was losing the will to fight the urge any longer. He lowered his voice. "What the hell were you thinking?"

Dylan looked confused, an adorable crinkle forming between his dark eyebrows. "About the kiss?"

Logan opened his mouth to demand to know *which* kiss he was talking about.

One had blown his mind apart, and the other had merely continued the job.

"These are our *friends*, not people we need to be fooling," he said, sounding a lot angrier than he really was.

And Dylan? Well, he looked flustered.

Eight field goals he'd kicked yesterday, and before each one, he'd looked cool as a cucumber. But he looked bothered now. His pale green eyes were wide, his cheeks undeniably flushed.

Hot and bothered, a body part that was definitely not his brain supplied.

"I wasn't aware," Dylan said slowly, carefully, "that we were really fooling anyone."

That was the sticking point, wasn't it? They weren't fooling anyone.

Even themselves.

Logan floundered. When it came down to it, he was just as flustered as Dylan was. He wanted to press him against the counter and taste him again. Kiss him so thoroughly that neither of them wanted to go back outside.

And God help him, Dylan looked like he wanted the same thing.

"At least," Dylan continued, shrugging hopelessly, "I wasn't trying to. I just . . . I just wanted to. I wanted to kiss you, so I did."

Logan understood perfectly.

He'd never claimed to be a genius, but this he got.

Dylan wanted him and didn't know what to do about it.

So Logan, throwing the last bit of caution to the wind, backed him up another step, until his back hit the edge of the countertop, and showed him.

His fingers tangled in the mess of hair always threatening to fall down into his eyes, and pushed it back, not holding him hard, but *firm*. Firm enough that he watched as the pupils in Dylan's pale eyes dilated. Oh, yes, he wanted him.

The how or the why wasn't important—not right now. Not when he had maybe a minute or two to kiss him before anyone showed up to bother them.

Leaning in, he watched as those gorgeous eyes fluttered closed, and he pressed his lips against Dylan's.

He'd intended for this kiss to be as gentle as the first one had. Careful. Not too much, too fast.

But then the moment their lips touched, Dylan wound his arms around his neck, tugged him in until there was nothing between them and kissed him back with so much passion that for just a second, his world rocked.

They'd only needed the match, and while Logan had supplied it, Dylan had lit it.

Logan's tongue stroked into Dylan's mouth and tangled with his own. The kiss turned wild, and that was his thigh that was humping Dylan's, wasn't it?

Everything had gone fuzzy in Logan's mind, anything resembling good sense drowned out by *want* and *now* and *Dylan*.

Someone was groaning, and Logan thought it might be Dylan, but then he realized it was *him*. Groaning and growling and desperate.

He nearly pulled back, because he was supposed to be the voice of reason here, the voice of *experience*. But then Dylan wound one of his legs around his own, his fingers pushing into Logan's shoulders, ten individual pressure points, and he somehow yanked him even closer, grinding in an absolutely filthy rhythm against Logan's body.

He knows what he wants.

And it's you.

Logan wasn't going to argue with that.

"Wow, uh, I . . ."

The voice was a whole lake of cold-ass water dumped on their heads.

Logan froze, his hands on Dylan's thighs.

He'd been about to slide them even further, cup his ass, pull him against him. Rut against him, hopelessly and helplessly, with their friends only a few dozen feet away.

He let Dylan go and took a step back, trying to get his breath under control.

Turning, he saw his quarterback standing awkwardly in the doorway to the kitchen. "Uh," Pax said again. "Sorry to interrupt. I didn't realize . . ."

That makes two of us, thought the part of Logan who was very amused by the irony in all this, *I didn't realize it either.*

Dylan had tried to tell him. He should have listened better.

And last night's "practice" kissing? A dead fucking giveaway, if he hadn't been so far up his own ass, mooning over someone he was convinced couldn't want him.

Well, at the very least, that fallacy had finally been put to bed.

"It's okay," Logan said, his voice unsurprisingly gravelly. He cleared it. Dylan hadn't moved. Hadn't spoken. Which made him feel a tiny bit better about how stupid he'd acted last night.

"The guys were wondering if you had any limes," Pax said apologetically. Like interrupting a kiss like that for *limes* was a crime.

And, Logan agreed with him, it sort of was.

"We have limes," Dylan said, speaking up for the first time.

Logan glanced back and watched, with shaky hands, as he opened the fridge. Sure enough, there was a square plastic container full of lime wedges that Dylan pulled out.

He set it on the counter and Pax took it, cradling it in his hands.

"Thanks," he said. And abruptly, he turned and walked out.

Logan let out the breath he hadn't known he was holding.

"Well, shit," he said. "At least it wasn't Tristan."

"Pax will keep his mouth shut," Dylan said.

Somehow, like everything else, they'd landed on the same page. *Nobody can know. Not yet. Not . . . not when we don't even know what we're doing.*

"Yeah," Logan said, though he wasn't quite as convinced as Dylan was. "I'll talk to him."

Dylan looked surprised. "You think you need to?"

"It won't hurt, right?" Logan shrugged. "I just don't want . . ." He cleared his throat. "This isn't about them, even though I know they're already all talkin' about us. They don't need to."

Dylan nodded in agreement. "Not yet."

"Not ever," Logan said before he remembered that since he'd been outed by Ricky, the world felt they deserved a full explanation of his personal life.

But Dylan hadn't been outed.

Well, not technically.

He outed himself. To you. When it came down to it, and you needed him.

Dylan put a hand on Logan's chest, turned him so he couldn't look away. "I guess," he said, a thread of amusement running through his voice, "I could've just told you the truth. That I like you."

"You tried," Logan said. "You said, *I've been having thoughts.*"

Dylan smiled. "I didn't say they were about you."

"No," Logan agreed. "But I wanted them to be."

"See?" Dylan laughed, like this was actually funny—and maybe it was, because it had turned out okay, at least so far. "I thought you weren't interested."

"Too interested, okay?" Logan said gruffly. He wasn't good at talking about his feelings. Might be the miniscule amount of experience he had doing it.

"Ah," Dylan said, smirking. "I still should have just *said*. That's what Jamie told me to do. Instead . . ." The smirk grew. "I apparently prodded the beast."

Logan leaned in. "Don't ever apologize for that. And," he added, "I hope you prod him a bit later, after everyone's gone."

Dylan's eyes glowed. "Don't think I could stop myself," he said. Logan hadn't known he could be so soft. So sexy. It was like seeing another side of the guy he already couldn't get enough of. He nearly leaned in again, took himself another taste, because Dylan was so irresistible.

But then Dylan straightened. "Who did you leave out there with the grill?"

"Sea Bass," Logan said.

Dylan swatted at him. "Go check on him. In a few minutes, we're going to have a ton of hungry players to feed, and if he burns or ruins anything . . ."

Logan grinned. Couldn't help himself. "You're cute like this. All bossy."

Dylan shot him a look that promised a whole lot more later. "You know it. Now get your ass out there, before Sebastian ruins our barbecue and we have to order pizzas."

Chapter Nine

Dusk had fallen and Dylan had lit the mosquito lanterns.

Had he even known he *owned* mosquito lanterns? Logan didn't know, but apparently Dylan did.

Whatever happened between them—whether they stayed only friends, who hooked up sometimes, or they became even more—he knew one thing for certain: he was never going to host another party without Dylan by his side.

Having grabbed a second beer from the big cooler on the other side of the yard, he dropped down into the chair next to Pax's.

The quarterback slipped his phone back into his pocket.

"Great party," he said.

Logan nodded, sipping his beer, taking in the crowd in the backyard. Half the team had shown up to support and celebrate their kicker. "Though I can't take much credit, other than the idea," he admitted. "This was mostly Dylan's doing."

Pax's forehead wrinkled. "But it was supposed to be *for* him," he said.

"Listen, if a guy wants to host a party, and does a damn good job of it, you don't stop him," Logan said.

Besides, he'd made sure, over the last few hours, that Dylan had plenty of time in the spotlight.

After they'd eaten, after all, there'd been almost nothing for him to do.

He was over by Tristan and Wade and the cooler now, Tristan trying to get him to have another beer—"you're only on three!" Tristan exclaimed loudly, still clearly trying to kill their kicker by insisting he match his field goal total. He'd had a good time. It was written all over his flushed, happy face.

Or maybe he's thinking about what you're gonna do later, when everyone finally leaves.

"Is that what you told yourself before you kissed him, too?" Pax asked.

"That's . . ." Logan didn't really know what to say. "We're figuring that shit out," he said.

Pax did not look convinced. "Just a week ago you were going around telling everyone that it was just a story you weren't correcting. That it wasn't real. That Dylan was straight. And now . . ."

Logan knew what it looked like. He sighed. "I know. Nobody is more surprised than me."

Pax's phone buzzed in his pocket. First, and then again, more insistently. He ignored it, but Logan could see his attention was divided, suddenly. He wanted to look at his phone, desperately.

Good a time as ever to change the subject, he thought.

"Who's that?" he asked casually. Even though he already suspected. And if he was right, then Pax had no leg to stand on.

"Uh, what do you mean?" Pax was a bad liar. It was written all over his face.

"Your phone," Logan said. Took another long drink of beer.

It buzzed again, like it knew, somehow, that they were talking about it, and Pax was unsuccessfully trying to lie about it.

"Nobody, really," Pax said. Unconvincingly.

"Right, uh-huh. 'Cause that nobody keeps textin' you. Like he can't stop." Logan paused. Couldn't help his grin. "'Cause it's a he, isn't it?"

Pax rolled his eyes. "It might be." Like he couldn't help it a moment longer, he grabbed the phone from his pocket.

The moment he saw the screen, his eyes lit. Like he'd been fucking plugged into the closest socket.

"It couldn't possibly be our illustrious quarterbacks coach, could it?" Logan guessed.

Pax flushed. "It could be."

"You're not supposed to be working. It's Monday, *and* it's a Monday after a win."

"It's not, it's . . ." Pax hesitated. "We're not talking about work."

Ah, there it is.

"He's just watching, um, some TV show, and texting me funny things, that's all. It's silly."

But that glow in Paxton's eyes didn't look particularly silly. Logan knew, because he recognized it.

Dylan had looked that same way, a few hours ago, when he'd kissed him in the kitchen.

He'd probably looked just like that, when Pax had caught them together.

"Ah, okay, well, if it's just silly," Logan teased.

"It's nothing, really. It's nothing." Someday, Logan was going to have to teach Pax to lie a little better. 'Cause he was absolutely fucking horrible at it.

"Same kinda nothing Dylan and I got going, I'd imagine," Logan said slowly.

"Oh, no, no. Nothing like that," Pax said hurriedly.

Nothing had happened between them, then. Which, Logan thought, made sense. Davis wasn't stupid enough to start fucking his quarterback. Even if he wanted to. Even if *Pax* wanted him to.

Davis was smarter than that. He'd already been through the NFL wringer, and he wouldn't do anything to compromise Paxton's future.

"Right, well, next time someone asks you about me and Dylan, it's the same kind of nothin'."

Pax's eyes grew wide. Sometimes Logan forgot how young he was. How naive.

He was twenty-five, but in NFL years? He was a baby. He'd only played a season and a quarter, and that first season, Logan thought, didn't even really count, because it had been such a clusterfuck.

"I wouldn't say anything," Pax said. Looking suddenly very serious.

Logan nodded. "We're . . . I don't know what we're doing, to be perfectly honest, and if the whole team finds out, starts gossipin', like they do, it's gonna make it harder to figure out."

Pax frowned. "But you're supposed to be pretending to be together."

"Oh, I don't ever forget it," Logan said wryly. "But that's . . . well, I think that's separate. Like a whole other thing."

Pax didn't look like he understood at all.

It makes sense. You don't even fucking understand. You just don't want him going and telling Tristan, who will tell everyone. And then everyone will interfere. They might even scare Dylan off and you . . . well, you can't take that chance, can you?

"If you say so," Pax pointed out dubiously. His phone was in his hand again, about point five seconds after it had buzzed.

"All I'm saying . . . we both have shit we need to keep hidden."

"You," Pax said, "are not as smart as you think you are. And," he added with a fierce grin, "you also happen to be the *worst* gossip on the team. Everyone thinks it's Tristan, but no, it's absolutely you."

"Which is why I don't want anyone talkin'," Logan said impudently.

Pax rolled his eyes. "There's not even anything to tell about me and Davis. He's my coach. He's helping me win games. He's helping me be the best QB I can be. That's it."

But the way Pax's voice hitched, just the tiniest bit, over Davis' name told Logan everything he needed to know. Maybe there wasn't anything to tell, maybe nothing had happened, but *oh*, Pax wanted it to.

Poor guy.

"Sure," Logan said.

"Why," Dylan said, turning to Logan as he made his way into the house with the last of the load of dishes and paper plates from outside, "did we think this was a good idea, again?"

Tristan and Wade, the last guests, had left less than five minutes earlier.

Dylan hadn't missed the way they'd winked and nudged each other, probably convinced that the moment they walked out the door, he and Logan were going to be all over each other.

Hell, he'd been convinced, too.

"Because it wasn't just me who wanted to celebrate how kick-ass you are," Logan said, his voice a deep rumble.

He considered approaching where Logan had his arms buried wrist-deep in soapy water in the sink, tucking himself against his big, broad back. Maybe sliding his hands down even lower. His nerves stretched tighter as he stared. It would be so easy to do it, but he wasn't just excited to do it, he was terrified, too.

It would be easier if Logan did it.

All he'd been able to get up the nerve to do was two kisses on the cheek—and the "practice" kissing that he'd wrapped up in a bunch of excuses before they'd even done it.

Why didn't Logan get over here? Why was he so fucking far away?

"Well, it was nice," Dylan said.

Logan turned. Lifted one of those expressive eyebrows. "Nice?"

"Okay," Dylan conceded. "A little better than nice. It was great, actually, to have everyone over."

"Great, because it turns out you're really good at doing it," Logan said. "If I'd organized this, it would have been a disaster. Not enough food. Warm beer. Mosquitos everywhere."

Dylan chuckled. "My mom runs a catering business. Did I ever tell you that?"

"*No,*" Logan said, laughing. "See, that's just fucking cheating."

"I used to help her all the time," Dylan said with a shrug. "So I guess this kind of thing comes naturally to me."

"It sure does," Logan said wryly. He flipped the faucet on and rinsed the last dish, setting it on the rack to dry. Then washed his hands, deliberately, slowly, and then dried them just as carefully, stretching out Dylan's nerves to nearly the breaking point. At some point, he was going to come over here, and if Logan wanted to make it easy on him, he'd kiss him and lose his mind again with how good it was.

It was this in-between uncertainty that had him ready to lose his mind, and not in the good kind of way.

If he told Logan that he didn't want to kiss again, he'd respect the boundary.

If he told Logan that he wanted to kiss a hundred times more, he'd probably be down for that, too.

Then finally, Logan turned. "So," he said, leaning against the countertop, his gaze assessing. "You freakin' out yet?"

For a split second, Dylan considered lying, and saying no, but Logan already knew. And what kind of friends would they be if he lied to him, especially about something as important as this?

"A little bit, yeah," Dylan admitted.

Logan's smile was soft, understanding. "It's a big step. One thing to have . . . what did you call them? *Thoughts*? And another entirely to act on them. We don't have to . . ."

But admitting to Logan that he was nervous wasn't him saying he didn't want to.

He did. A whole fucking lot.

"What if I want to?" Dylan interrupted before Logan could finish his sentence. "Because I really, really do."

"Alright. Why don't we . . ." Logan gestured towards the living room, and its huge TV. "We can watch something." He faux shuddered. "Maybe even finish the level of that horrible video game you like so much."

"Okay," Dylan said.

They headed towards the living room, Logan flipping the light off in the kitchen as they left. But before they got to the couch, Logan caught his arm and tugged him close.

Kiss me, Dylan internally begged. *Make it easy. Make me stop overthinking this.*

"Listen," Logan said seriously, his hand loosely encircling Dylan's wrist. Not holding him, but keeping him still. Keeping him close. Dylan could feel his body heat soaking through his light cotton tank. "Nothing has to change between us. You're my best friend. I didn't mean for it to happen when I suggested you stay here, but . . ."

"Me either," Dylan added wryly.

"But you are, and you matter to me. So we can . . . explore this, if you want. Or not. Either way is fine."

"What do *you* want?" Dylan asked.

Logan shot him a look. "I think I made my feelings pretty clear earlier."

"Okay," Dylan said. "Okay."

"We're friends. First. Last. Everything in between," Logan said, and it sounded like a vow.

Dylan felt himself relaxing. He wasn't committing to anything. They'd stay friends no matter how this fell out. He deliberately did not think about whether this was the same promise that Logan had made to Ricky—or any of those other guys he'd hooked up with. He'd admitted, under much duress, that there had been plenty of others before Ricky. But none after. *Nobody since Ricky, not til you.*

Dylan had a feeling that none of them had been Logan's friends, first.

"Let's play that level," Dylan said, and Logan let go of his wrist. He tried not to be disappointed that there hadn't been any more kissing. *There's plenty of time for that.*

He grabbed the controllers from their chargers, and tossed one to Logan, who caught it deftly.

It was mind-blowing how someone with such precise hand-eye coordination could be so fucking terrible at video games.

Dylan clicked the TV on, and they started playing. It was not a particularly difficult level, especially with two people, but it turned out that having to do most of the work made it a lot tougher than he'd expected. No matter what directions he gave Logan, he mostly just ran around, making it way more difficult to finish the level.

"Argh, no," Dylan exclaimed as he narrowly avoided dying again. He flopped against Logan's firm side. "You could be a little more help, you know."

"What? Me? I'm not helping?"

The dumb shit totally knew he wasn't helping. He kept his character running around, picking up everything that the bad guys dropped, but doing nothing to defeat any of them.

Dylan rolled his eyes, and settled more firmly into Logan's side. It felt nice. Comforting. With an extra zing of that sexual awareness that added just the right amount of spice.

"You're really terrible at this, you know," Dylan said, amused.

"Oh, I know," Logan teased right back. "But you like playing and I like *you*, so I don't mind. Also," he added, his voice dropping even lower, sending a shiver of awareness skittering through Dylan, "every time we play, I keep hoping that maybe you'll accidentally end up in my lap again."

"Oh?" Dylan turned a little, so he could see Logan's face. He looked damn pleased with himself, and his eyes were full of awareness—how close they were, how dim the lighting was in the room, how easy it would be to throw caution to the wind and grab exactly what they both wanted. "Is that what all this was about? You want me in your lap?"

"Let's just say if you fell into it again, I wouldn't be disappointed."

"What if . . ." Dylan took a deep breath. Set his controller down. Gathered his courage. "What if it wasn't an accident?" Then he swung a leg over Logan's body, perching lightly right where they both wanted him to be. In his lap.

For a moment that felt like it lasted an eternity, they both froze. It felt like a mirror of when it had happened, all those weeks ago, the defining moment when Dylan had begun to realize he didn't just think of Logan as a friend.

Then, finally, Logan tossed his own controller onto the couch, and reached up, tangling a hand in Dylan's hair, and tugged him lower. Then lower still. Until their eyes met. A breath away from a kiss.

He'd done this earlier, when they'd kissed in the kitchen, and Dylan had never known he'd liked having his hair pulled—had actually kept meaning to cut it—but now he couldn't wait for Logan to pull it even harder.

There was just something about the bite of pain, exacerbating all that anticipatory sweetness.

"I wouldn't care how it happened, as long as you're right here," Logan said lowly, and his other hand ran up and down his back lightly, like he was afraid to push too hard. Take too much.

But Dylan could see the hunger in his eyes. They both wanted this. Badly.

The knowledge resonated through him, and it felt real and natural and true to lean in and kiss Logan again.

The moment their lips touched, Dylan lost himself. It felt so good, their lips moving together hotly, wetly, Logan's fingers gripping his hair, pulling him and turning him, until he was exactly where they could kiss the deepest.

He'd been turned on plenty of times before—he'd been a teenage boy, hadn't he?—but there was something about the newness, about the differences he felt kissing Logan, that had him so turned on, he felt every touch like a bomb exploding over his skin. He was shaky. Sensitive. Yearning.

It was so easy to slide in closer, to rub his aching cock against Logan's firm stomach. Logan swallowed his groan, and then his hand was slipping lower, and then lower still, and *oh God*, he was gripping his ass in his palm, just as firmly as he held his hair.

He was caught, truly and completely, but was it really being caught if you were desperate for it, and never, ever wanted to escape?

Logan pulled back a fraction, and Dylan would have followed but Logan's strength stopped him. "Wait, wait," he said, breathless.

"For what?" Dylan demanded. "Is this where you tell me we should go slower?"

Logan smiled. Slow and sexy, it stoked the fire he'd already lit in Dylan even higher. God, he wanted this man. He realized then, it didn't even matter that he was a man. It was that he was *Logan*.

"No, it's where I double-check that you want me to keep touching you." Somehow, impossibly, Logan's grip on his ass tightened. It felt like a brand, like five individual brands. And then it softened, caressed. "And where I ask if you want to touch me, too."

"Yes," Dylan said, and leaned forward, capturing Logan's mouth again. It was so easy to slide into the easy, uncomplicated passion of the kiss. Back and forth, tongues slipping against each other, until Dylan felt the throb of need in his blood.

But then Logan pulled back again. The thread of annoyance did nothing to dim Dylan's arousal. In fact, it only seemed to make it more intense.

"What now?" he demanded.

"Easy," Logan soothed, and then he reached up and tugged Dylan's tank top off. "I want to feel you, that's all." And then his hands were on his skin, those big calloused hands tracing his spine.

Dylan had never undressed a guy before, but it wasn't so different, reaching down and pulling Logan's shirt off.

His tattoos, swirling over his pale skin, were evident even in the dim light of the room.

"What does this one mean?" he asked, tracing the swirls of a rose.

"It's for Texas." Logan's voice had gone low and dry and dirty.

Dylan's fingers slipped lower, circling his nipple. Logan's breath caught.

"And this one?" he asked, tracing the edges of the eagle, laid out underneath his pec.

"My grandfather, who served in Vietnam," Logan ground out.

Dylan's palm slid down his abs, tensing as he traced their ridges. He'd never seen anyone so big and broad and gorgeous, and he couldn't get enough of touching him. He stopped right above the waistband of Logan's shorts, his erection pushing the fabric out.

He'd touched his own dick plenty of times, hadn't he? That must be why this didn't feel weird or wrong at all. Or that strange, honestly.

That's 'cause you've thought about touching this *dick for ages.*

Logan sucked in a breath as his fingers brushed lower, right along the hard ridge of his cock. "You really want to do this," he said wonderingly. Like he wasn't questioning; just like he couldn't quite believe his luck.

"Might not be very good at it," Dylan admitted. "But . . . practice makes perfect, right?"

"I'm gonna . . ." Logan took a deep, shuddering breath. "Talk you through it, if that's okay?"

"If you want," Dylan said. They shifted a little, together tugging down Logan's shorts, his dick popping out.

It was big and flushed at the tip.

Now, Dylan thought, *this is where it's gonna get strange.*

But when he put his hand on it, gently at first, carefully, it didn't feel strange at all. It felt *good*.

"Oh God, just like that," Logan said. "Yeah, slick it down." His head hit the back of the couch, but he didn't stop watching even for a second, his gaze boring right into Dylan's as he kept touching his cock, gathering the precome and easing his way.

"Is this good?" Dylan questioned, even though the way his cock kept twitching in his grip made it clear that it was. He wanted to *hear* it.

He'd never had a fantasy about being talked through a hand job before, but he wanted to hear Logan's voice, rough and desperate, as he reassured him, his unassailable support wrapping him around like a warm blanket.

It was both completely, totally sexy, and utterly comforting.

Just like Logan himself.

"Yes, *yes*," Logan said. "Just like that, a little harder. Oh yeah," he groaned as Dylan's other hand joined the party, slipping down lower to cup his balls. "Tug them, yeah. God, that feels so good."

"Tell me more," Dylan ordered, as he gave Logan's cock a firm stroke. And then another. Not with any kind of real rhythm. Keeping him off-balance. Keeping him in control.

If Logan could hold him tight, trap him, then Dylan could turn the tables on him, too.

"Grip it harder. I like it . . . a little rough," he gasped as Dylan did exactly what he'd ordered.

"I like it, too," Dylan confided, even though he'd never known that before Logan.

He could already imagine being filled so full of this big cock, stretched out on the bed, as Logan gripped him by the hair.

Shit, they were gonna have to do that. Soon. *Next*, if Dylan had any say in the matter.

But then Logan's hand suddenly was right where he was hard and aching, and it was sliding into his own shorts, flicking open the button and the zipper like it was nothing.

Dylan's hand stuttered in its rhythm.

Logan smiled. It was soft and hot and challenging. "Can you take it as well as you give it out?" he wondered.

"Yes," Dylan hissed. Redoubled his efforts, sliding his fist up and down Logan's cock as the pleasure flooded through his body as Logan mirrored his own movements.

"Fuck, *fuck*," Logan crooned as he grew even wetter under Dylan's palm. He was close, Dylan could feel it, and he moved his fist faster, harder, knowing just what he liked when he was close—overwhelming himself with the ecstasy of it.

Logan's preferences clearly reflected his own, because he sank his teeth into his bottom lip, tasting blood, clearly trying to hold off his own orgasm as he brought Dylan right there to the edge with him.

For a split second, they both teetered on the edge, Logan's eyes wide, Dylan never looking away, never letting him breathe even for a second as he pushed them over.

He soared through his orgasm, panting as Logan wrung every bit of it out of him, and he did the same, hand moving on autopilot, as come splashed up his chest from Logan's dick.

Shuddering through the aftershocks, he came down slowly, Logan's grip loosening, his hand caressing instead of pulling. And then it was over, they were both a mess, and Dylan realized that his face hurt because he hadn't stopped smiling the whole damn time it was happening.

"Well, I think it's safe to say," Logan said wryly, "you liked that."

Dylan reached over and plucked his shirt off the couch, trying to wipe up the mess as best he could. There was a stripe of come bisecting the rose on Logan's chest, and he swiped a finger through it, grazing his nipple again, and loved how Logan shivered with the sensation of it.

Something to remember for later.

He stuck his finger in his mouth, wondering what it might taste like. He'd heard the taste of come could be awful, but he didn't mind it.

Next time, Logan was coming down his throat.

"God, you are too much," Logan said with a groan. "You're gonna fucking kill me. Too damn hot. Too damn everything."

"Am I?" he teased.

"Yes," Logan said, and ignoring the mess, closed the distance between them, kissing him firmly, insistently.

And *oh*, Logan might be the death of him, too.

Chapter Ten

If Logan had been worried that after Monday night's activities, his friendship with Dylan might change, he shouldn't have been.

They'd made out lazily on the couch for awhile, then Dylan had insisted on finishing the level of their video game, and *insisted* on coaching him through it. It seemed he'd finally figured out that while he wasn't very good, he was a lot better than he was pretending to be.

He just really liked riling Dylan up. When his eyes blazed and those soft lips curled into a smirk, he was impossible to resist.

It made him so fucking hot.

Then they'd gone upstairs, to their separate beds, and even though Logan had hesitated for a split second, Dylan had been chattering away about how practice tomorrow would be, and it seemed he hadn't even given it a second thought.

After all, nothing between them was official.

They were friends.

They'd kissed half a dozen times.

They'd hooked up.

As Logan had lain in bed, thinking of the day, not quite able to sleep just yet, he'd thought, *I don't even know if I want him here, with me.* He'd never wanted to share a bed with anyone before.

Not Ricky. Definitely not any of the other hookups that had come before him.

But Dylan was different.

It's 'cause you're friends, and you were friends first, and you're helpin' him figure his shit out, Logan told himself firmly before he finally fell into a dreamless slumber.

In the morning, it was like nothing had ever happened. Any awkwardness that was left, disappeared. Dylan made breakfast. They sat at the kitchen table, like they always did. Dylan brushed his foot with his own enough times, with an additionally playful grin on his face, that Logan knew it was on purpose.

Knew he wanted to keep touching him, even if he didn't have a good reason.

That you want to, that's enough. That's all I care about.

But they were friends. Friends didn't go around kissing each other all the time. Not in the morning. Not when they saw each other for the first time in a few hours. Not when they finished up practice.

The Piranhas had notched four wins in a row now, turning their season around after their initial two-game losing streak, and practice today had been both slightly more relaxed, as everyone was settling into the idea that they *could* be successful—and also more intense, because winning games meant that the coaching staff and the players all wanted to win more.

Logan sat down on the bench in front of his locker, dressed after his shower, and craned his head, looking for Dylan. He hadn't shown up yet, which meant that this might be one of those rare days he had to hang around the facility and wait for Dylan. Usually it was the other way around.

"Hey," Beau said, sitting down next to him. "You good?"

"Yep." He was sore of course, because it was the season, and the season meant you were in a continual state of soreness, but practice had been good. The line was gelling. He *felt* freaking amazing, painful muscles notwithstanding.

"Dylan's practicing some long kicks," Beau said. "He asked me to tell you, and he could also grab a ride with Pax. You know he's gonna be staying late."

Logan knew it. "You think that's a good idea?"

"Dylan catching a ride with Pax?" Beau asked, shoving his glasses further up his nose, a confused frown forming on his face.

"No, Pax working such long hours."

Beau shrugged. "He's getting better, so it's hard to argue with the results."

"No, just the methods," Logan grumbled.

"Take it up with Davis, then," Beau said. "I'm just the messenger here."

"But," Logan added, "you don't like it either."

Beau pressed his lips together. "That obvious, huh?"

"And I talked to Pax yesterday . . ." Logan trailed off. Not sure how much he should say. Not sure how much Beau had figured out. But Beau was one of the smartest, most observant people he knew. If he'd seen what was going on between Pax and Davis, then Beau had to be aware of it.

Beau sighed. "Nothing's happened. They just work . . . a lot."

"Yeah," Logan agreed.

"I'm aware of it. We're keeping an eye on it. Davis isn't stupid. He's not going to do anything to jeopardize his position with this team—or Pax's. That much I'm sure of."

It felt shitty to condemn Pax and his ill-advised crush to permanent unrequited status when he was hooking up with the guy he couldn't resist, and Beau and Sebastian were currently deep in the honeymoon phase of their relationship.

But that was the NFL for you.

Nobody had ever claimed it was fair. But that didn't mean it didn't fucking suck.

"Anyway," Beau said, standing up. "Should I let Dylan know that he'll need to catch a ride with Pax?"

Logan nodded. "Let him know I'll see him at home."

He stood, grabbed his bag and his phone, and he was just through the double doors at the end of the locker room when he ran into Helen.

"Oh, Logan, just the person I was hoping to find." She paused, glancing around him. "But not with your permanent shadow today?"

Did they really spend that much time together?

Yes, a voice inside Logan said wryly, *you fucking do, and you love it, so don't even think about apologizing for it.*

"Nope, he's still out on the field," Logan said.

"I wanted to let you know that the rumors seem to have died down, *mostly,* so that's great, but . . ."

There was always a *but* in these conversations. It was why, both in Minnesota and now in Miami, he'd tried his hardest to avoid the PR department.

But ever since Ricky and his stupid article, that had gotten a lot tougher.

"But," Helen continued, pasting on her most winning smile. If she guessed that might make him even more suspicious, it didn't show. "But I have a huge favor to ask."

"Of course you do." Logan wasn't even that annoyed; he was more resigned than anything else.

"There's a big gala here tomorrow night, on the field, to raise money for the Piranhas and Colin O'Connor's organization, The Rise Foundation. I'm sure you've heard of it."

Logan nodded. In fact, he'd anonymously donated money several times. A lot of money.

"It's my job to bring some current Piranhas players to the gala, to give the fans who've paid a lot of money someone to see. I'd really like for you *and* Dylan to make an appearance."

It shouldn't have come as anything like a surprise. Of course they weren't going to be able to *no comment* their way through this whole thing successfully. There were going to have to be a few times, like that time at the steakhouse, with those young fans, and with Matt, at the offensive line dinner, where they proved that they weren't just friends and roommates and teammates.

And you're not. You had your hands all over each other last night. That wasn't very platonic.

"You want Dylan and me to come and act like we're together."

"That's the story you're selling," Helen said bluntly. "When you didn't correct Ricky's assumption, that was the story you agreed to sell. And then there were those photos. They both made the rounds. People are taking it for granted that you're together."

"And you're looking for us to give them what they want," Logan said.

It wasn't even an unfair ask. Helen had done a lot for him. She'd written the statement, she'd dodged questions, she'd even ignored plenty of requests to put him on the podium in the post-game press conferences. And when she *had* put Dylan up on the podium last Sunday, to talk about his record-setting afternoon, she'd made it clear that he didn't have to answer any personal questions.

She'd taken a lot of flak for that from the media. And now she was asking for something in return.

Logan couldn't come up with a good reason not to give it to her. Any reason except one.

"I'll have to check with Dylan," Logan said. "Make sure he's okay with it."

Helen nodded, but the satisfaction on her face told the whole story. He'd agree to do it. They both knew it. After all, Helen had been there, in the conference room, two weeks ago, when Dylan had agreed to do what pretty much no other friend would have done.

"Let me know tonight, when you talk to him," she said, "and I'll send over the tickets. It's black tie. Make sure you both dress accordingly."

"Ugh, of course you didn't lead with that," Logan complained.

"I'm assuming you have a tux."

He nodded, because he did. He didn't *want* to, but he did.

He'd needed it for a family wedding a few years back. He just hoped it fit alright.

"Excellent," Helen said. "Text me tonight, and I'll get you the details."

Logan didn't roll his eyes as she turned away, but it was a near thing. He shouldn't be so annoyed at her assumption that Dylan would be willing to do this.

Except that it wasn't wrong. He would. He was just that kind of guy.

Logan decided to do a little work while he waited for Dylan to come home. He brought his laptop into the kitchen and set up on the island, grabbing a seat on one of the barstools. He'd just finished going through his emails and replying to both his business manager and his agent about a potential extension of his Adidas contract when his phone rang.

Glancing at the screen, he saw it was Landry.

"Hey, bro," he said, picking up the call and setting it on speaker so he could keep scrolling through his inbox.

"Please tell me," Landry said, in a voice edged with steel, "that you're dealing with this Ricky situation."

"Huh?"

"This horrible situation with your ex," Landry said.

"I don't know what you mean, we dealt with it. Dylan and I . . ." Logan trailed off. He didn't want to go into detail about how the fake relationship they weren't confirming was turning more real by the day, not yet, anyway. "Well, Helen has a handle on it."

"Does she? Is she watchin' these videos he's making about you and Dylan?"

"What?"

"You should sue him. Shut him up." Landry could be rather uncompromising. It was one of the things that had brought the most fuel to their brotherly rivalry over the years. It was just so fun to give Landry shit when he couldn't take a fucking joke. But he sounded really serious now. Too serious.

"I don't even know what he's saying," Logan said with uncertainty. He didn't *want* to know, if he was being really honest. "I'm sure it'll just blow over."

"I'm not sure it will. You should call your agent."

"What would he even do?" Logan heard the apprehension in his voice.

"Or call a lawyer," Landry said.

"What? He's just posting like . . . I don't know, dumb videos for attention." When they'd been hooking up, Logan had watched some of Ricky's videos and he'd not seen the appeal. "Are people actually watching them?"

"He keeps teasing this song, where he's like fucking broken-hearted over being abandoned for someone who left for the 'big city,'" Landry said dryly.

"Like Minneapolis isn't a freaking big city," Logan muttered.

"The only problem . . ." Landry sighed. "He's not mentioning you by name. He's not dumb enough to do that, apparently."

"I'll tell my agent, but I doubt there's much we can do," Logan said. It was better for him not to know. He didn't want to know how Ricky was going around slandering him, not if he couldn't do anything to change it.

It was why he'd tried so hard not to get angry about Ricky outing him. Because what could he do about it? Nothing. It didn't matter if he got pissed off, or ranted and raved about it, because it changed exactly nothing about the situation.

"I have to say, baby bro," Landry said, "I'm impressed with how you're handling this."

Logan almost wanted to laugh—at least so he wouldn't cry. He wasn't "handling this." He was only going forward because that was the only way that had been left open to him.

"Yeah, well . . . what else can I do?" Logan said.

"True." Landry's voice went softer. "You need me to go kick his ass?"

And Logan knew if he said yes, sure, go do it, Landry would. He'd go AWOL from the Bills, and he'd kick Ricky's ass, no matter what the consequences were, because that was the Banks family for you—they had your back through thick and thin.

"No, no, it's fine. Don't go kick his ass. Only because he's not worth you getting into trouble," Logan said gruffly.

"Sure thing, baby bro," Landry said.

But when Landry hung up, the first thing that Logan did was send two emails. One to his agent, Simon, asking him what he knew about what Ricky had been up to. He *didn't* search out the videos himself, because again, getting angry wasn't going to get him anywhere. The second one he sent was to Helen, asking her what they could do to help combat some of the negative publicity that Ricky was generating—even though he already had a feeling that they were doing it. Or rather, he *and* Dylan were doing it.

It was almost full dark, and he'd finished both emails by the time Logan heard the garage door open.

Dylan walked in and set his bag on the barstool nearest him, then glanced up and saw Logan. He'd been lurking, he realized, in a nearly dark kitchen, for an hour after finishing going through his inbox, waiting for him to show. Was he proud of it? Not really. But he'd done it anyway.

Officially, his brain supplied, *you are pathetic.*

"Oh," Dylan said, "I almost didn't see you there."

"Dark kitchens, those are my specialty," Logan said, hoping the joking note in his voice would be enough to avoid creeper status.

Dylan grinned. "Seems accurate," he said.

And now, even though he shouldn't be, Logan was thinking about all the times they'd stood in the kitchen.

All the times we kissed in this kitchen.

At least it was better than thinking about that backstabbing asshole, Ricky.

"I got cornered by Helen today," Logan said. "I guess O'Connor's foundation is holding a big fundraiser tomorrow. Black tie.

They want us to go." He paused. "I told her you'd need to be okay with it before I agreed."

Dylan was quiet for a moment, as he skirted past Logan, pressing a single warm palm to his shoulder. He was wearing his usual couch uniform of just a pair of shorts. Now that he knew he didn't need to bother, he hadn't thrown on a shirt—and he felt Dylan's touch, brief as it was, all the way down to the bone. Dylan opened the fridge, and pulled out the milk. Chocolate. Also grabbed a glass. Then hesitated and grabbed a second one.

A chuckle escaped out of Logan before he could stop it.

"You know me well," he said as Dylan poured him a glass.

"I'm only surprised that you didn't already have one in front of you," Dylan teased. "You don't have to live here to know chocolate milk is your one indulgence."

He hadn't mentioned anything about the gala. Logan found himself holding his breath.

There was a part of him, much bigger than he'd realized, that wanted to go with Dylan. Wanted more than just to get off together in the dark, on his couch, where nobody else could see. Wanted to keep pretending that it was more than that, if only because it felt so damn real.

"Black tie, huh?" Dylan said. "I guess I'm gonna have to figure out how to buy a tux in less than twenty-four hours."

"Or a really nice suit, you can go with that, you've got those," Logan said, hurriedly. He wasn't proud of it, but he kinda lived for travel days when Dylan would put on one of those suits that fit his body like a glove, hugging his legs and ass and chest and shoulders, and all the other parts of Dylan that he couldn't stop staring at.

"Yeah, maybe the dark blue with a black shirt," Dylan pondered.

"So, this is you saying *yes*, you'll go?" Logan said, tapping his fingers on the counter.

Dylan shot him a look. "Yeah, of course I will. I'm assuming, also . . . Helen wants us to play up the boyfriend angle, considering whose foundation this is for."

"That was mentioned," Logan said. "But if you don't want to . . ."

"Oh, it's fine," Dylan interrupted before he could actually vocalize any of his excuses or his apologies. "I'm in, for sure." He smiled, unexpectedly bright in the dim light of the kitchen. "Maybe it'll even be fun."

"Fun?" Logan raised an eyebrow.

"Yeah," Dylan said, after taking a sip of milk. "I'll be with you, won't I? And after . . ." He waggled his eyebrows, looking half ridiculous and half hot as hell, which was a situation that would've baffled Logan, except by now, he was used to it. "Maybe I can even strip you out of your tux."

Definitely one positive of the whole experience, because Logan had been having fantasies about that blue suit of Dylan's for some time now.

"I won't argue about that plan," Logan said.

"But tonight . . . *ugh*," Dylan said, a yawn suddenly erupting out of him. "I'm fucking wiped."

"Beau said you were practicing some long field goals." Logan drained the rest of his milk. Grabbed Dylan's empty glass on the way to the sink. Tapped him friendly-like on the ass as he walked by.

There was such a thing as a friendly, totally platonic ass tap, right?

"Sixty-plus yards," Dylan said with a grimace. "Over and over and over again. I'm beat. It takes a lot of precision and strength to kick that distance. My legs feel like Jell-O."

"You think you're gonna go out there and do sixty-yarders, then?"

Dylan shrugged. Not looking particularly convinced. "I think Coach likes the idea that I could. Enjoys having the potential in his back pocket, if he feels cornered into doing it, he can, but I didn't get the impression he actually intends to do it." He hesitated. "But here's the thing, that's the new requirement in the NFL. That's why the Raiders got rid of me. They've got that young kid now, from Grambling State, who can kick sixty-yarders on the reg. You gotta be able to go to the distance, and do it accurately. Fifty-yarders aren't even a challenge anymore, they're seen as gimmies. So, I gotta keep up or I'll get dropped. I need to do more, make sure I don't end up losing my touch."

"Coach wouldn't drop you," Logan said, even though he knew it happened. And that it happened a *lot* to kickers and other special teams guys.

Teams almost never stuck by kickers. If they went through a slump, generally, they got released without explanation or apology.

It was shitty, there was no way around it. But Coach wasn't like that. He saw the big picture.

At least that was what Logan kept telling himself.

And what, he *knew*, Dylan hoped too.

"Coach," Dylan said wryly, "is gonna do what's best for the team. You know that. If it's not me, then it's not me."

"But it *is* you," Logan said fiercely.

"Well, last Sunday bought me a lot of goodwill. There's a reason that record's stood for fifteen years," Dylan acknowledged.

"Damn straight," Logan said, and discarded all his good intentions of keeping his hands to himself, and tugged Dylan into a tight hug.

This is platonic, he told himself, even as he felt Dylan's body press into his own in half a dozen places, the sensation rocketing through him.

One friend, comforting and supporting another. Except that wasn't how it felt at all.

Reluctantly, he let Dylan go. It didn't help, with Dylan tilting his face up like that, like he wanted to be kissed.

Or maybe it was just his own desire, overwhelming his good sense.

He cleared his throat, moving back one step, and then another.

"We better get to bed. Long day tomorrow."

Was that a flash of disappointment in Dylan's eyes?

Or maybe what he was seeing was his own disappointment reflected there.

"Yeah," Dylan agreed. "I guess we should."

Dylan slipped his jacket on and took one last look in the mirror.

He looked good. Maybe he wasn't wearing a tux, but for a last-minute event, his dark blue suit, with its black shirt and subtly striped black tie looked good enough.

He wouldn't have cared, normally—dress codes didn't typically apply to players in gala situations; the organizers were happy to get them there at all—but he was going with Logan. And he was going *with* Logan. As his boyfriend.

Probably their first *and* last appearance as a couple.

He hadn't needed Ricky's article to remind him that Logan didn't *do* relationships. He'd admitted it himself.

So Dylan was going to enjoy this one opportunity to be Logan Banks' date.

Looking in the mirror, he was pleased with what he saw. The suit fit him like a glove—it was one he'd had tailored when he first signed with the Raiders—and the shirt and tie were perfect. Even his hair, which he'd fluffed up a little, using mousse to hold it, hopefully, in place, looked decent.

He flipped the light off as he walked out of the bedroom, and headed downstairs.

Logan turned as he walked in, his shoes making distinctive clicking noises on the hardwood floor, and Dylan felt his breath catch in his chest.

He'd thought he'd looked pretty good in the mirror before coming downstairs, but now, face to face in Logan, wearing a tuxedo that had undoubtedly been tailored to fit every inch of his incredible body, he felt suddenly insecure.

The black fabric of Logan's jacket slipped over his broad shoulders, hugged his torso, and flared out just enough to fit his hips. He'd shaved for the occasion, scraping away at least a week of scruff from his face, and *God*, he even smelled fantastic, Dylan thought as he tried to ignore the way his cock was hardening. No doubt totally ruining the line of his pants.

"Hey." Even his voice was lower. Gruffer. Dirtier. *No, that's your imagination talking right there*, he told himself firmly. "You look . . ."

Logan Banks downright licked his lips looking at him. Okay, so he hadn't cleaned up too badly after all.

"Why," Dylan joked, because if he didn't make them laugh, he was going to be the one to pin Logan to the countertop this time and they wouldn't be making it to any gala anytime soon, "does this always happen to us in the kitchen?"

"Better than the locker room." Logan's voice was still rumbling, deep and dark, and reminding Dylan of everything they could do one other place: the bedroom.

"True," Dylan agreed.

Didn't mean that he didn't want to drag Logan back upstairs right now and find a soft horizontal surface.

Hell, it wasn't like what they'd done together on the couch hadn't been one of the hottest sexual experiences of his life.

"You ready to go?" Logan was looking at him like he was thinking of staying behind too, but Dylan knew they couldn't. They'd promised Helen they'd attend. And Dylan couldn't deny that he was at least a little bit excited to finally meet Colin O'Connor in the flesh.

"Yep," Dylan said, turning and heading towards the door that led to the garage. He paused on the threshold, felt Logan's hand, warm and steady, on his back.

"I'm driving," Logan said, like it was a given, nudging him in the direction of his Range Rover.

It was such a boyfriend move, and Dylan was surprised, because as far as he knew, Logan didn't *do* the whole boyfriend thing.

Then he saw Logan hesitate as he headed around the car. For a split second he thought: *was he going to walk around with him, and open his door? Take the boyfriend thing to the next level?*

But he didn't.

Dylan told himself he wasn't disappointed. He didn't need anyone to open a door for him.

He slipped into the passenger seat and decided it was a really good reminder that Logan *wasn't* his boyfriend.

After they'd pulled out of the garage, Logan driving them towards the bright lights of downtown Miami, Dylan said in a teasing voice, "So, is this the full Logan Banks boyfriend experience, then? Do you have a dozen roses hidden anywhere? Boxes of chocolates? Should I be expecting an impromptu serenade?"

Logan's expression, tense around the edges, relaxed, and he smiled. "Would you be distraught to discover that there *isn't* a Logan Banks boyfriend experience?"

"No," Dylan said. "I kinda expected that you were making this up on the fly."

"Am I that bad at it?" Maybe if Dylan hadn't gotten to know Logan so well over the last two months, he wouldn't have recognized the worry in his voice. He'd hidden it well.

But Dylan *knew* him.

He was worried about this. He didn't want to let Dylan down. He *cared* about doing right by him.

It was such a Logan thing, so uniquely him, Dylan felt his heart beat a little faster in his chest. Even as he tried to tell himself that it didn't mean what he *wanted* it to mean.

"Not at all," he reassured. "Just be yourself. You're always enough, Banks. You know that."

"Yeah, but it's still nice to hear it," Logan said, tilting his head and shooting Dylan a look that made him feel not only warm and fuzzy, but inexplicably hot too.

He'd never imagined that anyone—especially a guy!—being a great friend, loyal and kind and thoughtful, would turn him on the way that Logan did, as easy as breathing.

But it was happening with enough regularity that it was difficult to keep denying.

"What about holding hands?" Logan asked a few minutes later.

The idea of putting his hand into Logan's, gripping it firmly, shouldn't send a thrill down his spine, but that was the state Dylan had been reduced to. "Are you asking if I'm okay doing that?"

Logan nodded as he pulled into the players' parking lot on the far end of the Piranhas complex.

"Logan," Dylan said, touched despite himself that he was checking in, making sure that he wouldn't do anything that made either of them uncomfortable, "I had my hand around your dick two nights ago."

Logan pulled into a spot and cut the engine. For a long moment he didn't say anything.

"Yeah, I know," Logan finally said, his voice gruff. Like he was thinking about it now.

Dylan sure was.

Wondering when he could do it again.

ASAP, that's when you want to do it again. You wanna reach over and press a palm against his fly right now, see if he's hard. See how long it would take to make *him hard.*

"I'm just saying, I think we've moved past asking if it's okay to hold hands," Dylan said softly.

Logan turned his head. The look in his dark eyes was intense. Dylan felt like he could see all the way down deep, all the way to his soul. Could see all those thoughts he'd had, and tried to hide. All the things he wanted, desperately, that he didn't know how to ask for.

"I just don't ever want to make you feel bad about this," Logan said quietly. Seriously. "Or push you into something you don't want to do."

Dylan reached over and it was so easy to grasp Logan's hand, resting loosely on the steering wheel, tangle their fingers together and squeeze. "You won't," he said. "I'm a big boy, I can tell you if things get…" *Too real. Too intimate. Too close to what I really want.* He cleared his throat. "You know, if they get uncomfortable."

Logan nodded. "I trust you." He hesitated. "More than anyone else, you know?"

Dylan had never quite believed people when they'd argued how easy it was to fall for a friend. He'd always imagined it must be difficult, moving people from one box to another, completely reframing the way a person fit into your life.

But it turned out that it was easy, a slow, gradual, blink-and-you'll-miss-it slide from friendship to something more.

Dylan was afraid he *had* blinked and missed it, because the feelings swirling inside him now, they weren't so friendly.

Definitely not platonic.

And they weren't just the getting-naked variety of not-platonic either.

Dylan gripped Logan's hand hard. Was gratified to see him barely even flinch. "I trust you, too. I wouldn't have done this for just anyone, you know."

Logan understood. It was clear from his gaze that he knew.

But he also must have realized that getting serious was the antithesis of what they needed to be doing, because he loosened his grip on Dylan's hand and smiled. "I'll keep that in mind, next time someone I know needs a fake boyfriend. You're only available on an emergency basis."

Only for you.

Dylan didn't say it.

Maybe he didn't need to.

Because Logan seemed to understand.

For another moment, they sat there, staring at each other, hands still loosely touching. Dylan knew, without a doubt, that it didn't matter how close they were, or how much they recognized how they were feeling, the time was coming for a reckoning—where the things he wanted and the things he felt were going to have to be said in plain fucking English.

But not tonight.

"Come on," Logan said, "let's go find Helen. Let her know that we held up our end of the bargain."

Logan heard the unspoken ending to his sentence, *so we can get out of here and we can strip each other naked.*

They found Helen at the locker room entrance onto the field, where she was directing the VIPs and players into the stadium for the cocktail hour.

"And then," she said to a couple in front of them, "we'll have dinner, with Colin O'Connor making a featured appearance and speech."

"At least we're getting dinner out of this," Logan grumbled.

"Dinner, and a chance to see you in a tuxedo," Dylan pointed out happily. "I'm good."

Logan laughed, just as Helen waved them forward. "Oh, you two," she said. "You clean up nice. The seating chart's over by the balloon arch, but before you go sit down and wish you'd never agreed to come, mingle and take some pictures, please?"

"Anyone in particular you want us to schmooze?" Dylan asked.

"Bless you," Helen said. She glanced over at Logan. "Is he always this accommodating?" Then she chuckled. "I suppose I don't want to know the answer to that question, do I?"

"Plausible deniability," Logan agreed. But he was smiling. *Proud,* Dylan realized as Logan reached over and took his hand in his own again, squeezing it, his expression warm and . . . Dylan couldn't place it for a second, then he realized what the emotion was. *He's proud of me. Proud of being here, with me.*

"As for anyone specific, I do want to get a few pictures with Colin, if you don't mind," Helen said. "For the press."

"Why am I even surprised? It's always the press," Logan said, but he was still smiling.

"Sounds good," Dylan agreed. He'd have probably asked for a picture with the famous quarterback, anyway, so it didn't bother him in the least that Helen had requested it specially.

As they walked into the stadium, hand in hand, Dylan was surprised at how completely the field had been transformed. The end zones were festooned with balloon arches, both in rainbow shades and also several in Piranha yellow and blue. There were dozens of white tablecloth-draped tables scattered over the middle of the field, hydrangeas in white and blue with trailing yellow blossoms in the center of each table, a tiny rainbow stuck into each arrangement. In the dead center of the field was a gigantic white tiered cake, decorated with more blue and yellow flowers. A small stage and microphone were set up on the opposing team's sideline. And that's where Colin O'Connor stood, in a pristine white dinner jacket and rainbow bow tie, laughing, with a group standing around him, all hanging on every single word he said.

"You ever met him?" Dylan asked under his breath as they stood at one of the end zones and gazed over at the ex-Piranhas quarterback.

"Once, briefly. After a game. My rookie year—the year he won the Super Bowl and retired after," Logan said. "You?"

"Nope," Dylan said wryly. "Us special teams guys . . . you know how it is. We're forgotten til we matter."

Logan frowned. "You aren't a special teams guy, Leonard. You're *my* guy. And you're also the guy who tied Bironas' record. Come on, let's see an old Piranhas legend meet a brand-new one."

"Oh, um, I'm not . . ." Dylan stammered, flushing, but Logan had a firm grip on his hand, and while he didn't drag him across the field, Dylan had a feeling that he *would,* if Dylan had resisted.

They were nearly on top of the group surrounding O'Connor when Dylan heard a voice behind them. "Oh, you look familiar," the voice said. "I feel like I *just* saw you someplace."

Dylan turned first, Logan following, and then the dark-haired man snapped his fingers suddenly. "Yes, you're Dylan Leonard," he said, clearly pleased with himself for remembering. He extended a hand, first to Dylan, who shook it, and then to Logan. "Nick Wheeler," he said. "You might know me better as this one's other half." He gestured absently towards where O'Connor stood, holding court. "But you two, I recognize both of you now. Great kicking, this last Sunday, Leonard. Very impressive. And, Banks? You're anchoring the line in a way that even *he* approves of."

It was clear from the twinkle in Nick's dark eyes that the *he* he was referring to was his husband.

"Appreciate it," Dylan said. "I was more surprised than anyone, honestly. I didn't even realize I'd tied the record until after the last kick was over."

"I wasn't," Nick said. "Neither was Colin. He knew it was gonna be a trenches game, defined by any small progress you could make, and you guys did just enough. He was fucking thrilled you pulled out the win."

"After last year, I bet," Logan said.

Nick made a face. "Let's not talk about last year, okay? Especially not in his hearing."

Dylan chuckled. "There were *some* high points, right? What about Pax?"

"Oh, he *loves* Pax," Nick said with a groan. "Don't even get him started on Paxton."

"Noted." Logan grinned. "He is a great guy. Great guy, great quarterback."

"Believe me, I know *all* about how great of a guy, and how great of a quarterback he is. Never gives up. Doesn't matter if the Piranhas are down, they're never out, not if he's in the huddle." Nick playfully rolled his eyes. "Like another ex-quarterback I know."

"Pax'll be thrilled to hear the comparison," Logan said. "I know he really looks up to Colin."

Nick nodded.

"Now what's this about some super dramatic love triangle that I keep hearing about?" Nick asked, in a teasing voice.

"Oh God, fucking Ricky again," Logan said. Sounding really annoyed.

Dylan was a little surprised. He'd seen some of the videos, for sure, because his mom kept sending them to him—even though he'd told her to stay off TikTok. He'd only been surprised that Logan hadn't mentioned them, but then maybe he wasn't aware of them, either, and Dylan had decided that might be a good thing.

But no, his vehemence meant that he *definitely* knew about the shit Ricky had been spewing.

Shit.

"I take it, it's not a real love triangle," Nick said slowly.

"Not even close," Logan said firmly. "He's just . . . he was just a hookup, you know?" He glanced over at Dylan, and Dylan could feel the heat, the affection in that look. "Dylan's the real deal."

And that, honestly, felt like the least fake thing he'd ever said.

"I'm glad to hear it. Colin's gonna want to meet both of you, for sure," Nick said.

Sure enough they watched as Colin's gaze rose up to meet Nick's eyes, and in a moment, he was politely but resolutely moving through the crowd surrounding him, coming to a stop next to his husband.

He was older than he'd been, a few silver strands lightening up the blond hair at his temples, but he still had those engaging blue eyes, and the warm smile. And his handshake? Firm as ever.

"You're Dylan Leonard," Colin said, shaking his hand, and then turning to Logan. "And Logan Banks. I've seen you a couple of times before," Colin said. "At games, of course, you're both awesome players. But also that horrible article, with the TikTok guy."

Dylan felt Logan tense up.

The team knew that their relationship wasn't real, but why would Colin O'Connor know? He wouldn't.

Dylan slipped an arm around Logan's shoulders, tugging him closer. "Thanks," he said warmly. Or as warmly as he could manage. "I kinda wanted to kick that guy's ass, honestly, but it turns out that it's pretty great, having everyone know. Right, babe?"

Logan Banks was not a babe.

Or else, Dylan had never thought of or referred to him as a babe before.

He'd never had a reason to.

Logan's gaze smoldered as they stared at each other. "Oh yeah, it's freakin' great," he enthused.

"And," Colin said, "congrats on tying Rob Bironas' record too. I saw Neal Fisher give a whole breakdown on the eight field goals you kicked, and I knew it was hard, because obviously it doesn't happen, not since 2007, but I had no idea it was such a challenge."

"Thanks. Been a momentous few weeks," Dylan said.

"If you ever need anything—support, someone to talk to, someone to *not* talk to, or anything at all. Even a cold beer with a friendly face, you just let us know," Nick said. "We spend a lot of time in California now, since Colin retired, but Miami is still home."

Colin nodded. "I keep meaning to come back and catch a game. Remind everyone that I'm still a Piranha. Now," he said, gesturing to Dylan and Logan, "I've got even more reason. I couldn't be prouder of you two, or Nicholson and Lewis, or even Beau and Howard."

Logan was still tense next to him, Dylan could feel every muscle in his body bracing for a blow but then he said, quietly, seriously. "We couldn't have done it without you, Colin. You set the stage for all of us. So thank *you.*"

Colin's grin widened. Softened. He cupped Logan's shoulder supportively, and squeezed. "I'm glad. Glad it turned out this way. Nothing's perfect, but we're gettin' there."

A photographer appeared, and they took pictures. Each of them with O'Connor, and then one with both of them.

Helen would be pleased, Dylan thought as they retreated back to where the bar was handing out flutes of chilled champagne and bottles of cold beer.

"So, that wasn't so terrible, was it?" Dylan asked. Logan had been quiet since they'd left O'Connor's side.

"I remember when he came out," Logan said. "I sat on the edge of my bed and I cried. Before he did that, before he gave that interview to Nick that changed his life, do you think he knew he'd change the rest of our lives?"

"No," Dylan answered honestly. He'd seen enough quotes from O'Connor over the years to know that he *hadn't* thought about it.

Not like he thought about it now. "But I am glad he did it, because he made it possible for me to do this."

He leaned in, and brushed another kiss across Logan's cheek. Lingering, the way he wanted to, on the feel of his lips on Logan's skin. On the slight prickle beneath his lips. Because even though Logan might have shaved for the occasion, it never took long for his scruff to grow in.

He didn't know if this was part of the fake boyfriend role he was supposed to be playing or his role as Logan's best friend. Or a combination of both.

Or maybe, even crazier, part of a role that they both wanted, but hadn't quite defined yet.

All that mattered was that they were here together.

Chapter Eleven

JUST BECAUSE LOGAN HAD looked up to Colin O'Connor didn't mean that he wanted to hear him make a speech.

The beginning of the gala hadn't been all that terrible. They'd run into Beau and Sebastian, shared a drink. He'd met one of his childhood heroes. He'd shaken his hand, and even managed to tell him a little of what he'd meant to him. And he was lucky enough to be here with his best friend in the world, who looked so fucking hot Logan wanted to peel him out of that blue suit with his teeth, *slowly.* Most important, the fake boyfriend thing, as silly as it was, meant that they both had a lot more excuses to touch each other.

Right now, Dylan's hand was on Logan's knee, the heat of it burning through his black dress pants, and Logan couldn't focus on O'Connor's speech to save his life. All he was thinking was, *move that hand a little higher, why don't you?*

And, *when can we leave? Right now? In five minutes? How about five seconds?*

Dylan nudged him. A few minutes ago, after they'd finished the main course, he'd leaned close enough that his dark hair nearly brushed his cheek, and then he hadn't returned to his original position—which was way too far away. All in all, a situation that made Logan happier than it should have, though he was beginning to come to terms with the fact that he wanted more out of this than just a fake boyfriend for these gala events and a guy he got off with sometimes. He just didn't know how to approach changing the parameters of their friendship—or even if he *should*.

Sounds like character development, bro, Landry would have told him. *It's always gonna hurt.*

But it didn't hurt right now. Right now, with Dylan practically in his lap, hand sliding from his knee up his thigh, the smell of him surrounding him, there was absolutely zero pain.

"What?" Logan murmured under his breath.

"You're not paying attention." Dylan's voice was low.

Logan glanced down at where Dylan's hand was now caressing his mid-thigh. Then back up into his amused greenish gaze.

"Really? I can't imagine why."

Dylan chuckled.

Up on the stage, O'Connor was tossing a ball from hand to hand, talking about the season he'd played for the Piranhas directly after he'd come out. There was no doubt some incredibly vital lesson he was trying to impart—about teamwork or loyalty or cooperation, no doubt—but Logan wasn't really listening.

He was thinking of those words on the locker room wall.

Equality - Perseverance - Loyalty

"And," O'Connor said, drawing his words out with a dramatic flair that Logan admired but knew he couldn't ever emulate, "that was how, by the twelfth game of the year, we were ten and two, and all hated each other."

A wave of laughter went through the audience.

Not many players here, Logan thought, *because none of them would think locker room strife is funny.*

But O'Connor was coming to his point now, pushing it home. "We ended up losing the last four games of the season, and then the wild card playoff game. Why? Because none of us gave a shit about each other. We were fifty-three separate pieces. Not one team. We have to learn to care about each other, we have to learn how to think about each other first, before we can ever find success."

O'Connor paused, for clear dramatic effect.

You could say what you wanted about him, but he'd clearly given enough of these inspirational speeches that he knew exactly what he was doing.

Even Logan was paying attention now, despite Dylan's hand on his thigh.

"At the end of the season, Coach pulled us all into the locker room. He'd had three words painted on the wall. *Equality.* Because that was something we were trying to build back then, this crazy idea that it didn't matter who we were, or who we loved, off the field, that we were all equal on it. *Perseverance.* Because we can't ever give up. Not on ourselves. And never on each other. And lastly, *loyalty,* because if you can't trust your teammates to have your back, no matter what, then you don't have anything."

Logan had never asked when those words had been painted on the locker room wall. He'd only paid attention to the fact that when he'd arrived in Miami to listen to their offer, Coach had taken him around the facility, and he'd seen them and believed, partly because of their existence, bright and undeniable on the wall, and partly because everyone he'd met here had seemed to not only pay lip service to those tenets but to truly embrace them.

O'Connor was winding down now, talking about how the microcosm of the locker room wasn't all that different from the much wider world. He was, Logan realized, leading up to talking about the foundation he ran, and how all the VIPs here were needed to help make that dream possible.

Money, basically.

Tomorrow, Logan would sit down and write a big check. Before, he'd always made sure they were anonymous, that they couldn't be traced back to him, but now, he could give freely and publicly.

He was thinking about the email he'd send his business manager when the crowd erupted in applause, and Logan looked up just in time to see O'Connor strike a pose with the ball, and then to his surprise, he threw it, a picture-perfect spiral.

Right towards Logan.

It was all instinct.

He raised his hands, pulling himself out of the chair, only to hook his foot unexpectedly around the base of the flimsy white wooden folding chair and he flailed, something he *never* did, still reaching for the ball.

Logan felt it brush his fingertips, but he couldn't quite reel it in, and instead, he fell backwards, hands empty, and unlike the turf he'd expected to hit, he felt his back collide with the edge of something. *A table*, he thought wildly, and suddenly he was falling back, taking the enormous white cake with him, chunks of buttercream raining around him.

The cake hit the ground with a soft *plop*, and he followed a second later, the whole second layer ended smeared across his middle.

For a second, he didn't move.

The crowd had frozen, silent and stunned.

Then, a voice cried out, "*ball*," and he rolled over, only to see the half a dozen players in attendance dive, shoving chairs and tables out of the way, for the ball lying innocently on the ground only a few yards away.

Sebastian reached it first, a smear of cake across the side of his suit jacket as he grabbed the ball from the ground.

Then he tossed it to Wade, who had to dodge Tristan, jogging in for the tackle in his pristine teal suit.

He was going to run right past him, Logan realized, and leveraged himself to his feet, swiping away frosting and cake, but he was a second too late, and only realized that because Dylan tackled him first.

It was a textbook tackle, surprising considering that the only time Dylan ever had the opportunity to practice tackling was the few times a year they put the special teams guys through the same paces as everyone else.

The ball popped out, and Logan grabbed it, reaching back and throwing, not quite as perfect a spiral as O'Connor's had been, but still pretty damn good, towards where Tristan had hopped up on one of the tables, and was tiptoeing across the surface, not disturbing a single crumb of bread or a single piece of flatware. He caught it, with one hand, and jumped down just as carefully, then took off like a shot, heading towards where O'Connor stood at the podium, jaw dropped, shocked at how his beautiful gala had devolved into a football game, with cake and frosting standing in for the mud and grass.

Dylan laughed next to him and reached over, wiping a smear of frosting from Logan's cheek. He didn't get it all, and he knew that neither of them cared.

He can lick it off later, Logan thought.

"Ladies and gentlemen," O'Connor said into the microphone, and he was laughing now as Tristan sidestepped and did a fun spin move right around where Sebastian was stalking him, shoving chairs out of the way as he tried to get to the ball, "this is exactly why we don't get nice things."

The crowd erupted in amused laughter and then applause. Thinking, Logan had to assume, that maybe this whole thing had been planned.

Tristan crossed the line next to the stage, and then with an impudent smirk, tossed the ball, still liberally smeared with cake, up towards O'Connor, who caught it.

A cheer went up through the assembled VIPs and *yeah*, Logan realized, *they think we planned this whole thing.*

They hadn't.

Because if they had, Logan definitely wouldn't have ended up in a tuxedo painted with stripes of frosting and dusted with crumbs.

"Shit," Logan said, still chuckling. "I'm covered in cake."

"Yeah, you really are," Dylan said. "What possessed you to go for the ball like that? I think he was tossing it to Tristan, who's behind us."

"Well, it was a ball and it's my first instinct to catch it," Logan said with a shrug. "I forgot the cake was behind me. Thought I was just gonna land hard on the turf, and you'd have to nurse me back to health. With a nice warm bath, maybe, and lots of cuddles."

Dylan laughed. "Now I'm just gonna have to get you cleaned up."

"Yeah?" Logan smirked. "With your tongue?"

Dylan's eyes darkened. Logan felt the impact of them like a brand, as they swept over him. How two buttons of his shirt had come undone in the struggle for the ball, and how there was definitely some sugar-like substance smeared across his chest. And his neck. And his face.

"I think," Dylan said, "that can be arranged."

Dylan had meant, of course, that he'd arrange it the very second they arrived back at Logan's house. He'd pull him upstairs, and he'd take each piece of the ruined tux off, one at a time, and he'd lick him clean. Until he was shaking and desperate and couldn't take another moment of torment.

But the moment they finally got back into Logan's SUV, and he smelled the sugar in the air, he couldn't resist any longer. He leaned over and licked up the side of his neck. "Yum," he said, "vanilla bean."

What he really thought was *yum, Logan Banks*.

Because that was the taste that really resonated, under the sweet sugary surface. Logan. Just Logan.

Dylan couldn't wait to take another bite, couldn't wait to savor the flavor on his palate, more fully, more completely.

More *privately*.

Still, they were fairly alone in the player parking lot, a handful of cars parked here and there, and Logan had happened, coincidentally, to avoid parking underneath one of the big LED parking lights that lit up the structure.

Besides, the whole world thought they were dating.

So they weren't exactly fooling anyone.

Logan reached out and tangled a hand in Dylan's hair and *tugged*, pulling him close, and then they kissed, hard and fast and overwhelming.

Dylan felt like he'd been on the edge for hours, desperate for a taste, and now he was getting one, and the effect it had on him was instantaneous.

He leaned in closer, needing to be pressed right up against Logan, despite the middle console that wanted to keep them apart, and he was just running his palm up Logan's gloriously muscled thigh, feeling it twitch under his fingertips, when Logan pulled back, breathing hard.

"If you're gonna suggest," he said, "that we take this to the back seat, I've got an even better idea."

Dylan raised an eyebrow.

"A *bed*," Logan said. "You know what that is, right? A nice, soft horizontal surface perfect for fucking."

He couldn't help the laugh that escaped. Sex had never been fun like this before. He'd never laughed so much while having an erection in his whole life. In fact, he didn't think he'd *ever* laughed while having an erection before.

Not til Logan.

"But that means," Logan said earnestly, a smirk turning the corner of his mouth up into a nearly irresistible draw, "that we need to *get* home, and that means, you gotta keep your hands to yourself or I'm never gonna be able to get us there."

"What? Me?" Except it was like his hands had a mind of their own, because they kept creeping up his thighs, loving the solid way Logan felt underneath his palms. Asking him to stop touching, even for ten minutes, was asking a lot apparently.

"Yeah," Logan said, his voice gravelly. "You can show me how innocent and sweet you are when we get home."

"That's you," Dylan said, leaning in for one last lick. Right up the sensitive tendon of Logan's neck. He shivered under his touch. "You're the one who's sweet."

"Plenty of time for that . . . *later*," Logan groaned. "Come on. I'm just about ready to bust out and pull you into the back seat, and I want more than just a quickie. I want to fucking . . . *savor* you."

That was enough of a dirty, sweet promise that Dylan readjusted into his own seat, reluctantly removing his hands from Logan's body.

"You'd better promise," Dylan teased as Logan started the car and began to drive out of the garage.

"That, and a whole lot more," Logan said. "Everything you want, I'm gonna give you. And the things you don't want? Think you don't like?"

"Yeah?" Dylan's mouth felt dry with anticipation.

"I'm gonna win you over a little bit at a time," Logan said. "Until you like it all. Until you can't get enough."

Dylan tucked his hands under his thighs, feeling the sweat dampen his palms. It was less than a ten minute drive to Logan's house at this time of night, but it was going to be the longest ten minutes of his life.

"You're making this really hard," Dylan told him.

Logan laughed as he pulled the Range Rover onto the freeway. "That the only thing that's hard?"

"Hell no," Dylan said. "And I'd have felt it myself, if you hadn't insisted on leaving the garage."

"Trust me, this is gonna be so much better," Logan swore. "I'm gonna have my hands all over you, my mouth all over you."

"Shit," Dylan ground out into the thick silence. "Shit. I want you so bad."

"Not freakin' out anymore?" Logan said with a grin.

"You freak out once," Dylan muttered, "right before you put your hand on a guy's dick for the first time, and you never hear the end of it."

"I'll take that as a no." His chuckle was dark. Dirty. So fucking sexy.

"I was thinking . . ." Dylan said, answering Logan's assumption with a suggestion of his own. "That maybe . . . you might want . . ."

"I might want what? To make you scream? That's definitely on the list."

"To fuck me. To hold my hair, hard, and bend me over, and fuck me."

There was nothing but silence.

Dylan watched as Logan's fingers tightened on the wheel until the whites of his knuckles glowed in the dim light of the car.

"You . . ." Logan cleared his throat. "You have got to stop talking like that, at least for the next five minutes, or we're going to end up in a ditch, and you're going to end up in the back seat, and I'm not going to be responsible for anything that happens after that."

"Promises, promises," Dylan teased. He knew he was prodding the beast, but he kinda wanted to see what Logan would look like with his control shredded to pieces, all his contained discipline destroyed.

"Behave." Logan shot him a dark look that *did* make a real promise if he could do what Logan asked, and Dylan felt a thrill shiver down his spine.

"Here's the thing," Dylan said, "I don't really think you want me to."

"For the next five minutes, I do," Logan huffed out in frustration.

"And after that?"

Logan chuckled. "I think you'll find me mighty eager for some misbehavin'."

It was the longest five minutes of Dylan's life.

Longer, somehow, even though it only lasted about four—Logan hitting the accelerator hard, his speed creeping up as they turned down the dark residential streets.

He jabbed the garage door opener with a sharp motion, pulled into the garage and turned the SUV off.

"No," he said firmly as Dylan reached for him. "We are gonna go inside, and go upstairs, like civilized fucking people."

"And what are we now?" Dylan asked, amused as he climbed out of the car.

"People," Logan said, prowling closer, like he was a predator who'd scented a particularly tasty bit of prey, "who fuck on the cold-ass garage floor, or half up the stairs, or against the kitchen counter or some other ridiculous stunt that will feel really fucking amazing at the time, but will make my knees hurt more than they should tomorrow."

Dylan burst into laughter. "Come on, then, old man," he said, pushing open the door to the house. He slipped his shoes and his coat off, leaving them at the kitchen table and headed towards the stairs. He felt the heat of Logan behind him, heard his steps on the hardwood treads. But Logan didn't touch him, not til he reached the top of the stairs, and paused, suddenly not sure where he should be headed.

His room?

Or the other way, towards Logan's master suite?

"My bedroom," Logan said, leaning in close, his voice low and sure, sending shivers down Dylan's spine. He pressed a hand to his back, broad and firm, and Dylan couldn't help it—he leaned into the touch. Wanting it, and craving even more.

Dylan had only been in Logan's bedroom a handful of times. He'd never had an excuse to walk in, even though he couldn't even count how often he'd lain in bed, late at night, sleep eluding him, wishing he could dream up some kind of reason to come crawl into Logan's bed, naked.

Logan pushed him more firmly down the hall, his hand slipping lower, until it was resting right above his ass.

Warm. Inescapable.

Except that Dylan had zero intention of running away. Even though it had only been two months, it felt like he'd wanted this for so long, and everything they'd done so far had felt so damn good.

The bed in Logan's room was huge, covered in a pale blue comforter, with darker blue sheets peeping out from underneath.

That hand kept pushing him closer, until Dylan decided, as good as this was, he wanted to do his own share.

He twisted, and caught Logan by the arm, pushing him firmly down, til he was sitting on the edge of the bed.

Delectable, in only a partially unbuttoned white shirt, bow tie hanging loosely around his thick neck, the cotton fabric pulling tautly around his even thicker chest. A glimpse of his tattoos just peeping out of the open neck.

He'd cleaned up most of the cake and frosting mess, but there were still remnants of it on his skin. Dylan knew it.

And he was going to taste it.

He leaned in just as Logan raised his head and their lips met in a fiery clash of tongues.

It would be so easy to lose himself in the kiss. It was all he'd wanted, all fucking night, just to taste Logan. To remind himself that this wasn't just a pretend relationship. That behind closed doors, they might not be holding hands and calling each other *babe*, but they couldn't resist each other either.

But he had *plans*. He couldn't just lose them in the feel of Logan's mouth, on the sensation of his lips moving against Logan's.

Dylan pulled back, and his fingers, which had dug into the white cotton of his shirt, slipped down, popping each button open deliberately.

The second the last one was open, he pushed the shirt off Logan's shoulders, and Logan crowded him closer, his hands gripping his back, then sliding down, grabbing a handful of his butt. Dylan's breath caught in his chest, and he almost got distracted again.

After all, it was so easy to get distracted, with all that gorgeous man spread out in front of him.

Leaning in, Dylan licked up his neck, savoring the sweetness laid over Logan's own delicious taste. His lips moved lower, finding the graceful curve of his collarbone, discovering a smattering of crumbs on the pec muscle right above his nipple. Dylan nipped there, then sucked, and he heard Logan's fervent groan echo through the room when he let go.

"Goddamn it, you're gonna kill me," Logan muttered.

"That," Dylan said, pressing a palm to Logan's quivering abs, "is exactly the idea."

It was fucking glorious to trace each of those muscles with his tongue, licking off the glaze of frosting there, leaving smears of wetness in their wake.

Logan was panting now, as Dylan neared his final destination: the rock-hard ridge straining against Logan's zipper.

"God, you're so hard," Dylan said in wonder as he traced it lightly with his fingertips.

"Yeah," Logan said, voice gritty. "I fucking want you."

Dylan glanced up, and could see it in his eyes. The look in them was intense, desperate, *needy*.

"Surprisingly," Logan continued as Dylan began to unbutton and unzip his pants, "the shock isn't me wanting *you*. Because, dude, you're fucking gorgeous. I'd have to be dead not to be attracted to you. It's *you* wanting *me*. That's the miracle. Makes me hot. Works me up like you wouldn't fucking believe." Logan chuckled darkly as his cock sprang out, flushed red. "Okay, maybe you might believe it."

"I believe it," Dylan said, and leaned in, licking experimentally at the tip.

There was no way that any cake or frosting could have ended up on Logan's dick—it had been totally covered by his pants—but he swore it was still sweet as he licked it, growing more and more confident as Logan's moans grew louder. Maybe it was the lingering sugar on his tongue, but Dylan found he couldn't get enough.

Three months ago, he'd never even dreamed about doing this.

Now he was blowing a guy in earnest, wanting to take him deeper and deeper, until they both lost their fucking minds.

"Shit, that's good, yeah, *God*," Logan muttered.

"You gonna talk me through this again?" Dylan asked when he came up for air.

Logan was definitely blessed in the cock department, and there was no way he could take it all, not unless he could magic away his gag reflex, but he remembered how Logan had liked his hand on it, too, and he twisted firmly, then even harder.

Logan's head fell back, expression blissed out.

"If I talk you through it," Logan groaned, "I'm gonna fucking come. And I thought you wanted me to bend you over the bed."

"Night's young," Dylan said.

"How are you so fucking perfect?"

"You said it yourself, it's a miracle," Dylan retorted impudently, and then bent down again, determined to wring every bit of pleasure out of Logan that he could.

Logan sighed happily as his cock disappeared between Dylan's lips again.

He felt so far removed from the guy he'd been before—the one who'd enjoyed being given blowjobs by the few girls he'd dated pre-Logan—but he could still remember the things they'd done that he liked. Curling his tongue around the head of Logan's cock, he sucked hard, as he slipped his hand up, cupping and tugging on Logan's balls.

Logan let out a strangled yelp as he sucked even harder, determined to make the man fall over the edge.

Then suddenly, every muscle in his body tensed and Logan didn't need to warn him for Dylan to know he was about to come—though he did, in something that he probably *thought* sounded like English—and then his cock twitched, and he was coming in long spurts down Dylan's throat.

He swallowed convulsively, choking a little, but doing pretty good, he thought, for his first blowjob.

Certainly, Logan didn't seem dissatisfied, Dylan thought as he leaned back and took in the drowsy, pleasured look on Logan's face as he gazed down at Dylan.

"A fucking miracle," Logan said softly. Reached down, and cupped his cheek.

"It was okay?" He hadn't meant to ask. Really, hadn't actually *worried* it would be good, because it was hard for it to be bad, but now he felt a frisson of unease. Logan had hooked up with lots of guys. Including Ricky. They'd all had experience, and Dylan hadn't had any. None at all.

Logan laughed. He leaned down and scooped Dylan right off the floor.

He wasn't a small guy. But Logan handled him like he weighed nothing, tossing him on the bed and leaning over him, stripping his shirt off, buttons pinging everywhere as he didn't even bother to wait.

And then his hands were on his chest, his stomach, his hips as he dragged Dylan's pants off.

His eagerness shouldn't have been so goddamn sexy, but it set Dylan on fire, until he was nearly panting by the time Logan got him totally naked.

But then, instead of touching him, the way he was desperate for, Logan rocked back on his heels and just looked. Like he was contemplating the very best method to take Dylan apart and then put him back together again, so that he'd never be able to feel pleasure again without thinking of him.

"You know," Logan said, so casually, like Dylan's dick wasn't hard as it had ever been, like he wasn't straining for even a single touch, "I've got a big cock."

"You don't have to brag, you know. I just had it in my mouth, anyway," Dylan teased.

"I'm saying it because . . ." Finally Logan touched him, fingers grasping his knee—Dylan hadn't ever imagined that someone touching his *knee* would feel good, but this felt fucking amazing—and he lifted his leg up, just enough that he could slide his other hand down, rubbing a thumb over his balls and then lower still, right where Dylan had never imagined craving another human being fucking him, but he did now. "Because I'm not small. And you've never done this before. It's a lot. We don't have to do it all at once."

"You don't think I'm gonna like it?" Dylan could tell him some things about how much he wanted it. Enough that he'd bought his own lube, secretly, on one of the trips to the grocery store he'd done without Logan, and even experimented with his own fingers.

It hadn't felt like Logan's fingers would. Or his *cock* would. But Dylan had learned enough to know that *yes*, he liked it. And *yes*, he wanted more.

"I think it wouldn't hurt to take some time," Logan said. His touch felt reverential. Careful. But still, unbelievably hot.

That shouldn't be possible. Someone being so cautious, it should have turned him off, but somehow, with Logan, it did the opposite.

Whether he's admitted it or not, he cares about you.

And Dylan cared about him.

"Okay, we can do whatever," Dylan said in a rush, "just . . . for the love of God, touch me, *please.*"

The seriousness of Logan's expression melted into something devilish. Something even, impossibly, sexier. "Oh, don't you worry," he said. "I'm gonna make you feel good."

Dylan heard him rustling in the drawer in the bedside table, and when he returned, he watched as Logan leaned over, one slick hand grasping his cock in a grip that had him seeing stars, so distracted that he missed the other hand entirely.

Until it was snubbing right up to his hole, every nerve ending screaming as Logan circled it with his thumb.

Then he slipped it inside, right as he gave a particularly bone-melting twist with his hand, and *yeah*, he'd promised he'd make him feel good, but this felt so much better than good. In a different *universe* than good.

But he wouldn't deny it, he was greedy for more, and strained, pushing his body towards where Logan was penetrating him. Wanting it thicker and wider and *deeper*.

"God, you really do want it," Logan said, his own gaze glazing over as he watched Dylan.

The look in his eyes alone, the wonder and disbelief and the *thrill* of it would have been enough to get him off. But then there were Logan's hands, working so expertly, taking him high, so high that he thought he'd cry if he didn't come, and then they'd pull back, with just enough restraint that he was thrashing around again, keening and straining.

Logan's thumb became a finger, became two fingers, became three fingers, and he was hitting him in exactly the right spot, the spot that had him nearly screaming with the pleasure of it as he worked him through it, pushed him right up to the edge and over it.

The aftershocks felt like they went on forever, or maybe that was Logan dragging them out and out until he was gasping, panting, really, with the remnants of pleasure that kept pulsing through him.

If it felt this good with just his fingers, how was it going to feel with Logan's cock?

Dylan felt his regular breathing returning slowly as Logan wiped down his chest and between his legs with a damp cloth.

And then, to his surprise, just when he was debating whether he should get up or not, Logan slid into the bed next to him, still naked, surprisingly graceful for such a large guy.

"Hey," he said, tapping Dylan on the shoulder, "you good?"

The last time they'd done this—the only other time—they'd cleaned up and gone back to bro-ing on the couch together, finishing the level that they'd been tackling on their video game.

But now, in the bed, Dylan found himself shoulder-to-shoulder with Logan, and it felt natural to turn over, and maybe they weren't expressly touching, not exactly cuddling, but it felt like they'd never been closer to that possibility.

Maybe, Dylan realized, that was what Logan wanted, he just didn't know how to ask for it.

He scooted half an inch closer.

"Yeah," he said, "I'm real good."

"I was worried I might've hurt you a bit, at the end." Logan's voice and his eyes were soft, and a little bit concerned.

"Hardly," Dylan scoffed. "I clearly loved it."

"And I," Logan said, his voice dropping lower, "loved doing it."

"Hopefully I can convince you to do it again?"

Logan chuckled. He reached out and tucked a strand of hair behind Dylan's ear. He was always kind and sweet, but he wasn't usually so tender.

It was the act that convinced Dylan that if he told the entire truth, came totally clean, then he might not be the only one feeling all of this.

That Logan might want this to be real, too.

"I don't think that's gonna be a problem," Logan said.

"So, we're doing this," Dylan said, gesturing between them. "And we're together all the time."

"You *live* here," Logan inserted, amused.

"Yeah, I do, but I don't want to leave, either, which . . . that isn't something I expected would happen."

"If it makes you feel better," Logan said, "you aren't alone there. I thought you'd hang out here for a week or two and then find your own place but . . ."

"But I didn't want to go?"

"And I didn't want you to," Logan finished for him.

This was it.

"It's not only that you're such a good friend," Dylan said, reaching out and stretching his palm across Logan's rose tattoo. Sensing his heart beat so steadily in his chest. It was amazing that something so reassuring, so steadfast, could also be so wildly sexy. But he was both, at the same time. Logan made Dylan feel comforted and safe, and also impossibly turned him on and set him free to feel anything, to *do* anything, to *feel* anything. "It's . . ."

"What else is it?" Logan sounded at least as invested in this conversation as Dylan was, so there was that, but it was also fucking terrifying to lay his feelings out like this.

Especially with a friend he valued as much as he valued Logan.

What if he didn't feel the same way?

What if sex was all it was?

You'll never know if you don't take the chance, Dylan told himself firmly.

"I like you, that's the other part."

Logan raised an eyebrow. Surprised, maybe, but not upset.

"Like *like* you," Dylan said, suddenly wishing that there was a better way to say this that didn't make him sound like a sixteen-year-old girl, and also that he could pull the blanket up and shield himself from the inherent embarrassment of it.

But he couldn't, because he was lying on the blanket, and also . . . maybe he should just own it.

Own his feelings.

So instead, he forced himself to meet Logan's gaze.

"I don't do relationships," Logan said. His expression was closed, and Dylan couldn't figure out a thing he was thinking or feeling. "Not ever. Not really because I didn't want to but because . . . it never seemed like the right person or the right timing, or worth the risk. So I don't know what the fuck I'm doing. But if I ever wanted to be with someone, like really *be* with someone . . ." He paused, and a giant smile bloomed across his face, and Dylan swore his heart skipped a fucking beat. "I'd want it to be you."

Happy, Dylan realized, *this is what being happy feels like.*

He'd been happy before, of course. The day he'd signed with the Raiders, and also the morning he'd woken up in Logan's house, realizing that someone had stuck their neck out for him, and they hadn't needed to. Plenty of times growing up.

But this happiness felt solid. Unshakeable.

Like he was going to be able to keep a piece of it, close to him, forever.

"Really?"

"Here I was, worried that I was going to push too hard, or make you too gay," Logan joked.

"Too gay?"

"I wanted . . ." Logan hesitated. "I wanted it to be something you wanted for *you*, not just something that you did to make me happy."

"I promise, this is something I really want." Dylan leaned in that last bit and pressed a soft kiss to Logan's lips.

"Good, 'cause, well . . . I'm kinda crazy about you. Didn't want to be, not at first, because it made things complicated. You're not supposed to be crazy about your friends." Logan slung a hand across his hip and tugged him closer. And now, yes, they *were* cuddling.

"Except," Dylan teased, "we were friends who desperately wanted to bang each other. I just didn't know that it was what it was, not at first. Remember that night we went out to sushi with Sea Bass and Tristan and Wade?"

"How could I forget?"

"I said I wasn't queer . . . but I was already thinking I might be. I feel bad about that. I . . . well, I lied."

"No," Logan said staunchly. "No, you didn't lie. You were figuring your shit out. I understand that. Sebastian understands that.

Wade and Tristan understand that. It's not ever cut and dried. We get that."

"Really?" Dylan couldn't help his surprise.

"Has that been bothering you this whole time?"

"Not this *whole* time," Dylan said. "But yeah, I guess. A little. I felt like I should have spoken up then. Told you the truth."

"You're telling me the truth now. And you didn't *not* tell me the truth before," Logan said firmly. "Do you know if Ricky had outed me even two years ago, I'd have been really angry? I wasn't ready then. And that was okay. Sebastian wasn't ready until just a few weeks ago, and he *still* doesn't want to talk about it. And that's his right."

Dylan nodded. He was beginning to see what Logan was saying. "Straight people don't feel the need to talk about how straight they are."

"No, they don't. So . . . like my nana said, you'd better give yourself some grace."

"I like that."

"And I," Logan said, tugging him close again, until they were touching in half a dozen places, and Dylan kinda wished they were touching in a dozen more, "like *you*."

Chapter Twelve

It was always a unique experience traveling to a different home stadium. Each stadium had such a different feel, a different vibe.

Some of them were great, like the Riptide's stadium in LA, or the stadium the Giants shared with the Jets in New Jersey, or even the field in Minneapolis. He'd really enjoyed playing there. Not like he enjoyed playing in front of the legions of Piranhas fans, but at the time, it was all he'd known.

Now, Logan knew there was no greater high than running out onto the field, set in the heart of downtown Miami, with the neon flashing lights and even Caribe, grandstanding for the crowd.

But tonight, they wouldn't be playing on home turf, but in Los Angeles—and *not* in the more queer-friendly stadium.

The Los Angeles Stars were most famous for their punishing defense, and for the exposés that had been written about them after Spencer Evans, the incredibly talented defensive end, had revealed their homophobia.

"Could get rough out here," Sebastian said to him, jogging up next to him as they made their way onto the field for warmups.

"Or it could be fine," Logan said. He wanted it to be fine. This was only the second game he was playing since coming out. When he'd originally considered doing it, when it had been *his* choice, he'd considered that to be a factor: which stadiums the Piranhas would be visiting.

But in the end, Ricky hadn't left him any choice, and he'd noticed, almost right away, where the Piranhas would be visiting shortly: the Stars, coming right up on the schedule, only the second game after Ricky's article.

Supposedly they'd undergone a culture overhaul since Spencer Evans had called them out on their bullshit, but Logan was from Texas. He knew how deeply ingrained prejudice could be; how difficult it was to root out completely.

Sebastian shrugged. "Isn't it weird how different two teams can be that share the same city?"

"The Riptide is a damn good football team," Logan said, eyeing the opposite side of the field, as the Stars in their bright yellow and red began to arrive, "but still, I would've rather played them. Even on a short week."

This week they'd drawn the short straw, with the Thursday night game. Less time to prepare for the Stars, but more time next week, and even, if they could pull off a win, maybe a few extra days off.

"It's gonna be just fine, no matter what happens," Sebastian said, slapping him on the back. "I promise you."

"Shouldn't I be promising you that?"

Sebastian laughed. "Okay, sure, if you want."

Logan assumed a dead serious expression. "Sea Bass, I promise you it's gonna be alright."

"Oh, now I feel tons better," Sebastian retorted wryly. "If anyone gives you shit, I'll just come kick their ass."

"You'd probably have to beat Paxton to it," Logan said, glancing over at where their quarterback was going over some plays on a tablet with Davis.

Sebastian grinned. "Exactly, man, we've all got each other's backs."

He jogged off, to warm up with the rest of the defense.

Logan started making his rounds, starting with Pax and Davis.

"Feelin' good?" he asked, as he approached the pair.

"Ready to win," Pax said seriously.

Logan wished he possessed the natural ability to lighten people up—specifically their quarterback—the way that Tristan could. But Tristan was down field, catching passes from the receivers coach.

"We'll take it one play at a time," he reminded Pax.

Davis nodded. "The Stars' defense, while not as good as they were when they had Evans, aren't slouches. We're gonna put up a fight, each and every play."

"They're gonna rush you, every play," Logan reminded Pax. "But we're gonna keep you upright, dude, okay?"

Pax nodded.

He knew the guy had taken it way too much to heart when they'd managed to move the ball enough to get Dylan all those field goal attempts, but never made it into the end zone.

He'd been riled up in every offensive meeting this week, spending far too many late hours, if Beau was to be believed, huddled with Davis and Coach Randy, the passing game coordinator, trying to find a way to be more effective.

Sometimes Logan wondered if he let himself take a breath and let the game come to him, whether he might find what he kept searching for.

But Pax was stubborn and determined and had decided that working as hard as humanely possible was the solution—and wouldn't listen to anyone who might try to tell him differently.

Logan jogged over to where the rest of the offensive line was warming up. He slapped each of them on the shoulders and back, checked in with everyone, getting updates on injuries, making sure that everyone was mentally ready for the struggle to come.

"We," he said as he started to stretch his back, "are gonna keep Pax in this game, okay?" he said. "I don't care what it takes. You know they're gonna be coming, so prepare for them coming and deal with it."

Rob, the left tackle, nodded seriously. "The tape's wild. I've never seen a team that blitzes this often. Maybe the Steelers."

"It made sense, when they had Evans," Brock, the right guard, pointed out. "But it's not necessarily solid strategy now."

Brock was a beast in the weight room, and a beast in the video room. He was another reason why Logan had been plenty happy to leave Minnesota for Miami. He liked guys around him who didn't just throw their strength around, but who had minds and knew how to use them.

"Hey, we let them figure that out the hard way," Logan said. "Everyone get taped up, and ready to go. I want to run a few drills, get the line totally gelled before we face these guys, okay?"

He was technically not the offensive captain—that was Pax, the quarterback—but he, with Rob's help, led the line. He made sure they were ready. He made sure they knew their place. Every game, he told them what to expect, and where to expect it from. He got some of his info from Coach Randy, who watched plenty of tape himself, and from Beau, who was every bit the analytical genius everyone said he was, and also from his own study.

He'd watched the last four Stars games in preparation for this one. Brock, he was sure, had watched even more.

If in the middle of the game, Brock saw something key that he recognized, he'd make sure to tell him.

Warmups ended, and they ran the drills Logan had envisioned.

Pax went out with Zach, who was the punter and the special teams captain, and Markus, the defensive team captain, and won the coin toss, choosing to take the ball now, instead of deferring to the second half.

Dylan was in his typical spot, by his practice net, removed from where the rest of the team was gathered around the benches.

He always kept himself separate this way—so he could focus, Dylan had said once—but this time, unlike all the others, he glanced up as Logan got ready with the offense to jog onto the field.

Their eyes met.

Logan had already wished Dylan good luck—even though, he'd teased, he really didn't need it when they'd been back in the locker room.

He knew how Dylan liked to keep his focus exclusively on the job he'd need to be doing for the next few hours, and he wanted to respect that.

But right now, Dylan was staring at him, and his warm, sweet gaze felt like a caress against his cheek, reminding him of what they'd decided only a few days ago.

If I ever wanted to be with someone, like really be with someone . . . I'd want it to be you.

He'd never imagined that he'd say those words to anyone. Or that he'd *mean* them.

With Dylan, he did.

And to his surprise, Dylan felt the same way.

How cute had he been, the other night? Desperate and horny, for sure, which had been a revelation in and of itself, but then the sweet, sleepy, bashful Dylan who'd confessed just how much he liked Logan?

If he hadn't been in deep before, he was now, there was no longer any point in denying it.

And the last few nights, sharing orgasms and then sharing a bed?

Logan didn't think he could ever go back to the way things were before, when they'd just been friends.

"Earth to Logan . . . are you there, Logan? Or are you lost in the sea of luuuuurve?" Tristan teased, jerking Logan's attention back to the loose huddle they'd gathered before heading onto the field for the first drive.

It was too much to hope that the rest of the guys wouldn't realize *very* quickly that whatever was between him and Dylan wasn't fake in the least.

"The sea of luuuuurve?" Paxton repeated in disbelief.

"Yeah, you wouldn't know anything about that," Wade retorted.

"I wouldn't," Pax said—Pax *lied*, Logan was ninety-nine point nine percent sure he did. "But I would know about playing a damn good football game. So let's do that, okay?"

Dylan watched as the Piranhas' offense moved down the field with confident certainty, Pax passing the ball quickly, getting it out of his hands in the nick of time before the blitzing defense got to him.

The running game was a lot tougher going, Kenyon barely managing to eke out a yard or two at a time before he'd get tackled to the ground.

The quick plays meant that going downfield was impossible, but Tristan was still fighting through all his deep routes, running hard at every opportunity.

Still, with the tough, aggressive Stars' defense, Dylan kept his leg warm, half-expecting that he'd be called out to kick another field goal.

You can do that again. You can kick another eight field goals, if that's what this team needs to record a win. You could even kick nine, break Bironas' record.

It was third down and the offense was just past midfield, when Tristan ran another one of his trademark long button-hook routes, stretching out the play, when he snagged the ball right out of the air, and took off, his legs carrying him past the Stars' cornerback—who wasn't, Dylan observed, nearly as dynamic as either Sea Bass or even their rookie, Rose—and twenty seconds later, he crossed the goal line, grandstanding for an LA crowd that didn't look very pleased.

Dylan gave one last stretch, getting ready to head out onto the field to kick the extra point.

Tristan, still exclaiming about how fucking awesome it had been, that he'd made that last move to evade the corner's tackle, passed by him and Dylan patted him on the back, getting a flashed smile in return.

Then he turned, and there was Logan—beaming even through the visor of his helmet. There was something irresistible about his smile, about *him*, that made Dylan want to keep looking and never stop.

So Dylan, who never let himself get caught up in distraction before a kick, found his gaze lingering on Logan's back as he headed towards the bench, where Pax and the rest of the offense was sitting, catching their breath and sipping on their cups of Gatorade.

He was smiling, still, beaming actually, as Pax gestured at something on the tablet Davis had handed him.

"Leonard!"

Dylan glanced up and Coach Roger was standing there, an impatient frown on his face.

"You gonna go kick the extra point?" he demanded to know.

"Yes, yes, of course," Dylan said, and jogged out, with the rest of the kick formation. But he felt off. He didn't have time to do his last set of prep kicks, and, he thought, *whose fault is that? Your stupid dick's.*

But was it his stupid dick's fault when he didn't hit the ball quite as he'd intended, and it veered wide right, missing the upright by a few feet.

The crowd booed as he walked off the field, disgusted with himself and not even trying to hide it.

"It's alright," Coach said, slapping him on the back as he passed by him. "Shake it off, shake it off, it happens."

It *did* happen. Dylan just never wanted it to happen to him.

He worked as hard as he did so that it wouldn't.

Skirting around the back of the bench, he came to a stop in front of his net. Stopped. Took a deep breath. Set up his ball on the holder. And kicked three practice kicks in a row.

Because in a minute or two, after the commercial timeout was over, he'd have to go kick off, and the last thing he needed was to fumble the ball again.

"Hey."

Dylan glanced up, and it was both the best thing in the world that Logan was standing there, his helmet dangling from one hand, the eye black under his eyes smeared, and the worst, too.

He didn't know what to say. What had happened? He couldn't even explain it to himself. He definitely couldn't figure out how to explain it to Logan. And he *should*, because he'd let Logan and the offense down. He'd let *himself* down.

"I've got to go kick off," Dylan said.

"Yeah, I know," Logan said. "I just wanted to say . . ."

But instead of saying it, he trailed off, like once it had come time to say it, he suddenly wasn't sure *what* he should say.

"It's all good," Dylan said, hating the forced cheerfulness in his voice.

"That's right, you kicked *eight* field goals last week. You tied Rob Bironas. You're a kicking god. Don't forget that."

"I won't," Dylan said.

And he hadn't.

He'd just gotten . . . what? Momentarily distracted? Flustered by how hot Logan was? How much he liked *liked* him?

Dylan pushed the thought away. "I gotta go," he said.

And this time, when he kicked off, his foot hit the ball squarely without a single ounce of hesitation. Everything was good.

He was good.

But after the kickoff, he came back to his bubble, and didn't feel fine.

Kicked a dozen or so practice balls into his net. Then a dozen more.

Watched as the defense let the Stars get behind them and run for a sixty-yard touchdown.

Normally, at this point, they'd be tied. But no . . . Dylan had let his team down. Had let *himself* down. And so they weren't tied, they were already down a point, and the first quarter was only half over.

He kicked another ten or so kicks in, and watched with frustration as the offense sputtered out at least fifteen yards out of his range.

The Stars' defense was blitzing every single down, without fail, and Dylan could see, when he let himself look at the field, that it was throwing Pax's timing off. Could read the frustration in every line of his body as he'd sit down on the bench, next to Kenyon and Davis and Logan, and try to figure out how to make the next series better.

But in the meantime, the Stars scored three times in three possessions, and by halftime, the Piranhas were down 21 to 6.

In the locker room, Dylan usually stayed apart. His focus was the most important skill he had as a kicker, and if he let himself get involved in the halftime locker room scene, it could affect him.

Today, he nearly drifted towards where loose knots of players gathered, going over plays, trying to fix what had inexplicably broken.

Sebastian was talking in a low voice to Micah, who had his head down in his hands. He'd given up two of those touchdowns, and Dylan supposed that halftime could have gone as badly as it had a few weeks ago, but instead, Micah seemed to be really trying to overcome his challenges, not distract by pinning them on someone else.

Logan looked up as Dylan hovered nearby, not sure whether he should say anything to him or not.

It wasn't his usual way. But the simmering frustration bubbling up made him want to join in, not sit by himself and stew even further.

"Hey," Logan said, his expression lightening as he glanced over in Dylan's direction. "You okay?"

"Yeah, yeah, of course," Dylan said. Even though he didn't really *feel* okay.

But then nobody in the locker room did.

They'd been in such a groove the last few games—taking control and setting the tone, that it felt really weird to be the guys being pushed around on the field.

"Even without Evans, the Stars are no joke," Logan said, exhaling in a long, heavy sigh. "But we've got a plan."

"Me too," Dylan said wryly. "Kick better."

"Hey, you're gonna be fine, and we're gonna get you some more opportunities. Our timing . . ." Logan trailed off.

"It's off. They're rushing you so fast that Pax has to throw immediately, and it's throwing off the receiver routes and the blocking for Kenyon."

Logan's frustration melted into a soft smile. "You wanna come coach the team?"

Dylan couldn't help but chuckle. "No, no way. Standing on the sidelines most of the game? Just gives me a different perspective. I'm removed, can see things that sometimes you guys can't."

"Beau sees it. Just a matter of fixing it," Logan said.

"You will," Dylan said firmly. Because he did believe it. The sheer amount of stubborn determination on the offense—between Pax and Logan and Rob and Tristan and Wade, never mind Kenyon, who was essentially incapable of admitting he was ever wrong—would carry them through. Dylan had faith.

Logan didn't say anything, just shot him a look that pointed out everything that he didn't say: that he should have the exact same kind of faith in himself.

And he did, he really, truly did. He knew, logically and unemotionally, that he could make those kicks in his sleep.

It wasn't his logic that worried him.

It was the emotion seeping in through the cracks. The cracks that he'd willingly let happen. That he'd practically invited by becoming so close to the other guys on the team, by letting Logan in so close.

He wouldn't trade those cracks for anything, but they were making it hard.

Just make it easy, he told himself.

"Kick some Stars butt, okay?" Dylan said. "For me?"

Logan nodded, a sudden grin dawning over his handsome features. "Will do."

There was nothing that Logan wanted more than to do what he'd promised.

What he committed to, body and soul.

But, as the clock ticked down to the end of the fourth quarter and the end of the game, it seemed like kicking Stars butt was not in the cards.

They'd let themselves get pushed around, instead.

The second half had gone better than the first, but they'd still only gotten close enough once to potentially give Dylan a chance at a field goal.

And Coach Dawson hadn't thought it was close enough.

Sure, it was a fifty-six-yard try, which was not an inconsiderable distance, but instead of going for it, and giving Dylan the okay, Coach had punted the ball instead.

The defense had held firm, not giving up any more points, but it hadn't mattered, because the offense hadn't been able to move the ball enough.

It was like a bad deja vu of the first few games of the year, when they'd all been on different pages, and hadn't been able to connect to get the ball moving.

Logan let out a long breath as the final seconds ticked away.

One loss wasn't the end of the world, but he hated how they'd lost: like they were moving backwards, not forwards.

Like they'd let their worst impulses overcome them, yet again.

Practices, Logan already knew, were going to be brutal next week.

Coach and his staff wouldn't take this lying down. He could already see Asa's frown, the deep furrow in his brow, as he flicked through his tablet, trying to figure out where they'd gone wrong.

And how they could fix it.

It seemed everyone was thinking of that, because the locker room was quiet after the loss, and so was the bus ride back to the airport.

Dylan took the seat next to him, and Logan wasn't surprised to see that he didn't seem to feel like talking either.

He'd wanted to erase the failure of that missed extra-point kick with another one—with that long field goal try that Coach hadn't let him attempt.

Logan had seen him on the sidelines, trying to convince him to let him go out and do it, but Coach had just shaken his head twice. Then a third time.

"There's always next week," Logan said, as Dylan stared out the window.

One of the things he cherished most about Dylan's friendship was that they never ran out of things to say to each other, and yet, at the same time, they were comfortable saying nothing, just sitting, never feeling obligated to fill the silence.

Logan could have stayed quiet now, but he didn't want to. He wanted to erase that crease between Dylan's eyebrows. Chase away those ghosts in his eyes.

But then, he had his own share. If he'd just been a little faster, a little stronger, a little smarter, maybe they'd have moved the ball better.

Logically, he knew this loss wasn't on him.

But it was hard to convince your heart of that when it was aching with it.

"There's eleven more weeks in the season. Ten more games," Dylan said, not turning his head to look in Logan's direction.

"Yeah, exactly," Logan said. Trying to believe it himself, which was probably why he sounded less than convincing, even to his own ears.

"Listen, you don't have to do this," Dylan said after a long quiet.

"Make you feel better?"

Dylan finally glanced over at him, expression solemn.

"Maybe I'm trying to make myself feel better, too. These games . . . they never feel good. When it feels like the whole team's off-kilter and out of sync. When it feels like we failed in all three aspects of the game. But it's not just your fault. It's not just mine, either."

"But it's easy to believe it," Dylan said.

Logan nodded.

Dylan's hand slipped over the seat divider, and brushed his own, squeezing it briefly. "It sucked, yeah, but you know what? We're gonna get up tomorrow, and it won't feel so shitty. This is the worst it's gonna feel."

Logan chuckled. "You say that now, til practice starts this week."

"Okay, fair," Dylan said, cracking a smile now. "Practice will definitely be the shittiest it's gonna feel. I'm gonna kick so many extra points I'm going to be doing it in my sleep."

"If you get too aggressive, I'll just boot you out," Logan teased.

It was a good reminder, Logan decided, as Dylan grinned, that no matter what had gone wrong in the game, they still had this.

And this wasn't going away.

In fact, he couldn't deny, as he reached back over and grabbed Dylan's hand and held it firmly, that it was only growing stronger.

"Sebastian texted," Logan said, a few days later when Dylan walked in from the garage, two grocery bags hanging from his hands. "He wants to go out tonight, to the club."

"Ugh, really?" Dylan retorted as he set the bags on the counter. Not sounding particularly pleased. Logan hadn't really wanted to go anyway, but Sebastian had begged—or at least what passed for begging when it came from Sebastian Howard—and he hadn't had the heart to say no.

He *had* said that he needed to check with Dylan first, and Sebastian had retorted how friends and roommates didn't usually plan their Saturday nights around each other—and Logan couldn't disagree. But they hadn't decided yet whether they were going to tell their friends that their fake relationship had become very real indeed.

Real enough that they were spending nights in each other's beds.

Real enough that the first thing he wanted to see in the morning was Dylan's face—and the last thing, too.

"He said he's got a whole deal going with the manager of Hibiscus," Logan said. "We don't have to go . . ."

If they didn't, Dylan was going to have to be the one to tell Sebastian though.

Of course, if that was how it went, the chances of them keeping their real relationship secret much longer were basically zero.

"Isn't Hibiscus the place that we went a few weeks ago? Where Beau and Sea Bass were all over each other?"

And I didn't dance with you, because I really wanted to, way too much, and I knew that if I touched you, I'd never be able to keep my hands to myself? Yep, that's the place.

"Yep, that's the place."

"And I danced, but you didn't." Dylan turned back from putting the jugs of milk into the fridge.

Logan opened his mouth to explain, but Dylan continued. "Listen, I know you will, because didn't Ricky mention that was something you guys liked to do together?"

"It was very Taylor Swiftian, dancing by the light of the refrigerator," Logan said, rolling his eyes. "I'm only surprised he didn't put that in the dang song he recorded."

"Oh, I'm sure that'll be on the next one," Dylan said. He leaned back against the counter. "Would you dance with me, if we went tonight?"

"I mean, *yeah*, of course."

"But you didn't before." Dylan frowned. "You sat *by your-self* and stared at your phone."

"I . . ." Logan gave in. "I didn't want to . . . I wanted it too much, okay? I wanted to dance with you. And I thought you'd probably freak the fuck out if I came up behind you, grabbed your hips and my dick accidentally made contact with your ass, okay?"

Dylan grinned. "'Accidentally,' huh?"

"I can't really help it when you're around, to be honest," Logan said with a shrug.

"Oh, I'm not complaining. I just . . . I thought . . ."

Logan reached for him, tugging him into his arms. "Self-preservation, okay?" he mumbled into Dylan's shoulder. "That's what I was doing. Poorly. But I was *trying* to do it."

Dylan pulled back and there was an undeniable twinkle in his green eyes. "I get it," he said. "I've just never been any good at that stuff. I wanted you . . . so I took you. Any way I could have you."

"You can have me. Any way you want me." Logan meant it.

"Well, tonight, I want you on the dance floor . . . and off of it . . ." Dylan trailed off with a knowing smirk.

"So I should tell Sebastian we're in?"

"Yeah," Dylan said with a nod, turning away from Logan's arms. He was tempted, for half a second, to grab him back. "Yeah, we're in."

"You know . . ." Logan hesitated. "It won't be a secret, then. Whatever . . . whatever it is we're doing."

"Oh, I thought what we were doing was being boyfriends," Dylan said matter-of-factly, head still in the fridge, voice echoing through the empty space.

"Uh, yes, that," Logan stammered. Surprised, even though he shouldn't be at this point, that Dylan wasn't freaking out at the idea of being someone's boyfriend.

He was freaking out a little at the thought of being someone's boyfriend, if only because he'd never done it before. *Thank you, Levi*, he thought, *for putting* that *thought in my head.*

What if he was bad at it? What if he fucked it up? What if he let Dylan down? What if Dylan got tired of him and broke his heart? What if he ended up with only a shadow of what he'd had—a shadow of what he truly wanted?

Logan pushed those annoying questions and worries aside. Maybe he might be bad at this. Maybe he might make mistakes. Maybe it wouldn't always be perfect, but at the very least, he'd always have Dylan in his life.

That was the only thing that mattered.

"So, yeah, I'm sure they'll find out." Dylan stuck his head out. "I forgot to get cream cheese for the bagels. I think they probably already know. Or have guessed."

"That we don't have cream cheese for the bagels?"

"No," Dylan said with a chuckle. "That we're together."

"Oh . . ." Logan thought of the text that Sebastian had sent, teasing about how he had to check his Saturday night plans with Dylan. Suddenly, it seemed very likely that everyone *had* guessed.

Maybe even before they'd realized it themselves.

"Yeah," Dylan said knowingly.

"You're okay with that?"

"Listen," Dylan said, setting the last of the bananas into the fruit basket and turning back towards Logan. This time, his arms wound around Logan's neck and he tugged him low, until their gazes were level. "Listen, I was willing to be your boyfriend, in front of everyone, and it wasn't even true. Now that it's true, do you really think I'm ashamed or worried about what people are gonna say?"

Logan shook his head.

"Are *you* ashamed or worried about what people are gonna say?" Dylan asked archly.

"Absolutely not," Logan scoffed. How could he be? Any guy would be proud to have a guy like Dylan at his side. Funny and sweet and loyal and hot as fucking hell. And *accomplished*. He made Logan look a million times better, just because he was smart enough to recognize what Dylan brought to the table.

"Then, I think it's okay," Dylan said softly. "But if you're not good with it . . ."

"I'm good with it," Logan said before he could finish. "I'm real good with it."

"So does that mean you're gonna come up behind me," Dylan said with a smirk, "and put your hands on my hips and *accidentally* brush my ass with your dick?"

"It's a promise," Logan said, and kissed him.

CHAPTER
THIRTEEN

Dylan leaned back against the bar at Hibiscus and watched as his boyfriend walked over to him.

It was a really good word, *boyfriend*, though he had lived most of his life not really appreciating it the way he did now.

Probably most of that was Logan, and not the actual title itself, but they'd become so inextricably linked in his head that he wasn't sure where one started and the other ended.

"So it's official now, isn't it?" Tristan leaned over, sucking up his vodka soda noisily through the straw.

Dylan rolled his eyes. "Are you asking or are you stating?"

"Well, *stating*, obviously, because it was clear to everyone with a pair of eyes that you two were gone for each other. You just didn't see it yet."

"Yeah, we do now," Dylan admitted.

"Good." Tristan sounded very pleased. Then a sudden expression of confusion creased his face. "Though I gotta wonder, does this mean you're gonna get *two* lectures from Coach?"

"Two lectures?"

"Yeah, like the whole Coach talk about *don't let this relationship affect you on the field or I'm gonna bury you under it?*" Tristan said as Logan finally reached them. He slung a casual arm around Dylan's shoulders, but it didn't feel casual. Dylan could feel the half dozen places where they were touching like bombs going off inside of him. He'd managed to go seven weeks living with this man and not touching him with the intent of getting him naked, Dylan thought incredulously. How was that even possible?

"Who's burying who?" Logan asked.

"Didn't Coach threaten that if you and Dylan couldn't keep your shit off the field? We *definitely* got that speech. And I know Sea Bass got it too, when he admitted that he was dating Beau," Wade asked, slipping in next to Tristan.

"Oh, we got it, but it was a little different . . ." Dylan trailed off. Suddenly, a little bit uneasy because talking about this while Logan was at the other side of the bar was one thing, and it was entirely another doing it in front of him—even though they'd talked about it this afternoon, just the two of them, and they'd been on exactly the same page.

"Exactly," Tristan said with a sharp nod. "Your relationship wasn't legit, and now it is, so you should get it again."

"Oh, it's legit now, is it?" Logan teased. "How did you figure that out?"

Tristan rolled his eyes. "I was just telling your *boyfriend* that. It wasn't ever fake, we all knew that."

Wade nodded, looking like he might burst out laughing at any second.

Okay, it had probably been obvious.

To everyone else.

"It was supposed to be fake," Dylan added, "but well . . ."

"It just wasn't?" Tristan said, and *he* was laughing now, too.

"You said it yourself," Wade added, "*it would have to be the right guy.* I bet you already knew it was going to be Logan." He nodded sagely at his own theory. "'Cause when you know, *you know.*"

Maybe Dylan should be more annoyed that Wade was right.

But he was cute, and he was cute with Tristan, and he could throw a block that brought tears to Logan's eyes.

It was hard to dislike him, even on principle, when that was the case.

"Where's the lie?" Dylan said with an easy shrug. He turned to Logan. "You want a beer?"

"Sure, why not? Today's practice sucked enough that I could probably use more than one," Logan admitted.

"God, let's not even talk about it," Tristan said with a heartfelt and dramatic—but likely not even dramatic enough—groan. "Especially because here come Pax and Davis, and they've been on a rampage."

"We lost," Logan reminded him mildly.

Tristan threw him a glare. "Before that, even."

"Two Coronas, with lime," Dylan said, after he'd gestured to the bartender and he'd sauntered over.

He went to grab them from the under-counter cooler, and when he finished setting them on the counter, sliding slivers of lime into the tall glass necks of the bottles, he looked a little more closely at who he was serving.

"Hey, you're Logan Banks," he said. "You're a freaking beast, man."

"He sure is," Dylan said with a smirk that made Logan blush.

Tristan whistled, very loudly.

The bartender snapped his fingers. "Someone was in the other weekend, askin' about you, specifically. Short guy, blond hair. Claimed he was famous on TikTok."

In the middle of squeezing his lime, so the juice would drip into the beer, Dylan's fingers froze.

"Said he knew you," the bartender continued. "Real well, if I understood it right."

"Ricky," Logan muttered under his breath, a storm cloud descending over his features, when only a second before, he'd been as happy and relaxed as Dylan had seen him since the loss to the Stars.

"Yeah, I think that was his name," the bartender said.

"I didn't know Ricky was in Miami," Dylan said carefully.

"Me either." Logan did not sound particularly happy about that fact.

Dylan couldn't blame him. He was clearly here for one reason and one reason only: to cause more trouble than he'd already been causing.

"Well, shit," Tristan said, his expression saying it all. "That asshole thinks he can just show up here and what?"

"Create drama," Wade grumbled.

"Who's making drama?" Pax had just walked over with Davis trailing behind him.

Normally, coaches didn't come to player gatherings, but ever since Sebastian and Beau had started dating, it had opened the door to Davis coming with Paxton.

It was clear to anyone with eyes why that was.

"Logan's ex. That jerk who outed him," Wade said.

Pax frowned. "I thought he was back in Minneapolis?"

"Apparently not anymore," Logan said. His tone made it clear he didn't want to talk about it.

But nobody else apparently got that message.

"He even came here, to Hibiscus, because he must have seen some of the pics I know made the rounds, from last time we hung out," Tristan pointed out.

Anyone who thought Tristan was dumb only needed to spend approximately ten seconds in his company to realize that the sassy attitude and bleached-blond tips he'd recently adopted were only surface-deep.

The guy was crazy smart *and* intuitive. He'd even guessed about Dylan before Dylan had even properly guessed about himself.

"Well," Paxton said slowly, "if he's here for drama or for trouble, then he'll figure out pretty quick that we don't take any shit. Especially," he added, giving a reassuring pat to Logan's back, "when it's one of our own."

Logan rolled his eyes, but he still looked inordinately pleased. "Even if he does his normal shit, it's fine. I talked to my agent and to Helen, they think he's an annoyance who will just go away if we ignore him long enough."

"You don't know that for sure," Wade pointed out.

"I do know that even if he does, it doesn't matter," Logan said bluntly. He turned towards Dylan, who realized he'd been holding his breath. "I'm with Dylan now. I want to be with Dylan."

It wasn't a fairy tale. Their lives were full of too many sweaty locker room smells and dirty socks and sore muscles and secret, hidden fears that they weren't quite good enough to make it for it to be anything resembling a fairy tale.

But when Logan staked his claim, pulling him against him and kissing him proudly and sweetly in front of everyone . . . it kinda *felt* like a fairy tale.

"Damn straight," Pax said, and Dylan saw he was grinning when Logan finally lifted his mouth and Dylan could kinda, *sorta,* think clearly again.

Damn, but Logan could kiss.

Each and every time their lips met, it felt like he lost the thread completely. And usually, he didn't even give a shit it had disappeared.

"Wow," Tristan said teasingly. He turned to Wade. "I think we're gonna have to go home now, after that little display."

Wade chuckled, gazing down at his boyfriend with a loving look on his face. "We just got here, babe. And before . . ."

"Trust me," Davis spoke up before anyone else could remind Wade that there was a rule in place about over-sharing, "we really don't want to hear about what you did before you showed up."

"I could stand to hear a little more," Sebastian teased, finally arriving, his hand tightly locked with Beau's. "How 'bout you, babe?"

"You're just saying that because we've *all* had to hear a little too much about Wade and Tristan," Beau retorted, but his expression was fond.

"I don't know about all y'all," Logan said, sliding a hand across Dylan's back. He felt hot and cold all over, and *God*, he was absolutely not going to get an erection in front of all their friends. It was *not happening*. "But I came to dance with my boyfriend and you're just clutterin' up my game."

"Game? Game? What game?" Tristan spluttered before Pax whacked him on the back.

"Behave, rookie," Pax said, grinning. "Logan's got plenty of game. He got Dylan, didn't he?"

"Damn straight," Logan said, and turned to Dylan. "Come on, I promised you a dance, and this one is nice and slow."

Sexy too, the intoxicating beat of the music thumping in his blood as Logan took his hand and led him out to the dance floor. It had been practically empty when they'd gotten here half an hour before, but now there were a surprising amount of people crowded onto the rooftop. The weather was perfect—hot, of course, because even in October, Miami was hot, but there was a nice breeze, and the humidity was lower, and as a result, people had come out in droves on this Saturday night.

Logan found them a dark corner, and before Dylan could ask what he wanted to do, he'd gripped his hips, just as he'd promised, and his touch was like a brand, the imprint of his fingers sending earthquakes of feeling rumbling through him.

Sweat trickled down his neck, under his hair, and when he glanced up at Logan's face, his dark eyes were burning into him.

It reminded him of late nights in bed, frantically moving against each other, desperately trying to get close, to *be* closer, and slow, easy mornings, when he'd wake up hard as a rock and Logan's hand would be right there, easing him through his orgasm.

Their knees bumped, as the song segued into something even steamier, hotter than the thick, muggy Miami air.

Logan must have been thinking about it too, because his hand slid around Dylan's hip, tugging him even tighter against him, and Dylan buried a moan in his throat at the feel of his undeniably hard cock, pressing into his thigh.

"You feel so damn good," Logan murmured, his voice deep and dark and barely audible, but Dylan could hear it, because it felt like his whole body was a goddamned tuning fork. If he'd known it could be like this . . . such a possessive, all-encompassing desire . . . but Dylan didn't think it could be. Not with anyone else. Just with Logan.

It's you who feels that good, Dylan wanted to say, but the words died in his throat, as Logan ground against him, in a filthy rhythm that left his mouth totally dry.

"Goddamn, I wanted to do this last time we were here but I thought I'd scare you away."

"What, that *this* would scare me away?" Dylan teased, grinding back and watching as Logan swallowed hard, his Adam's apple bobbing.

"Isn't scaring you away now," Logan said.

It was doing the opposite. The fact that he made Logan hard, that he'd made Logan hard long before he'd ever guessed that he did, made him want to throw caution away with both hands. He wanted to drag Logan to an even darker corner and put his hands everywhere he'd ever dreamt about.

Dylan tilted his head back and the hungry look in Logan's eyes was unmistakable. They weren't fooling anyone anymore, that much was certain—but right before Logan's mouth descended onto his, someone jostled him, and he glanced back to see Tristan grinning back at him.

"Hey, guys," he said excitedly. "Long time no see."

Logan groaned. "What are you doing here?"

"What?" Tristan said innocently, as he waved his arm in the air, no doubt letting Wade know where he was. "Am I cramping your style?"

Logan glared and Dylan couldn't help but throw his head back and laugh.

"Hey," he said under his breath to Logan, "we came here to hang out, it's all good. You can get all up in my business later . . ."

Logan had still been resisting taking the final step of fucking him, but Dylan couldn't lie; by this point he was desperate for it. Despite that, Logan kept hesitating. However, there was a look in his eyes tonight that promised any resistance left would be crumbling, soon.

Tonight, Dylan promised himself.

"Don't worry, I will be," Logan said, and it sounded like a vow.

"So," Tristan said, his hips moving sinuously with the music, "you two trying to get arrested for public indecency already?"

A second later, Wade arrived, and then Sebastian and Beau. Davis and Pax were still over by the bar, their heads close together as they watched something on a phone.

Logan followed his gaze and groaned a little—probably not because Dylan moved about half an inch away from his body, to a slightly respectable distance. "You guys left them alone? You know all they're gonna do is work."

"Probably," Sebastian said with a shrug. He shot Logan a look. "You want them doing anything else?"

"Beau is *right there*," Logan reminded him.

"Yep, I'm here, and I'm not blind, either, thank you very much," Beau inserted.

"None of us are," Wade said solemnly.

"Are we here to worry about Pax and Davis or are we here to dance?" Tristan demanded archly.

"Dance. I came here to dance with my boyfriend," Dylan said, really enjoying *one*, how the word rolled so perfectly off his tongue, and *two*, the way Logan reacted to it. His fingers tightened on Dylan's hip, and if he played his cards right, he was only about ten minutes away from practically throwing Dylan over his shoulder, finding them a cab, and then fucking him so good he'd probably never get over it.

Except, he reminded himself, *you promised to come and hang out with Sea Bass and Beau and the other guys. And hanging out usually means more than ten minutes.*

"He's even doing a credible job of it," Tristan said, eyeing the way Logan was moving with Dylan. "I'm impressed."

"I'm not."

Logan yelped, and oh *yeah*, those fingers dug into his hip even more, and Dylan gloried in the evidence of his strength.

It was hot when Logan was gentle, despite the tightly controlled power of his body, but it was even hotter when he forgot himself and let some of it off the leash.

"I expected it," Dylan explained with a low chuckle. "Have you ever seen the man play football?"

Tristan considered this. "Daily, actually. And yeah, I can see it now." The look he gave Dylan was full of approval. "You've really been paying attention."

"From the beginning," Dylan admitted.

And yeah, that was totally a groan coming out of Logan's throat.

"You," Logan panted as he tried to simultaneously use one hand to punch in the numbers to the front door keypad and use his other to unbutton Dylan's shirt, "are a fucking tease."

"Am I?" Dylan laughed. He couldn't help it. Logan was so worked up, he'd spent the entire cab ride home from Hibiscus sitting on his hands, because he'd whispered, tone urgent and distraught, that if he didn't, he was going to do something he'd regret.

"Not something *I'd* regret," Dylan couldn't help but reply.

"Yes," Logan had said between clenched teeth. "Because you're gonna want me to do it when we can both get naked and you can scream the house down without anyone else to hear."

Dylan couldn't exactly argue with that—or that he *had* teased him. A lot. On purpose.

"You're the worst," Logan said as he finally got the code right, and they stumbled into the foyer, half of Dylan's shirt hanging off his shoulders, and he wasted zero time jumping into Logan's arms. "And also, the best."

"I really am, aren't I?" Dylan said, grinning. Logan was like a solid tree—so big and broad and surprisingly easy to climb, especially when Logan's hands slid under his ass and gripped him hard. "If I'm the best, then you should do whatever I say."

Logan nibbled at his bottom lip, causing Dylan's breath to catch in his throat. "What do you say, then?" he murmured.

"Fuck me," Dylan said. "God, *please*."

Logan chuckled, the dark sound of it cresting over his nerves, wrenching them even tighter as he began to take them up the stairs to his bedroom. "I suppose I gotta stop waiting for you to change your mind."

He deposited Dylan on the edge of the bed, and leaned back, watching as Dylan shrugged out of his shirt, his gaze growing hotter and hotter along his skin, singeing him at the edges.

"Am I the only one gettin' naked here?" Dylan asked as he slipped his shoes, then his socks off, his fingers lingering on the button of his tightest jeans.

He'd worn them, hoping to be irresistible.

But he was learning that all of this was window dressing. Whether he was wearing old baggy sweats or his best suit, Logan wanted him anyway.

"Yeah." Logan's voice was deep. Gravelly.

"Okay, you can watch, then, and enjoy." Dylan popped the button and then slowly, as slowly as his own fraying self-control would allow, lowered the zipper. He shimmied out of one side, and then the other, Logan gasping when he realized he'd worn nothing under the jeans.

"You're gonna be the death of me, you know?" Logan's drawl was so sexy, he nearly shivered with the sound of it.

"Death of both of us, I hope," Dylan said.

He watched as Logan went into the drawer he recognized now and pulled out not only the bottle of lube, but a condom this time. He'd bought that box of condoms himself, a few days ago, and deposited it in full view of Logan, with an impudent wink, into the drawer in the bedside table.

Dylan had always been someone who knew what he wanted—and knew, without a doubt, that what he wanted was Logan.

"I'm thinkin' . . . you've started to like this part, haven't you?" Logan's question wasn't even a question as he gently pushed Dylan back with one hand and began to circle his hole with a wet thumb on the other.

"I don't mind it," Dylan said, his sentence punctuated with a gasp that made it clear just how much he fucking loved it.

Any minute now, Logan would lean in and he'd touch his cock, jerking it slowly as he fingered him, or he'd lean in even further and the hot, wet heat of his mouth would send him into a place so blissful nothing felt quite real.

He was nearly there now, with Logan's thumb sinking in, and then he gasped as another finger followed right after the first.

"You gotta forgive me," Logan said, sounding out of breath already, even though Dylan knew the kind of shape he was in, "I . . . I . . ." He sounded unsteady. Desperate.

The place you pushed him to, Dylan reminded himself smugly.

"I gotta have you too," Dylan murmured, reaching down and curving his palm around Logan's cheek.

The one thing Dylan wouldn't deny was that each and every time they did this—not every time they fooled around, but enough, because *Dylan* couldn't get enough—it was easier. He might, under extreme duress, admit that Logan had been right and they'd needed to work up to it.

But right now pleasure was spiraling through him, with only the tiniest hint of pain, as Logan slid another finger in, stretching him out. Making sure he was good and wet.

"How did you say you wanted it again?" Logan's voice was breathless.

"Oh, you *know*, 'cause you've been thinkin' about it every day, and every night, too," Dylan said, his own not nearly as steady as he'd hoped.

Logan's fingers slipped out of him, but before he could turn over and tangle his fists into the bedding, bending over for Logan to *finally* fuck him, Logan dipped his head and kissed him. Warm and sweet and slow.

Loving, Dylan realized, *he's kissing you like he loves you, and he doesn't want it to just be hot, dirty fucking between you—though you both want that too.*

Dylan realized that he didn't want only that either, and he reached up, clutching his fingers into the collar of Logan's shirt, kissing him back with just as much emotion.

Then finally, it ended, Logan stepping back and quickly shedding the last of his clothes and reaching for the condom.

"You ready?" he asked.

Dylan didn't answer. At least not in words. He turned over and pushed himself up on his knees, digging his fingers into the bedding. Squeezing his eyes shut. He was suddenly strangely a bit nervous, even though he was ready. What if he didn't like it? What if all his fantasies had been wrong?

At first, all he could feel was the warmth of Logan's naked body as he crowded in close, and then, gloriously, he reached up and tangled a hand into Dylan's hair, and suddenly, he was gripping it and yanking his head back with just the perfect amount of force. His cock slipped in the first inch, and Dylan gasped at the insane pressure of it, the feeling of being trapped between it and Logan's grip.

Then, like he'd been made just for him, Logan slipped in, slowly but surely, the rest of the way. Dylan bit down hard on his lip. It hurt, just a little, the burn of it blending with the twinge from his scalp. But Logan's hand slipped around him, wrapping his fist around Dylan's cock gently, coaxing more and more pleasure out of him, until it felt like the pain melted into it, like the pain almost made it bigger, better, until it nearly took him over completely.

He groaned, and then Logan began to move.

Logan knew that Dylan was going to be tight.

He'd squeezed his fingers like a vise every time he'd fingered him in the week leading up to this, and so he'd *known*, of course, being Dylan's first time that it would be difficult to go slow enough. That he'd need to be patient.

He hadn't ever expected that the need to take him, to feel him all the way around him, to make sure that Dylan never wanted anything else, would overwhelm him. Make him so shaky with the desire that he'd nearly lose himself in it.

Slow, slow, slow, he repeated in a constant litany, just so he wouldn't forget, and wouldn't hurt him—at least more than he wanted to be hurt.

Because caught like this, between Logan's fist in his hair and his undeniably big cock, probably hurt. But from the way that Dylan kept moaning and pushing back into it, garbled praise falling from his lips as he bent over and just took it, Logan couldn't help but think he was loving this just as much as he was.

He smoothed his other hand down Dylan's back, and then gripped his hip with it as he began to thrust a tiny bit faster.

Logan had always prided himself on bucket loads of self-control but Dylan emptied them like it was nothing, and the way he kept pushing back on his dick, like he couldn't get enough? The way he whimpered every single damn time he drew back, like he never wanted to be without it inside him? Logan didn't know how long he could hold on, hold off on coming his fucking brains out.

"God," Dylan moaned into the comforter, "just like that, but *harder*. Fuck me like you mean it, Banks."

Logan wasn't stupid. He wasn't going to take orders from someone who'd never done this before. But the slick squeeze of Dylan's ass around his cock was so intoxicating, it was impossible to resist following the instruction and he began to thrust harder, and then harder still, half an ear listening to Dylan groan louder and louder—and the other, totally caught in his own incredible pleasure.

No doubt about it: it *was* incredible. Actually, it was fucking life-changing.

His hips stuttered as he felt everything inside him tense up, and he realized then, he needed to get Dylan over the edge before he totally lost it.

"Touch yourself," Logan said, leaning over and murmuring it practically into Dylan's ear. "Make yourself come on my cock. I want to feel it." And then he began to fuck him hard—the kind of fucking he'd always been afraid to do, the kind of fucking that stripped you raw and made you hallucinate stars and all that other shit that they always talked about in romance novels.

Dylan's body tensed up underneath Logan's, and he only had a second to prepare himself as Dylan's orgasm pulled him right along with it, the rhythmic clenching undoing him one pulse at a time.

It felt like it went on and on, far longer than anything Logan had ever felt before, and then, suddenly, it was over, and he was releasing Dylan's hair, almost like he'd forgotten he was still holding it, and sliding out of him, watching as the man he loved—*oh God, the man he loved*—collapsed onto the bed.

Logan felt frozen in time, the realization still pinging around his brain.

It was just the endorphins. And the really, really fantastic sex. But he knew it wasn't. This had been coming for some time, and he might have seen it on the horizon, but he'd never felt this way before.

It was like he was being remade, one molecule at a time, and now it was over, and he looked down, and he wasn't only himself anymore. He was Logan, who was in love with Dylan.

"That," Dylan said, his voice slurry, "was fucking amazing."

"Yeah," Logan said, clearing his throat. Not sure which part he was agreeing to—the part where the sex had blown apart his brain, or the sudden realization that this was probably going to be it for him. "I . . . uh . . . I'll be right back."

And yes, he totally cowardly escaped into the bathroom. Got rid of the condom. Wet a washcloth so he could help Dylan clean up. And then stared at himself in the mirror. He looked the same, a little wild around the eyes, maybe, but he looked the same.

Would Dylan be able to tell?

Would it freak Dylan out if he knew?

Don't be an idiot, you're the first guy he's ever been with, he's still gettin' used to that, you can't spring the L word on him too, on top of everything else.

Logan knew that voice was right, but even then it was hard not to say anything, when he walked back into the bedroom, and saw Dylan rolled over on his side, come streaked up his stomach and torso, the biggest, silliest grin he'd ever witnessed on the guy spread all across his face.

"Here, let me help," Logan said, crouching by the bed and helping to wipe Dylan clean. "Or we could take a shower . . ."

"I'm not moving," Dylan said firmly. "I feel too goddamned amazing to move. If I move, I'll probably *not* feel so amazing, and as far as I'm concerned, that would be a real fucking shame."

"It would," Logan agreed, and washcloth disposed of in the laundry hamper, slid into bed next to Dylan. His green eyes were soft in the dim light of the room. "So, I guess that was pretty damn good," he said. Which, really, *understatement.*

"Yeah." Dylan was still smiling. "Thank you for giving that to me. For . . . for being patient and understanding and knowing what I needed, just when I needed it."

Always. I'm always gonna do that for you.

Logan had never felt so fiercely protective of anyone in his life, even though he'd been defending and safeguarding his brothers and sister, and then his fellow players, for his entire life.

But it had never felt like it did now, with Dylan.

"It was absolutely my pleasure," Logan murmured. He slung an arm around Dylan's shoulders, and pulled him in tight. He'd never understood why people liked to cuddle after sex. But once he'd finished touching Dylan, he found he didn't want to let him go just yet. Wanted to prolong that skin-to-skin contact.

You are absolutely, one hundred and ten percent fucked up in love, that voice proclaimed again, loudly and with certainty.

Logan knew he couldn't argue with it anymore.

Chapter Fourteen

"LEONARD," COACH ROGER, THE special teams consultant, barked in his direction. "Come on. Let's kick some more. Fifty more, I think, should do it."

Dylan had known that the practices after missing the extra point in the last game were going to be brutal, and so far he hadn't been proven wrong.

Coach Roger had been on his ass at every practice for the last few days, and at first, Dylan had welcomed the pain. Thinking that it might actually set him straight, get his head out of his ass, and give him the reset he felt he needed.

But now, on day four, it just felt like Coach Roger was being an ass because he enjoyed being an ass. Truthfully—he was the one guy on the coaching staff that Dylan hadn't immediately liked. Coach Asa was awesome; blunt and honest but with a heart of gold hidden under his cotton polo shirts. But of course, the one coach that Dylan couldn't connect with was the one he needed to work with the most closely.

It's still worth it. You still love playing here. You still want to play here. So make it work.

"We just kicked *fifty* extra-point shots," Dylan said, wiping his face with a towel. It was brutally hot this afternoon, unseasonably so for October, and after running drills, *way* too many drills, so many drills that they'd started to feel more like torture than conditioning, Coach Roger had set him on the long field goals—the ones that Coach hadn't even let him try in the last game—and then they'd done the fifty kicks, all at the exact distance of the extra-point kick: thirty-three yards.

And during each and every kick, Coach Roger had critiqued his form. Shouted when he deviated even a sliver from the way that he did all his kicks. By the fiftieth kick, he was exhausted, and his temper simmering, even as he told himself that what they were doing was necessary.

"Yeah, and you missed one last game. You know where kickers who miss extra points end up?" Coach Roger barked at him.

Dylan knew, and he'd been trying, ever since the miss, not to think about it. But he had, anyway. It was just plain inevitable.

Because Miami was where he wanted to be. Not just because of Coach Asa or Beau or the family vibe of the team. Or the whole-hearted acceptance the team preached and then stood behind.

He couldn't deny any more that Logan was a huge part of why he wanted to stay in Miami. He was falling for the guy, he knew he was, even though the relationship part of their friendship was new.

Or . . . new-*ish*.

Dylan couldn't pinpoint exactly when it had begun, but . . . probably before he had ever really acknowledged it to himself.

But Logan was also, right along with being an enormous benefit to being in Miami, a distraction, too. He knew it, even if he didn't want to acknowledge that either.

"They end up off the team," Coach said, when Dylan didn't respond. "They end up on the couch, and nobody's callin'. So," he added, clapping his hands in a way that made Dylan want to punch him, "let's see another fifty kicks, okay?"

"Okay."

Everyone else, Dylan could see, was beginning to file back into the locker room.

But he'd be here at least another hour. If not longer.

He saw Logan's unmistakably large body, as he headed towards the locker room. At the last second, he turned and gazed right over at Dylan. Dylan shrugged. And gave him a little shoo motion.

Logan nodded, understanding, and turned to go take a shower.

Dylan had driven today, so Logan would catch a ride with one of the other guys.

"You ready to play yet, Leonard?" Coach Roger repeated, his voice harsh. "Or are you gonna make eyes at your boyfriend again? Let yourself get distracted?"

The first practice after he'd missed the kick, he'd admitted, when questioned by Coach Roger—who did, despite his many annoyances, understand that kicking was far more mental than it ever was physical—that he'd gotten distracted right before he'd kicked.

Coach had been the one to make the connection as to *what* he'd been distracted by, and it was most annoying that he'd been right.

Dylan hadn't confirmed, but he hadn't denied it either, and Coach Roger had taken way too much pleasure out of needling him about it.

It was bad enough that he knew he'd done it; it was extra bad that Coach kept bringing it up.

"I'm ready," Dylan said firmly, with certainty. "Let's go. I could do this all fucking day."

"Sure you could," Coach Roger said shrewdly.

But it was enough. He'd prodded Dylan enough and now even though he was fucking hot and fucking tired, he was going to kick a hundred of these just to prove him wrong.

He grabbed a ball and jogged out to the tee, still set at exactly thirty-three yards, and made himself go through his entire routine, the deep breath he took, the pause, the arm movements, everything, sending the ball straight down the middle of the uprights.

One down, ninety-nine to go . . .

Dylan chugged three Gatorades on the ride home, grateful at least that he was clean, and had the precious AC blowing on him full blast.

He parked next to Logan's Range Rover, and grabbed his bag from the back of his BMW, and staggered—not walked—to the door that led into the house.

Logan was sitting on one of the barstools in the kitchen, lights turned down low, in his regular uniform of just shorts and nothing else. "Hey," he said, when Dylan walked in. "You stayed late."

"Roger is a sadist," Dylan said, dropping his bag on the floor. "At first I thought I might like it . . ."

Logan grinned and inserted, "Yeah, I can see why you might."

And okay, yeah, he liked a little bite of pain when they were fucking. That was hot. Coach being an asshole was the opposite of hot.

"Anyway, he made me kick another fifty extra points. So I kicked a hundred, for good measure."

"You feel better about it now?"

"No," Dylan said, sliding onto the barstool next to Logan's, and resting his head on his shoulder. He had nice big broad shoulders, perfect for a head. Perfect for *Dylan's* head. "But I will, in a few days, when we play again, and I can lay the memory to rest."

"I had an idea, when I saw how long and crazy your practice was," Logan said softly, reaching out and brushing a still-damp strand of hair out of his eyes, "but if you're wiped, then we can forget about it."

Dylan was tired, yes, but he was still curious. "What did you have in mind? If it's ride you like a stallion, that's not happening."

"No," Logan said chuckling. "You just have to sit here and talk to me, and let me uh . . . well, pamper you, I guess. That's the theme anyway. Pampering."

"Pampering?"

Dylan glanced over and saw the cardboard box and its distinctive design. Logan had done what he'd promised, when Levi had initially sent the first date box—he'd shoved it deep in his closet, and Dylan hadn't seen it again. He *had* seen the parade of subsequent boxes, only to notice that they all disappeared.

"Yeah," Logan said. Cleared his throat. "Levi was right about one thing. I've never done this dating thing before. I don't know how to be good at it. And I want to be good at it."

"You're good at it, I promise," Dylan said.

"Not just the sex part," Logan insisted. "The date part."

"We go to dinner. We went to Hibiscus together, the other night."

"Yeah . . . but that was all Sea Bass. And we have to eat, don't we? No, I wanted to do something special, that . . . I came up with on my own."

"So you thought you'd use one of the date boxes that Levi sent you as a joke?"

Logan made a face. "Okay, not *entirely* on my own."

"Right." Dylan was charmed. Logan wanted to be good at dating *for him*.

"And maybe it was a joke—or *Levi* thought it was a joke, but the thing is serious," Logan said. "I opened it up, and yeah, it's totally freaking serious."

"Well, let's do it."

"Excellent." Logan rubbed his hands together. "Go change into something more comfortable."

Dylan looked at his t-shirt and shorts. "More comfortable than this?"

"Well, at least . . ." Logan reached over and tugged up the hem of his shirt. "I don't want to make a mess."

"What are we doing on this date?" Dylan asked, mystified. "Finger painting?"

"Not exactly." Logan chuckled. He tugged over the open box and began to pull various bottles and containers out of the box, followed by a handful of printed cards. "We're gonna make our own mud mask treatment, and then ask each other what they call conversation starters, and then it's time for a foot soak."

"A foot soak? That sounds nice, actually," Dylan said, sighing happily. His feet *did* hurt. It was definitely all those kicks.

"But the mud mask is messy I bet, because . . ."

"Your childhood experience with mud?"

Logan laughed. "My number one rule: don't leave Levi alone with mud, *ever*."

"Well, good thing he isn't here," Dylan said. He picked up a container actually labeled "dried mud."

"It says here," Logan said, "that we're supposed to put on the mood playlist first."

"There's a mood playlist for mixing up a mud mask and smearing it all over each other?"

"It doesn't say anything in the instructions about smearing it on each other . . . but . . ." Logan's eyes lit. "I like that idea. A lot."

Logan had whipped out his phone and he found the playlist on Spotify, linking it in with the sound system scattered through the house, and the music began playing softly. With the lights turned down low in the kitchen, it was actually *almost* a little romantic.

Logan was definitely not as bad at this as he feared.

He read off the instruction card, and they mixed up the dried mud with water and with the salt exfoliant and the essential oils, only splashing a little of it on the counter and the floor.

"Shit," Logan said, as he scooped up a finger full of the mud, "it's fucking cold. Close your eyes. I don't trust myself not to accidentally get mud in them."

"Oh great," Dylan muttered, but he shut them. This, he realized, as he felt the first swipe of cold mud—and yes, it *was* cold—across his cheek, was more about trust than exfoliation.

"Almost done," Logan said, as he continued to paint his skin with the mud mixture.

"Wish I could see you, sticking your tongue out in concentration. Bet it's adorable," Dylan teased.

"Adorable, huh?" Dylan could hear the pleasure in Logan's voice. "You think I'm cute?"

"I thought it was kinda painfully obvious I find you totally irresistible," Dylan said wryly.

"Awww," Logan cooed. "There, you're done. Time for me."

Dylan could already feel the mud beginning to dry on his face, and when he opened his eyes, he could feel it crack a bit as his skin shifted. "How do I look?"

"Hot as hell," Logan proclaimed. "Now make me just as handsome as you."

Dylan scooped his fingers into the container of mud, and after Logan's eyes fluttered closed, began to smear it across his cheeks and forehead.

"You know," he said, "it might have been better to do this *after* you shaved."

"But you like my scruff."

And sue him, he totally did.

It reminded him exactly who he was kissing. Who he couldn't wait to get into his bed.

Not that he could ever mistake Logan for anyone else—there was such a distinctive way he kissed and touched Dylan and just plain *was*. Even if he was clean-shaven, Dylan could pick him out of a hundred people.

And it would be him he'd want, every single time.

"Just a little," Dylan teased, as he continued to spread the mud all over Logan's face. A plop of it fell to the counter, and Dylan laughed, scooping it up.

"What are you doing? Making a mess?"

"Yep. Totally. Channeling my inner Levi," Dylan retorted.

"If you were channeling your inner Levi, I'd open my eyes to a kitchen full of mud, and, babe," Logan said seriously, and Dylan's heart flipped, and then flopped, "you'd never do that to me."

"Oh, is that what we're doing now? Cute nicknames?" Dylan wiped the last of the mud across Logan's forehead. The mud on his cheeks was mostly dry, but Dylan still had to resist the urge to drop a kiss there.

"We're on a date, aren't we?"

Dylan laughed as he walked over to the sink to wash his hands. "Good point. How long are we supposed to keep these on, *babe*?"

Logan's smile was so wide, it cracked the mask. "Twenty minutes," he said. "Come back over, it's time for the conversation starters."

"I wasn't aware we needed help starting a conversation," Dylan teased.

"We don't, but . . . these are supposed to help us get to know each other better. Though . . ." Logan waggled his eyebrows, further splintering the drying mud on his face. "I like to think there's a better way to get to know you. You . . . naked . . . underneath me . . ."

Dylan would have to be a lot more exhausted for that image to not send a frisson of excitement up his spine. "I thought," he said, "we were supposed to be doing this *without* sex."

"Ugh," Logan groaned.

"Hey, that was *your* idea," Dylan reminded him. "You wanted to be good at this too."

"Well, how am I doing so far?" Logan asked in his most Texas drawl.

Dylan leaned across the counter. "So far so good. What about these questions you wanna ask me?"

"Okay, first one. And this is a doozy, so prepare yourself." Logan shot him a smirk. Which would've been adorable anyway, but it was extra endearing, because of the mud currently drying all over his face. "What's a very ordinary action that you find really attractive?"

"Huh." Dylan thought about this. "When you always use a glass for the milk, even though you desperately want to drink right out of the container."

"I promised you that first day, didn't I?" But the pleasure in Logan's eyes was so strong, Dylan could feel the warmth of his look from the other side of the counter.

"Actually, I believe you promised you wouldn't drink the last of the milk, a promise you didn't keep almost immediately . . . but I appreciate the effort to use a glass. Every time you do it, I almost jump you, it's so sexy."

"Because I use a glass and don't drink right out of the container?" Logan's voice was full of disbelief.

"Hey, it's because I know how much you *don't* want to, and that you're doing it only for me," Dylan said.

"True, true," Logan admitted. "And at first, because I didn't want you to leave."

"Now, *that* deserves a mud kiss," Dylan said, circling the counter and pressing his lips firmly against Logan's, despite the dried mud.

Logan's eyes were soft as he leaned back.

"What about you?" Dylan asked.

"God," Logan said quietly, "I don't even know where to begin. That you go to the grocery store, that you know where the mosquito lanterns are. That you laugh with Levi, when he calls. That you continue to tutor me in video games even though I suck, and we both know I'm never going to get better. That you introduced me to Han Solo, the Eighth Wonder of the Universe. None of those things should make me hot, but all of them do. Every single damn one."

"Eighth Wonder of the Universe, huh? Should I be jealous?"

"Never," Logan said and tugged him back, closer this time. Dylan put his chin on Logan's shoulder, trying not to get flakes of dried mud on his skin. Of course if he did, then he'd have to take a shower and so would Dylan and well . . . a naked and wet Logan could never, ever be bad.

"You say you're bad at this," Dylan said quietly, "but you're not. You make me feel safe, and you make me feel free. To be exactly who I am. No judgment."

"How can I judge?" Logan wondered. "When everything you do just makes me like you more?"

For a long moment, they just stood there together, Logan's arms encircled around Dylan's waist, Dylan's chin on Logan's shoulder. Then Dylan pulled back. "What's the next question?"

"Next question?"

"If you don't ask me the next question, I'm gonna drag you upstairs and into bed and that's before we even take all this mud off."

"Mud sex?" Logan sounded like he wasn't sure whether to be happy or dismayed by this possibility.

"Next question," Dylan said adopting a stern expression.

"Okay, this is a good one. What do you worry about the most?"

Dylan felt his insides freeze. There was no way that had cropped up on purpose. They'd gotten this stupid date box months ago. And it wasn't like Logan could have picked these questions.

"Uh . . . you go first," Dylan said.

Logan's gaze narrowed. "What's going on?"

"Nothing, I just have to think about the answer for a minute." Dylan was uncomfortably aware that he wasn't quite being honest. But he didn't want to lie either.

Logan looked skeptical. "Okay. My biggest worry? Uh . . . that we lose more games than we win. That Coach loses his job. That we all end up separated. I want to keep us together."

Logan's worry wasn't all that different than Dylan's own. But Dylan's had an extra fillip of additional shittiness to it. He didn't even want to think it, never mind say it out loud. But Logan had asked, and maybe, Dylan thought, he deserved to know.

"I worry about that too," he admitted. "But I guess my biggest worry is . . . well, more detailed."

Logan raised a mud-covered eyebrow. "More detailed than losing more games than we win and Coach losing his job and us all being separated?"

"I'm afraid that dating you has distracted me and made me a bad kicker." He said it really fast, so fast that maybe Logan wouldn't pick out each individual word and know what they all meant separately, never mind together. But Logan was so smart; it was one of the many reasons Dylan was crazy about him. He frowned.

"You think . . . you think *I* made you miss that kick in the last game?" Logan sounded incredulous. And yes, it was absolutely ludicrous. Dylan knew it, which is why he hadn't wanted to say it.

"No, no, of course I'm the one who missed it," Dylan said hurriedly.

"Then I'm not sure I understand."

"It's . . . it's a stupid superstitious thing. I admitted, to Coach Roger when he asked, what I was thinking about right before I missed, and well, he said kinda offhandedly that yeah, that was the thing that had changed. I was dating you now. I was rock solid before."

"And you'll be rock solid again. You missed *one* kick, Dylan. A freaking extra point."

"And some more in practice. Not a lot, but some."

Logan rolled his eyes. "What about you tying Bironas' record? You did that after we were dating."

"Not for real," Dylan said.

"But Coach Roger doesn't know that. As far as he knows, we've been dating for weeks."

But the issue wasn't *only* Coach's take on it; it was Dylan's own.

Logan's words were exactly what Dylan had both been hoping for and dreading—all at the same time. Cold, hard logic, which both made him feel better, and also worse.

"It's stupid, I know."

"No," Logan said, surprising the hell out of Dylan. "No, it's not. Football players are madly superstitious. I played with a guy in college who wouldn't change his cup all season long. Do you know the kind of smell he and *we* endured? It's better I don't even describe it. Football players can be really caught up in the details of things, but kickers? I know they're worse. Anyone can kick a ball and do it well a couple of times. You guys do it well *hundreds* of times, under the worst circumstances and the most insane pressure imaginable. So it tracks."

"I don't want to be that guy, though. The one who doesn't change his cup."

Logan cracked a smile. "Trust me, you would never take it that far. Now I know you're freakin' out about missing that kick and Coach Roger isn't helpin' you forget about it."

"Well . . . yes and no," Dylan admitted.

"Did you or did you not kick an extra fifty kicks after practice because you wanted to prove that you're just as good as promised?" Logan's voice was stern.

"A hundred, actually."

Logan frowned. "Listen, something I should have said before and I didn't . . . another unconventional thing that I find incredibly attractive about you? How good you are at your job, and how dedicated you are to being better. That's insanely hot."

Dylan couldn't help but smile. "Yeah?"

"Yeah. It's so hot that I sometimes get distracted when you kick, like, a clutch field goal in a game and I have to remind myself that this is not the time to drag you back into the tunnel and stick my hands down your pants."

"Now you see why I'm in trouble?" Dylan took a step back and began to pace in front of the island. "It's the same with me. You're so intense and focused and I . . ." Dylan froze, realizing what he'd just been about to confess. "And I like you so much," he finished. Awkwardly. *God, would Logan notice?*

Earlier, Logan had said, *How can I judge, when everything you do just makes me like you more?*

Like, he'd said. Not love.

But Dylan had just nearly slipped and said, *You're so intense and focused and I love you.*

Because he did. There was no question in his mind that it was one hundred percent love.

Was it love for Logan too? Dylan hoped so. Late at night, when Logan snored quietly next to him, Dylan believed that it was.

How could it be anything else?

"It's like," Logan said, a glimmer of a smile on his face, "you can see right into my brain. 'Cause it's the exact same for me."

Was it? God, Dylan hoped so.

"Come on," he said, reaching out and taking Dylan's hand. "Let's wash this awful mud off our face."

It took time, and they got more water and mud flecks around the sink than *into* the sink, but Dylan had to admit after he was finally clean that his skin felt good.

Logan must've thought so too, because he couldn't stop touching his face either.

"I didn't think it could be this soft," Logan marveled as they trooped upstairs with the packet labeled "Foot Soak."

"Isn't that supposed to be *my* line?" Dylan teased as they walked into Logan's enormous bathroom with its big tub.

"Well, if you feel like sending a compliment my way, I'm not gonna stop you," Logan said, eyes twinkling as he leaned in, plugging the tub and starting the water. "And don't worry, if you don't, I brought these."

He pulled the conversation starter cards out of his pocket.

Dylan groaned. "I hope all of them don't make me question my existence."

"They won't," Logan promised. Hesitated, when Dylan shot him a look. "I might've already read them."

"Studied them, more like," Dylan said, laughing. Amused, even though he shouldn't be.

"I wanted to make sure I had good answers! I wouldn't go into a game unprepared, especially if I wanted to win."

"Am I something you need to win?" Dylan asked archly.

Logan's gaze grew soft and he reached for Dylan's hands, squeezing them. "Not a game to beat, but someone to win *over*, yeah."

It was funny, or it would have been if Dylan's heart hadn't been melting a little bit further, because he'd been won over from practically the first moment.

Clearing his throat, Logan glanced away. "Oh, I think we need to put in the foot soak stuff now."

Dylan couldn't blame him for changing the subject and focusing on the tub and its rapidly filling contents. Logan had never had a serious relationship—or a relationship at all—and he was in new territory, and Dylan had never had a relationship like this either. He'd certainly never felt this way before, like it felt like every time Logan's heart beat, Dylan's couldn't help but beat, too, right with his. He'd dated, but it had never felt like this before.

"Now," Logan continued, "I think for this, it's better if we . . ." He slid down his shorts, and Dylan wasn't surprised to see he wasn't wearing anything underneath. He felt a burst of heat. But he couldn't help laughing either.

"You are so transparent," Dylan said, still chuckling as he followed suit, joining Logan on the edge of the tub, submerging his feet into the water. The water was hot and fragrant, and it did feel damn good.

"Time for another card," Logan said, interrupting the blissful silence. "Oh, this is a good one." He flashed Dylan a sly smile. "When we met, what was your first impression of me?"

Dylan rolled his eyes. "Are you sure these are the actual cards?"

"Swear to God," Logan said.

"Well," Dylan said, pretending that he was thinking hard. "I guess I thought, who is this idiot yahoo who wants me to go live with him even though I'm a stranger?"

Logan laughed and elbowed him in the side. "It's a good thing you're cute."

"Is that what you thought, the first time we met?" Dylan asked.

"Not the very first thought, but yeah. We were . . . uh . . . in the kitchen, I think. Having a beer, the night you moved in. And you looked over at me, and I thought, *oh shit, I think I'm in trouble.*"

"Did you really?" Dylan was delighted.

"Then you walked into the kitchen the next morning only wearing these little black shorts and I didn't just think I might be in trouble, I *knew* I was in trouble."

Dylan laughed.

"It wasn't that funny at the time," Logan grumbled.

"Oh, it is and it was," Dylan insisted. "'Cause it wasn't that much time after that I nearly dropped a weight on my foot because you were doing that horrible ab sequence."

"I remember that." Logan sounded awed. "That was because of *me?*"

"Yep. It was a real . . . uh . . . illuminating moment." Dylan paused. That night he'd been in the shower, trying for some private time between him and his dick, and the person he hadn't been able to stop thinking about was Logan. It might not have been the only time he'd come face to face with his growing attraction, but it had been one of the very first times. "But if we're talking very first impression . . . I felt like I was comfortable with you, and I didn't really understand why, but it felt . . . natural, I guess . . . to go home with you."

"It felt natural to ask, I asked before I even thought about it. You were sittin' in Kelly's office, and you looked up at me and I suggested it before I could even think it through. Like you said, it just felt right. Like you were supposed to be with me."

Dylan leaned over, resting his head on Logan's shoulder. "Secretly," he said, "you knew I was the only person on earth who would make you better at video games."

Logan chuckled. "Yeah, that was it."

"You needed *something*," Dylan said.

"You," Logan said, and Dylan turned his head and met Logan's mouth in a hot, sweet kiss.

He'd known before, less than hour ago, that it was love for him. The realization had come to him in a blinding flash of brilliance, but now he settled into it, the heat of it warming him all the way through.

And now he knew, without a single doubt in his head, that he'd needed Logan too.

Chapter Fifteen

"Simon," Logan said, clicking the accept call button on his phone. They were on the bus, heading to the hotel for their game in the Meadowlands the next day. "What's up?"

He could always tell when it was bad news. Simon always hesitated for a split second, giving away his qualms before he even spoke. And he knew, before Simon ever said a word, that it had to be about Ricky.

Logan reminded himself to tell Simon that he should never, ever play poker.

"After your email about Ricky, you know I reached out to his rep."

"Yeah," Logan said. "You said you did, and that you said there was nothing we could do, because he wasn't mentioning me by name. We even talked to that lawyer friend of yours."

"There *wasn't* anything we could do, until now."

"What happened?" Logan asked apprehensively. Next to him, he could feel Dylan tense.

"He approached us, through his agent, wants to meet with you personally, and then he agrees to stop mentioning the situation on his TikTok."

"The man fucking outed me by lamenting about his languishing TikTok career, and I'm not even gonna go into what he did to

Dylan, or all the other shit he's done after. And *now*, he wants to talk?"

Logan felt his temper begin to creep up on him.

Simon sighed again. "That's what he says he wants. A conversation. I suggested an NDA after that, and he didn't quibble."

"What does he even want? To apologize?" Logan gave a short bark of incredulous laughter. "I don't fucking think so."

Maybe he'd made his peace with how Ricky had outed him, because he'd had no other choice, but that didn't mean he was prepared to offer his forgiveness. Not after what he'd done to Logan and then all the bullshit he'd spouted about him afterwards.

"He didn't say what he wanted, but I did tell him you'd consider it."

"No," Logan said inexorably.

"Seriously, though, it's not a bad option. And if he does do it again, then we're covered. If we've got the NDA . . . we can sue the hell out of him if he takes a step out of line."

"No," Logan said again in an even harder voice.

Dylan glanced over, not only obviously interested because of what he'd said twice now, but probably *how* he'd said it.

"Logan," Simon said persuasively, "I think you should agree to meet with him."

"How many times do I have to say it? No. I won't do it. I'm not interested in whatever bullshit he has to say. He's said plenty already. All he's done since he outed me is talk."

Simon sighed. "Alright," he said with resignation. "I'll pass that along."

"And," Logan added, "tell him to stay away from me."

"I thought he was in Minneapolis?" Simon asked in confusion.

"He was supposed to be, but a bartender at one of my local clubs said he was in, asking about me."

"Hmmm," Simon said noncommittally. "If he *does* approach you, and gets belligerent, we could always put in for a restraining order."

"What I'm saying is he better not approach me at all. Pass that along, too."

Logan was not a violent person, but he was plenty pissed off. Why did Ricky keep fucking pushing him? He refused to be pushed into something he didn't want to do, but even his self-control had limits.

"Will do," Simon said. Then he changed the subject, injecting a purposefully cheerful note to his voice. "I hope you guys have a great game."

"We will. Comin' home with another W," Logan said, and after saying goodbye, hung up. Trying to take a few deep, calming breaths.

"Your agent?" Dylan guessed.

"Yeah," Logan said. "Wishin' me luck for tomorrow."

"He also called about Ricky, didn't he?"

"You shouldn't be this smart, you know. It's annoying."

Dylan shrugged. "It's not a huge leap. He's in Miami. That can't be a coincidence."

"It's not."

"He wants to talk to you," Dylan guessed.

"It's not happenin', even if he hadn't pulled all that other bullshit, it's still not happenin'." Logan knew how warm his gaze was, as it rested on Dylan. He was crazy about the guy, had never felt like this for any other person before. It was new and terrifying and exhilarating. "I don't know what he'd get out of it, talkin' to me. He's said plenty, hasn't he? And I've got nothing to say to him, at least nothing he'd want to hear. But I guess he told Simon that he'd sign an NDA if we met."

"And you don't want to do it, even to get that? Even to get him to stop talking about you?" Dylan asked, zero judgement in his voice.

"No." But Dylan was his guy; he deserved more of an answer than he'd given Simon. "It's not worth it," he said. "If it was you . . . maybe . . . but just for me? No way. He can hang himself with all his bullshit. It's not going to change anything. It's not going to win me back."

"I sort of got the impression he didn't have you before, before," Dylan said wryly.

And that was true, wasn't it? He'd never really given Ricky a chance. But then, before now, he'd never been interested or invested in turning any of the hookups he'd enjoyed into more.

"He didn't then and he doesn't now," Logan said with finality, not wanting to discuss it any further.

He couldn't deny that he was glad when the bus pulled up in front of the hotel less than five minutes later, and they were grabbing their stuff, and filing into the lobby, a group of them gathering in front of Kelly, who was giving out room keys and room numbers.

Rookies roomed together—and Kelly had long since learned it was better to put Wade and Tristan together—but veterans got their own rooms. Before they'd left for New York, Dylan had admitted to Logan he wanted to stay in his own room.

Logan couldn't say he exactly understood, because he'd discovered that he actually slept *better* with Dylan than without him, but he knew Dylan was trying to keep his focus laser-sharp, and if that meant sleeping alone the night before the game, then he was willing to give Dylan whatever space he needed.

"I thought," Tristan said, as they headed towards the bank of elevators, "that you two were practically inseparable these days."

He pointedly glanced down at the two different room numbers that Kelly had scrawled on their key cards.

"It's called focus," Logan said, before Dylan could attempt to defend his choices, "and you should try it sometime."

Wade, standing next to them, laughed, and Tristan shot him a dirty look.

"Who says a few exceptional orgasms don't keep my focus sharp?" Tristan teased.

"Please keep your exceptional orgasms away from my good night's sleep, okay?" Dylan said.

"Oh, Kelly learned her lesson. We're on a different floor now." Wade sounded both a little embarrassed about this, and also, at the same time, definitely a little bit proud.

"A blessing for the rest of us," Pax added dryly.

"She also learned not to put them on the coaches' floor. Remember the time they ended up next to Coach?"

"Oh, I do," Logan said, enjoying the flush that was currently creeping up Wade's neck.

"I think what I'm hearing," Tristan said, as the elevator doors opened with a ding, "is that y'all are jealous of how good a time Wade and I have."

"That is not what we're saying," Davis said with a chuckle, but Logan caught the split-second moment he glanced over at Pax.

The yearning in that glance.

The desire to keep the whole floor up all night.

And the resignation that it would never happen.

It passed between one blink and the next, but it was all there, and Logan felt not just sorry for him, but curious too. Wasn't there a way that maybe they *could* keep the whole floor up? Surely that dubious honor shouldn't entirely fall to Wade and Tristan?

But then Dylan poked him in the side as the floors ticked by. "You sure you're okay by yourself?" he asked quietly.

"I'll be fine," he said. And he would be. He understood Dylan's need to be alone, and while he'd miss him, he understood how important this game was. The Jets had only one loss this year, and were looking like stiff competition. They were all going to have to be at the top of their game to come out of this with a win.

"Okay." Dylan looked uncertain, but didn't say anything else.

The Piranhas held their walkthrough in one of the big ballrooms downstairs, then after, they had a big family-style dinner, and Coach dismissed them about ten, after a few last-minute positional meetings, to get a good night's rest, and be awake and alert early tomorrow, because the bus would be taking them to the stadium at ten, so they'd be ready for a one PM kickoff.

Dylan gave Logan a quick hug in the hallway, and a kiss that lingered, before setting off for his own room, a few doors down.

Logan let himself into his room, deciding that he'd take a hot shower and then relax in bed by finding a movie on TV.

He'd just settled into bed, the remote in his hand, when he heard a knock on the door. He glanced down, looking at his pair of gray boxer briefs.

Normally, he wouldn't answer the door nearly naked, but he had a feeling he already knew who it was.

And when he got up and opened the door, he wasn't wrong.

Dylan stood on the other side, a pair of loose shorts on, and a t-shirt he'd clearly thrown on, because it was inside out.

"Everything okay?" Logan asked, as Dylan walked in, and the door shut behind him.

"Yeah, yeah, it's fine," Dylan said impatiently. He was pacing around the room now, Logan watching as he nearly wore a path into the cheap hotel carpeting.

"It doesn't *seem* fine," Logan observed.

Sure, he'd hoped that Dylan *might* change his mind and end up in his bed after all, even if it was only to sleep, but he hadn't anticipated that Dylan would be so worked up about it.

Dylan stopped abruptly, in the middle of his path, and turned towards Logan. There was a wry look on his face, almost full of disbelief. "I can't believe I'm saying this," he said, and he *looked* like he couldn't believe it either, "but I think you should talk to Ricky. Hear him out."

"We already talked about this," Logan said. "I don't need to hear anything he has to say."

"No, you don't, but I think he has some things he needs to say to you."

Logan scoffed. "An apology? He can be sorry all he wants, but I'm not obligated to forgive him, after what he did to me, and *especially* after what he did to you."

Dylan rolled his eyes. "Yeah, after what he did to you, for sure, because he won't keep your name out of his mouth, but what did he do to me? All he did was make me realize sooner how much I liked you, how attracted I was to you, how *not straight* I was. So I guess that backfired on him."

"I guess it did." Logan couldn't say he felt bad about that.

"He was jealous. That's why he dragged me into it, and that's why he won't stop." Dylan continued pacing. "I was lying in bed, trying to fall asleep, and this thing, I couldn't stop thinking about it. I've thought about it before, a couple of times, but this time, it just wouldn't go away. I just felt like . . . I knew how he felt. And I thought you should know, that if you're not talking to him because of me, that's ridiculous and you should hear him out."

"It's not because of you," Logan said dryly, sitting down on the bed. He was pretty sure that was true. "It's because it's a waste of time. His and mine. And because I'm a little afraid I might just punch him in the face."

"Okay but . . ." Dylan turned, and he seemed to be bracing for something. "The thing I kept thinking was, *if I had you and lost you . . . would I be acting any differently?*"

"Except, he never had me," Logan reminded him. "And yes, you would be acting differently. You wouldn't have done anything that he did. You're . . . you're a good guy. A great guy. You're *Dylan*."

Dylan shot him a look, and it skewered Logan, right in the heart, right where guilt he felt over how he'd acted before rested. "Yeah, but love makes you do crazy things."

Logan stared.

"And no, I shouldn't be saying it like this, about him, in any kind of relation to him, but . . ."

Logan didn't let him finish. He stood up and caught Dylan on his pass by, tugging him into his arms and holding him tightly, not letting him move. Not letting him look away. "Did you just say that you love me?"

Dylan nodded, mutely, like he'd just lost his words.

"You love me and you think he might have too, and that makes you feel sorry for him, because he never got the chance."

Dylan nodded again.

Logan sighed. Happiness and a truly extraordinary joy flooded him, tinged with something else.

Guilt, that part of him yelled, *you feel guilty, because Dylan is right. You never gave Ricky a chance.*

"I understand why you feel that way, about Ricky," Logan said slowly, "and we're gonna talk about that . . . that other thing in a minute . . . but first I wanna say . . . I was never gonna fall for him. It just wasn't like that between us. We barely talked. With you? I can't *stop* talking to you. I wanted to *know* you, Dylan, and I've never felt that way before, never felt comfortable enough to open myself up like that. But with you, I did."

Dylan nodded a third time, his heart in his eyes.

"And as for the other thing . . ." He couldn't stop the smile anymore; the joy made it impossible, and the truth was, he didn't *want* to stop it. "I love you, too."

Dylan threw his arms around his neck and hugged him tightly. So tightly it felt like he might never let him go. And frankly, Logan was good with that.

"I love you so much, I didn't think I could, but I do, and it's you, it's only ever gonna be you," Logan whispered into Dylan's hair. "And I'm sorry for Ricky, truly I am, but I don't want to hear what he has to say. I . . . I just don't."

"Okay," Dylan said, pulling back, but only about an inch. Just enough he could look Logan right in the eye. He was glowing—as happy and relaxed as Logan had ever seen him. "Okay, that's your call, and I'll respect it and I'm sorry . . . sorry that I said it like that, when we were talking about Ricky . . ."

"Did you just apologize for telling me you love me?" Logan hadn't thought he could be more charmed, and yet, here he was, charm piled on more charm.

"I guess?" Dylan said sheepishly.

"Don't apologize for that," Logan said, and leaned in, kissing him firmly. For a long time. Until he was pretty sure if he played his cards right, Dylan wouldn't be going back to his own room tonight.

But then, Dylan pulled back. Reluctantly. But he still moved back a foot and then another. Right out of Logan's arms.

Logan had told himself that he wouldn't ask—that he definitely wouldn't beg, but in the end, he couldn't help himself.

"Stay," he said softly. "I want you to."

"What about tomorrow?" Dylan's gaze was serious.

"What about tomorrow? You're gonna go out and kick some extra points, and maybe a field goal, and we're gonna notch a win."

Dylan shot him a reprimanding look that shouldn't have made him hot—but it did. "You know it's not that easy. If it was, anyone could do it."

"I know. But I've got faith in you."

"And that," Dylan said, "means the world to me."

"We don't even have to have sex, though I'd hardly complain if we did, I just . . ." Logan hesitated. He'd never said this to another person before, but then he'd never told someone who wasn't a family member that he loved them either. "I just want you here with me. I just *feel* better when you're here."

Dylan's eyes lit up, and like a magnet being pulled towards its twin, he leaned in, one hand resting on Logan's shoulder. "I know how you feel," he said, "'cause I feel the same, but . . ."

"But?" Logan raised an eyebrow.

Dylan sighed. "I see you, and I'm . . . overwhelmed. There's no other word for it. I'm just flooded with emotions. And that? That is incredibly fucking distracting, even when I don't want it to be. Even when I try to block it out. So yeah . . . maybe I didn't miss that extra point because we started dating, but I let you get into my head, because I didn't want you to be anywhere else."

Logan didn't know what to say. He'd believed that Dylan's concern that he was a distraction wasn't all that serious. That it was all in his head, and it would pass. But maybe it wouldn't. And fear, the kind he'd never experienced before, not in any football game, not ever in practice, definitely not in any of those hookups he'd indulged in, began to weasel its way in.

"What are you saying?" he asked.

"I'm saying . . ." Dylan smiled, and just the ease of it, the way it lit up his face, helped banish a little of it. Dylan wasn't breaking up with him. He wasn't leaving him. He was just trying to explain to Logan how this had all affected him. "I'm saying that I need space. That's all. As much as I don't want to take it, I also want to win football games. And I want to play on this team. With you. So to do that . . ."

"You need your space. I get it." Logan understood. Didn't necessarily *like* it, but he couldn't help but understand. Football and this team mattered to him, too, and if it didn't matter to Dylan, if he didn't give a shit, then Logan had a feeling that he wouldn't have fallen for him the way he had.

"You," Dylan said, sliding his hand down, til it lay right over his heart, "are kinda the best."

That fear, Logan realized, was why people avoided relationships, because it was never going to entirely go away, not when he loved Dylan so completely, but it was also a really fucking good reminder to protect what he had and to cherish it.

"So I've heard," Logan said, grinning. "Come on, give me one more goodnight kiss, and then it's bedtime. I need my beauty sleep, don't I?"

Dylan tilted his head up, his mouth just a breath away from Logan's own. "Yeah," he said, and suddenly the air was thick between them. With love and want and a staggering kind of desire that Logan didn't know how to handle, either. Then when their lips met, it was like touching flame to bone-dry kindling.

Logan staggered back to the bed, Dylan grinding against him, their mouths moving together in one kiss that seemed to spin on and on, his hands reaching down and grabbing Dylan's glorious ass, pulling him hard against him.

They'd gotten off together in the shower this morning, with a long, lazy reciprocal hand job that had left him gasping when he'd finally come, but it felt right now like that was an eternity ago.

He'd loved Dylan yesterday, and the day before, and the day before that, and he'd known it was true, but he hadn't known that Dylan loved him, and that they fucking loved *each other*. The emotions swirling through him, when he touched him and Dylan touched him back, were so intense. And, well, he'd never been lucky enough to feel like this before.

Logan fell onto the edge of the bed and Dylan straddled him, fingernails digging into his shoulders, the bite of pain only making the pleasure more intense.

Dylan pulled back a fraction, pupils blown wide, breath coming in shallow pants, lips red and swollen. He looked so fucking hot and so fucking *his*, Logan nearly devoured him all over again. "I think," he said unsteadily, "that maybe we should have kept it to a kiss on the cheek."

Logan was hard as a rock in his loose boxer briefs, so turned on that it felt like all Dylan would have to do was reach in and wrap his hand around his cock and he'd lose it.

"Except that kiss on the cheek you gave me? That first day? Kept me up nights. Lots of nights."

Dylan grinned. "I'm not complaining, are you?"

Logan gave him a long, exaggerated thrust. Dylan moaned, throwing his head back as he ground against him. "Not in the least," he admitted, voice growing rough. "I just took a shower and I'm gonna make a mess."

Dylan's eyes were jewel-bright. "So am I." And he began to thrust more purposefully, and then their lips met again, and Logan was absolutely, one hundred and ten percent not proud of how intense it got, but Dylan stayed with him every step of the way, giving just as good as he got, and when he fell off the edge into a surprisingly intense orgasm, Dylan shaking above him at nearly the same time, he realized that he'd never been happier in his whole goddamned existence.

This, to make Dylan groan like that as his orgasm rocked through him, was as good a purpose in life as exceptional blocking and keeping his quarterback's jersey clean.

"I . . ." Logan's breath faltered. "I love you, you know."

Dylan smiled. He looked peaceful. As peaceful as one could look after they'd just come their brains out. "I do know. And," he added, brushing a kiss across his cheek, "I love you, too."

Dylan told himself that he was fine. That he was good.

After they'd cleaned up, he'd gone back to his room and hadn't given in to the extreme temptation to just curl into Logan's big, warm body and spend the night tucked up next to him. He'd left and walked back to his own cold, empty room, and had, surprisingly, fallen asleep quicker than he'd imagined he would.

He had his good night's sleep.

He'd had breakfast.

He felt focused and ready.

But now, standing on the sidelines, watching the offense begin to move down the field at the Meadowlands, he no longer felt quite as fine as he had before.

Uncertainty was creeping in.

He went back to his net, kicked two practice kicks and then a third, and shouldn't have felt relief surge through him as Wade broke out of his pattern, caught Pax's pass, and slammed right through the line into the end zone.

"You got this," Coach Roger said, clapping him on the back as he finished his last warmup and waited for the refs to call the touchdown official, so he could go out and kick the extra point.

He *did* have this—Coach was right. After all, how many of these had he kicked during the last week?

Way too damn many.

He knew Logan was out there somewhere, on the field, or milling around near the sideline, but he didn't look for him.

Didn't trust himself to.

After, he promised himself, as he jogged out onto the field for the extra-point try.

He got set, as he had done so many thousands of times in the past. Eyed the ribbons barely fluttering on the ends of the poles, knew he wouldn't have to compensate for much wind. Dug his back cleat into the ground, met the long snapper's eyes, and counted down, and then the moment the ball left his hands, swung his leg back and nailed the shit out of it, sending it sailing between the two uprights.

It was a picture-perfect kick, and Dylan didn't realize how much he'd not just wanted it, he'd *needed* it, needed the reminder of his own skill and conviction, until he saw it split the goal posts in half and felt a nearly savage thrill of success crest through him.

Logan was waiting for him on the sideline, a bit of hesitancy in his expression—like he wanted desperately to abide by the space that Dylan had said he needed, but he also wanted to tell him just how proud he was.

But he didn't need to, because the pride was unmistakable, shining in his eyes.

"Fucking awesome kick, babe," he said, slapping Dylan on the shoulder.

"Thanks, *babe*," Dylan retorted in a teasing voice.

"Knew you could do it," Logan said.

"Knew I could too," Dylan said with a grin, really *feeling* it now.

He turned away, to go back to his bubble by the net, and Coach Roger caught up to him.

"Great kick," Coach Roger crowed, sounding just about as pleased as Dylan felt.

"Felt good," Dylan said. "Felt real good."

"Well, you worked hard enough this week." Coach paused. "Just keep focused, okay? No more moony looks towards the offensive line bench."

Dylan rolled his eyes, but he couldn't argue with that assessment. Making this one kick had felt damn good, but he was going to need to do it again. And again. And again.

And he did, kicking three extra points for the Piranhas' three touchdowns.

The Jets couldn't get their own offense moving, because Sebastian was all over the field, disrupting plays, batting down balls, and double-teaming their best receiver along with Micah Rose.

As the clock ticked down into the fourth quarter, the Piranhas were still up twenty-one to three, and they had the ball, Pax moving the ball down the field confidently, really beginning, Dylan thought, to come into his own.

Davis was still pacing relentlessly on the sideline, but now, every once in awhile, he'd at least crack a smile when Pax threw a particularly sweet pass right into the teeth of the Jets' defense.

There was only thirty seconds left in the game when the offense finally came to a spluttering halt, around the thirty-eight-yard line.

It was a long field goal, and it would be his first try of the game. He glanced over at where Coach Roger was deep in a huddled consultation with Coach. He had a feeling that Coach was going to just punt the ball—but he hoped that Roger was in there, advocating for Dylan, hoping to give him the chance.

Dylan decided that if anyone was going to advocate for him, it was going to be *him*. He walked over, feeling purposeful.

"Coach," he said, "let me try it."

Coach glanced up at him. "Leonard, it's a fifty-three-yard try."

"I can do it," Dylan said stubbornly. He believed that he could. He kicked fifty-three-yarders—and longer—every practice. And even more, he'd kicked them in games, too. Only a couple of times, sure, but he'd still done it.

"Leonard," Coach said with resignation in his voice, "I know you can. I absolutely believe that you can, but I *need* you and your confidence to show up every Sunday. I don't want to jeopardize that."

"You won't, sir. I promise that."

Coach looked at him with a hard, penetrating stare. Dylan had been picked apart by coaches and team bigwigs for years, but he'd never experienced anything quite like Asa Dawson.

"What if you miss?" Coach asked archly, raising an eyebrow.

Next to him, Coach Roger looked shocked, like he couldn't quite believe that he'd asked that question. But this was Asa Dawson, and he did things differently. It was partly why he'd been so damn successful in Tennessee, and why he was trying to do the same thing in Miami.

He didn't always go the normal route. That opened him to criticism, especially when he lost, but then, he hadn't lost much in Tennessee. But the jury was still out in his Miami experiment.

"Uh, well, then I miss," Dylan said. Not sure how he should be answering the question.

"Are you gonna fall apart? Question your identity and your skill and your place on this team?"

Dylan considered this. "I don't know," he said, and that was the honest truth.

He wanted to say, *no, of course not*, but he also knew himself, and he knew the chaos missing the extra point last week had thrown his mind into.

Coach sighed. "I'm gonna regret this," he said, but then he was waving him onto the field. "Go give it a try," he added. "Ball's yours."

Dylan deliberately did not look around to see if Logan was watching. Didn't even let himself have even the slightest chance to get distracted by his big, sweet, mountain of a boyfriend.

"We doin' this?" Zach asked as he took one last kick into his net, and then headed onto the field for the attempt.

"We're doin' it," Dylan said firmly.

It was a long kick, and the angle was awkward. He thought, almost fleetingly, of the question Coach had asked. *What if you miss?*

If he missed . . . well, he'd go back to the drawing board.

He wouldn't take it personally—at least that was what he told himself before refocusing on the task at hand.

Checking the angle once, then twice, and then a third time. Then the wind. Unlike earlier, when it had been calm, it was all over the place, sending the ribbons fluttering one moment, and stilling them completely the next. This kick, even if it was shorter, would've been difficult, if only because the wind made everything unpredictable.

The ref blew the whistle, and when his foot connected with the ball, it felt good. Except that, in the end, it wasn't.

Dylan watched as the ball soared and missed the left upright by what must have been less than an inch.

He stared at it, at the trajectory, and wondered where he'd gone wrong.

Except he thought that maybe he already knew.

You asked yourself what would happen if you missed.

Chapter Sixteen

The thing about missing a fifty-three-yard field goal that had no impact on whether the Piranhas won or lost, was that it didn't matter much to anyone else except Dylan.

Nobody gave him the side eye, or kept their distance, or even mentioned it. In fact, Dylan thought grumpily as he packed up his stuff out of the locker, it felt like they'd all forgotten that he'd kicked it at all.

Winning erased a lot of ugly warts, that was for sure.

Logan leaned against the locker next to Dylan's. "You ready to go?"

"Yeah," Dylan said. He was more than ready to leave and forget what had happened here—which was stupid, because they'd won the game. He'd kicked three solid extra points, without even a moment of hesitation. But then that last kick had happened. A kick he'd encouraged Coach to let him make, even though Coach had clearly known it was a bad idea.

And it had been, Dylan realized. He'd gotten cocky. He'd become too sure of himself and his success, and in the end, it had come back and bitten him in the ass.

How often had he said, over the course of his football career, that it didn't matter how you kicked in practice, only how you kicked in the heat of the moment, when the entire game was riding on you?

He'd forgotten that, and it was his own fault.

The bus took them to the airport, and then they boarded. From the beginning, Logan and Dylan had shared a row. But every so often, he could see Logan glancing over at him. Unsure. Questioning. Wanting to say something, but not sure what to say.

Maybe he should just put his headphones on and watch something. Or take a nap. But he was too cranky to sleep. Annoyed with himself. Annoyed with Coach, who should've stopped him. Even a little bit annoyed with Logan, who kept hovering like he *wanted* to say something, but didn't.

They'd just reached altitude when Logan finally gave in.

"You know, the wind was all over the place," Logan said, "it's not your fault that it just barely missed. And fifty-four yards! That's a long-ass kick, babe."

Dylan shot him a look. Bless him, he was trying. And he loved him for that, but what he really wanted was silence so he could work through all this shit.

Because yes, he was feeling a *little* bit sorry for himself, and maybe he just needed some time to properly wallow.

"You a kicking expert now?" Dylan questioned.

Logan flushed. "No, no, of course not, but I . . . I don't want you to feel bad about it. You took a chance, took a shot, and sometimes . . . sometimes that doesn't work out."

"No, sometimes it doesn't," Dylan said. He didn't want to say that it didn't work out for guys like him—for *kickers*, specifically, or special teams guys, or players that hadn't been blessed with the perfect combination of physical attributes and skill and luck that pretty much guaranteed them a spot on the roster—because it wasn't Logan's fault that he was basically the epitome of all those things: the right size and shape, with the competitive mindset, and the intense agility, and on top of that, the luck that had seen him land with one NFL team, find success, and then land with another.

"You're beating yourself up about this," Logan said.

Clearly he didn't want to let this go.

"Can you just . . . let it lie, okay? It happened. I'm not happy about it, but I'll get over it."

"After you kill yourself in practice this week? Kicking God knows how many attempts? Letting Coach Roger boss you around, letting him make you feel like you're not worthy?" Logan's voice was arch. Dylan hadn't looked at him. Didn't want to see the sympathy in his eyes. He wanted Logan's love and his admiration, not his pity.

"I know what I'm capable of," Dylan said, not even bothering to try to hide his grumpiness. After all, Logan had spotted it anyway.

There were pros to falling in love with your best friend.

There was also one big fucking con—that it was nearly impossible to hide your bad mood from them.

"I know you're beatin' yourself up about that, but this was a solid team win," Logan said, lowering his voice, laying on the charm heavy and thick. And the accent too. Funny how Logan always sounded more from Texas when he was trying to get something he wanted.

"Yeah, it was." Dylan couldn't argue with that. Didn't want to argue about that. Frankly, he didn't want to argue with Logan about any of this. If Logan would just *stop*, then he wouldn't have to.

Finally, Logan seemed to sense that, because he fell silent. At least for five minutes. Then he spoke up again.

"You convinced Coach to let you try that, didn't you?"

"Why does it matter?" It didn't matter, because Coach had let him, and he'd let him down. Let *himself* down. He'd gotten his shot, and the wind or the angle or just his own doubt had blown it.

"It matters," Logan said firmly. He turned the tablet in his hands towards Dylan. "I think you should watch this, before you continue this whole pattern of blaming yourself."

On the screen was a video from a post-game press conference. Coach was sitting by himself at the table, with the pop-up Piranhas backdrop.

"What's this?" Dylan asked.

"Just watch," Logan said, and hit the play button in the middle of the screen.

Logan had turned the volume down, but the plane was pretty quiet, and he could hear Coach's voice clearly as he answered a question about Pax and the offense, running more efficiently. He glanced over at Logan, who just gave him a smile. "Just keep watching," he repeated.

Dylan rolled his eyes. "I don't know what . . ." But he stopped speaking abruptly, his attention suddenly caught by the next question that a reporter was asking Coach.

"Are you going to do anything about the Leonard situation?" the reporter asked. They were off-screen, but there was almost a smugness to their tone, like they couldn't wait to hear just how Coach was going to punish Dylan for missing the extra point last week and the field goal this week.

"Do anything?" Coach had a puzzled look on his face. "What would I do about it?"

"He's clearly a wreck, not capable of the high-stakes pressure of an NFL team," the reporter clarified, and Dylan couldn't help it, he cringed a little. Hitting pause on the screen he turned towards Logan. He'd had good intentions—Logan loved him and he wouldn't have anything else—but this *hurt*. He didn't want to hear other people talking about him like this, like the worst version of the insidious voice in his own head, telling him that he wouldn't be able to cut it.

"No," Logan said firmly, and hit play again. "Watch it."

Dylan rolled his eyes but he kept watching.

Coach visibly sighed on the screen, looking displeased. "I guess we're really doin' this, aren't we? Okay, let me be real clear. Crystal clear, so there's no confusion and I don't have to take any more of these stupid-ass questions. Dylan Leonard is a highly skilled kicker capable of play that lives up to and perhaps even exceeds the level that I expect from a Miami Piranhas player."

"But . . . he missed last week. Missed this week," the reporter interjected.

Dylan was surprised at the angry venom that suddenly flashed in Coach's eyes. Like the reporter hadn't just insulted Dylan, he'd insulted Coach, too, and every single one of the brain cells he held dear.

"Oh, so we're doin' *this* now, too. Okay. Let me be real clear, *again*. Yes, Dylan missed that extra-point kick last week. It was only the second time he's missed an extra-point kick between four years in college, at Michigan State, which is, I might remind y'all, a highly reputable institution that plays in the Big Ten, an exceptional, exceedingly competitive conference, and then during his three years with the Vegas Raiders. And yes, he missed today, but . . . y'all, that's on me. We could've punted, or even gone for it on fourth down. Pax was yellin' in my ear, begging for the chance to go for it. But I gave the ball to Dylan and I don't regret that. Not for a single second. But I do regret not sendin' him out there with a full boat of confidence. I questioned him." Coach sighed heavily. "I know better and I questioned him anyway. So if he missed today, it's not 'cause he's washed up or inconsistent or won't win us games 'cause he can't make the kicks. It's 'cause I underestimated him, right at the time when I shoulda been believing in him the most. Now that's my problem to fix, between Dylan and me, and we're gonna do it, so you don't have to worry about that. But what you should worry about . . ."

Dylan held his breath. Not sure he could even blink.

"What you should be worryin' about is what you're doin' to these guys. 'Cause what you're doin' is what you *shouldn't* be doin', which is underestimating them, the moment something doesn't go right. It's not just you, the media, houndin' on them for every little damn thing, it's the rest of this coaching community, having no faith and no loyalty, believin' that one special teams guy is just the same as another. The Riptide discarded Neal Fisher like he was trash, because he lost them the Super Bowl. One play, one kick, and he was out, even though he'd had a Hall of Fame career playin' for them. That was a goddamn shame, and let me tell you, I won't be doin' it here, not in Miami. Football is mental as much as it is physical, but you're eroding what gives these guys their confidence, day by day, game by game, by pickin' them apart. I won't let you do that with my team. 'Cause they're mine, my goddamn players, and the only person they need to have faith in, besides themselves, is me. So, no, no changes, no adjustments, no alterations. Dylan has my full support, and my full endorsement." Coach leaned forward, and even on the video, Dylan could see the laser focus of that gaze as it landed on each and every reporter at the press conference. Challenging each and every person who might have the nerve to reply. "Next question."

Logan plucked the tablet out of Dylan's hands and tucked it away. "So?" he asked.

But Dylan didn't know what to say. He'd been shocked, no doubt just like the rest of the sports media, into silence.

He knew Coach valued loyalty. That didn't come as a surprise.

But Coach's brand of loyalty was something he'd never experienced either in college or the NFL, and wasn't something he'd ever expected that he *would* experience.

It was thrilling and it was humbling and Coach's words helped Dylan see the mistakes they'd both made right before that kick.

Coach was right; he'd questioned his capability.

But Dylan had questioned his *own* capability. The moment he hadn't known how to answer Coach's question about if he missed, he should've told Coach to forget it. That he wasn't ready. That he wasn't focused.

He'd wanted to show off, but the mental prep, it just wasn't there.

"How did you know about this?" It must have *just* happened. How had Logan even known that Coach had said those things?

"Pax told me. Right after it happened. I guess he was next up at the press conference and he heard the whole damn thing. Said you could've heard a penny drop, it was so quiet." Logan chuckled. "I knew you had to see it, too."

"Coach asked me, just like he said, what would happen if I missed," Dylan said quietly. "He asked me if I'd freeze up after, if I'd question myself. I told him I didn't know. What I should have said—what I should have *believed* was that I wasn't going to miss."

"The wind . . ."

Dylan shook his head. "Yeah, it could've been a factor, but no, the problems started and ended with me not believing enough in myself. For doubting if I had enough focus. If I had believed I could do it, if I'd believed that I was ready and prepared, which I was, I wouldn't have had to go back to my own room."

"It was okay that you did." Logan was so goddamned supportive, it made Dylan want to weep.

"I know it was, but I shouldn't have had to. But . . ." Dylan heard the determination rise in his own voice. "But I'm gonna get there. I know I will."

"Obviously, my opinion on this means jack all, but you gotta know . . . I know you will, too," Logan said.

Dylan grinned. "I know."

"That," Logan said, relaxing back into his seat and slinging an arm around Dylan, tugging him close, "was a damn fine speech though."

"I think Coach missed his chance as an orator."

"Oh, no, he didn't. He's right where he needs to be," Logan said fervently.

He'd obviously won his boyfriend over big-time, when he'd supported Dylan, but it was more than just that.

So many coaches treated players like they were disposable pieces, that they could be moved around and replaced, sucked in and used up, all to get that precious Super Bowl win. But players were people too, and they deserved respect, no matter what.

It seemed, Dylan realized, that he had finally found a coach—and a man—who believed that.

Now he just had to believe it himself.

"I think," Sebastian said, as he looked around at the various players who'd gathered on this Monday evening, "that we should make this a weekly tradition after a win. Sushi and then drinks up here, just in time for the sunset."

"You do realize, in December and January, that means we're gonna be eating at like four in the afternoon, right?" Beau said, nudging his boyfriend, who started laughing. Logan slung an arm around Dylan and pulled him close.

They'd started the day by sleeping in, and then eating a late breakfast, interrupted by a pair of what Logan considered truly exceptional orgasms, and then he'd even gone to the store with Dylan.

Dylan hadn't said anything, but the knowing gleam in his eye had told Logan that he'd realized just what he was trying to do: distract him from the way he'd missed that field goal yesterday.

"Yep." Sebastian sounded like he didn't give a shit. "We win, we gonna celebrate. I don't care if it's two in the afternoon."

"I love the optimism," Pax said. "Winning in December and January. Sounds great to me." His tone was wistful. This was Pax's second season, and during the first, they'd lost nearly every single game, including a ten-game losing streak on the back end that had led to the head coach and all the front office staff losing their jobs.

Pax didn't talk much about what that season had felt like, but Logan knew it must have been brutal.

He and Davis were similar that way; they didn't talk about their pain, they just buried it.

The quarterback who'd replaced Davis was set to be arraigned in a few weeks for beating and nearly killing his wife and several other women, and you'd never know from Davis' stoic poker face that it affected him at all, but Logan knew it had to. If it had been him in that position, he'd have been so incredibly pissed off that it would've been painfully obvious. And maybe Davis *was* angry, but just like Pax, he pretended that anger didn't exist.

When Davis' team had rejected him and insisted on signing the asshole for a ridiculous amount of money, there'd already been swirling rumors of what kind of person he was. Just about everyone had known about the abuse, and they hadn't cared, because they were blinded by the shine on a potential Vince Lombardi trophy. They hadn't cared either that they'd destroyed Davis' reputation in the process. After the hack job they'd done to him, no other team had wanted him, and he'd ended up retiring early. And Logan knew that no team had ever called him again, not until Coach Dawson had offered him the quarterback coach's job.

But again, sitting here with Pax, set a little ways apart, like he always was, obvious affection for his quarterback in his eyes, you'd never guess how shitty the hand he'd been dealt was.

In different ways, Logan thought, glancing around the group, they'd all been hurt, and were recovering, finding a new opportunity here in Miami, with the Piranhas.

Nobody had thought Sebastian could play corner anymore, and teams had passed on him, until Beau had decided that he'd make a great safety.

And Beau? If Logan had a twenty-dollar bill for every time someone brought up his homosexuality, wondering why his Southern-famous father hadn't kicked him out at seventeen, when he'd come out, or made some snide comment about how his brilliance was actually nepotism, he'd be rich.

Dylan had been traded to the Piranhas by a team that hadn't really wanted him either; they'd been enamored of someone younger and more exciting.

Logan had wanted out of Minnesota, lured by the freedom that Miami promised.

Tristan had fallen pretty far in the NFL draft because too many teams had considered his social media presence and his LGBTQA+ outreach a liability.

Coach had gathered them together here, and it reminded Logan of what he'd said yesterday.

'Cause they're mine, my goddamn players, and the only person they need to have faith in, besides themselves, is me.

Logan knew then, that even if they didn't win in December and January, even if they didn't make the playoffs or win the division, it didn't matter, because this team was special anyway. Not because of their individual parts, but because of the whole, because of what they made together. Coach had designed it that way.

"Can we win in December and January?" Beau grinned. "Absolutely. And it's gonna happen. 'Cause we're gonna make sure of it."

A cheer went up from the group. Logan stood, stretching out his stiff legs. "Hey, anyone need anything?" he asked.

There were a handful of nods, and Logan went over to the bar to order the drinks, as well as to get another couple of beers for him and Dylan.

Even though they'd just come from the sushi restaurant that Sea Bass had introduced them to, Logan glanced over at the menu on the counter, wondering if he should order some appetizers for the group. None of them had driven—there were so many horror stories about athletes and alcohol and getting behind a wheel—but it wouldn't hurt to soak up the beer he was currently ordering.

"Can't go wrong with an order of mozzarella sticks," a voice from the past said.

Logan knew before he even looked up who it was going to be.

His white-blond hair was shaded orange and pink and purple in the setting sun, and he looked undeniably good, as much as Logan wished he looked otherwise.

Logan even remembered when he'd found him attractive.

But no more.

He'd burned that bridge, and then salted the ground behind him.

"Ricky. I thought I warned you to stay away," he said coldly. He'd thought if he ever ran into Ricky, he wouldn't want him to know how angry he'd been, how infuriating his behavior had made him, how much of a betrayal his outing had been. But now, he discovered that he didn't give a shit. He wanted to grab Dylan and get out of here. Pull every string he could to keep him away. Lean on him until he buckled. Broke.

"I've been trying to find you," Ricky said, tilting his head and shooting Logan that flirtatious half-smile that had used to work him up. He'd almost forgotten about it, like he'd nearly forgotten about Ricky, after he'd left Minneapolis.

Now, right along with the anger, there was the guilt. Right on schedule.

He knew he shouldn't feel it. Ricky had paid him back in spades for whatever he'd done to him—or whatever he *hadn't* done. But he still looked back on his time before, all the relationships he hadn't had, hadn't pursued, all

"I know," Logan said with a hard voice.

"You come here a lot. Kind of like that bar in Minneapolis . . ."

But Logan didn't want to reminisce, he didn't want to swap old stories, he had zero interest in being nostalgic over a time when he hadn't really been happy.

He'd been making time until he could *really* be happy.

Was that Ricky's fault? Not really. But it sure was Ricky's fault that he'd outed him. Sure was Ricky's fault that he'd badmouthed him constantly, ever since he'd decided his career was more important than whatever they'd shared, even if it had only been sex.

"I don't want to talk about it, and I don't want to talk to you. I thought I'd made that clear," Logan said.

Ricky looked surprised.

Because of course he did.

"What?" Logan retorted. "You thought I'd see you again, and like . . . not be able to help myself? Fall at your feet and grovel maybe? After outing me, and then all the shit you said about me afterwards? And for what, to help your career?"

"You weren't paying attention to me," Ricky said low and agonized, through clenched teeth.

"Yeah, well, that's what happens when you break up. Except that we didn't do that, did we? We just stopped hooking up. It ended. It happens."

Ricky opened his mouth and snapped it shut again. "Fine," he said. "If you want to do it this way, *fine*. You never listened to me. You never listened to what *I* wanted."

That was true. But it also hadn't been what Logan wanted, and listening wouldn't have made a damn bit of difference.

"So you decided, what the hell, why not punish me for not wanting what you did?" Logan felt his anger, the anger that he'd tried for so many weeks to push down, to ignore, to pretend didn't exist, because it didn't change a fucking thing, swirl to the surface. "And not just that, let's continue to talk shit, and spread bullshit rumors, not just about me, but about my new guy?"

"You weren't going to get back together with me, so I figured, why not get something out of it," Ricky said petulantly. Clearly proving that he'd learned nothing. That he'd never been the guy who Logan should've been with, anyway. No matter how he'd felt about him.

Logan snapped.

He took a step closer and then another. Pressed Ricky against a barstool. He was *much* bigger than Ricky, had inches on him and at least a hundred pounds of muscle. "Why not throw me under the fucking bus, huh?" Logan said in a voice he recognized as dangerous. To Ricky. To himself.

"Hey, everything okay over here?"

Of course Dylan had come over to see what was wrong.

He didn't want them to meet; he didn't want Dylan tainted by Ricky's avarice.

But then he realized that it didn't matter, because there was no way that Dylan could ever be like Ricky. Even though he'd claimed that love could make you do crazy things, it wouldn't ever make Dylan act like Ricky.

Logan tilted his head. "Ricky was just leaving."

"Doesn't look like he's leaving," Dylan observed calmly.

Ricky struggled just a little, but Logan had him trapped, and he couldn't escape.

"I'm trying to make sure he understands that he's leaving, and he's gonna keep my name and *your* name out of his mouth going forward."

"But . . ." Ricky struggled again. "I haven't actually said . . ."

Logan had never seen Dylan's face morph into something so hard and uncompromising but it did now. "You said enough."

"Any promises you make aren't worth shit, but when my agent sends over an NDA next week, I expect you to sign it," Logan said.

Ricky shot him a disbelieving look. "But . . ."

"No," Dylan insisted. "You're gonna sign it. If you want to be famous, you're gonna do it some other way."

"I don't know why I should even listen to you," Ricky sneered. "I don't *have* to do anything."

"You *owe* him," Dylan said. "You owe him your silence, because you outed him against his will, before he was ready. That was really shitty, no matter how you felt about him."

Logan watched as regret flashed across Ricky's face—it was just a second, almost too quick to see, but he saw it, and the anger he'd been holding on to ever since Simon had woken him way too early that Tuesday morning all those weeks back finally evaporated.

Leaving him feeling empty and disgusted. With Ricky. And a little bit with himself.

He let him go.

Ricky shook it off.

He hadn't agreed to sign anything, but Logan decided he didn't give a shit anymore. Ricky was a bug, and he'd just been squashed. Even if he kept screaming about him, it didn't matter anymore.

Ricky turned to go, but then, suddenly, fear bloomed across his face.

Logan looked over, and there were the other guys approaching, and they all looked really pissed off.

"You must be Ricky," Sebastian drawled. His body language was relaxed, but Ricky tensed when he said his name.

"That's me," he said.

"I thought so," Sebastian said. "Though I told Tristan over here, that it couldn't possibly be you, because you'd never be stupid enough to show your face here."

"I would?" Ricky didn't stutter but it seemed like a near thing. His skin had gone pasty gray. Sebastian could be intimidating as hell when he wanted to be, and he was working every inch of that right now.

For *Logan.*

"Yeah," Tristan said, stepping up. "Because you had to know that we protect our own, and we're plenty pissed that you keep fucking him over."

"That wasn't the plan," Ricky argued.

"No," Beau said, "I'm sure the plan was to make him regret ending things with you, and make him want you back, but you realized pretty damn quick that wasn't going to happen, didn't you? And then it didn't matter, so you decided to take whatever attention you *could* get."

"Guess what, that was real shitty," Wade said gravely.

Ricky glanced from one guy to the next, all the way down the line.

"Here's the thing," Pax added. He was the quietest of them, but his voice was as frigid and judgmental as Logan had ever heard it, "we don't take it well when you fuck one of us over. It's like you've fucked all of us over. You want to do that, Ricky?"

Logan saw Ricky's Adam's apple bob as he swallowed hard. "No."

"I didn't think so," Pax said with satisfaction.

"I'll . . . I'll . . . anything you want, I'll sign it."

"That's what I thought," Dylan said.

"If we find out that you didn't sign anything or you keep blabbing . . ." Beau let his voice trail off. It was hard to re-member sometimes that he was his father's son, but it was right there, in between the space of every word, the threat of it. Logan had learned that's how Coach did things; he used the threat, sometimes he didn't even say it out loud, because the threat alone was enough.

And it was enough for Beau, too, because Ricky seemed to visibly shake with the impact of it.

"I won't, I won't, I swear," Ricky said, tone vehement.

"Except," Sebastian said, "that your word isn't worth shit. But I guess we don't have a choice."

"I fucked up, I know, I just . . ." Ricky's voice broke. He glanced over at Logan, and he'd have to be made of stone to not feel a pulse of guilt at the anguish, finally visible, in that look.

"I get it, it would really suck to lose him," Dylan said, and for the first time, he sounded a tiny bit sympathetic.

But not all that sympathetic.

"Yes," Ricky said. "But I loved . . ."

"But that doesn't excuse what you did or how you did it," Dylan interrupted. "And if you really loved him, you wouldn't have said any of that shit about him in the first place."

"That's not love," Wade agreed quietly.

"Just sign the NDA," Logan said, stepping in between Ricky and the rest of them. They'd made their point. Maybe Ricky had driven over him and then backed up and down him a few times for good measure, but they didn't need to do that to him. They didn't need to stoop to his level.

"I will," Ricky said. "And . . . God, I really am sorry. I shouldn't have . . ."

"No, you shouldn't have," Logan said. He forgave him, but that didn't mean he had to give Ricky the satisfaction of saying it out loud.

"I guess . . . I guess this is goodbye."

"Yes," Logan said, but he didn't really believe it was, not until the last of Ricky's blond hair disappeared down the stairs.

"Well, that was real dramatic," Tristan said, hopping on a barstool. "Anyone else parched after that little demonstration?"

Dylan tucked himself under his arm. "You okay?" he asked quietly.

Logan nodded, and discovered, to his own surprise, that yes, he was. The anger was gone, and with it, the guilt. He'd settled what he'd needed to with Ricky, and he didn't really think he'd be bothering any of them again.

He might be selfish, but he wasn't stupid.

"How did any of you know?"

"Oh, we've been keeping an eye on him," Tristan said knowingly. "A real close eye."

"I had to stop him from using our TikTok to go after him," Wade said.

"I just wanted to set the record straight," Tristan insisted.

"You were gone so long, well, we knew something had happened, and Dylan was still with us, so we knew you hadn't snuck off to a dark corner for a quickie, like Tristan and Wade . . ."

"Hey," Dylan said, after they'd gathered the drinks Logan had ordered and were carrying them back to the table, "we're not Tristan and Wade, okay? We can control ourselves."

"I don't know about that," Logan said, leaning down and pressing a long, lingering kiss onto Dylan's cheek as the group laughed. "Let's not make any promises we can't keep."

"That sounds about right," Dylan said.

"And seriously, guys . . . thank you. I thought I didn't need that, but I kinda did, I think." Logan glanced around the group as they all smiled at him. They were his teammates. His friends. His *brothers*. He'd never thought he wanted more of those, but then he'd met these guys and they'd slotted themselves into his life, like they were always meant to be there.

And Dylan?

His best friend *and* the love of his life.

He'd been so lucky to get him, and for that alone, Ricky hadn't deserved his fist in his face.

"You did," Tristan said staunchly. "His trap needed shut."

"Yep, and we were happy to do it," Pax added.

"He had it coming," Sebastian said. "And so did you, because you're our friend, our brother, you know?"

"Yeah, I know," Logan said, smiling because he *did* know it.

CHAPTER SEVENTEEN

It was Wednesday morning, early still, and Dylan knew where he'd find Coach.

In his office, bent over his laptop or his tablet, hard at work on next week's game plan.

"I'll meet you in a few," Dylan told Logan as they parted in front of the weight room.

He'd wanted to talk to Coach Tuesday, the first day back in the facility after the game *and* after the speech he'd made at the press conference, but since he'd become friends with Beau, he'd learned what Tuesday mornings were like for Coach and his staff.

Sometimes they went over every play of the game, in slow motion, breaking everything down, looking for ways to improve, new ideas to try, plays that weren't working that needed to be tweaked or discarded entirely.

So yesterday he wouldn't have been able to catch Coach by himself. But today . . . today he could, if he got to his office early enough.

Sure enough, when Dylan walked around the corner, the door to Coach's office was open, like it always was when he wasn't in meetings, and he was bent over his desk, intently studying something on his tablet.

He knocked on the edge of the doorframe. "Hey, Coach?"

Coach glanced up. He had, from the very beginning, instituted an open-door policy. If his door was open, you were free to come talk to him about anything. "Dylan," he said warmly, a smile lighting up his face. "Come in. I was hoping I'd be able to catch you this week."

Dylan walked in and took a chair opposite Coach's. "I just wanted to say that I really appreciate, more than you know, what you said in the press conference after the game."

"Of course I support you. I traded for you. I wouldn't have done that if I didn't have faith in spades," Coach said wryly, leaning back in his chair.

"Not just that," Dylan said, "but the rest of it, too. About the NFL chewing players up and spitting them out when they don't perform perfectly. The stuff you said about Neal Fisher. They want us to be confident but do everything they can to erode that confidence, every day."

"They do, and it's a damn shame," Coach said, nodding.

"You've never done that."

"Except I did," Coach retorted, kindly. "The moment you needed me to believe in you, I questioned you. I know how the kicking game works. I know how it's five percent physical, ninety-five percent mental. And I killed your confidence, right before you went out there. I'm sorry for that, Dylan."

Dylan considered the apology. Truly considered accepting it because he believed that Coach meant it, meant every word of it. But then he shook his head, because even if he had done exactly what he said, Coach wasn't responsible for him and his actions.

"No," Dylan said. "Maybe no, don't say that again, because it didn't help, but I didn't believe I could do it before I went out there. I was all twisted up, trying to *be* confident, and I forgot to just . . . be confident. I kept looking for ways to make myself that way, to believe I could do it, when all along, I should've just *known*."

Coach tilted his head, clearly considering this. "Why?" he asked. It was one of his favorite questions, so Dylan should've seen it coming.

"I thought . . ." God, it was hard to admit this. Hard to admit this to himself, even. Harder still to admit this to a man he greatly admired and respected. "I thought I'd let myself get distracted. By Logan."

Coach's smile was unexpected. "Am I allowed to say I'm not surprised?"

"Yes, because I think . . . I think you give that speech for a reason. You make it jovial and kind, and you make us think that you'd never believe we'd actually let a relationship get in the way of how we play on the field, but you're still saying it, aren't you?"

Dylan had thought a lot about this during the last few nights, ever since the press conference. And he thought he'd figured it out.

Coach got up and stretched his legs. He was still tall and fit, and while his dark hair might be graying a bit at the temples, Dylan realized when he looked at Asa, he didn't *feel* old. He still felt young and hungry.

"I say it because I know it happens," Coach said. "I know just how hard it is for love not to get in the way."

Of course he would. Beau hadn't just sprung out of thin air. Coach had been married, a long time ago. Before he'd even gone to Tennessee to coach, if Dylan remembered his Wikipedia history right. When he'd been traded to the Piranhas, he'd looked up every bit he could on his new coach—and the brilliant, and jovial but lonely image he'd put together in his mind had felt pretty accurate once he'd met Asa Dawson. In so many ways, it had always been him and Beau, against the world.

"When I was at Tennessee . . ." Coach continued, and then trailed off, a wry smile on his face. "Well, that's ancient history, but there was someone I'd have thrown everything away for. It would've been a stupid-ass decision, so I'm glad I didn't, but at the time . . . man, I could've given a shit what happened on the football field, even though it was *my* football field, and what we did on it mattered a whole goddamn lot. I knew it, but I let the wanting of it tempt me away from it. For a time."

It dawned on Dylan, watching nostalgia and regret and maybe even the remnants of love, of a different, happier time, flash across Asa's face, that who he was talking about couldn't be Beau's mother. She'd been gone, off in New York, when Coach was at Tennessee. At least according to Beau and to Wikipedia.

Dylan wondered if Beau knew about his father's failed love affair.

And, because one of his flaws was curiosity, he couldn't help but wonder who it had been.

"I'm not going to let that happen. Not anymore," Dylan said firmly. Even though what he really wanted was to ask who it had been and why it had clearly ended so terribly. Relationships ended for so many reasons, but Dylan had a feeling that Asa's hadn't ended because he hadn't been in love.

He had been, and from the look on his face, Dylan thought he might still be carrying it with him now. Even still.

Dylan knew then that he didn't want to feel like this in a year or in five or in fifteen. He was going to do everything he could to keep Logan close, and, he realized, the thing that would destroy their relationship faster than anything was him losing his focus and letting Logan distract him. He'd end up resenting him, not loving him, and that would erode away everything they'd built together.

"It's about, if you don't mind the advice, finding the balance," Coach said, resting a hip on the edge of his desk.

Like he knew just what Dylan was thinking, and knew just what he'd needed to hear.

"What do you mean?" Dylan asked.

"I mean . . ." Coach's smile was kind. Understanding. "You're never *not* gonna have him in your thoughts. You can't push him out entirely. So . . . find the balance. Find the way he and football can peacefully co-exist."

"You think they can?"

Coach nodded emphatically. "I do. Course, I never got there, but that doesn't mean you can't, Dylan. You've got a strong will and plenty of determination. I wouldn't bet against you. How many times have they counted you out? Ruled you down? You never accepted any of that. Not once."

He hadn't, Dylan realized. They'd been rejecting him and, like Coach said, counting him out, every single year. He wasn't big enough. He wasn't tall enough. He wasn't strong enough. He didn't kick long enough. He'd jumped from team tryout to team tryout after college, six of them in total, before he'd finally landed with the Raiders, who had then turned and moved on only three years later. But he'd never wavered, Dylan realized, he still knew exactly who he was and what he wanted.

And what he was going to do next time he jogged onto the field.

He tilted his chin up. "No," he said, agreeing with Coach, "I never did."

"And you won't." Coach's tone was kind—but oh, it was firm. Like he was telling Dylan that he believed in him without ever saying the words. Though, Dylan thought, he'd said those too, at the press conference.

Those had been for the reporters.

But this was for him, and he understood, more than Dylan had even realized, that the person who needed to believe in him wasn't him, or Logan, or Coach Roger, or any of his teammates and friends—but *him*.

Nobody could do that but Dylan himself.

"No, I won't," Dylan said, and finally, for the first time in what felt like months, he truly believed it. The ice-cold certainty not of perfection, but of belief.

Coach's face broke into a warm, genuine smile. He stood and patted Dylan on the shoulder. "Givin' up isn't in your DNA, Leonard. Just remember that."

"I will."

And he would. Dylan had a feeling this conversation would linger for awhile. He'd parse it out, think it over when he couldn't sleep, and he'd return to it whenever he felt even the slightest chance that he might waver.

That wasn't all though, as he said his goodbye to Coach, and made his way deeper into the practice facility, heading towards the locker room to get changed for practice. He'd think about what Coach said and *how* he said it, and how he seemed to know just how Dylan was feeling.

He'd wonder, Dylan knew, because he knew himself, just how that was possible.

And he'd wonder what stories he was keeping hidden.

"Shit, that practice sucked," Logan said, giving his back one final stretch as he leaned over the bench in front of his locker, bracing his palms against it.

"No fucking joke," Rob said, from the other side of the room.

It had been brutal. Hot, for the beginning of November, and the coaches, feeling buoyed by their 5–3 record, had been focused and determined to wring the most out of the players that they could.

But even though it had been indisputably rough, Kenyon and Tristan were still shaking their towel-clad hips to whatever song was playing through the overhead speakers. They looked like they were about ten seconds away from launching into a full dance-off. Pax was eyeing them both with fond amusement, and Davis had claimed the big recliner in the middle of the room, his plastic-laminated play card resting on top of his face as he tried to grab a quick nap.

Logan groaned as he pulled his briefs up and threw on a t-shirt.

Dylan walked in from the field then, flashing him the kind of bright smile that had won him over from the very beginning and now made his whole chest expand with love and affection. It was amazing, feeling this way. Terrifying too, but mostly amazing. Now he knew why nobody who felt this way ever wanted to keep it a secret.

"Hey, you look tired," Dylan said, sitting down on the bench, and prying off his cleats. He pulled off his tank and Logan told himself that he was absolutely worn out, too worn out to be even the tiniest bit aroused by seeing Dylan's naked body.

But yeah, that was the other thing about love. It was hungry. And it felt like, no matter the circumstances, he was always hungry for Dylan.

Since he'd met with Coach a few days ago, he'd been more settled, happier, more quietly confident, and nobody was happier for him than Logan.

"I think I need some beauty rest," Logan said, not too tired to smile at his boyfriend. "Maybe a nap when we get home?"

Dylan smirked. "Is it really a nap if we're both in bed and both naked?"

Tristan tossed a wet towel in their direction. It landed in front of Logan with a wet *plop*. "And you say Wade and I are terrible," he called out in a teasing voice.

"You and Wade *are* terrible," Pax retorted.

"Yeah, it's just mean to rub our faces in all the orgasms you're having that we're not," Davis said.

Logan was looking for it, so he noticed how Pax's tanned face flushed even darker when Davis said the word *orgasms*.

Probably the exact way he'd have looked if Dylan had said it. Probably the exact same way he'd look *now* if Dylan was stupid enough to use the word *orgasms* around him.

But Dylan was brilliant and knew him, and knew better than to deploy that particular word unless actual orgasms were soon to follow.

Logan's phone beeped, and he glanced down. He'd put some social media accounts, the ones that tended to break big NFL news, on alert. And he noticed, as he looked at the screen, that he wasn't the only one because suddenly it seemed like the whole room had gone quiet and most of them were looking down at their phones.

During Tom Taylor arraignment, the headline read, **charges dropped.**

Logan swallowed. Tom Taylor was the quarterback who'd replaced Davis on the Charleston Condors. Who'd been known, by just about everyone, as the guy who beat his wife. And his girlfriend. And his mistress.

Several of the women, ones he'd apparently discarded, had finally banded together and filed charges against him. But that hadn't mattered at all to the Condors. Even though they'd had a totally solid franchise QB in Davis, they'd pursued Taylor, and signed him, giving him an absolutely ridiculous amount of guaranteed money.

Making every other team in the NFL wonder what was wrong with Davis Abernathy.

Now, Taylor wasn't even going to face a judge and jury.

Logan clicked on the article, and saw that the women, no doubt under insane pressure by the media and certainly by Taylor and his legal team, had recanted their story.

He'd just finished reading through the article, and looking up, met Dylan's concerned gaze. He'd read it too, then.

This was absolute bullshit, and he'd be angry if he didn't even *know* Davis Abernathy, but he did, and he was extra super-duper pissed off because none of this was fair.

Sure, professional football wasn't fair, but at the very least Taylor should've had to answer for his crimes—not be rewarded for them.

"Davis." Pax's voice was low. Concerned.

Logan looked over to where Davis was sitting in the recliner. He'd moved. Now he was hunched over, head nearly in his hands and Logan realized that he was making some kind of choked noises. Like he couldn't quite breathe.

Like he didn't even *want* to breathe. Like it was being pulled out of him one labored gasp at a time.

"Davis," Pax said a little more sharply, and Logan looked closer, realized he was trembling. *Shaking.* His phone fell out of his hand

and hit the floor, breaking the silence that had fallen over the room.

They all knew the story. Knew Davis. Knew just how he'd been fucked over.

"He was supposed . . ." Davis' voice shook and then cracked. "He was supposed to fucking *pay*."

"I know, I know," Pax said, and suddenly, he was kneeling on the floor in front of Davis, his head tipped up towards him. "I know."

"He needs to *pay*," Davis repeated, breathing still coming in fits and starts, the heaviness of it loud in the silent room. Someone, maybe Tristan, had turned the music off. Everyone was staring, right at where their quarterback sat at the feet of his coach.

Logan had a feeling that Davis didn't want Taylor just to pay for what he'd done to those women—which was definitely worth it, on its own—but to pay for the way he'd tangentially ruined his career.

Pax laid a hand, so fucking gentle, on Davis' back. The other on his knee. Tipped his head even closer to Davis' own, their foreheads nearly touching. Logan nearly looked away. It was too much. Two people who shouldn't be intimate but clearly were. It felt like they were all looking in on a far too private moment.

Davis' breathing got more difficult, more forced, the sound of him nearly choking too loud in the awkward silence.

"It's okay, I need you to breathe, I need you to look at me, and I need you to breathe," Pax said quietly. Firmly. "Look at me, Davis. Just at me. That's right. It's just you and me."

Logan could see Davis' chest heaving, harder and harder. Caught a glimpse of the total panic on his face right before he buried it in Pax's shoulder.

"That's right, just breathe for me. Breathe in and out. It's just us. Just me and you," Pax soothed in a calm, easy voice.

Logan felt his eyes prick with sudden, unexpected tears. Then he felt a hand, warm and firm, reach for his own. Dylan squeezed his fingers. There were tears in his eyes too.

They watched, together, along with the rest of the team, as Pax talked Davis through what Logan thought had to be a panic attack.

He'd never personally had one before, but he had seen Lyla have one before, and his mother, once. He knew they happened, and he had a rudimentary idea of how to deal with them and how to help, but he'd never been in Pax's shoes before.

Never been the person that they hung on to like a lifeline. Because that was how Davis was hanging on to Pax now. Like he was the only sane sense in a world gone topsy-turvy.

Finally, after what felt like an eternity, but was only a minute or two, Davis' breath began to steady, but Pax didn't let go of him. He just kept murmuring, over and over, that he had him, that he needed him to stay calm and steady, that he had him, that he'd take care of him, that anything that happened, they'd face it together.

Nobody moved, until a voice in the doorway to the locker room spoke up. "That's enough," Coach said sharply. "Let's finish gettin' dressed." He walked over to where Pax and Davis sat, and out of the corner of his eye, Logan saw Pax finally move, and when Davis lifted his head, his face was streaked with tears.

Reluctantly, Logan turned away, but didn't let go of Dylan's hand. "I'm going to go hop in the shower," Dylan said. "You sticking around or are we headin' home?"

"Home," Logan said. He felt unsettled by what had just happened, and even though he couldn't explain it, there was nothing he wanted more than to hold Dylan—to just *hold* him. Let him know that he was cherished and loved and adored and that Logan wasn't going anywhere.

"I was gonna say . . ." Dylan dropped his voice. "I think we should get outta here."

"I'll meet you at the car," Logan said. When he turned back, ready to pick up his bag and leave the locker room, Pax and Davis and Coach were all gone.

"That really sucks," Tristan said quietly as he came over with Wade. They both had their bags on their shoulders. "I can't imagine what that feels like."

"I think it feels really shitty. Just like it looked," Logan said.

Both Tristan and Wade nodded.

"You think that's why . . . uh . . ." Wade hesitated. "Why the Condors released him?"

The panic attacks. Of course. No team was going to want a quarterback with panic attacks.

It wasn't fair, but then this was football. It didn't give a fuck about fairness.

"Maybe," Logan conceded. "Or maybe they happened after. You know . . . *after*."

"Maybe," Wade said. He didn't sound convinced.

But Logan wasn't sure what to think.

All he knew was that he hadn't seen a lick of surprise on Paxton's face. He'd known. And he'd known exactly how to deal with Davis when it happened.

Paxton had told him, and Logan had been convinced that he wasn't lying, that they weren't together. That they weren't involved. Logan had believed him, but now he suddenly wasn't so sure. Could two people be that close and *not be* sleeping together, especially when the desire was clearly there?

He didn't know the answer to that question, and as he picked up his bag to leave the locker room, he realized he was glad he didn't have to know the answer. He had Dylan, and they weren't just sleeping together, they were friends, they loved each other, and they had each other's backs. He didn't have to worry about that at all.

But as he went to go wait by the car, Logan knew he'd worry about it for Pax and Davis instead.

"We gonna talk about the elephant in the room?"

Dylan spoke up when they were almost home.

They'd both been quiet since climbing into Logan's SUV for the drive home.

"Pax told me they aren't fucking," Logan said. "And I believed him then and I kinda still believe him now. He had this frustrated look on his face I recognized a little too well."

"Ah, before *we* started hooking up, then," Dylan teased, a glimmer of a smile flickering across his face.

"Yep," Logan acknowledged. "At the barbecue."

"I wonder what Coach is gonna do. He's gonna have to do *something*, but God, I can't imagine him punishing either of them. Not after that," Dylan said. "I told you, he seemed to really understand what I went through. Had some good advice."

"You and your curiosity about Coach's tragic love story," Logan said with a chuckle. "It's cute, really."

"It ended, doesn't that automatically mean it's tragic?"

Logan pulled into the driveway and hit the button to open the garage door, pulling the SUV into the empty space.

"Apparently you're some kind of closet romantic," Logan teased as he opened his door and grabbed his bag from the back.

Talking about Coach's supposed failed love life was at least easier than untangling the mess of Davis and Pax.

"Not so closeted around you," Dylan said, slinging an arm around him as they made their way into the house.

Dylan tossed his bag on the barstool and turned towards Logan. "Seriously though," he said, his face growing solemn. "You think he's gonna fire Davis?"

"For having a panic attack because the guy who destroyed his life is gettin' away free and easy?" Logan shook his head. "That's not Coach."

"Any other coach might," Dylan pointed out.

Logan knew it. "Yeah," he agreed reluctantly. "But not Coach. You heard him. You heard his . . . well, it was like a freakin' manifesto. He meant every word. And he called Davis, didn't he? When nobody else wanted him? He's not going to do what everyone else did and just throw him away. That's not him."

"Can I just say," Dylan said quietly, tugging Logan into his arms, "I'm so fucking glad that I have you? That I get to do this? That I can look over at you on the sideline and know that you're mine, no bullshit and no doubts and no questions?"

Logan closed his eyes, melted into the way it felt to hold Dylan close. "You can. Every day, if you like."

Every day but game day, he thought but didn't say, because even though Dylan said he was feeling a lot better, a lot more like himself, Logan wasn't going to push. If that was what Dylan needed—time and space to narrow his focus—then Logan would give him that. He'd give him anything he goddamn wanted.

Every dime in his bank account. His body. His soul. His heart.

Chapter
Eighteen

Dylan knew he shouldn't be nervous about meeting his boyfriend's family. How many times had he casually chatted with Lyla and Levi and Landry while they'd been on speaker-phone with Logan? More times than he could count.

He'd even overheard some of Logan's conversations with his parents, Larry and Linda.

"They're really into the letter *L*, aren't they?" Dylan had teased Logan one night when they'd been sitting on the couch, a movie playing in the background.

Logan had blushed. "Don't even get me started," he said. "I threatened to change my name when I was a kid because of it. Bad enough being the middle child . . ."

"What did you want to change it to?" Dylan had been really curious.

Logan had impossibly gone even redder. "Kal-El," he mumbled under his breath. "I wanted to change it to Kal-El."

"Superman!" Dylan crowed. "See, you *are* a nerd after all. A closet nerd, which is almost the best kind."

"What's the best kind?"

"Oh, that's easy," Dylan had replied, "the kind that's willing to roleplay Han and Leia in the bedroom."

Logan's smile had turned sly, then, impossibly, he'd said, "Princess, there aren't enough scoundrels in your life."

Dylan shook the memory clear of his head. He shouldn't be thinking about the night of hot, nerdy-as-hell sex they'd had that night, not when he was about to meet Logan's parents and his sister, who'd flown in from Texas to watch the Piranhas play Dallas.

Logan had arranged for them to go to dinner on Saturday night, meeting at a restaurant a few blocks away from the team hotel.

"We should, barring Lyla acting up, be able to squeeze back in right before curfew hits," Logan said, as they took the elevator down to the lobby, where they'd meet his family.

"Lyla acting up?"

Logan grinned. "She might be the oldest, but that doesn't mean she's innocent."

"Well," Dylan said dryly, "she's a Banks, isn't she?"

"Truth," Logan chuckled, tugging Dylan more firmly against him, tucking a hand into the back pocket of Dylan's jeans. "You nervous?"

"About meeting your parents and your sister?" Dylan hesitated. "A little, I guess. Mostly because I want them to like me."

"*I* love you, and that's all that really matters, but honest to God, they're gonna love you, Dylan. They couldn't do anything else."

Dylan raised an eyebrow as the elevator dinged and opened, and they walked into the lobby.

"Listen, they're so happy that I've finally got a boyfriend, they could give a shit about how awesome you are, but hey, the good news is that you *are* awesome, so that's just an extra bonus."

"Are *you* nervous?" Dylan questioned.

Logan's flush told the whole story. "Never brought a boyfriend home before," he muttered. "And there's Lyla to worry about . . ."

But before Dylan could ask what *that* was about, they'd crossed the lobby, and Dylan immediately spotted the big, tall man who was an undeniable, if older, clone of Logan.

The woman next to him was tall, too, with dark auburn hair, bright eyes and a kind smile.

The younger woman with them, in her early thirties, Dylan recognized from the pictures in Logan's house, and she was even more gorgeous in person, with her long, chestnut hair and charming smile.

Then, suddenly, when she spotted them, it morphed from charming to silly, Lyla making an exaggerated grimace with her expressive features. "Oh my God, baby bro," she said as they approached, "you said you'd fallen for Dylan, but you really . . ." She rolled her eyes. "You *really* fell for him, didn't you?"

Logan punched her in the arm, and then pulled her in for a quick hug.

"Mom, Dad," he said, turning to greet his parents. "Meet Dylan."

Linda gave him a long look and then immediately pulled him into a big, warm hug. "It's so good to meet you," she said, sounding like she meant every word. "Logan's told us so much about you."

"So much," Lyla inserted with a bright smile. "He wouldn't freakin' shut up about you."

"Lyla," the older man warned, and held out his hand. "It *is* good to meet you, Dylan. We've all been lookin' forward to it."

"It's true," Linda said.

"Come on," Logan said gruffly, "we've got reservations. I found a good place you might like, Dad. Burgers the size of your head."

"Even my head?" Larry raised an eyebrow. Which, Dylan was amused to see, was almost an exact replica of the way his son did it.

"Even *your* head?" Lyla asked, shooting her brother and her father a teasing smile.

"Even my head," Logan said with an exasperated sigh. "I forgot how obnoxious you can be, especially when Landry's not here to keep you in line."

"Landry doesn't keep me in line," Lyla pointed out. "I keep *him* in line."

"That," Linda said, taking Dylan's right side as they exited the lobby and stepped onto the street, "is not necessarily true."

Dylan had gotten the impression that Landry, the younger by two minutes, was still the alpha of the family.

"Logan told me that you two are going to see Levi in a few weeks," Larry said, as they turned down a side street. "During your bye."

"Yeah," Dylan said. "I guess the only one I won't have met is Landry."

"Oh, and he's *real* excited to meet you," Lyla said, and Dylan couldn't help it, he laughed. He liked this big, loud, noisy family. It was so different from his own. Not better, or worse, just *different*.

"Levi said he sent you guys some gifts? Something about date in a box?" Linda asked.

"Oh, God," Logan exclaimed. "Like twenty-five of them. They never stop coming. Lyla, you datin' anyone? Need a date in a box?"

Dylan chuckled. "They're actually pretty fun."

"What on earth is a date in a box?" Larry wanted to know as he opened the front door to the restaurant.

The hostess immediately waved them over, probably recognizing both of them. That was something Dylan hadn't quite gotten used to yet. But he had a feeling that if he stayed in Miami—and stayed with Logan—he'd need to, because it was going to become a regular thing.

"Let me show you to your table," she said, giving Logan a bright smile. "Such a fan," she added. "Good luck tomorrow! We're all rooting for you."

"Now," Larry said, when they'd finally settled down at a big corner booth, "who's gonna tell me what this 'date in a box' thingamajig is?"

Dylan laughed. "It's like a group of activities you do together, or a craft you create together, and then there's also a playlist you can put on, that fits with the theme of the box, and some questions you ask each other. Deep stuff, stuff you wouldn't normally talk about."

Lyla looked surprised. "And Logan did this? With you?"

"Who else would I do it with?" Logan grumbled.

"I'm just shocked, it's not like you," Lyla teased. "Opening yourself up? Doing crafts? Doing activities? Answering questions about yourself?"

Logan rolled his eyes. "Laugh it up," he said. "So *are* you dating anyone?"

Lyla laughed. "Not anyone I'm willing to do a date box with," she said.

"I don't know, it's pretty cool," Dylan said, standing up for his boyfriend. "We like it a lot."

"Such a romantic," Linda teased. "I'm so glad to see it."

"That's right," Logan said, slinging an arm around Dylan and pulling him close. "I'm a romantic now, and don't you forget it."

"I have to say," Dylan said as they walked down the hotel hallway towards their rooms, "I really love your family."

"Do you?" Logan was pleased. It wasn't that he'd believed Dylan wouldn't. He loved his family, too. But they could be a lot to deal with, on their best day, even missing Landry and Levi. Dylan had grown up with just his mom. He was probably used to quiet. Reasonable, rational conversation, and quiet steadfast affection. Not incessant teasing and one-upmanship and the kind of loud, noisy love that had always permeated the Banks household.

But Dylan had clearly warmed to the Banks vibe immediately, dishing out as good as he got, and by the end of the night, he's not only exchanged phone numbers with his mom, he'd had several hushed conversations with his sister, which Logan already knew wouldn't bode well for him.

"Of course I do," Dylan said, sticking his tongue out at Logan. "They're great, and you know that."

"They also drive me nuts, half the time," Logan admitted. "But yeah, they *are* pretty great."

"My mom is too. Quieter though, a little less in-your-face, but I think you'll like her."

"Is she anything like Lyla?"

Dylan pondered this for a second. "No, not really."

"Then I'm sure I'm gonna love her," Logan said with a big smile.

They came to a stop in front of the room that Logan had been assigned, and he pulled out his room key. He hadn't even said a word about wanting Dylan to stay with him. Dylan had made his feelings on the situation clear, and Logan was going to respect that—or die trying.

"Well," he said, turning towards Dylan, "I guess you better give me a nice big goodnight kiss. One that'll last me all night long."

Dylan tilted his head, considering this. "I'm not sure I can do that."

Logan rolled his eyes. "Not even gonna try, huh? Am I that repulsive now?"

"No." Dylan grinned, and plucked the key card out of Logan's hand, sliding it through the slot on the door. "You're hot as hell, so damn hot I've been thinking about stripping you naked all evening."

Okay, Logan thought, *I can get behind this. Sex now, then separate rooms later.* He wasn't *happy* about it, but sex with Dylan was basically impossible to turn down, especially when he wanted it too. Had spent the whole dinner watching as he charmed the hell out of his entire family, and made himself a place in the middle of it, like he belonged.

But it was especially hard to resist when he was being bossy like this, pushing Logan into the room and letting the door shut behind them, caging him against the wall.

"So is that a *no* on the goodnight kiss, then?" Logan teased—just to see how it made Dylan's eyes darken. Just to convince him to close the last few inches of distance between them, and kiss him, confident and sure, nothing like the hesitant first kiss they'd shared.

"God, I want you," Dylan groaned as Logan's hands slid down his back, gripping his hips, digging his fingers into his jeans, pulling him in close so he could feel every inch of Logan's hard cock. "No," he corrected, "I fucking *need* you."

"What do you need, baby?" he asked, between long, deep kisses that left him reeling. How was it possible that each time they came together it was more intense than the last?

Logan didn't know but he didn't want it to end.

"God, I can't believe this, but I can't help it. Not when you looked so *ugh,* perfect at dinner. You need to fuck me," Dylan said, his tone desperate and pleading, and Logan didn't need him to say anything else. Flipped their positions and then dragged him over to the bed, shedding clothes as they went. Dylan's shirt ended up shading the lamp in the corner, Logan's shoes and then his socks creating a trail from the entryway.

Logan landed on the bed, clothed just in his briefs, and then Dylan was on top of him, leaning in and kissing him hard, tongue delving deep, stroking against Logan's own, undulating against him in a way that was going to rapidly destroy his self-control.

Pulling down Dylan's boxer briefs, he grabbed a handful of that fucking incredible ass and held on, Dylan keening against him as he tried to get impossibly closer.

"Bag," Logan mumbled breathlessly as Dylan finally broke the kiss, "I've got what you need in the bag . . ."

But Dylan was already crawling off him, digging through the bag sitting on the bench at the end of the bed, giving Logan a view of his bare ass and gorgeous, muscled thighs that he wouldn't forget anytime soon.

He took the opportunity to shuck his own briefs, and ran a testing hand over his hard dick, hissing as the pleasure surged through him.

Dylan tossed a condom wrapper on the bed and Logan was just about to ask where the lube was, but then he realized, opening and shutting his mouth with a shocked hiss, that Dylan's fingers were already wet and working himself open.

"Fuck," Logan moaned, "you gotta let me see."

Dylan shot him a cocky, smug grin and turned, giving Logan a view that was going to live in his dreams forever. That incredible ass, curving into thick thighs, two fingers fingering himself open.

"Feels so good," he panted. "Feel so full."

"Gonna feel fuller in a minute," Logan muttered. "Get over here. I wanna feel you."

Dylan crawled over the bedspread, looking like a fucking wet dream, and Logan curved his hand around that ass, sliding a saliva-slick finger in alongside Dylan's own.

Throwing his head back, Dylan groaned, as Logan wiggled it, slowly loosening him up enough to take his cock.

"Fuck, that feels so good," Dylan cried out. "God, *please.*" He reached out, hands scrambling for the condom he'd tossed onto the bed, but Logan's hand, clamped down on his thigh, kept him from squirming too much—or too far.

"You want it," Logan said, trying to get ahold of his own slippery control, "you gotta listen, okay?"

Dylan's mouth worked and then went slack. Then his eyes fluttered shut, and he didn't move as Logan reached for the condom, tearing it open and rolling it down onto his cock, hissing as the latex enveloped it.

Logan leaned in, gently pulling Dylan's fingers out and slicking down his own cock with the excess lube. "Now," he said, murmuring roughly into Dylan's ear, right before he gave the lobe a nice little bite, "you gotta take it, okay? Take what you want."

Dylan's eyes opened, pupils blown huge and dark. His gaze didn't leave Logan's face. He only reached down, circled one wrist of Logan's, and then pushed it up, until it came in contact with the headboard. The other, he moved lower, then lower again, until it was resting against Dylan's hip.

"These," Dylan said, licking his lips, like he was already imaging how it was going to feel when he sank down on that hard cock, "stay where they're at. Okay?"

Logan nodded. "I won't move them. I promise." He gripped the headboard's wrought iron accent with one hand and dug his fingertips into Dylan's hip with the other, and was glad he did, because then Dylan was positioning himself and then sinking down, slowly, inexorably, and the gradual, drugging drag of pleasure, the hot tightness enveloping him was enough to make him just about lose his mind.

"Fuck," Logan groaned. Strengthening his grip. "Fuck, you feel so good."

Finally he bottomed out, and for a long moment, neither of them moved or spoke. Dylan's head was thrown back, eyes screwed shut, hands braced on Logan's chest, and he keened as he began to finally move. Maybe, Logan realized belatedly, they weren't exactly quiet either.

But that concern disappeared almost as quickly as it had raised its head, because then Dylan began to move a little faster, fucking himself down on Logan's cock, and it felt so goddamn amazing that every thought in his head except for *hold on, make it good, make it great, make him see how much you love him,* was just plain gone.

Dylan's fingers curled into Logan's chest, digging into his skin, and reflexively, he dug in harder, too, leaving what was sure to be a whole hand's worth of fingertip bruises across his ass.

I'll kiss each and every one of them, after, Logan thought, and then didn't think at all. Bracing his legs on the bed, he thrust up, Dylan leaning over, cock rubbing against Logan's abs, and it was a hot, quick, furious race to the end, both of them moving hard and fast, sweat beading along their skin, until Dylan cried out, tightening impossibly around him, and Logan fell right into orgasm with him.

Dylan collapsed onto his chest, still shuddering and twitching around him, and Logan's hand, no longer gripping with force, swept gently up his back. Loving him. Appreciating him.

"That was unbelievable," Logan murmured into Dylan's shoulder. "Unfuckingbelievable."

Dylan gave a tired chuckle, but didn't move his head. Didn't move at all. "We keep besting ourselves, it seems. Not that I'm complaining."

"I'm not," Logan said. "Not even a little."

He was waiting for the moment that Dylan would get up, they'd clean up a little, and then he'd leave.

If he was being perfectly honest with himself, he was dreading it.

Was he pathetic?

Absolutely.

But at least he owned his own pathetic-ness.

Finally, Dylan did move, unsticking them, and walking over to the bathroom. It had fallen dark in the room, but he didn't flip the light on, just ran some water, and when he came back, he had a damp washcloth for Logan, who'd finally managed to lever himself upright.

"Thanks," he said. "I could've . . ."

"Naw," Dylan said, his smile lighting up his face even in the dimness of the room. "I got it."

They cleaned up, and Dylan sat down on the edge of the bed, a little bit gingerly.

"You okay?" Logan asked, suddenly concerned. They *did* have a game tomorrow, and he knew Dylan had been worried—and he also knew how hard he'd been working to get his head right.

The last thing he wanted was for some physical discomfort to ruin everything he'd been working towards.

"Oh, I'm fine," Dylan said, eyes twinkling. "So much better than fine. Nothing to worry about. We both got a little . . . uh . . . enthusiastic in the end." He chuckled.

"A little? I think that was the most athletic sex I've ever had."

"And the best," Dylan said, pressing a kiss to Logan's bicep. "Definitely put the best in there, too."

"The thing is," Logan said, wrapping an arm around Dylan and tugging him in even closer, enjoying the feel of their naked skin touching, "it's always the best because it's you. I love you so much."

Dylan grinned. "I know," he said.

"Ugh," Logan said with a groan. "Will I ever live *Star Wars* sex down?"

"I don't know . . . do you even want to? That was pretty damn good, too."

"Next time," Logan said, "you get to wear the wig and the dress."

"It's a deal," Dylan said with a nod and a big smile. From the anticipatory gleam in his eyes, Logan thought he might even be looking forward to it.

Then he reached out and grabbed his t-shirt off the lamp and Logan's heart sank. Just a little, because he knew Dylan loved him. He knew Dylan wanted him. He knew Dylan wasn't going anywhere—except for tonight.

He should be able to live with that.

He'd lived without the guy for twenty-seven years before this. But now he was imprinted so deeply, so firmly, that when he wasn't around, Logan felt lost. Not a lot. Just a little. Just enough that he always wanted to reach for him, even when he wasn't around.

"Hey," Dylan said, after he'd shrugged his shirt back on, and then pulled up his boxer briefs. "I'll be right back."

"What?" Logan was confused. "Aren't you going back to your room?"

Dylan smirked. "Do you want me to?"

"Absolutely not, but I also want you to do whatever you need, and you said . . ."

"I know," Dylan said, putting a hand against Logan's mouth. "I know what I said. But I was . . . well, I was struggling. And I'm not struggling now."

"Good," Logan said. Believing in him—same as he always had. Nothing had changed for him, but he could see the quiet confidence in Dylan's eyes now. When for awhile there . . . he'd seen the questions in them. The doubt. The uncertainty.

All of which was now laid to rest.

"That means . . ." Dylan paused. "You're not getting rid of me. Tonight. Tomorrow night. Or any other night."

"Thank God," Logan said, tugging him back into his arms, and wrapping him up tightly, "because that's where you belong. With me."

As the huddle on the field broke, Dylan glanced across the field and met Logan's eyes. Through the visor of his helmet, his face was damp with sweat, a streak of mud next to one eye. It had been a wet, rainy day. Humid, too, because this was Miami, and even in November, it was hot.

Dylan didn't need to hear Logan to know what he was thinking.

We gotta get this done, so you can get it done. Get the W.

It was late in the fourth quarter, and the Piranhas were down by one, and the feeling had been building in the back of his skull the whole game, as the Piranhas and the Cowboys traded touchdowns, that it was going to come down to this. Time was going to run out, and if they were lucky, Pax would be able to drive them down the field one last time, just far enough that Dylan could kick a field goal and win the game.

And he wanted this one, wanted it more than he'd wanted one in a long time.

Wanted to watch the ball soar between the uprights, wanted to feel the triumph roar through him in one big dizzying wave.

For the first time in what felt like months, he knew he could do it.

Could see it, could feel it, could even *taste* it.

Logan nodded, and Dylan nodded back, communicating across the field.

He'd make sure Dylan got his shot. And when he got it, he was gonna take it.

"This is it," Beau said, sliding up next to him, his ubiquitous tablet in his hands, his hands-free microphone pulled down off his head, resting around his neck. He looked tired—exhausted, really. It had been a really tough game, the Cowboys playing them hard and close, with a strong defense, and an offense that never seemed to give up. And the rain, arriving in a cataclysmic downpour every so often, hadn't helped.

Everybody was wet and worn out.

Ready for the battle to end.

Davis was on the other end of the sideline, and he looked so tense that every time Dylan looked at him, he'd worried for him.

Neither Davis nor Pax had said anything about what had happened in the locker room, and nobody had asked, but Dylan knew everyone had been thinking about it.

He shook away the distraction, and thought, *I'm gonna finish it.*

"You look confident," Beau said, glancing over at him. "Like you're just waiting to be called out there and you already know you're gonna make the kick."

"I am," Dylan said calmly. "On both counts."

Beau raised an eyebrow. "I like it," he said. "Let's end this misery. I'm wet in places I don't like to be wet, and I even changed during halftime."

Most of the team had. The locker room had smelled like an unfortunate combination of wet dog and a sweaty sauna that hadn't been cleaned in too long. It had been a quiet halftime too, Coach not making any big speeches, just everyone with their head down, trying to get dry (at least temporarily), and trying to come up with a solid game plan that would see them through the second half.

But now it was nearly over, only forty seconds left, the Piranhas with one timeout left, and the Cowboys just burning their last one.

Dylan and Beau watched as Pax connected with Wade on a crossing route, and he fought through two defensive tackles, elbowing his way through the wet and the muck, just crossing the twenty-yard line, grabbing the first down.

But all Wade's fight had meant was another few precious seconds had ticked off the clock, and there were twenty-three of them left. Coach called for the final timeout and this time when he looked over at Dylan, he wasn't questioning what would happen if he missed. And Dylan? He wasn't thinking about it either.

He nodded in acknowledgement. Beau patted him on the shoulder as he turned to get another few warmup kicks into his net, before making the one kick that would either win or lose them this game.

The timeout wound down, the last few seconds ticking off the clock, and he jogged onto the field.

Zach, the punter, was also his holder, and he tested the ground, squishing into the wet soil. "Ugh," he said, "it's a mess out here."

"Yeah, this isn't ideal," Dylan said, but the conditions didn't make him feel any less confident. He'd kicked in wet conditions. He'd kicked in snow. He'd even kicked once in ice—an experience he didn't *want* to repeat, that he likely, as long as he stayed in Miami, wouldn't be repeating anytime soon. "But we're gonna make it work."

"Damn straight," Zach said, grinning at him. "You look good."

"Everyone keeps sayin' that," Dylan said.

"Must be true, then," Zach said with a laugh.

Dylan laughed too, and it chased away the last shadows, the last little cobwebs that were still living in the corners of his mind.

He was focused. But more than that, he was calm. Prepared.

He could make this kick.

He *would* make this kick.

The rest of the kicking team drifted into formation, and Dylan saw each of them carefully testing the ground. Making sure that they could get the grip they needed to push off, that they were missing any massive wet spots.

He checked his particular square of ground too, but made sure not to step too hard into any one spot, because he didn't want to turn an ankle or get stuck in a depression right when he needed to move quickly and efficiently.

"Got it?" Zach asked, and when Dylan nodded he got into position. The ref tossed the long snapper the ball and then blew the whistle.

Everything narrowed.

The world collapsed into four things: the ball, the uprights, his body, and the wind, just barely brushing his cheek.

He never wondered if he'd miss.

He only believed he'd make it.

The ball snapped, and Zach caught it. In a precisely choreographed, precisely timed set of moves, a set they'd done a hundred times, a *thousand*, Dylan's foot swung back, and just as Zach got the ball down on the ground, positioning it perfectly, they connected.

In its simplest form, kicking a field goal was one of the easiest things you could do on a football field, harkening back to childhood days on the playground. There was a ball, and you kicked it. If you were lucky, you kicked it really far, and if you were really damn lucky, you kicked it pretty straight.

Dylan kicked it far and he kicked it straight.

The ball arced through the air, a perfect kick, and went straight through the uprights right as time expired.

Triumph surged through him, just as he'd expected and he turned, just catching Zach as he catapulted into his arms, shouting some babbling nonsense about getting it done.

And the truth was, they had.

Maybe it was just one kick, one win, one more link in the chain of a season, but it was more than that to Dylan.

It was proof.

Solid, irrefutable proof.

The team spilled onto the field.

Dylan slipped in the mud as Beau jumped against him, Sebastian too. Then Tristan and Wade. Pax, shouting and pumping his fist. There was Coach, too, with the biggest goddamn smile he'd ever seen on his face.

"Dylan!"

He turned towards the voice—he'd been turning towards this particular voice for as long as he'd recognized it, and now it just felt natural, instinctual, *right*—and there was Logan. He wasn't just smiling, he was fucking beaming.

"I knew you'd fucking do it!" he yelled, and then they were colliding, pads hitting pads, their face masks knocking against each other, but the brightness in Logan's eyes, the unmistakable affection, the loyalty, the *love*.

"I did too," Dylan said, and the look on Logan's face . . . he'd do anything, go anywhere, conquer anything, just to keep seeing it every single damn day.

"I know," Logan said, and that was really why he felt that way, wasn't it? Because Logan had known. Logan had always known.

Even when he hadn't, not really, because he couldn't have, he'd still *known*.

Why else would he have reached out to him the way he did, all those months ago?

"I love you," Dylan said, because any other words felt inadequate for the feelings surging through him, overwhelming him.

Logan's fingers tightened on his arm. "I know that too," he said.

And even though the field was full, of players, coaches, and media, Dylan didn't see anyone else.

"You know anything else?" he teased.

Logan's gaze was so steady, Dylan couldn't look away, even if he'd wanted to.

And he didn't.

If he was really lucky, he was going to be looking at Logan for the rest of his life.

"Hmmm," Logan said, a teasing glint lighting up his eyes. "I don't know . . . can't think of the words . . . not sure what I'm thinking . . . feeling . . ."

Dylan grinned, and knocked their helmets together again. He wanted to kiss him, but all this metal and plastic was in the way. "How about . . . you love me, too."

"Yep," Logan said, "that's definitely it."

Make sure to check out *Playing by the Rules*, Pax and Davis' story, which is out now!

To read a bonus scene from *Playing the Player*, AKA *Yes, Coach has a past, and you're going to find out more about it*, click here.

INTERESTED IN READING MORE OF
BETH'S BOOKS?

CHECK OUT A FULL LIST OF TILES
BY SCANNING THE QR CODE
OR VISITING HER WEBSITE

WWW.BETHBOLDEN.COM/BOOKLIST

WANT TO FOLLOW BETH?

MAKE SURE YOU NEVER
MISS A RELEASE?

SCAN THE QR CODE BELOW
OR VISIT HER WEBSITE
FOR A SOCIAL MEDIA LIST,
NEWSLETTER SIGNUP,
AND SO MUCH MORE!

WWW.BETHBOLDEN.COM/ABOUT

www.ingramcontent.com/pod-product-compliance
Lightning Source LLC
Chambersburg PA
CBHW060428310726
48977CB00001B/97